'An epic drama starring an unforgettable heroine.
Keane . . . has a wicked eye for the ruthless, fiercely
factional criminal underworld and her books never fail to
pack a powerful punch'
Lancashire Evening Post

'Mills & Boon meets *Peaky Blinders* in a mix of heaving
bosoms and cut-throat razors'
Sun

'A brilliant historical crime read'
Bella

'This thrilling and twisty crime novel is perfect for fans of
Martina Cole'
My Weekly

'A gritty and enlightening read'
Yours

'No one delves into the underworld like Keane!'
Woman's Weekly

'Authentically gritty!'
Crime Monthly

G000320276

About the Author

Dubbed 'Queen of the Underworld', Jessie Keane is of Romany gypsy stock. She was born rich, in the back of her gran's barrel top wagon, and her family thrived until their firm crashed into bankruptcy and became poor. Her father died when she was a teenager and she fled to London to escape grim reality, finding there a lifelong fascination with the criminal underworld and the teeming life of the city.

Twice divorced and living in a freezing council flat, she decided to pursue her childhood aim to become a writer. She sold her wedding dress to buy a typewriter and penned her first Annie Carter book, Dirty Game.

This was followed by five more Annie Carter books, all *Sunday Times* bestsellers, then Ruby Darke arrived in *Nameless, Lawless* and *The Edge*. Jessie's stand-alone novels include *Jail Bird, The Make, Dangerous, Fearless, The Knock* and *The Manor*.

JESSIE KEANE

Dead Heat

HODDER &
STOUGHTON

First published in Great Britain in 2024 by Hodder & Stoughton Limited
An Hachette UK company

This paperback edition published in 2024

1

A CIP catalogue record for this title is available from the British Library

Paperback ISBN 978 1 399 72098 4
ebook ISBN 978 1 399 72096 0

Typeset in Plantin Light by Manipal Technologies Limited

Printed and bound in Great Britain by Clays Ltd, Elcograf S.p.A.

Hodder & Stoughton policy is to use papers that are natural, renewable
and recyclable products and made from wood grown in sustainable forests.
The logging and manufacturing processes are expected to conform to the
environmental regulations of the country of origin.

Hodder & Stoughton Limited
Carmelite House
50 Victoria Embankment
London EC4Y 0DZ

www.hodder.co.uk

To Cliff the ideas man. Thank you, Foreman.
See? I said you'd get a mention.

An eye for an eye . . .

Exodus 21:22–25

PROLOGUE

1994

At just turning forty, Mrs Christie Doyle looked damned good. She should have, too, with the amount that was spent on the upkeep of her toned body, her white-blonde hair and her serenely beautiful face. Looking good was all part of the deal she'd made years ago with her husband Kenny Doyle – she understood that and it was the least she could do, not to shirk her side of the bargain.

Sometimes, Christie looked around at the people they knew and she wondered about them. Were they happy? Bored? Contented? Restless? She herself was a bird in a gilded cage and she knew it. She had the house – well, houses, but *this* one she always thought of as home was a place in a countryside valley set just twenty miles outside of London. There was also the Primrose Hill house that was now worth into the millions, and the Malaga villa Kenny had kept after their brief Spanish sojourn, using it for boys-only golfing trips. She had the husband and the flashy sports car on the drive (which she hardly ever used; she was nervous of cars) while Kenny favoured his silver Roller.

She had *everything*, didn't she?

Cue hollow laughter.

She had been Kenny Doyle's wife for just over twenty years and only she knew the full story behind that. The sad tale of a young love thwarted, a lifelong affair of the heart missed out on by the merest fraction.

If anyone ever asked her about it she would have just shrugged and said it was all far in the past, which was true enough. Very true. Get half a bottle of fizz inside her and she might even tell you more. But mostly, she wouldn't. Discussing it – even after all this time – was like a hot, burning pain in her gut.

Sometimes she still dreamed of Dex. And of the crash, the one that had happened when she was just four, the one in which her parents died. She still has a vague, troubling memory of her mother, crying in the front passenger seat, with her father at the wheel. The rain, the swoosh of the windscreen wipers – and then the huge whoomph of the fire as it took hold. Just bits and pieces, horrible hazy little snatches of memory. Meaning nothing, not now, not after all this time, but unsettling; disturbing – yes, *haunting*.

The past haunted her.

She thought it would haunt her until her dying day.

I

1958

The thing Christie Butler sometimes remembered about the crash that should have killed her was the rain. Then the lights, slashing through it and into the Ford Anglia saloon's fuggy interior, dazzling her. Just those two things, really. Everything else was unclear. She was four years old and she was tired, drifting off to sleep. The windscreen wipers whooshed back and forth, back and forth, soothing her. The family had been to the seaside for the day and the weather had been bright blue and sunny. Wonderful. Now, the weather had turned and there was a rumble of thunder in the air, but she wasn't afraid of that because she was a big girl, her dad always said so, and the noise was just the angels moving the furniture up in heaven.

Christie's mum Anna was in the front passenger seat, holding her little red transistor radio on her lap, and the Everly brothers were singing 'Wake Up Little Susie'. Mum's right hand was on Dad's thigh. They seemed tense, whispering: but it had been a good day, Christie was sure it had, down on the coast, taking in the brisk sea air, eating ice creams, collecting bits and pieces from rock pools, putting tiny pink crabs and bright anemones in the little red bucket Dad had bought her today, so that she could examine them more closely.

'But you must always put them back in the sea where they're safe,' Mum warned her. Dutifully, Christie did.

'I had to say something,' Dad was saying to Mum. 'How could I not, when that bastard . . . ?'

'Graham!' said Mum, glancing back at Christie. 'I know. It's awful. I understand.'

Dad had said a *bad word*.

Now they were homeward-bound and whatever the adult concerns of her parents, for Christie it was all good. She was so tired! There was just the slashing rain and the strobing lights of other cars, but inside, in here, there was warmth and music. Dribbles of water were running down the window beside her and they were nearly home – Christie knew that – nearly home and then Mum would tuck her up in bed and Dad would kiss her goodnight and all would be well. Her eyes flickered closed.

Then, the bend in the road. A *sharp* bend. *Lights*. Christie tipped hard sideways and her eyes shot open at a small shriek of alarm from her mother. The lights were blinding. And then there was a noise so loud, a sensation of impact so massive, that Christie tumbled off the back seat and into the footwell behind her mother's seat. There was the hideous sound of tearing metal. *Blistering* heat.

Christie wanted it to stop. Wide awake now, she was frightened. Bewildered. There was an inrush of air, stark cold air from the front of the car and suddenly, shockingly, the car wasn't moving anymore. The engine stopped. The windscreen wipers halted mid-sweep. Christie could hear the *tick-tick-tick* of the engine cooling. The Everlys had stopped singing 'Wake Up Little Susie' and she could hear her mother, crying Nothing from Dad. Dad was her hero; he could cope with anything, do anything. Why wasn't he speaking, moving, doing something?

Dripping.

The rain.

Or maybe not. She could smell oil like when Dad checked over his car engine, something like that. Still there was no sound from him. No movement.

She crouched there in the footwell for a long, long time; it felt like forever. Mum stopped crying and Christie was afraid to call out to her because if she didn't get an answer, what would that mean?

Eventually there were sirens, and then someone with a big red face yanked the door beside her open and, his mouth smiling, his teeth crooked, he pulled her out.

'Come on, lovey, let's get you out of here,' he said.

Christie was too frightened to move, though. She was only four, not much more than a baby, clutching the teddy bear she'd been given on the day she was born, that she didn't like to be parted from, that she had even taken with her to the beach today.

She shook her head. She wanted Mum. Needed to hear her voice. But Mum wasn't speaking; she wasn't crying. And why was Dad not moving?

'It'll be all right,' said the man reassuringly, but she could see something in his eyes that said different. Christie let him help her out then, let him drape a blanket around her and carry her quickly away – but over his shoulder she saw the soaking, petrol-shedding mangled mess that was Dad's precious little Ford Anglia.

Christie had a horrible feeling that things would *never* be 'all right' again. She was bundled into the back of a big bright ambulance and there were shouts outside, people saying *get back, get back!* There was a *boom*, a rush of noise and the sound of crackling flames. People were shouting. Christie asked the people in the ambulance, were Mum and Dad coming too?

'They're coming later,' said a man, smoothing a hand over her hair, pushing her down onto a bed. His mouth was smiling, like the fireman's had been, but his eyes weren't. 'Sit down, poppet. Let's look you over, all right? Everything's going to be fine.'

It was a lie, Christie could tell.

Later, she would know that she was the miracle girl, the little blonde cutie who had been in the papers, the one who was meant to have died along with her parents in a tragic blazing wreckage when the family car had spun off the road. And quite a few times, over the years that followed, Christie wished that had been the case.

That she hadn't been the miracle girl at all.

That she had perished; that her life was over and done.

2

Days followed after the crash – endless empty days. People came and asked her questions. Words, adult words, floated above her head but she just wanted her mum and dad. Grim faces stared down at her. Someone said *adoption* and there were raised voices, hushed meetings. While it all went on, Christie stayed at the house of her father's brother and sister-in-law, Uncle Jerome and Aunt Julia. She sat on a little bed in their spare bedroom, in their big house that was so much grander, so much more *fashionable*, than her parents' house had ever been.

Christie had loved her parents' house. There, Mum had brushed out Christie's hair every night, kissed her and called her 'little angel', then tickled her and laughed. Christie remembered that. And standing on a chair to kiss her father goodnight.

'Go and pester your mother,' he'd say, smiling as she dropped butterfly kisses all around his scratchy chin, fogging up his thick black-rimmed glasses. 'Go on.' He'd laugh, and lift her down and say: 'Sweet dreams. I love you.'

Her parents' house had felt warm, like Mum was warm, like Dad was too. But they were gone. Here, in this grand Victorian place with its high ceilings and big chandeliers, there was no warmth. There was nothing but a vast expression of wealth. Expensive wallpaper. Lush sofas covered in

purple velvet. Persian rugs, all gold and blue. Tables made
with marble from Italy and deeply padded dining chairs.
Dazzling gold leaf. Money on show, wealth clearly visible,
everything laid out to impress.

'We had to take her in, of course we did,' she heard Aunt
Julia hissing to her husband as she and Uncle Jerome stood
one day in the open door to their master bedroom. 'You know
that. What else could we do, Jerome?'

From where she sat clutching her teddy bear, the one she
had taken to the seaside on that last trip with her parents, that
she had clung to when the fireman pulled her out of the car,
Christie could see them. They radiated tension. Big bearded
Uncle Jerome was pulling his hands through his wavy dark
hair – so like Christie's father's hair – and leaning into his
wife, whispering replies. Then Aunt Julia's eyes met hers.
Christie saw Julia tap her husband's arm.

'She's listening.'

Jerome looked back over his shoulder, gave Christie a sickly
smile. Ever since the crash, Uncle Jerome had looked funny,
like he was ill. He still did. Aunt Julia and Uncle Jerome went
on into the master suite, and Uncle Jerome closed the door
firmly behind them.

★

And so Christie's future was arranged. This was the way
her life was going to be, from now on. Mum and Dad were
gone somewhere, up to heaven everyone said. A nice lady
had sat her down in a strange office along with Aunt Julia
and Uncle Jerome and it was all signed and sealed and
agreed that Christie would be given permanently over into
their care. They were her godparents after all and loved

her very much. She would become a part of their family. Wouldn't that be nice? the lady asked her.

Christie didn't say a word. She thought *nice* would be to have her sweet, gentle mum and her lovely dad back again. And not to have to think, *never* to have to think again about that night, that crash, the awful moment when she heard the flames begin and knew that they were gone.

But somehow she couldn't help it – she *often* thought about the crash. It truly haunted her, filled her dreams. To her intense embarrassment, she would sometimes wet the bed like a helpless baby, waking in terror, clammy, damp, tearful, humiliated by her own weakness, sobbing her heart out, crying out for her mum and her dad.

'It doesn't matter,' Aunt Julia would say, but Christie could see that the mess and inconvenience of this intruder child, relative or no, annoyed her. Tight-lipped, she would cram Christie's dirty sheets into the washing machine, remake the bed. 'Think nothing of it. Nothing at all.' She would say it, but she didn't mean it. There was anger in every line of her body.

'She's difficult,' Aunt Julia told everyone, dismissing Christie's symptoms of distress.

'She'll settle,' said Uncle Jerome, who rarely spoke to Christie and didn't seem to much care whether she did or not. Mostly, he ignored her, but one day he kindly put Christie's dad's surveying theodolite in the corner of her bedroom – to comfort her, she supposed: and it did. Just a bit.

Christie understood, even at so young an age, that Uncle Jerome had enough to contend with, raising his own kids. He wasn't keen on the idea of raising his brother's too, but they were godparents so what could you do? Social services had trampled all over everything in the early stages after his brother and sister-in-law's deaths, and him and Aunt Julia had been filling in forms for what felt like months. He was irritable, grief-stricken, not himself.

There'd been arguments between him and Aunt Julia over the whole business. How would it look, Christie had heard Aunt Julia say, if they, as godparents, as close relatives of the dead couple, now refused to do what they had once solemnly sworn they would do – and look after Christie?

People would forget, Jerome said. Adoption might be best. But Julia was adamant. God's sake, they had two of their own. What was the difference, one more?

Christie knew she wasn't welcome so she tried to be invisible, silent as a ghost. She knew Uncle Jerome didn't really like having her around the place. That he thought she was spooky. She sleepwalked, sometimes. Once, Uncle Jerome said he'd heard the back door being unlatched and, roused from sleep, he'd followed Christie out into the garden, down to the dark woods, near the biggest of the sheds where the cars and bikes and spare parts for lorries were kept. She'd been standing there, silent, eyes blank.

Jerome complained loudly to his wife – was that creepy, or what? He knew you mustn't wake sleepwalkers. Wasn't that a fact? So he had taken Christie by the shoulder and led her, unprotesting, back up to the house and indoors and up to her bedroom.

But after a fashion, eventually, Christie did settle. She lay in bed at night. No one kissed her goodnight; no one read her a bedtime story. She thought of her mother and father and sometimes it frightened her that she could barely remember their faces. She missed them so much. She thought of Mum's orderly, scented, welcoming home and compared it to this one, which mostly went uncleaned, unloved. Christie had heard her dad once use the expression 'all fur coat and no knickers' and that did suit Aunt Julia. Aunt Julia would almost swoon with delight at the thought of dinner with the bank manager. She loved all that.

She'd come from a dirt-poor family struggling on a council estate and when Jerome and Graham had started their building business and the money began to roll in, Julia was in heaven. She would greedily lavish expensive dresses, suits, coats, jewels on her person and on her kids – though never on Christie. She had more chandeliers put up, fabulous settees brought in, costly wallpaper hung on the walls and rugs on the floor – but she would never wash up, or dust, or sweep. Piles of dirty laundry lay all over the kitchen. Julia threw dinner parties but the stove she dreamed up ever more elaborate recipes on was black and crusted with grease; the sink was filthy. The lino on the kitchen floor was usually sticky with grime.

Eventually – when the business was starting to do really well – Julia hired cleaners, but she treated them badly and so there was a high turnover of staff and long periods when the place went back to its normal shambolic state. Left to Aunt Julia, even little Christie could see they would all have drowned in their own muck.

And then there were her aunt and uncle's own kids, Ivo and Jeanette. The favoured ones, the ones who had always received fabulously expensive presents while Christie got something far simpler. Mum and Dad had given her a home-made rocking horse and a little sweet shop toy so that she could play at grocers. Her parents had never been able to afford anything grand, because every spare penny had gone back into the family's growing building business, but that hadn't mattered to Christie. She had adored whatever her parents gave her because those presents had been given with so much love.

'Is that *all* you got?' Jeanette would say to Christie every time she got a present. 'Look – *I* got *this*.'

And she would show her cousin some costly item, her eyes glittering with avarice and spite, all the while watching for Christie's reaction. Always, Jeanette was disappointed, because Christie wasn't jealous. Even early on in life, she knew the true value of what her parents had given her.

Jerome and Julia's kids had never been especially close to Christie before the fatal crash occurred. They had mingled only at rare family parties – birthdays, bonfire nights, Christmases – so when they had, to their shock, found her suddenly installed full-time in their house, an unwanted interloper, they watched her like vicious cats given a new toy to play with. There was Ivo who was ten when Christie moved in, and Jeanette who was six.

'I don't suppose they'll let you stay for long,' Jeanette lost no time in telling her young cousin, coming in one day and plonking herself down on Christie's bed without invitation. 'And you needn't think you can play with any of my toys.'

But where else would I go? wondered Christie, feeling a shiver of fear. She had seen pictures on the TV of people on the streets, without a home to stay in. Was that her, now? She had to stop wetting the bed! Aunt Julia was sick of it, and if Christie carried on doing it, there must come a day when Aunt Julia would take her out and dump her somewhere, leave her to cope on her own.

'And what's this?' Jeanette snatched Teddy from Christie's arms.

'Teddy,' said Christie. Teddy was bedraggled, chewed up, with brilliant amber-yellow eyes, a smiling mouth, a shocking-red ribbon around his neck. Christie loved him and always kept him close. He was a reminder of her life as it had been before *that* night; the way it had been before everything broke apart.

'You're a big girl now,' snapped Jeanette. 'Too big for ted-dies. And anyway he's not even a Steiff. I've got a Steiff bear – they're very valuable. This one's no good. I'll look after him for you.'

And Jeanette took Teddy away, throwing a taunting grin back at Christie over her shoulder as she left the room and went into her own. She was back within half an hour, bring-ing Teddy with her. She threw Teddy down on the bed beside Christie.

Christie took one look at the bear her dad had given her on the day she was born and she let out a shriek.

Jeanette had dug out his bright yellow eyes.

Teddy was *blind*.

3

There was a huge and, for Christie, bewildering crowd of people at the church for her parents' funeral. Christie's parents had been popular; there were lots of WI ladies there to see Christie's mum decently buried, and men from the golf club, business associates and old pals of her dad's, all wanting to pay their respects. People hugged each other. People cried.

Aunt Julia held Christie's hand as they walked up the aisle and took their seats at the front of the church. Julia was nodding here and there, acknowledging the other mourners, and then she did the most peculiar thing: she leaned down and kissed Christie's cheek.

'Poor lamb,' she said, loud enough for everyone within ten feet of them to hear.

Aunt Julia had never, ever kissed Christie before. She had never even seemed to *notice* her that much, not really, but now Aunt Julia had told her that she would be her 'second mum'. Christie didn't want a second mum; she wanted her own mum back again. Staring around at the faces of the other mourners, Christie could see that everyone looked both sad and approving of Julia's gesture.

And then when everyone was seated, some black-suited men brought in the two long flower-laden boxes and laid them gently on covered tables at the front of the church.

One of the black-suited men was Uncle Jerome, whose bearded face was paste-white and sweating. He lowered the coffin containing his brother Graham's remains onto the table and came and sat by Aunt Julia, Christie and his two children.

Then the organist struck a chord and the congregation rose to sing 'Abide With Me'. After that, they all sat and the vicar droned on about dust and ashes and being reborn in heaven. Then it was time for speeches. Some of the men who had worked with Dad on the building business he had run with Uncle Jerome, contacts on local councils, electricians, plumbers, bricklayers, carpenters, the labourers from the many J & G Butler Ltd building sites, all said a few words. Then it was Uncle Jerome's turn.

His hands shaking, his face bleached with stress, Jerome read from a pre-written note, saying that Graham had been the best brother imaginable, the best business partner, the best friend, and that he would miss him until his dying day. Then he folded the note, stepped down, said 'sorry' and rushed down the aisle and out of the church, his hand over his mouth. The whole congregation could hear him retching outside.

Then there were more hymns, and presently Uncle Jerome came back inside, still looking upset, and sat down. He glanced at Christie, then away. Jeanette, grinning, kicked Christie's leg. What Christie couldn't quite take in was that *her parents*, her sunny smiling mother, her big cuddly bear of a father, were inside those two boxes. That they were dead, never to return. People – the vicar, for instance – talked about meeting again in heaven, but did you? And if you *did*, then why was Uncle Jerome so upset? He would see his brother Graham again, and Anna his sister-in-law.

Then the thing was over. The men carried the boxes out into the churchyard, lowered them into the ground. Everyone went back to Uncle Jerome and Aunt Julia's grand Victorian villa. There were cakes, drinks, and soon the thing became a party. Christie escaped into the garden, walked down to the bottom of the plot behind the vast sheds that housed the monstrous yellow JCBs and the HGV lorries, the dumper trucks and vans and tarpaulin-covered heaps of spares that were used on sites all around London and down to the Home Counties.

Christie thought she was alone, but one of the shed doors nearer to the house was standing open and Dad was always saying these were valuable items, these diggers and trucks; they were always to be locked up securely. Mostly, they were, and Christie had been told never, ever to go near those sheds, that it was dangerous. She went to the open door and looked inside.

Ten-year-old Ivo was sitting up in one of the JCBs, working the controls. Her cousin was fascinated by the diggers and she knew that Ivo couldn't wait until he was old enough to actually drive one. Then he saw her standing there.

'What do you want?' he snapped.

'Nothing,' said Christie, and moved on, going right down to the bottom of the plot where there was a big line of oaks, a thick hedge, mounds of sharp brambles. Christie always felt she could lose herself down there, forget her new Butler 'family' and their horrible house, make-believe that everything was still all right and that soon Mum and Dad would come and collect her and take her home.

But now she knew Mum and Dad weren't coming back for her. For a while, she had thought and hoped and prayed that they would; now she was sure they would not.

All she had was *this*.

When they'd had their fill of cakes and beer, people started strolling in the gardens and she hid away in the shrubbery, nearly invisible in her sombre black funeral dress, but she heard someone say as they passed by: 'Such a tragedy. So awful. Poor little kid. It was a miracle she survived at all. They say they only just got her out of the car in time before the flames . . .' The voice trailed away.

'But she's lucky to have Jerome and Julia take her in. They're *such* good people,' said another.

4

Christie's Butler cousins, Ivo and Jeanette, were already
attending the Church of England primary school nearby
and when Christie was five she too was led to the school
gate by Aunt Julia. She barely ever saw Uncle Jerome, who
was usually busy touring the building sites, disturbing workers leaning on shovels and having to, as he put it, 'fire their
backsides', immediately.

It was obvious even to Christie that Uncle Jerome struggled with the plans her dad had read so easily, getting into a
bad temper over the pressure of running the business alone
whenever he was at home so that they were all glad to see
him go when he departed for work.

'Lazy bastards,' he would moan at the tea table, while
Ivo stuffed his face and Jeanette pushed her food around
the plate. 'As if I ain't got enough to contend with, with
Graham . . .' His voice tailed off. He couldn't say it.

'When I'm old enough I'll be a site foreman,' said Ivo.

At the school gate, Christie was left in the care of a grey-
haired woman in a fur coat. She was taken into the tall red
brick school building, shown her cloakroom peg and the
toilets, and then there was assembly, the headmaster bald
and bespectacled, saying prayers and then playing classical
music, the sort of music Christie could remember her dad
liking. Sometimes she had gone out in the Anglia with her

dad to the building sites. She'd loved that. Everyone seemed to have liked him. He never seemed to have trouble with his workers like Uncle Jerome did.

Christie could remember her dad at the kitchen table in their small cosy home, his dark head bent over site maps, his big square dark-rimmed glasses slipping down his nose. She remembered scrambling up onto his lap and looking at the plans in fascination.

'How's my girl?' he'd say, kissing her cheek.

There was no Dad anymore. Now there was school and lessons and little bottles of milk to drink, and biscuits, then home for lunch while some kids stayed at the school as Christie would have preferred to do. But she was given no choice. She and Ivo and Jeanette were taken back down the hill to the house, given sandwiches and tea, then escorted back up to the school. Then there was needlework and English, the times table and painting, and then time for home again at three o'clock, and the best thing about the little school was that, because they were different ages, there was no need for Christie to set eyes on her cousins during the school day *at all*.

Christie did well at the quaint little school. She made a friend called Patsy, who joined the school on the same day she did. She did even better when Ivo hit eleven and departed for the local comprehensive, a couple of miles down the road. Then she never had to see him at all during the day and that was absolutely fine with her.

Her cousin was a huge boy for his age, broad-chested, with long thick wavy hair that spread out to his shoulders, making him look intimidating. He had tiny features – small pig-like eyes, a dainty little nose, a pinched cat's bum of a mouth. He always smelled sweaty; whenever he came near, Christie's nose wrinkled in disgust. She didn't think he ever bothered to wash himself. He had muddy-brown eyes like Jerome's, and tended to shove anyone who was in his way – Christie included – out of it, and quite roughly too. She hated Ivo and she *definitely* didn't like sallow, skinny, spiteful Jeanette – she was never going to forget or forgive her for gouging out Teddy's eyes.

But slowly, Christie did settle down to something like normality. The bed-wetting eventually stopped, but bad dreams still plagued her. The huge *boom* of the explosion when the crash happened. The rain. The *drip, drip, drip of liquid*. Sometimes, she dreamed of her parents' faces, smiling at her. Those dreams were nice. But sometimes – and this was awful, embarrassing – sometimes she walked in the night, in her sleep, and awoke in the kitchen, or standing barefoot on the lawn in the back garden. Sometimes she got as far as the big sheds where the lorries and JCBs were kept, and twice she was found asleep on the concrete hardstanding outside the door of the shed closest to the house. This gave Ivo and Jeanette even more to taunt her with.

'You're a ghoul,' said Ivo.

'You don't even know what that is,' said Christie.

'It means a freak,' purred Jeanette. 'You're a *freak*, Christie. Everyone knows it.'

'Fucking right,' said Ivo, who'd picked up colourful language and not much in the way of education at his new school. He skived off, was frequently in detention and had somehow accumulated a large mob of equally thuggish lads around him.

'Should we be worried about Christie doing that? Isn't that just bloody peculiar?' Christie heard Uncle Jerome asking his wife one day. 'God's sake! Sleepwalking! She's mentally disturbed I reckon. *You* know. From the crash.'

'It'll pass,' said Aunt Julia. 'The bed-wetting did, didn't it. This will too. You'll see.'

5

Soon it was time for Christie to go to secondary school. She was bright but she sat – and spectacularly failed – her 11-Plus exam, which would have seen her go to the same grammar school her mate Patsy was now attending. Not that Patsy, clever though she was, ever tried much at school or attended as she should. She skived off whenever she could, meeting up with dodgy boys in fast cars.

'It doesn't matter anyway,' said Patsy. 'I'll come over to you; you come over to me. We'll still see each other.'

Christie was sent to the same sink secondary school as Ivo and Jeanette. The only good thing about that was that Ivo left the school at about the same time she started there, so at least there was some respite from him.

Patsy's frequent visits were a comfort but she wasn't getting on with her cousins. Ivo was always digging at her, calling her names and loitering around her bedroom door. Jeanette was forever yanking at Christie's hair and cheerfully excluding her from shopping trips with Aunt Julia, staring at her with raw hate and calling her a moron.

The thing was, by the time Christie hit thirteen, she had become startlingly pretty. Often she saw Aunt Julia, when the family were getting ready to go out to this show or that, looking at skinny sallow mousy-haired Jeanette, her own daughter, and then at Christie – and Christie could see that her aunt was far from delighted with the comparison. And Jeanette? She was so envious of the way Christie looked that it nearly killed her.

At thirteen, Christie's hair was long, thick, straight and a Nordic silver-blonde. She had sleepy sea-green eyes and the almost languorous aspect of a swan; she was tall, long-necked, elegant. Boys turned their heads and looked at her. A couple of them asked her out, but she didn't go. Then one day she hobbled home from school, her guts aching. Going to the loo, pulling her pants down, to her horror she saw blood on them.

She had stepped out of the bathroom, light-headed with fear. Jeanette was passing on the landing, and Christie grabbed her arm.

'I'm bleeding,' she said, wide-eyed with terror.

'What?' Her cousin wasn't interested.

Christie pointed. 'There. Down there. I'm bleeding.'

'Oh.' Jeanette's eyes narrowed. Then she smiled her thin spiteful smile.

'You're bleeding to death,' Jeanette told her.

'*What?*'

'It happens sometimes. To some people. First their parents die and then they do. Best just go to bed and stop there. You're dying, dingbat.'

Her cousin walked on, along the hall, into her room. The door closed behind her.

Christie stared after her, her stomach cramping, blood starting to snake down her thighs.

She was dying!

Alone, frightened, she took to her bed and turned the sheets red with her blood. Then Aunt Julia was calling up the stairs that tea was ready. Christie just lay there. She heard Ivo and Jeanette go down, laughing, chattering. Then there was more activity and someone – Jeanette? – impatiently called her name. Finally Aunt Julia came up the stairs and into Christie's room. She swept the sheets back and her mouth pursed with disgust.

'I'm dying,' Christie sobbed.

'You're not dying,' said Aunt Julia in annoyance. Her lip curled as she stripped the bed of the soiled sheets, tutted over the state of the mattress.

Not kindly, Aunt Julia took Christie into the bathroom and scrubbed her shrinking private parts with a harsh, cold soapy flannel. The iron scent of blood filled the air. Then she brought a belt and a packet of sanitary towels and showed Christie how to put them on.

'Does this happen often?' asked Christie, who didn't even have a notion about the birds and the bees. No one had ever spoken to her about it.

'Once a month,' said Aunt Julia.

Christie couldn't believe it. She would bleed every month? God, how awful. 'And . . . I'm not dying?'

'No. You're not.'

'Does this happen to everyone?' asked Christie.

Julia gave a grim smile. 'Only to women,' she said.

*

Julia felt an uncomfortable shiver of guilt then. Maybe she should have talked about this to the girl. But honestly? She wasn't – had truthfully *never* been – interested in her. The kid made her feel uneasy. And God knew, she had problems enough with her own brood. Teenage Ivo had started getting into bother with the law, stealing and cheating, teaming up with that wild Cooper boy and the unruly Millican clan. The Millican lot had been caught by the local bobby trying to break into cars, and she heard that Ivo and the Cooper boy had got clear of that by the skin of their teeth. She couldn't believe it. She felt shamed by it. If anyone ever found out, she would be mortified.

Her husband was a businessman, a respectable person – well, inasmuch as any businessman ever could be. Sometimes she knew that Jerome did blur the lines with his dealings, slipping backhanders to local councillors, taking lorryloads of substandard, dried-out Tarmac off council hands and laying it here and there, knowing full well that the surface wouldn't last and there would be potholes galore soon to follow.

But then, didn't everyone do that? Of course they did. Only the saintly Graham, Jerome's dear departed brother, had ever objected to the idea. Julia always told herself that Graham – God rest him – had been a fool. Everything was fine; everything would be OK. So she had troubles with Ivo – yes, it was unfortunate but it was true. He was a handful and his father clearly couldn't manage him. Also – and this irked her but she couldn't deny it – her daughter Jeanette was disappointingly plain. Sometimes Julia would watch Jeanette and Christie out in the garden and she would find herself contrasting the two of them. Christie with that slow, unnervingly sensual gaze that she turned on people; her perfect glowing skin, her taut young girl's figure, curving and ripening into womanhood now – and Jeanette, who was still scrawny, who would probably *always* be scrawny, her skin unfortunately yellow in tone, her eyes down-slanted at the corners under her thin mid-brown brows.

An ordinary-looking girl you'd pass in the street.

Just that.

Not like silvery, alluring Christie with her hypnotic sea-green eyes. Not like her *at all*. Her own daughter couldn't hold a candle to Christie's sombre beauty. It was ironic, it was in fact *maddening*, that this kid, this unwanted intruder in their family's life – and how could she think of Christie as anything else but that? – had turned out so pretty. It just wasn't fair, was it?

*

Later, Christie caught up with Jeanette.

'You told me I was bleeding to death,' she said when she came across her in the kitchen, buttering a sandwich for herself. She never made one for Christie. Not ever.

Her cousin shrugged and grinned and something went *snap* in Christie's brain. She took Jeanette's head in her hands and slammed it into the chopping board.

Jeanette yelled for Aunt Julia, who hit the roof when she found her daughter sobbing in the kitchen, a buttered white slice of bread stuck to her face.

'She did it!' yelled Jeanette.

Christie didn't deny it; she was *glad* she'd done it.

She was sent to her room – without lunch, without dinner, without supper.

She didn't care.

6

Cousin Ivo didn't lose his bad ways as he grew. He remained a constant source of worry to Julia. She began to fear the tap on the door, the phone ringing, the police saying he'd been caught doing something *really* bad. Of course, she told herself, he'd just fallen in with a rotten crowd. Jerome always said, 'Ah it's just boys being boys, nothing to worry about' – which was the perfect excuse for him never to interfere in his wayward son's life.

Julia thought there was *plenty* to worry about. Particularly when one of her newly cultivated girly mates, hardly able to contain her glee, let her know that a local mobster called Kenny Doyle had started getting Julia's son to do jobs for him.

Julia didn't know what these 'jobs' involved, but she had heard all about Kenny Doyle. He was a flashy type, intimidating, always showing up in the latest and most expensive car, and where the hell did a simple East End boy get the cash for things like that? Jerome was a businessman. He had worked long and hard – of *course* he had – on the *bona fide* business of J & G Butler Ltd, building it first with his brother Graham and then pressing on with it on his own after Graham's sad passing.

Some time after his brother's death, Jerome – now sole owner of J & G Butler Ltd – had bought out the small arable farm next door and this farmhouse was now the 'official' business premises. The fences and hedges between the two properties had been cleared so that now the Butler plot was massively extended, a double-width Tarmacadamed drive-way laid right the way down to the bottom of the plot to accommodate the heavy plant that was often stored down there in the sheds. Julia liked to look out at it all, her little kingdom, and she felt proud of Jerome when she did. Jerome, she told herself, had *earned* the money to throw around on posh motors. But this 'Kenny'?

Julia thought that Kenny was a hard-eyed crook and she didn't like the way he strolled into the house and lounged around tossing swearwords back and forth with Ivo – and yes, even Jerome – casual, uncaring, *not* treating her with any respect at all. She hated that. Truth was, Kenny rather frightened her and she suspected he frightened Jerome and maybe even Ivo too. But there it was: Jerome was too toler-ant. He had *always* been too tolerant. He'd been too soft with Graham his brother, God rest his soul of course, and after all they'd been equal partners in the business. It wasn't up to Graham to lay down the law the way he had.

Then came the day when Jerome found one of the big yel-low diggers stored out back scratched all to hell, dented and damaged. He'd tackled Ivo about it, and this was awful, Julia thought, this was *terrible*, but she did feel that even Ivo – his own son – frightened Jerome a bit now. She had heard Ivo – and she couldn't bring herself to believe the evidence of her own ears, not really – she had heard Ivo order Jerome out of his own armchair by the fire.

'Oi! Out of there. You're in my seat,' said Ivo.

At first, when she'd heard their son say that, she was convinced that Ivo was joking with his dad, that he wasn't serious. But then – to her amazement and alarm – Jerome stood up and vacated the chair. And it was clear, from that moment on, that Ivo was really in charge. And Ivo was answering to Kenny Doyle.

Still, Jerome tried lamely to reassert his authority when the digger – a priceless piece of machinery, and bought with a massive loan agreed with their bank manager over a luxurious dinner in a swish Mayfair hotel – turned up so badly damaged. It wasn't even paid for, and there were bits hanging off it already!

'It's not on. Who's been using the bloody thing anyway? All the sites are closed on the weekend. Was it you, Ivo?' yelled Jerome.

'Shut up, old man,' said Ivo.

'You *what*?'

'I said, shut up. Look – I did a bit of business for Kenny, if it's anything to do with you. Which it *ain't*, by the way.'

Jerome blustered. 'I'm *paying* for that sodding thing,' he pointed out.

'You want to go on with this?' Ivo asked. 'Only, I don't think you should.'

It was a clear warning – and to Julia's horror, Jerome backed down. The son had the upper hand in the house now. Then on the news on Monday they heard about ram raids on banks around the area and that a JCB had obviously been used in several of the raids. Things were changing. Jerome wasn't in charge anymore. Ivo was. Or rather – his puppet master, that villain Kenny Doyle.

It was Julia, not Jerome, who plucked up the nerve to talk to Ivo.

'I don't like the way all this is going,' she said. 'Your father told me about the damage to the JCB. I want you to stop seeing that bastard Kenny Doyle. I suppose using our machines for his dirty business was his idea? It's a miracle we haven't had the police at the door yet.'

'No,' said Ivo. 'Actually it was mine. I suggested it. And there's no question of me stopping seeing Kenny – get that right out of your head. I want to get in good with Kenny. He's a mate.'

Julia didn't swallow this. She had seen Kenny here, in her house, and she knew that Kenny was not a 'mate'. Big as Ivo was, Kenny was bigger, and he had a nasty habit of grabbing the younger man around the neck in a headlock, laughing all the while, and she could see that Ivo was sick with shame when he did that. But he never complained. He took his resentment out elsewhere. She knew that Ivo picked on Christie – just as she knew Jeanette did – but what the hell could you do? Kids would be kids, and Julia guessed neither of hers had ever got over having Christie thrust into the family dynamic so unexpectedly. Christ, she hadn't ever really gotten over it *herself*.

She didn't want to think about that, anyway. Thinking about that reminded her of that horrible funeral years back, the two coffins laid out side by side, and she had nightmares about that enough without adding to her own woes.

Julia came to hate the atmosphere around the house. Sometimes it seemed to her that ever since Graham and Anna had perished, everything had gone wrong. It was as if her and Jerome, her *family*, were all sliding down a steep slope, crashing ever nearer to the bottom; everything was crazy, out of control.

She visited the graves, sometimes. She didn't *like* to go there, not really, and she *never* took Christie, although she supposed maybe the kid would have liked to go. But Christie didn't ask and Julia never offered. She went alone, put some fresh flowers down, and hurried off. Sometimes she paused to say a prayer. But she didn't believe in heaven, or God, or anything really. Born on a council estate, dirt-poor and always struggling in childhood, scraping the ice off the inside of the house's metal-framed windows in the wintertime, running to the outside lavvy because of course they didn't have an indoor one, and then her brother had hanged himself and she had wanted so much, so *desperately*, to escape all that, so she had married, snatched in haste at the first man who'd offered, and that was Jerome.

She'd abandoned that poor background, cast it out, refused to even remember it. When they first got together, Jerome had been going places, greasing up the cronies he culti-vated on the council, securing lucrative building contracts, and Graham – the bright one, the studious one – had gone to evening school, learned to read and understand site plans and to use the surveyor's theodolite; they'd made a good team and the money had started to flow into the firm they had proudly set up together: J & G Butler Ltd.

But now – unwillingly – Julia *did* remember where she'd come from, she *did* remember her roots, because the place she lived in now might be big and grand but the *atmosphere* in the Victorian villa she occupied with her own family was exactly like the one she had left so far behind all those years ago. Troubled. Edgy.

Ivo was running riot. She couldn't deny it. Had to acknowledge it and acknowledge too that there was sod-all she could do about it. Jerome was afraid; he'd lost his brother, who had always been his staunch supporter, his right arm; he'd lost his 'head of the household' position – and along with all that, she had to admit, he'd lost the very last vestige of any respect she'd once had for him.

7

'Must be mating season,' Ivo said with a smile as he watched two flies, joined together, climb up the paintwork on Christie's open bedroom door.

Oh Christ, thought Christie. She was almost fourteen and Ivo was nearly twenty, and whenever his eyes crawled over her she shuddered. Everything Ivo said to her these days had revolting sexual overtones.

'Got to find out the facts of life from somewhere,' Ivo had said when she climbed into the front of the Transit for a lift to school one day and found books up on the dashboard. Filthy, lurid-covered paperback books with busty half-dressed women on the covers, books that she was *sure* he had placed there deliberately for her to see and squirm over.

Christie knew about the facts of life now. They'd covered that subject in secondary school, which had been embarrassing enough. She didn't want to know more – certainly not from Ivo – and she *definitely* didn't want to see his disgusting reading matter.

After that she'd started to be more careful not to be late for the bus. Ivo made her flesh creep, and she avoided him wherever possible.

'Isn't it horrible,' he'd commented with a smirk at her when they passed by horses in a field when the whole family was out for a walk and his parents were out of ear-shot. 'Think of those mares, forced to mate every year. Think of the stallion jumping up on their backs all stiff-pricked and just *ramming* it into them, time after time. 'Course, they like it. They're in season. Women do too. You know that, don't you?'

Christie never answered. She never answered *anything* Ivo said to her. She took refuge in silence. He was disgusting. Christie could feel her face curdling with loathing every time he came anywhere near her. Like now. Here he was again, leaning on the open door of her bedroom, smiling at her as she sat on her bed trying to read.

Christie got up, crossed the room, and shut the door in his face. She heard him chuckling as he walked away. There was no lock on her door and she began to think about that, about lying here in the night and Ivo's room just across the hall.

'Could I have a lock on my bedroom door?' she asked Aunt Julia one day when they were both in the kitchen.

Julia, who was scrubbing her painted nails at the sink while studiously ignoring the pile of dirty dishes stacked high on the draining board, turned and looked at Christie in surprise. 'Why would you want that?' she asked.

'Just . . . for privacy,' said Christie awkwardly. There was no way she could tell Ivo's mother that he was hanging around her like a bad smell, trying to intimidate her by saying horri-ble, suggestive things.

'We don't believe in locks in this house,' said Julia firmly.

When Patsy came over, it was a relief. And it was an even bigger one when Christie was able to escape to Patsy's parents' house.

'I don't like that Ivo,' said Patsy. 'He's such a creep.'

'I know,' said Christie, grateful that she still had her friend, that there was still *someone* to talk to, someone who understood.

She wished so much that she could still see Patsy every day, as she had when they were at primary together, but that was impossible. At home, Christie got too nervous to even go to the upstairs bathroom on her own. She would use the one downstairs, but there was a frosted glass window in there and the bathroom was right alongside the pathway that led into the kitchen so she felt that people – *Ivo* – could look in on her, see her in the bath, on the loo, anything. She had seen him hanging around outside there once or twice, whenever he knew she was in there.

'Could we put a curtain up in the downstairs loo?' she asked her aunt, but she knew what the answer would be.

'Whatever for? Don't be silly. That's frosted glass – nobody can see you.'

So, no curtain. And Christie was *still* sure that Ivo lurked outside whenever she was in there. So in the end she avoided using the toilets at home altogether, and used the school ones instead, no matter how much discomfort it caused her. At weekends, she just had to wait until she knew Ivo was out until she could go.

It was horrible. Her mirror told her what Ivo clearly saw – she'd grown pretty. She had – and this was worse – grown *breasts*. At almost fourteen she had a womanly figure and she had to avoid swimming on days out with the Butlers because Ivo would look at her. She *hated* for Ivo to look at her. So life with the Butlers was a nightmare. She crept around the place, hid away in the grounds. The bed-wetting that had plagued her as a child reappeared on occasion and Jeanette and Ivo had a great laugh about that. She sleep-walked again, too. Mostly she kept out of everyone's way and wondered if she would ever be free of these people, this place.

And then – quite suddenly – it got worse.

8

When Christie came up the stairs to go to her room one teatime after school and saw that Ivo's door was wide open, she didn't really – not at first – pay any attention. He was standing there inside his room and he grinned at her. Then she looked down and realised, with a crashing sense of horror, that he wasn't wearing any trousers or underpants and that his *thing*, his penis, was swollen and upright. She'd never seen a sexually aroused man before and it shocked her. Aghast, heart pounding sickly in her chest, she moved on quickly to her room, went inside, shut the door.

He'd intended that she should see him; she knew that. *The filthy bastard.* He knew she always came upstairs at this time and he'd planned for her to see him undressed and aroused. Hoping that it was a one-off, Christie kept to her own routine but he did the same thing the next day. The day *after*, she very casually asked Aunt Julia to come up with her to look at a stain on the curtains in her room and very carefully did not speak to her on the way up the stairs.

On the landing, she saw that Ivo's bedroom door was open and that he was there, partly clothed again, disgusting. She darted into her room, Aunt Julia trailing behind her and Christie was rewarded almost immediately by an outraged cry from her aunt.

'Ivo!' Julia shrieked.

Christie heard a mad scrambling from Ivo's room. She could picture his panic. This was his mother, not his intended victim. He'd be *embarrassed*, the horrible sod. Well, *good*.

'What on earth are you doing, walking about like that?' his mother demanded.

Christie paused at her bedroom door, looking back at her aunt still out there on the landing, whose expression was scandalised. Christie could see all sorts of unbidden ideas forming in Julia's head – that Ivo knew it was Christie who usually came up, alone, at this time. That Christie had asked her for locks, curtains – and the bed-wetting had started up again, and the sleepwalking; that Christie was clearly behaving in a disturbed manner. And now – this. Ivo, nearly naked and in a state of arousal, lying in wait for his cousin.

'Put some bloody clothes on!' barked Julia. 'You shouldn't be walking around like that!'

The door to Ivo's room slammed shut. Julia pushed Christie into her room and went inside after her, closing the door onto the landing.

★

Julia was no fool. This incident embarrassed her, shamed her. Her son, a sex pest! And there was that niggling worry at the back of Julia's mind that her own brother had been troubled, a bit *strange*. He had, in the end, taken his own life. Was Ivo headed the same way? To mental disorder, and death? And that Ivo should be doing this stuff to his cousin, who had been raised here since she was four years old, as *part of the family*. All right, it wasn't a burden any of them had welcomed, but Julia at least had done her best for the poor little bitch. She was sure she had.

'Where's this stain you were talking about? Just a bit of mould I expect, where the curtain's lying against the windows-ill and the moisture's run down the glass . . .'

Now Julia had seen the evidence of Ivo's behaviour with her own eyes, but she chose to ignore it. She had to favour her own child over Christie. What else could she do? She'd made a good home for them all, hadn't she? And maybe she'd misunderstood the situation. She might be jumping to conclusions about Ivo, and everything would turn out all right.

9

All Ivo's mates had a habit of hanging around in the Butlers' kitchen, chatting, laughing – all the Millican clan, and
the Cooper boy, Dex, the one who never seemed to quite
fit in. Christie actually rather liked the Cooper boy. He
was handsome and jokey; he made her smile. He wasn't
scary like Ivo. She couldn't help wondering what he was
doing, hanging around with this mob. These lads got up
to all sorts, and Ivo was their ringleader. The police called
several times about this crime or that in the local area.
Uncle Jerome kept out of the way when all this was going
on. He was wary of his own son – Christie had seen that,
witnessed it, many times. And Aunt Julia was in complete
denial. Her boy Ivo was a thug, mixing with other thugs,
and he was worse than that too, but Julia refused to see
any of it because it reminded her of the deadbeat streets
she herself had come from, of her own troubled, tangled
roots, and she didn't want to think about any of that, not
now, not ever.

The atmosphere in the house was brooding, awful, when
Christie turned fourteen in April. Then Ivo was twenty in
June. It had been a long, unseasonably hot day and the family
were turning in for the night. All was quiet; all was still. And
then, just as Christie was about to put down her book, turn

out her bedside lamp and go to sleep, the door creaked open and there he was.

He'd stopped lying in wait for her half-naked after his mother caught him doing that, and there had been no further instances of that behaviour for several months – although Aunt Julia was still refusing to let Christie have a lock on her bedroom door.

But Ivo's stalking of her seemed to be over, and Christie had been relieved. Now, this. He was standing there wearing only a pyjama top, holding a magazine over his private parts. Quickly, he pushed the door closed behind him and held a finger to his lips.

'Shhh,' he hissed. 'Just want to talk.'

'Get out, Ivo,' snapped Christie, shrinking back in the bed, her heartbeat suddenly frantic. If she screamed, would anyone come? Would Aunt Julia come and rescue her? Or would she just ignore this, like she ignored everything else?

Christie thought she knew the answer to that. And Uncle Jerome? He would ignore it too. There was no way he was going to confront Ivo, because Ivo – his own son – scared him.

'Aw, don't be like that. Look, I'm covered up, see?' He indicated the magazine. It was a girly magazine. Christie could see naked women on there; her stomach clenched with disgust at the sight.

'I *said*, get out,' she repeated.

The magazine fluttered to the floor. Christie turned her head away.

Ivo bent and picked the thing up again. He came over to the bed and sat on the edge of it. Christie shrank back. Ivo dropped the magazine again. 'Oops. Look at that. Thing keeps falling to the floor, don't it? But look. Look, Christie. Look how much I want you.'

Christie's mouth was dry as dust. She cringed back against the pillows, drawing her nightie tight around her. She couldn't look. Didn't want to. 'I'll tell Aunt Julia,' she said.

'She won't do nothing,' said Ivo confidently. 'So come on, Christie. Let's do it, yeah? Don't you want to? Don't you like to do it?'

'Get out,' whimpered Christie.

But Ivo wouldn't go. And that was, at fourteen, Christie's first experience of sex. It hurt, and he smelled – and afterwards she was nearly sick with horror.

10

She lost count of the number of times Ivo sneaked into her room. She didn't want it; he did. And her not wanting it made not a blind bit of difference to him.

'You're getting thin,' Aunt Julia said to her one breakfast time. 'You feeling all right?'

'Fine,' said Christie, and left the house as soon as possible to be out of there before Ivo came down. Just to see him made her stomach heave. She couldn't stand even to have him in the same room as her.

School was a daily nightmare. She sat alone. She missed Patsy. She hated the school. It was massive and the teachers were dead legs just waiting for retirement, miserably working out their final years as best they could. The communal showers after gym were humiliating, embarrassing. She withdrew, skived off, and got lectures from Aunt Julia about calling the family into disrepute with her behaviour – which was pretty bloody rich, Christie thought.

'The school inspector came round. Where on earth were you? I thought you were in school!' Julia ranted.

Christie had been walking the roads, sitting in the woods, doing anything that didn't involve being at home or being in that damned school. She didn't care and nobody even noticed that she was sliding into a deep depression.

The night-time visits from Ivo went on.

And then one day when she had endured gym lessons – which she hated – and afterwards subjected herself to the misery of communal showers in the girls' changing rooms, Christie was called into the headmistress's study. The kind-eyed head looked at Christie and smiled. Miss Harper the gym mistress was there too.

'Is there anything you would like to talk to us about?' the head asked gently.

Ivo's face loomed in her mind's eye, Ivo who was getting worse in every way, cultivating his criminal contacts, bragging about 'joining up' with one of the local hoodlums called Kenny Doyle, subjecting her to those revolting night-time visits.

Christie shuddered. 'No,' she said.

The head took a breath, seemed to need to compose herself.

'Only,' she said, 'Miss Harper has noticed something.'

Christie didn't have a clue what this was about. Had she broken the rules again? Run through the showers with a towel around her, hating to feel so exposed? She did that sometimes. That must be it.

'Miss Harper has noticed that . . . perhaps you would like a family member here with you, Christie. Would that help?'

Christie thought of Uncle Jerome, Aunt Julia. 'No,' she said.

'You live with your aunt and uncle – is that correct? They are your legal guardians?'

'Yes,' said Christie.

'You wouldn't like them here, to support you?'

Christie stared at her blankly. 'Why?'

'There seems to be . . .' The head paused, groping for the right words. 'Miss Harper reported to me that you look . . .'

'What?' Christie turned her gaze on the gym mistress, standing across the room, her colour high with embarrassment.

'Dear girl, is there any way that you could be, well . . .'

'Well what?'

The head took another deep, calming breath. 'Pregnant?' she suggested.

11

When she got the call from the school, Aunt Julia came and collected Christie, grabbing her roughly by the arm and saying nothing to her, not a word, all the way home on the bus. It was only when they got home that Julia spoke, and that was not until she'd checked the house was empty. She hustled Christie upstairs to her bedroom, sat her down on the bed and, quivering with fury, demanded to know how this could have happened.

Christie, silent, stared up at her aunt.

You *know* how this happened, she thought. I warned you. I asked you for a lock on that door. You said no. You saw Ivo, the way he was behaving. Christie took a breath and said it, out loud. All of it. That Julia had known this would happen. That she hadn't actually cared. Oh, she cared *now*, now that it seemed some shit might stick to her own family and – most particularly – to that rotten bastard she'd given birth to.

Aunt Julia lunged forward and slapped Christie, hard.

'You take that back!' she yelled. 'You take that back *right now*, or by Christ . . .' Julia seemed to grab hold of herself then. She stalked back and forth in front of Christie, arms folded over her middle as if to prevent herself lashing out again. She was nodding her head, her eyes ferocious as they fixed on the girl sitting there. 'I should have known, right from that start, that you would only ever bring us trouble.

And haven't we always been good to you? Haven't we given you a roof over your head, food on the table, everything anyone could want?'

Everything except genuine affection, thought Christie. In their various ways, every member of the family had been unwelcoming to her. Spiteful to her. Dangerous or damaging to her.

'And now *this*,' Julia raged on. 'You're just bloody trouble, Christie. You're a fucking nightmare, and you know what? *You should have died in that crash.*'

Christie stared up at her aunt. Julia had never said anything like this before. She had tolerated Christie. But here was the truth, out at last: Aunt Julia wished that she had never been burdened with her.

★

Seeing the look on Christie's face, Julia tried to get a grip on herself.

'I'm sorry, all right? Sorry. I shouldn't have said that. Now what the *hell* am I going to do?' Julia muttered, pacing, her eyes fixed on the girl, the problem. A disgrace to the Butler family if this ever got out. But oh damn it she knew, she *knew* that this baby had to be Ivo's. Her oversexed fool of a son had done this, brought this shame crashing down upon them all. And – oh God – if it should get out . . .

No. It couldn't.

It *mustn't*.

Imagine what all her friends, all her *kids'* friends, would think about it. They would laugh and sneer and they would cut her out of their charmed circle, when she had strived so hard to be a part of it all. She and Jerome donated to local charities, were always seen at posh dinner dances; they dined out with the bank manager, were on first-name terms with their – admittedly rather dodgy – accountant. Jerome had joined the golf club. They were *respectable*. And she wasn't having anything, not *anything*, ruin that. Particularly not this wretched girl who had inflicted this crisis upon her.

Julia knew exactly what her own roots were, where she had come from. That awful estate. Still she could never forget it: the burned-out cars up on bricks, sofas shedding their stuffing in front gardens, thugs loitering on street corners, their vicious dogs snarling and barking on choke chains, nobody going out at night for fear they could be mugged or worse.

When she had met Jerome, him and his brother Graham had seemed to be from a class above. They'd been going places, building their own business from the ground up. She had known that Jerome could get her out of the fix she was in, with her idle uncaring parents, her high-strung and fatally flawed brother, as eager – obviously – to escape the dismal reality of life as his sister was. Well, her brother Tony had died – but *she* had escaped. Jerome had taken her away from all that, and there was no way – *no way at all* – that she was ever going back there. So none of her friends, no one even in her family, with whom she had very little contact anyway, must know what had happened. She had to make sure of it, and she knew how to do that.

That very day, Julia made the call.

12

Once, Mrs Violet Thursday had been a nurse. But that had been years ago. Now she was a grey poodle-permed woman of nearly seventy and making a meagre living from dressmaking – and other services that had nothing to do with fabric or fittings. She didn't look happy to see Julia Butler standing on her doorstep. Mrs Thursday had a tiny bungalow at the bottom end of the estate, where pensioners usually chose to live and where there was never too much trouble with yobs of an evening. There were grape hyacinths of a stunning Delft blue in her front borders, their intense deep shade warring with the acid yellow of tiny spring daffodils. Gnomes peeped out here and there from the shrubbery.

Julia was holding Christie by the hand.

'What can I do for you?' asked Mrs Thursday, glancing first at the girl and then the woman.

'Can we come in?' asked Julia.

Mrs Thursday's lip trembled slightly. 'I don't do it anymore. Can you people get it through your thick heads? I don't.'

Julia stepped up, looming over the smaller woman.

'Like fuck you don't,' she hissed. 'Carol Bartlett said you done it for her daughter not long since and you know *damned well* you did it for me, once.' She glanced at Christie and lowered her voice. 'Back before I was married. You know you did.'

Julia could see the recognition of that fact in Mrs Thursday's rheumy eyes. Julia had slept with an immigrant from the West Indies and got herself up the duff. Disastrous timing, because not two months after Winston's departure for his homeland she had realised she was pregnant. Then she met Jerome and slept with him, but he would have known instantly that the baby wasn't his. The dates would be wrong and the colour of the child was sure to be, too. So she had called on Mrs Thursday to get rid of it. Then and only then had she been free to marry Jerome and escape the estate and her own shambolic family background.

'Is it the girl then?' asked Mrs Thursday, eyeing Christie.

'Well you didn't think it would be me, after all this time, did you?' Julia sneered. 'Thank God that's all over.'

Mrs Thursday crossed her arms over her middle and bit her lip.

'I told you,' she said. 'I don't . . .'

'You'd bloody better,' said Julia sharply. 'Or the police will be hearing about what you *have* been doing, and for quite a few years too. It's against the bloody law, and you know it. What's that thing? Oh yeah. It was contrary to section fifty-eight of the offences against the person act. Eighteen sixty-one. That's the *law*, Violet. You knew it then and you know it now.'

Mrs Thursday went pale. 'I just wanted to help those poor girls, that's all,' she said defensively.

'Well now you can help *this* girl,' said Julia, and pushed past Mrs Thursday and went inside, dragging Christie with her.

★

Christie was let into a bedroom and the door was closed. She was grateful at least that Julia stayed in the other room while Mrs Thursday got on with the business.

'Take off your knickers and lie there on the bed, dear. On that towel. That's it.'

Mrs Thursday went off to the kitchen and returned five minutes later with a large steaming bowl of water, which she placed on the dresser beside the bed. She laid out items beside it – a Higginson's syringe like nurses used for enemas, a bar of Lifebuoy soap, a grater, a bottle of what looked like disinfectant, another towel. She grated the soap into the water, added the disinfectant, stirred it all up. The pungent whiff of the soap nearly made Christie heave.

'Now. Just go floppy, all right? Just relax and we'll soon be done.'

It didn't hurt. It felt odd, as if she was being inflated inside, like a balloon. At last, Mrs Thursday said: 'Now tomorrow you'll feel a bit of pain and then it'll all come away. All right, dear? Now get dressed. All done.'

Aunt Julia paid Mrs Thursday, then took Christie home.

The first thing Christie noticed when she went to bed that night was that there was a bolt on her bedroom door. With deep relief, she used it.

*

Next day, she couldn't go to school. Her stomach cramped and she started to bleed. She went downstairs to the bathroom, half-crouching, barely able to stand. Thank God everyone – Ivo, Jerome, Jeanette, Julia – were all out. She bolted the door on the bathroom and sat on the loo and before very long she could feel the blood streaming out of her and there was a lot of pain. She gasped and wished her mother was there with her. She sat there for nearly an hour, then – not daring to look in the bowl – she flushed the chain, washed herself at the sink, and went back upstairs to bed.

'It's all sorted,' Aunt Julia told her later. 'I let the school know you'd lost the baby and that you won't be back there until next week.'

'Did they ask about the father?' asked Christie.

Aunt Julia's lips tightened in irritation. 'We're never to talk about that. All right? It's sorted – that's all that needs to be said. I said it was a fling and that the boy's moved away with his parents. And your Uncle Jerome's given a donation to the school for the new gym complex, so everyone's happy.'

Everyone except me, thought Christie after her aunt had gone again, wondering if anyone could ever help her, if she could ever be free of these people, this place, this *nightmare*. She felt sick, hot; she stumbled down the stairs to tell Julia, and fainted dead away at the bottom.

13

She'd been ill. She told herself that. Yes. Flu or something? Anyway, now she was better. She saw Dex alone one day as she passed by the games room – which had once been a dining room but which now contained a full-sized snooker table, a dartboard, a skittles alley and a games table set out with a very expensive ivory chess set.

She paused in the doorway. Dex was sitting at the chess table, setting out the pieces. He looked up at her.

'Do you play?' he asked, indicating the board.

Christie shook her head and said something that had been playing on her mind for a long, long time.

'You really shouldn't hang around with Ivo and his crowd,' she said. 'And no, I don't play chess.'

Dex looked at her in surprise. 'Why shouldn't I hang around with Ivo and the lads?' he asked.

'Because they're bad news.'

'What, you're saying your own cousin is bad news?'

'He is. They all are.'

Dex's blue eyes narrowed as he stared at her face. 'How do you know *I'm* not bad news too?'

That unblinking blue gaze unnerved her. She could feel herself blushing. 'I don't.'

'Come in here. Sit. I'll show you how to play.'

'I don't know anything about chess.'

'Not the Queen's Gambit? Not the English Opening? The Albin Counter-Gambit?'

Christie laughed. She moved into the room, sat down opposite him at the chessboard.

'I don't know what you're talking about,' she said.

'But you're warning me off your cousin.'

'Yes. He's . . . he won't be any good for you.'

'These are pawns,' said Dex. 'That's a knight, that's a bishop, there's the king and the queen.'

'You might as well be talking Swahili.'

'The aim is to achieve checkmate.'

Their eyes locked: held.

'Or maybe you'd prefer to play some other game?' asked Dex.

Christie stood up. 'I don't have time for games,' she said.

'That's a pity,' said Dex, smiling.

'Bye,' she said, and left the room.

14

Kenny Doyle was to rise to the top of the criminal pile over the years, but when he started – and he started early – it was small stuff. Just thieving. Then he graduated to rolling. Currently, he was engaged in his rolling profession, by beating a teenage girl's head against a brick wall. She wailed loudly in protest, a sound that got *right* on Kenny's nerves.

'Shut the fuck up,' he told her, giving her head another whack.

She was a tiny thing who a minute before Kenny grabbed her had been standing shivering under the dim sodium glare of a street light, dressed in a short skirt, high heels and a top that clung to her pathetically minuscule breasts.

Then Kenny showed up and now she was down a dark alley with him, her head bleeding and aching. Hysterical tears streamed down her skinny cheeks.

'Next punter you get, and the next, and the next, you bring them all down here to do the deed. You got that?' he told her.

Terrified, the girl nodded, snot and blood all over her face.

'Or I'll slit your throat. You got *that*?'

She had.

So began Kenny's proper criminal career. He only slipped up once and spent six months in jail. He was determined never to repeat the experience, but it proved useful. Locked up among fraudsters, enforcers, con men, burglars, forgers and bank robbers, Kenny quickly realised that he was a mere beginner. But beginners could learn, and Kenny didn't waste the time he spent behind bars. He talked to experienced cons and when he was out, he had a fistful of new contacts and a firm determination never to be in that situation, ever again.

The British underworld was flooded with cash and Kenny was out to get some of it. On the sink estates, just like the one he had grown up on, there was cannabis aplenty, smoked as oil, resin or leaves, and the mark-up was an extraordinary one thousand per cent. Black marketeering around London's docklands proved staggeringly profitable for him and then Kenny was in a position to open a host of small businesses to front whatever under-the-counter dealings he now chose to exploit. He formed a crew of lads around him, and soon the rolling of underage prostitutes was a thing of the past. Kenny moved on to hijacking lorryloads of spirits and cigarettes to augment his income from the drug sales. He got a few 'long firms' going. Pretty soon, he was *minted.*

The only way was up, and Kenny was soon bristling with money to burn. He started wearing flashy suits and driving high-end cars and making a killing. He joined the Masons and got police in his pay. He became what he had always wanted to be: a face. And if they saw him coming, people – very wisely – stepped aside.

15

By the time he got the formal invitation to visit the boss of one of the larger firms in Broadmoor down in Crowthorne, Kenny Doyle was very bad indeed, but in his youth he'd just been a bit edgy, a bit devil-may-care, just a bit *wrong*.

An only child, he had been spoiled by too much maternal devotion and grew up thinking he could rule the world. A lively curly-headed child, he turned into an athletic teenager and then into a big solid bruiser of a man, barrel-chested and thick-necked as a bull. At seventeen he knocked his father down after the old man got drunk and punched his mum in the face. He wouldn't have that. No way. Drunk or sober, he just wouldn't. Mum was an angel, a saint. And his mum, in her turn, worshipped the ground Kenny walked on.

It didn't do him any good, of course. With his super-inflated ego and his growing gang of various old East End families like the Butlers, the Millicans and the Coopers, all gathered around him and up for trouble, Kenny could easily have spent the better part of his life inside, doing time. But Kenny was no fool; he made use of such people only to the extent that they could be trusted not to fuck up.

The Cooper boy had been OK for small things, petty things, deliveries and such, although Kenny thought that

Dex Cooper did have a mouth on him and was too damned clever for his own good. One of these days Kenny reckoned he was going to have to give that arsehole a slap and calm him down. The Millican clan were best for cars. Stealing them, then shipping high-end motors out of the country using old dockie connections – their dads and uncles. As for Ivo Butler, well, Ivo was useful as a breaker of heads, arms, legs. He enjoyed his work, too. You had to watch him, though. See that he didn't go over the top.

Kenny's favourite quote was this: 'They say crime don't pay? Well that's bollocks for a start. It pays like a bastard, and I should know because I *am* that bastard.'

His *second* favourite was: 'You don't need luck if you got money – and fortunately I got both.'

Kenny was nearly thirty when he visited Broadmoor to take the next step up in his career. What you had to remember – what in fact you could never forget – was that Broadmoor was not a prison, but a high-security mental hospital, containing some seriously dangerous people.

Kenny had on his best togs, one of the sheeny suits he favoured; he had to look his best. He got out of his car and went through door after metal door manned by huge grim-faced screws. The slamming of those doors echoed in his head, reminded him of his brief stint in stir. He imagined being in here, banged up on a life sentence. He was searched, identified, led to a seat, told to sit down.

Buzzers sounded; doors clanged. It was cold in the interview room. He waited. Wondered if he ought to be doing this. Wondered if this might be a step too far, if he was getting too up himself. But then it was too late. Cole Mason came through the door. He was bald and massive, with the gentlest blue eyes Kenny had ever seen. He had killed a handful of men in a variety of amazingly violent ways, but he could have passed for a priest.

Jesus, should I be doing this? wondered Kenny.

But Kenny had grafted for this, seen this as his final aim, for years. He'd started as a legit doorman on the clubs – and having found that he was very useful with his fists he had drifted, inevitably, into debt collection and protection rackets. From there it was building societies, small bank jobs. That was when the Butler connection came in handy, Ivo Butler and the JCBs his family firm kept for use around all their many building sites.

Now Kenny was working his way up in the world. Everything was *sweet*. Particularly so when one of the old firms – *this man's* firm – Kenny had done a job or two for acknowledged him at last. Cole Mason was inside Broadmoor Prison on a life stretch but he was also running a multimillion-pound business sponsoring debt-collecting agencies and other businesses on the outside – and taking a large cut of the profits.

As an up-and-coming face Kenny had written to Mason and asked for his endorsement in return for a retainer of, say, a thousand pounds a month. Not even expecting a reply, Kenny got one. *Come in and see me,* said Mason. And so here Kenny was, almost – to be honest – shitting himself with fear and wishing he hadn't been so damned ambitious. But he was here now. He had to go with it.

'I've been hearing word of you,' said Mason, scrubbing a shovel-like hand over his huge bald dome of a head.

'Really?' This gratified Kenny. He was king of his own muck heap but these people, Mason and the like, were the real deal.

'You're a sound man,' said Mason. 'People have vouched for you. You must know the Butler boys, Graham and Jerome? I knew Graham well, back in the day. Straight as a die, quiet, real solid type. Shame about the way he went, poor bastard.'

'Yeah, it was tragic,' said Kenny. Truth was, he hadn't known Graham Butler at all, or the wife – Anna – who had perished with him in that car crash long ago. But he knew Jerome, he knew the story, knew that Graham's daughter Christie had been very young at the time of the crash and that her tiny size and young years had probably been the saving of her. She'd survived – and been moved in, he'd heard, with Jerome and his family.

'You never know the day, do you?' asked Mason. 'Or the hour.' Mason cleared his throat and then said: 'Incidentally, a thousand pounds a month is a fucking insult.'

Kenny spread his hands, tried to look cool. 'It's a starting figure, Mr Mason. A suggestion. That's all. I meant no offence.'

'Well it's a fucking insult,' said Mason, and suddenly brought one huge fist down onto the metal table that stood between them.

Kenny jumped. He could feel sweat starting to trickle down his back. Mason smiled sweetly.

'One thousand five hundred pounds would be acceptable though,' he said.

'I could do that,' said Kenny, moistening his lips.

'Will you do it?' asked Mason.

'Yeah. Of course.'

'Then we have an agreement.'

Kenny nearly ran out of that place. He was a tough bastard but there was tough and tough. When he'd got home and changed his underwear and had a drink, he had time to finally be pleased about the way things had gone for him today.

Onward and upward, he thought.

He was *in*.

16

A proper weekend-long visit to the Butler place by Kenny Doyle was like a royal progress. At sixteen, Christie watched in fascination as the news of Doyle's imminent arrival threw the whole household into a whirl of activity.

'What does he like to eat?' Aunt Julia asked, hoping Kenny hadn't realised how much she'd disliked him when he'd called round in the past. All right, she *still* didn't like the man, he was still a crook and scary as hell but she knew the family needed the money – iffy or otherwise – that Kenny Doyle was happy to shove their way.

'Stuff. Food. No bother,' said Uncle Jerome, then paused, looking at Ivo. 'Steaks, though. Fillet only. Turbot. He likes that. Lobster. Nothing but the best, right?'

Ivo nodded.

The house had a new cleaner and she soon had the place gleaming, neat, everything functioning perfectly. A stained chair cover or a squeaking door could throw Aunt Julia instantly into a panic.

'So get it fixed,' said Uncle Jerome. 'Don't bother me with it for fuck's sake.'

Aunt Julia, who was strictly an indoors woman, was busy planning menus and the placement of dining chairs; then, realising it was summer, she thought that everyone would of course move out onto the patio.

She spied the state of the garden and nearly collapsed.

The large elaborate fishpond with its central fountain of Venus arising from the depths had several wellington boots floating in its murky waters. Slimy green blanket weed covered the surface, studded with dull dead goldfish. The fountain, clogged by years of neglect from a succession of hapless part-time gardeners, didn't work.

Beyond that, the overgrown lawn was full of clover and moss and there were buttercups – thousands of them – in bright yellow profusion. The edges of the lawn were undefined, the borders thick with weeds, a few struggling plants knocked flat and choked by bindweed.

'Oh Christ,' she said, and hired a gardener, pronto.

Christie observed all this with faint ironic amusement. Yes, it was a royal progress and Kenny Doyle was clearly the reincarnation of Henry VIII, passing through the countryside throwing his subjects into uproar in the balmy summer months. She knew from her history books that Henry had often fled the city of London in summer where the plague was running riot, killing off rich and poor alike. It wasn't going to kill Henry – he made very sure of that. He decamped with his whole court to the countryside, bankrupting many a small lord who had to royally entertain him and his minions for weeks on end.

So it was with the Butler clan. There was a month of furious activity, unknown men coming and going with machinery. And then, suddenly, everything was neat and tidy. The fountain spewed clean water. The lawn was returfed. Not a door in the house squeaked or stuck. There was not even a small stain on the carpets, or the furniture. Everything was perfect. There were new dresses for Aunt Julia and Jeanette. Not for Christie, of course. And new bespoke Savile Row suits for Uncle Jerome and Ivo.

'Just keep out of the way,' Aunt Julia told Christie ahead of Kenny Doyle's visit. 'Don't want you getting under his feet.'

Patsy marvelled at all the fuss when she called over to see Christie.

'Gawd, what's all this?' She laughed.

'Royal visit,' Christie told her. 'Kenny Doyle's coming.'

'I've heard of him. He's a proper big noise. You met him then? Spoken to him?'

'Not yet,' said Christie. Sure, she'd seen him come to the house before, but she'd always kept out of his way and she intended to continue doing that.

When the cavalcade of cars arrived, jostling for space in the long, long drive that led all the way down to the big sheds at the bottom of the plot, she stayed down there, sitting under one of the oaks, watching the squirrels and reading a book – and dreaming of Dex Cooper, hugging the thought of him to herself. Up at the house, she could see people moving around on the patio, she could hear Mama Cass singing 'It's Getting Better' on Uncle Jerome's new stereo. Loud laughter burst out now and again.

When the light began to fade into a vivid burnt-orange sunset and she was getting hungry, she considered what to do now. Obviously, she had to go back up to the house. She didn't want to. She knew her arrival back on the scene would seriously annoy her uncle and aunt, and she'd be confronted by the disgusting Ivo. But there wasn't enough light to read by now, and the lamps were being lit on the patio, and if she was quiet she could just scoot through the house unnoticed, grab a sandwich in the kitchen, then get back up to her room, bolt the door and go to bed. She scrambled to her feet, brushing twigs and dirt from her thin summer dress.

'Hello,' said a voice nearby.

She turned, surprised.

There was a man standing not ten feet away from her. He was wearing a shiny navy-blue suit, threads of gold silk woven into the fabric; it gleamed in the fading light. He was a big man of maybe thirty, well over six feet tall, and heavy with it, padded with muscle and sheer bulk. He had a round face, a nose that looked as if it had been knocked sideways once or twice, deep-set dark eyes that made her think of a shark cruising by, unblinking. Curls of smoke rose from the big Cuban cigar he held in his right hand.

'Hello,' she said in return, and stepped forward warily. Since the trouble with Ivo, since the realisation that men could hurt you both inside and out, she was careful around men in general.

He switched the cigar to his left hand and held out his right. 'You're Jeanette aintcha? I'm Kenny,' he said. 'Kenny Doyle.'

Christie stared at him. So this was the one all the fuss was about. She glanced up toward the house. It seemed, all at once, a very long way away. And the light was fading fast now. Very fast indeed. But he was holding out his hand and she supposed she had better be polite.

'Hello,' she said again, and shook his hand, not wanting to.

'We haven't met yet, have we, Jeanette?'

'I'm not Jeanette. I'm Christie. Her cousin. And no, we haven't met.'

'What are you doing down here on your own?' he asked, holding her hand, not letting it go.

'Just reading.'

'Oh? Reading what?'

She shrugged. 'Nothing much.'

'You ought to come back to the house.'

'I was just going to,' she said, pulling her hand free of his grip. 'What are you doing down here, anyway?'

That seemed to amuse him. He smiled. Yeah, like a shark, she thought, and in that moment she glimpsed in him a brutal type of authority she had never met before. No wonder the Butler clan went apeshit, *this* pitching up on their doorstep expecting to be entertained.

'I was just taking a walk,' he said. 'Didn't expect to have company. Sometimes – don't you find? – you can get tired of that.'

Christie did find that. She was surrounded by enemies, all day, every day. Solitude was always a relief.

'Come on, let's walk back together,' he said, holding out an arm, ushering her before him.

Christie walked back up to the house with him. They didn't speak. Once they were on the patio, everyone seemed to fall back, make way. Then Aunt Julia rushed up with a big shit-eating grin on her face. She shot an anxious look at Christie, then her whole attention was on Kenny.

'We thought we'd lost you!' She laughed. It sounded forced, false.

'Just taking the air. And meeting Christie.'

'Ah.'

Ivo came out through the French doors. 'Playing then, Ken?' he asked, a pack of cards in his hand. His face looked hopeful, servile. Christie couldn't get used to that.

'Sure. Why not.' Kenny turned, took Christie's hand. 'Good to have met you,' he said.

'Were you nice to him?' Aunt Julia hissed urgently, her hand tight on Christie's arm, bright red painted nails digging into the flesh, when Kenny and the other men – but not Dex

Cooper or his little brother Alex; neither of them had shown up today – had disappeared into the games room.

Christie shrugged. 'I suppose,' she said, enjoying her aunt's discomfiture. But Aunt Julia wouldn't leave it there. She tapped on Christie's bedroom door later that night, when all the men had retired to bed.

'What did you say to him?' Aunt Julia queried. 'When you met him in the garden?'

'Nothing much,' said Christie.

'He said he liked you,' said Aunt Julia, as though this troubled her.

'Did he?'

'You were nice to him, I hope? Polite?'

It was only then that Christie fully appreciated how deeply afraid her hated relatives were of this Kenny Doyle person. She tucked this fact away in the back of her brain for future reference.

Christie shrugged. *Yeah, sweat, you horrible old mare.* She remembered Julia when they'd gone for the abortion at Mrs Thursday's place, Julia who had acted like it was all Christie's fault, not that bastard Ivo's.

'He said he liked to be alone sometimes. That's all,' she told her aunt, and left it at that.

17

Over the time that followed, Kenny found he was able to say that he was a member of the Cole Firm and was even allowed to meet other big names, big faces, in person, vouched for as he was by Cole Mason.

Membership of this exclusive criminal club meant international connections and easy access to a multifaceted network of top criminals. These people were the top players of the underworld. The jobs got bigger and easier. Kenny started dealing exclusively with those contacts that came through Mason's firm, and the deals were always rock-solid safe. He hung on to the Butler clan, whom he'd known all his life and were in his pocket; they'd never betray him because they knew he'd cut their bollocks out if they did. And betrayal was even less likely now. Crossing Cole Mason or anyone in his crew – and that now, to his delight, included Kenny himself – was suicide. Lonny and Ian Millican did a couple of things on their own and got banged up for it on a long stretch, but that never touched Kenny. Nothing ever touched Kenny now. He was top-drawer crim, beyond reach. As for his old oppo Dex Cooper, well who knew? Dex had dropped out of the scene. He didn't see him anymore.

On his way home one day, feeling triumphant and wanting to brag about it, Kenny called in unannounced at the Butler place. He found Ivo sitting in the kitchen with his scrawny little sister Jeanette.

'Hiya,' said Ivo, looking up from the day's paper. Tony Jacklin had won the US Open, Kenny saw. And the new Tory Prime Minister Ted Heath was promising strong and honest government. As if.

Jeanette beamed up at Kenny. Thought she looked appealing, no doubt. *Ugly little runt,* thought Kenny.

'Got a moment?' asked Kenny, and Ivo nodded. He cocked his head toward Jeanette. *Fuck off.* Her smile dropped and she got up and left the room, slamming the hall door pointedly behind her.

'Let's go outside,' said Kenny, not entirely convinced that Jeanette wasn't listening on the other side of that door.

Ivo lumbered to his feet and they went out and stood in the sunlit garden. Things were back to normal out there. The equipment sheds loomed down the bottom of the plot but up closer to the house it was now the usual grubby chaos. Discarded pots and deflated footballs floated in the fish pond. Tatty old bits of plastic furniture were scattered here and there. The grass, untended, was long and thick with weeds.

'So what's the crack, boss?' asked Ivo, rubbing his head, stretching his arms up, yawning.

'You need a bloody gardener here,' said Kenny. He hated untidiness, disorder. It offended him.

Ivo grinned and didn't comment.

Kenny told Ivo that he was going up in the world.

'To where?' asked Ivo.

'I got a recommendation off Cole Mason.'

Ivo stepped back in surprise. 'What, *the* Cole Mason? The one who got life for the archway murders?'

Kenny nodded. 'There'll be a lot more breaking work coming your way. You up for it?'

Ivo puffed out his flabby cheeks. 'Just say when and where. And before that – say how much.'

'Double what it was before.'

'Three times,' said Ivo.

Kenny looked at him askance. He stepped forward and his eyes were unfriendly. A flare of fear erupted in Ivo's eyes. 'Don't take the piss,' Kenny advised. 'We can make good money. Both of us. But no piss-taking, all right? I don't like it.'

Ivo held out his hands, palms up. 'All right, all right.' He laughed nervously. 'Want a beer?'

Kenny's eyes narrowed, then he drew back, nodded. 'Yeah, why not? Go on.'

Ivo went back into the kitchen. Kenny stood there, feeling revved up, successful. Then he saw *that* girl, the one he'd seen here before, coming back down the garden, passing close by the sheds where all the building machines and equipment were stored. Her thick straight white-blonde hair, hanging loose upon her shoulders, caught the sunlight and lit up like polished silver.

Christ, he thought. *Now that's what you call a looker.*

She went round behind the sheds, vanished.

Ivo came back, handed him a beer.

'Is that . . . what was her name? Christie?' he asked, pulling the tab.

'What?' Ivo looked around him, pulled the tab on his own beer, drank and belched.

'The blonde one. Down there.' He pointed. 'I've seen her here before.'

'Oh yeah. My cousin. She lives with us.'

Kenny felt jolted. This was the child who'd survived the car crash that had killed her parents, the parents that Cole Mason had mentioned. 'How old is she?'

'Sixteen.' Ivo's eyes were on Kenny's face. 'Wouldn't trouble yourself too much over her though, mate. She's a cold cow. Frigid as a block of ice. And bloody demented.'

'There's smoke coming from that shed down there,' Kenny pointed out. 'Isn't there?'

Ivo looked. Wisps of smoke were indeed curling up into the sky. Wisps – and then clouds of it.

★

'Jesus!' said Ivo, and started running.

It was the shed with the JCBs inside it.

He puffed and panted his way down the garden and found Christie standing there, a box of matches in her hand. She was *smiling*.

Shoving past her, Ivo snatched down a fire extinguisher from the shed wall and fired the thing at the flaming rags that were threatening to engulf the machines, his pride and joy.

The fire was out in an instant. Ivo, gasping for breath, coughed and turned a murderous look on his cousin.

'You do that?' he bellowed.

'Yep,' said Christie, tossing the matches onto the concrete floor.

'*You* . . .' started Ivo, then Kenny appeared in the doorway.

'Everything all right?' he asked.

'Yeah. Some old cloths caught fire, that's all. Accident,' said Ivo.

Christie smiled sweetly at her cousin, knowing that *she* knew this was a small act of revenge. That he hadn't let his abuse of her go. That she never would.

'Come on,' said Kenny, his eyes on Christie. 'Let's go back to the house, yeah?'

'Sure,' said Ivo, scowling at her.

'Why not?' said Christie, smiling.

18

Kenny visited the Butler home more and more frequently. Julia seemed to be watching Christie all the time these days, and finally she drew her to one side and said: 'Listen, Christie. You are never, ever, to tell anyone about what happened. You do understand that, don't you?'

'What?' Christie said, although she knew exactly what Julia was referring to. Her rape by her cousin Ivo. The scandal, the illegality of the abortion that had followed.

Julia grabbed Christie's arm and shook her. 'Don't play dumb. You have a lot you owe us for, you know, and it would be nice if you were at all grateful. But you're not, are you?'

Christie said nothing.

'So look,' Julia ploughed on. 'Not a word, OK? These things happen sometimes.'

Christie was staring at Julia's face. They *what*?

'Ivo would be in a lot of trouble if this ever came out,' said Julia.

Good, thought Christie. That suited her fine.

'And of course it would reflect badly on you. The girl always gets the blame. Everyone would see you as a tart, thinking you'd led poor Ivo on.'

Poor Ivo?

'It wouldn't do you any good if you blabbed about it,' said Julia, and Christie saw sweat break out on Julia's cheeks, heard – clear as a bell – the edge of desperation in her aunt's voice.

The poor cow, thought Christie. *She isn't even convincing herself. She's just covering up for that arsehole because he's her son.*

'I want a curtain up at the bathroom window downstairs,' said Christie.

Julia stopped talking and stared at her niece, open-mouthed.

'Christie . . .' she started.

Christie shook her head once, very firmly.

'I want that curtain up and I want a *stronger* lock on my bedroom door and I want that fucker Ivo kept away from me. You speak to him and you make it clear that if he sees me coming he walks the other way. You tell him that. He won't listen to Uncle Jerome – he tramples all over him and we both know it – but if you warn him of the implications he'll take it from you. Or I promise you – I talk. I talk loudly. To the school head. To the police.' She paused. 'And maybe even to Kenny Doyle. He likes me, you know. I can tell. And then there'll be trouble. And also – you'll never be able to hold your head up among your charity pals ever again. Your name will be *mud.*'

★

Julia's face drained of colour while Christie spoke. Was this the same quiet, placid girl they'd taken in, given a home to? The language! The *threats*! 'Now just hang on . . .'

'No. That's the deal.' Christie looked down at Julia's hand on her arm. She looked up, into her aunt's face. 'And take your damned hand *off* me,' she said.

Next day, there was a stronger lock on the bedroom door.

A curtain went up in the bathroom window.

And Ivo left Christie alone. Particularly now that Kenny Doyle was taking an interest in her.

'Kenny Doyle don't care about you,' said Jeanette to Christie one day.

'Oh?' said Christie.

'He wants to shag you, that's all.'

Christie looked at Jeanette's sharp, sour little face. She thought of her blinded teddy bear, and of all the casual, careless cruelties her cousins had inflicted on her over the years.

'Well he certainly wouldn't want to shag *you*,' she said calmly.

Jeanette's mocking smile faded. 'Look,' she started angrily.

'No,' said Christie. '*You* look. If I told Kenny Doyle just half of what's happened to me since I moved in here, you cow, he'd rip all of your throats out. You do know that, don't you?'

She could see that Jeanette did. She'd gone pale.

'Good,' said Christie, and walked away.

The tide was turning in her favour.

And *Kenny Doyle* was making that happen.

19

It was months later when Christie was passing through the kitchen, studiously ignoring the crowd of men in there. At the sink, the cleaner refilled her bucket and rolled her eyes at Christie, smiling. Poor woman had her work cut out, trying to keep this hovel tidy. There was a young man standing beside the cleaner, filling a glass with water, chatting to the woman, and Christie felt something like a jolt in her chest as she saw it was *him* – Dex Cooper.

Christie hadn't seen him for quite a while. Truthfully, she still had quite a crush on him. Now she was struck anew by his treacle-blond hair, his tanned skin, his laughing blue eyes that met hers now for a lingering instant and then moved away.

She walked on up the stairs to her room, bolting it carefully behind her.

Everything was as normal once again – whatever normal was, in the Butler household. Ivo ruled the roost. Uncle Jerome kowtowed to him. Jeanette was spiteful whenever the opportunity presented itself. Aunt Julia posed with her charity pals. Christie kept out of everyone's way. Aunt Julia and Uncle Jerome attended their charity dinners at the golf club, mixed in with bank managers and other people who owned businesses.

Jeanette came up with the idea that they could all go out down the local Palais one Saturday night, and after an initial desire to say a flat no, Christie thought, why not? She'd shear off from her detestable Butler cousins the moment she got there.

The noise inside the Palais was astonishing, the group up on stage just a gang of ragged youths who thought they were going to make it big-time and never would. Some of the boys who hung around with Ivo were there, drinking too much and making pests of themselves with the girls. Christie, in her C & A pink crochet dress, kept clear of them and of Ivo. She wandered off to the bar. And there he was, quite unexpectedly – Dex Cooper. He turned his head, looked at her with those stunning blue eyes.

'I know you, don't I?' he said. 'Christie, yeah?'

Christie was wary of men. Ivo had made her that way. But it was hard to deny that she'd always liked the look of this one. She had, from the very first moment she'd seen him. No matter what had been done to her, whatever she had endured, she couldn't help but be drawn to Dex. But . . . he *must* be a villain, of course he was, to be mixing with Ivo's lot. And she didn't need that in her life.

'Let me buy you a drink, at least,' he said.

'Coke,' said Christie. 'Please.'

'Still at the Butler place?' he asked as the barman went off to fetch Coke for her, lager for him.

'Still hanging around with my cousin?' she returned.

'Why, are you worried about me?'

She was. She didn't *want* to be, but she was. He seemed too damned *nice* to be anywhere near Ivo's orbit.

The barman put her Coke down on a beermat.

'Well – thanks for the drink,' she said, and walked off.

'Hey!' he called after her.

Christie paused, turned. She couldn't quite suppress a smile. He was watching her. She felt that strange sensation again, just like she had in the games room when she'd seen him there, and in the kitchen. A tightening in her chest. Her stomach turning over.

'I'm Dex,' he said. 'Dex Cooper.'

'I know who you are. You're one of Ivo's mates, so you and your little brother Alex are probably both crooks.'

Dex Cooper was doomed to go to the bad, to set out on a life of petty thievery and prison time. She told herself that, very firmly. She was very sure of what she needed now, and of how to get it.

'That's harsh,' said Dex. 'That's a nice name. Like Julie Christie? You look a bit like her.'

'Thanks for the drink,' said Christie again, and walked on.

20

The Butler family were right to be nervous around Kenny Doyle. He was a big beast in every way. Undoubtedly a criminal. Big, powerful, and with a legion of hard men to call on should the need arise. Christie thought that it probably did arise, often. He was an entrepreneur, he told everyone. She knew that wasn't the full story, not really. She heard that he'd been running all sorts of scams.

Patsy had taken up with Mungo Boulaye, another gangster type who was in very tight with Kenny Doyle, and Mungo had told her he and a few of his pals, Kenny included, had been busy working 'long firm' rackets. Christie had no idea what that was but Patsy obligingly filled her in. Patsy, despite her supposedly superior education, had a powerful yen for bad boys. She always had, always would. She had fallen *hard* for Mungo.

'They take out a short-term let on a warehouse,' Patsy told her patiently. 'They get some fancy letterheads printed and get some dodgy references and then they set up as distributors. Then they order bulk goods from manufacturers and pay on the nail. So everybody's happy, right?'

Christie really didn't follow. How the hell could you make money when you were doing nothing but shelling it out? But she nodded.

'Then all of a sudden the business takes off,' Patsy elaborated. 'On paper anyway. The suppliers think they've hit pay dirt; they're happy as clams. Orders are doubled. The firm's already proved it's credit-worthy so these new orders are all on the knock – washing machines, fancy record players, TVs, you name it. Then . . .' Patsy paused.

'Then?' echoed Christie, but she thought she knew.

'Then *wallop*.' Patsy slapped her hand down on the kitchen table. 'It's all prearranged. Everything's sold off to receivers all over the country. Nothing left in the warehouses but a pile of bills, a few empty boxes and some cobwebs. The firm having appeared to be so kosher, it would be months before the suppliers wised up – and by then they'd be off doing another job somewhere else – somewhere far, far away – with their pockets stuffed with cash.'

So this was the sort of thing Kenny Doyle got up to with his 'entrepreneur' bollocks.

Christie felt a stab of pity for the manufacturers, getting so comprehensively caned. Even high-powered businesses had people running them, people with families, employees, bills to pay, and Kenny and his cohorts were screwing them. So Kenny Doyle was hardly a prince among men. But she reminded herself – and this was the crucial thing – *the Butlers were afraid of him*, and that was enough.

When Kenny – at last – asked her out on a date, she accepted, pleasantly aware that she had Kenny squirming on the hook of his desire for her, that he was hot for her, fascinated by her, found her so cool, so alluring, that he visibly shuddered with wanting her whenever he came close. And she tried to forget all about Dex Cooper.

21

Not that forgetting Dex was at all easy.

Things changed with her cousins though. As if all that had happened in the past between them was forgotten – as if, in fact, it had *never happened*, Ivo play-acted the indulgent cousin to Christie, and began regularly including her and his sister Jeanette on trips here and there. A big group of them hung out together, went down the Palais, to the local stables, to the pictures.

On one trip to their local fleapit of a cinema, Dex was two seats away from her – Ivo sitting between them – and they were watching a rerun of *Fathom*, with Raquel Welch up there on the big screen in all her wondrous physical perfection. Dex was laughing, teasing Christie because she'd broken one arm of her glasses – she was a little short-sighted and later would switch to contact lenses – and she'd stuck it back on with Sellotape. Well, she hadn't broken her glasses; Jeanette had. She'd snapped the damned thing off like a twig and laughed about it. Christie had stuck it back on. She was used to repairing damage.

Christie was an endless source of amusement to Dex, it seemed. She never minded that, though. He'd come to one of the Butler Christmas parties with a large brunette on his arm, but he'd barely given the girl a glance. All his attention had been focused on Christie in her elegant, soberly cut black velvet dress. She'd made it herself. She looked grown up in it. She *was* grown up. Although Kenny was hovering around, wanting her, and she knew he'd be a safe bet and could easily keep the poisonous Butler clan at bay for her, she couldn't seem to shake off this *longing* for Dex Cooper. She was seventeen when she realised fully for the first time that Dex was as seriously, deeply attracted to her as she was to him, and his fixation with her on that night of the Christmas party, the sweet, stomach-churning triumph of it, was forever lodged in her brain.

For that one magical evening she'd held him completely in the palm of her hand, and she knew it. The brunette had been furious but Christie had never been so happy. Never. Not before and certainly not since. That had been the happiest time of her life. No question. No doubt. She'd fallen in love – and it was wonderful.

★

Jeanette had suggested a night out to see some concert or other with the songs from *The Sound of Music* at the local theatre, and Christie said yes because she'd loved that film.

They went in one of the company's flatbed trucks. There wasn't much room in the cab. Ivo was at the wheel, Jeanette squashed in beside him, and – to Christie's shock – Dex Cooper was sitting there on the passenger side; so where on earth was *she* going to sit?

'Sit on my lap,' Dex suggested, smiling, and she did, nervously, facing away from Jeanette and Ivo.

Ivo was heavy on the accelerator and hard on the brake. Dex put his arm around her, holding her steady. He was warm and his arm was strong and suddenly she didn't

care if they ever got to the bloody theatre. She was exactly
where she wanted to be, her face tucked in against his
shoulder, her rotten cousins at her back, unseeing. If she
tried hard enough, she could pretend that they weren't
there at all.

And then it happened.

Dex tilted her face down to his with a hand on her chin,
and he kissed her.

She kissed him back. One kiss turned into two, then three,
then four. Dex's arm tightened around her as their mouths
moved together. Five kisses. His tongue outlined her upper
lip, then her lower, then slipped inside, tasting her, teasing her
tongue, exploring her, until Christie felt a heat, an unknown
and until now *unimaginable* heat, stealing through her body,
weakening her limbs, awakening feelings that she had never
even known existed.

Oh God, don't stop, Dex. Please *don't stop* . . .

Then – too soon, far, far too soon – they arrived at the
venue.

She found the performance long-winded but what did she
care? She was sitting beside Dex in the dark auditorium. He
didn't touch her, didn't even try to hold her hand, but he was
there, and there was this wild electric hum of desire in the air
between them.

What had she been thinking, setting her cap at Kenny
Doyle? Kenny was safety, protection, but *this* was the one
she truly wanted. Dex might be flighty, bad, *wicked*, but she
wanted him and she knew damned well that he wanted her.
When Dex had touched her, she'd felt a warmth that she
hadn't known since that awful day, that last day at the beach
with Mum and Dad; she'd actually felt her poor frozen heart
begin to thaw a little.

On the way home after the concert they all piled back into the truck but this time, unthinking, purely by accident, she got in so that she was *facing* Ivo and Jeanette. So Dex didn't kiss her again. He didn't, obviously, like an audience, and waves of disapproval were already wafting over from prim-mouthed Jeanette and mountainous Ivo behind the wheel.

Regret filled Christie – and *crushing* waves of disappointment.

22

Christie was just going into her bedroom after the concert trip, about to get ready for bed, when Ivo came bursting into the room, barging past her, closing the door behind him.

'What . . . ?' she started. She didn't like him in here. This was her one, her only, private space in the house and here he was, the big ugly bastard, invading it all over again.

'What the fuck was all that?' snapped Ivo, his skin tinted red with some inner outrage.

'What?' Still floating on cloud nine after those deep, drugging kisses with Dex, Christie could only stare at her cousin dumbly. 'What d'you mean?'

'What do I mean?' Ivo reached out one spade-like hand and shoved her, hard.

Caught unawares Christie flailed back, her knees hitting the bed. She fell.

To her horror, Ivo was on her in an instant, pinning her down. She was drenched in the smell and feel of him. The sweat. The damp, hot feel of his big body pressing her into the mattress made her shudder, disgusted, sickened, drowning in memories, *horrible* memories.

'You don't behave like that,' he spat into her face. She could feel his damp breath on her mouth.

'What, I . . . ?' She tried to twist her head away from his, and failed.

'*You know.* Don't keep saying you don't. Acting the fucking tart. Embarrassing me like that. It's not bloody on.'

'I didn't. I . . .' Christie didn't know how to respond to any of this. She could barely breathe and all she could think was that he was spoiling it, ruining what had been so magical, so pure.

His eyes glared into hers. 'You did. And it ain't happening again. You better know that too. You belong to *me.*'

Ivo grabbed her throat. For an instant, one brain-fogged, panic-ridden instant, Christie couldn't even draw breath.

'You don't ever do that again. You hear? You leave Dex bloody Cooper alone,' Ivo snarled.

Christie could only nod. If she didn't, she was afraid he might kill her.

Next day, Ivo was loitering near her bedroom door again when she came upstairs. She halted on the landing.

'What?' asked Christie coldly, ready to turn tail and run straight back downstairs if he started anything.

'Message from Dex,' he said.

'*What?*'

'He says to tell you he ain't interested. Says he got a hard-on with you in the truck, but then he'd have got that with any bit of skirt, you're nothing special. So he said to tell you to piss off.'

Ivo went downstairs, leaving her standing there in shocked silence.

★

Ivo was pleased with his work. That was her, the frigid little cunt, told. Then he drove over to the Cooper household and Dex's mum answered the door. She called for Dex and he came and looked at Ivo.

'Bad news I'm afraid pal,' said Ivo.

'What?' asked Dex.

'My cousin Christie don't want nothing to do with you. The way you behaved, mate, really . . .' Ivo tutted. 'Getting your tongue halfway down her throat, I mean. She didn't want it but she was afraid to say so. So she asked me to do this and I'm telling you now. She's not interested and she's said you're to keep clear. Got it?'

Dex was silent, staring at Ivo.

'That clear?' said Ivo.

Dex nodded slowly. 'Yeah. It's clear.'

★

The next Christie heard about Dex was that he was going abroad, emigrating. But he did come to the Butler house the day before he left, just once, to say goodbye to them. That evening was etched into Christie's memory and she carried it with her into her future years, holding it to her like a talisman, a warding-off of evil; the vision of Dex, the Dex she loved but who had rejected her. He was suited and booted, handsome as a film star with his straight treacle-blond hair and his blue, blue eyes. But he barely looked at her.

It was true then, all that Ivo had said.

Then Dex left.

'Best thing that could happen, him fucking off like that,' Ivo said. 'Told you he wasn't interested, didn't I.'

After that, Christie was determined that she would never, ever allow herself to fall in love again.

She mustn't.

It was too painful.

23

The next time Christie and Kenny Doyle met, she was eighteen years old. More important, she was heartbroken – literally smashed in two. She'd fallen head over heels in love with Dex like a fool but he'd just taken advantage of her in the truck. Told her to – and this hurt – 'piss off'. He'd left the country, left her here with these people she hated.

Then there came another 'royal' visit. Kenny Doyle, His Fucking Majesty, was calling in at the Butler place for the weekend with a collection of mates who were really his courtiers, his hangers-on, his arsehole creepers. They – and Ivo and Uncle Jerome – laughed uproariously whenever Kenny cracked a joke, listened to every comment he made as if it was all pearls of wisdom, which Christie quickly concluded was not the case.

Kenny Doyle walked into the house on Friday night, and the Butlers grovelled. They fed him, offered him the world on a plate, gave him the best bedroom in which to rest his head; nothing was too good for Kenny. Christie kept well out of the way, moving from one room to another throughout the day whenever she heard the whole mob of them coming, filching bread and cheese to eat from the kitchen whenever she thought the coast was clear. Finally at dusk she went out into the garden and then, despite the night drawing in, she went up past the equipment shed to the oaks beyond and sat there, hunched in a coat, reading the newspaper by the light of her torch, seeing the usual parade of horrors in there: the Duke of Windsor being buried in England, a plane crash at Heathrow, Napalm being dropped onto Viet Cong children by American planes.

She was trying hard not to think about Dex, but she felt wasted, devastated, choked with tears whenever her mind groped its way in blind anxiety to the empty space where he should have been.

'Hey – Christie?'

The voice startled her. She sprang up, wiping at her cheeks, blinking furiously. If any of them saw her crying, they'd mock her. Poke fun at her. They loved to do that. But it wasn't them. It was *him*, Kenny Doyle, standing there in another of his flashy suits, this one grey with a silvery sheen to it. Kenny's suits always had a metallic thread running through them, sometimes silver, sometimes copper, sometimes gold. It was if he thought that, by covering himself in good fortune, he could draw even more of it to him. He wore a grey silk shirt, a grey knit tie. He looked expensive. He was greedy, Kenny Doyle, Christie had long since realised – greedy in every way. For money. For prestige. For food. Probably also for sex. He looked like the gangster he was. He looked *dangerous*.

'Sorry, didn't mean to make you jump. I saw the torch-light. Thought it must be you. Haven't seen you all weekend,' he said.

Christie said nothing. Had he seen her tears? She didn't think so.

'What's up? Something upset you?'

He *had* seen them.

'No. Nothing,' she said, starting back toward the house. All she wanted was to be left alone. To reach the sanctuary of her bedroom, to close the door on the lot of them, Kenny Doyle included.

'You don't say much, do you?' he asked, half-smiling, falling into step alongside her.

There was nothing to say. She was torn in two, the heart ripped out of her. She didn't care if she lived or died, not anymore. She'd lost her parents, endured years of torment and abuse – and now, the final death knell. Dex was gone.

'Hey.' He stopped her with a hand on her arm. 'Hey, come on. Talk to me.' His dark eyes were intense as they rested on her face. 'They treat you all right, do they? I know you lost your own folks . . .'

'It isn't that,' she said, and walked on.

'No? Because I promise you, I can have a word. Sort it out. You understand?'

Christie stopped walking. She stared up at him in the half-dark of the garden and suddenly she was seeing clearly, seeing *him*, as if for the first time.

For so long, she had been desperate for a way out.

Now Dex was gone and that hope was over.

But she had found her exit, and Kenny Doyle was *it*.

24

They married in London. Aunt Julia was far more excited by the idea of a wedding than Christie herself. Jeanette was excited too, not only at having Christie – at long last – kicked out the door, but also at the prospect of being a bridesmaid alongside Christie's old school pal Patsy.

It wasn't a big ceremony, although the Butlers, always eager to be looked at and admired under Julia's leadership, had pushed for that. Christie didn't want it. So she and Kenny pitched up at Chelsea Register Office with just two bridesmaids, Uncle Jerome, Aunt Julia, and Ivo.

It was over very quickly, confetti thrown, photos taken outside, then a few modest days in a hotel and Kenny was soon off doing business – and then Dex showed up again.

★

Christie was sick with rage and disappointment, furious at the fates that had caused her such misery in her young life. Had Dex come back three days earlier from his travels abroad, she knew she would never have married Kenny Doyle. But then to Dex she was just another girl, another *nobody* he'd enjoyed a kiss and a fondle with, that was all. She had loved him utterly, completely – but he had turned his back on her, easy come, easy go.

Now he knew she was married. He probably assumed she was *happily* married, too. Not that he cared, either way.

Christie would never forget standing in her aunt's grubby kitchen, fresh back from what passed for their 'honeymoon', her husband of three days leaning against one worktop, the – oh all right, why not say it if it was true? – the *love of her life* leaning against the fridge door, talking about Argentina, about his mum and dad, about everything except what had just happened – Christie's marriage to big-time crook Kenny Doyle. Kenny was giving it a load of chat, trying to impress like he always did, while Christie just stood there, somehow smiling but feeling sick.

When Dex left and Kenny had cleared off somewhere to meet someone, Christie went into the bathroom and vomited. Then her aunt was knocking on the door, asking if she was all right – as if she actually cared, which Christie knew she did not. Her aunt wanted to know the dirt; that was all. Her eyes would gleam with insatiable curiosity as she asked, why was Christie so upset? Was she ill? Was she perhaps – and this would be accompanied by furtive, gleaming, avid glances at Christie's stomach – pregnant, oh, and was that the reason for the rush to get married?

'I'm fine,' Christie managed to say, but tears were cascading down her face as she flushed the chain and sat down, shaking with shock, on the closed loo seat. And yes, it was grief; it was heartfelt, utter *grief*.

Was this God, punishing her for marrying a man she didn't love? Taking those vows and not meaning a single one of them, just to escape from life around Ivo?

Nice trick, God. Neat. Get me married off to fucking Kenny Doyle and then you let Dex come back in the door again.

Kenny was away for a week after Dex's visit, and she thanked God for that. She was supposed to be looking for a London house, money no object, and after a few days of lying in bed, wanting to do nothing, feeling that awful over-whelming sense of loss, she finally crawled out and showered and got on with it. What else was there to do?

She found a narrow four-storey Georgian house in up-and-coming Primrose Hill for herself and her new hus-band. It wasn't terrific, it wasn't perfect, but it was away from the Butlers, far away, and that was all that mattered. After packing up her few possessions in a rented van, she moved out of her uncle and aunt's place and into her own.

'You mustn't be a stranger,' said Aunt Julia.

'That's right,' said Uncle Jerome, and Christie saw it in their eyes – their awareness of the sea change in their rela-tionship with their niece. Christie was tightly linked to Kenny now, and they had just better watch their step or there would be repercussions. Bad ones.

That applied to Ivo too. He hovered in her bedroom doorway, watching as she moved out, losing his grip on her and hating it but too scared of Kenny to even try raising an objection.

Aunt Julia called at the London place within a week of Christie's exit, laden with armfuls of gifts, but Christie saw her coming and didn't answer the door.

A week later, Ivo came and knocked for a good half hour. When he finally gave up, Christie looked outside. He'd brought chocolates for her. A bloody gift! That fat, over-weening git, that *rapist*, did he think they were *sweethearts* or something? And when she hadn't answered the door he'd opened them himself and eaten half of them. The mangled box with a few chocolates remained there on the step, ants swarming over them, a silent rebuke. Later Christie picked the remains of the gift up and took it through to the kitchen and tossed it, shuddering, into the trash.

Uncle Jerome came the week after that, leaning in his usual casual fashion against the door frame, one arm above his head. She waited until he'd gone, and then she could relax again.

'Anybody call?' Kenny asked her that evening, coming in and kissing her cheek.

'Nope,' said Christie, and put his dinner on the table.

The Butlers no longer existed for her.

Within the first year of her marriage to Kenny Doyle, they took the hint and didn't call anymore.

25

Of course, as a married man, Kenny expected sex and Christie had braced herself for that. Memories of sexual encounters with Ivo made her wince. But Kenny was always scrupulously clean, painstaking in his toilette. She liked that. Physically, she didn't find him repulsive. He was a handsome man. Gypsy-dark. And this was part of the deal she had agreed to when she stood in the register office and promised to love, honour and obey. Maybe there was something about reproduction in there too, something about kids perhaps, but she hadn't listened to any of that or maybe she had even imagined it. The wedding day had passed in a fug of numbness for her. She'd agreed the deal to get out from under the Butlers – and nothing the registrar said had really interested her in the slightest.

'You may kiss the bride,' he'd said. An elderly gent, bespectacled, benign. He had smiled at her encouragingly. She was very young. Nineteen!

It was no surprise to Kenny, she knew, to discover that she wasn't a virgin when they went to bed. She'd prepared herself for the wedding night. Got the Pill, made sure there'd be no 'little accidents'. The idea of an unexpected pregnancy made her shiver. Vague memories surfaced when she thought of the possibility of it, of Ivo panting in her face, pounding her into the bed, of Mrs Thursday and a nauseating hospital scent of soap and disinfectant.

The actuality of Kenny naked and sitting on the bed waiting for her when she emerged in her nightdress from the en suite did shock her. But this, she reminded herself, was the deal. Kenny had kept his part of it, married her, got her out from Ivo's control, and now it was her turn to keep hers.

'Take it off,' he'd said when she approached the bed.

'What?' Her heart was hammering so hard in her chest that she thought it was going to come straight out through her ribcage. Her mouth was dry.

He smiled. She couldn't take her eyes off his body, which was gold-toned from tanning out in the Costas with all his dodgy mates. He was heavy with muscle. Intimidating. She'd always seen him fully clothed, flashily dressed; yes, this was a shock.

'Come on, I don't bite,' he said. 'Come closer.'

Christie approached him. Kenny reached out, took her hand. 'Don't worry,' he said. 'It's going to be fine. Now come on. Take it off.'

He couldn't be stalled any longer. Christie knew it. She'd kept him at a distance during their courtship but now it was no longer possible. She'd lingered in the bathroom, putting off the final moment, but she couldn't delay now. She gritted her teeth, lifted the hem of the nightie and quickly pulled it off, over her head.

She heard the breath catch in his throat.

'Wow. You're beautiful,' he said.

'No I'm not.' Ridiculously, she wanted to cover herself. Somehow, she resisted that urge.

'Gorgeous,' he said, and reached out, cupping her breast in one big hand. With the other he pulled her down onto the bed. 'It's going to be all right,' he said.

And it was, really. He tried to be restrained, to take it slowly, but in the end he couldn't. She felt his surprise when he slid into her and found no barrier. Maybe he would think she'd been using tampons. She hadn't, but he would think that. Or maybe he would think she'd had a multitude of lovers, which wasn't the case either. She didn't – oh, and this was shocking, she knew it was – she really didn't much care what he thought. She was here, she was Mrs Kenny Doyle, and she was safe now. Dutifully she faked an orgasm, because she knew he would expect that. He'd had lots of women, she supposed. That didn't bother her either – not in the least.

That first time set the pattern for their lovemaking. He was eager, she was cool but made the right noises. She usually made the effort and screamed a bit, clung to him. But of course you couldn't get away with that sort of deception indefinitely. She sensed Kenny cooling off within five years of their wedding day, and she was anxious about that. She didn't love Kenny – of course not – she was still foolishly, hopelessly, *agonisingly* in love with Dex Cooper – but she *needed* him. They discussed children. Christie played along with the idea, noted how it turned Kenny on all the more, made him far more excited about the whole business of sex with her.

'I think I put a baby in you just then,' he whispered to her in the dark one night, lying on top of her, still inside her.

'I think so too,' she lied. The Pill made her feel very sure that he hadn't.

'You came so hard,' he whispered, kissing her ear, half-laughing. 'You were like a wild thing. You scratched my back.'

'Sorry,' said Christie, thinking that maybe she had over-done her performance.

'No, don't be sorry. That's the best way to get a baby, isn't it. I heard that. When you both come together.'

'I don't know – is it?'

'Damned sure.'

She hadn't 'come' at all, not once, not ever, with Kenny, but she had put on a very convincing performance in that department. There was no way Kenny could have impreg-nated her. She had her secret supply of tablets and she was diligent when it came to taking them. She didn't want kids. Not a girl for sure because she was frightened of what could happen to her – the world was a dangerous place. And not a boy either, because who knew what sort of monster he might grow into?

So she maintained the lie. Kenny kept waxing lyrical about kids; she kept taking the Pill.

She was careful about keeping her little secret from him.

Once, a chippy male doctor looked at the very expensive ring on her left hand and asked her: 'Does your husband know you're taking these?'

Instantly she'd changed to another doctor – and this one was in private practice in Harley Street, where no one would dream of questioning a female patient in such a way, married or not. She had it all under control. Sorted. And then she got home one day and found Kenny had been rummaging through the kitchen waste bin. She'd tucked the empty foil packet way down at the bottom under a mountainous pile of teabags and banana skins, but when she got home there was Kenny with the damned packet in his hand.

'What's this?' he asked her, very sharp, although he knew perfectly well what it was.

When Christie didn't answer, he said: 'I knew it! I bloody thought so. You've been taking these damned things and I thought there was a chance you were going to get a kid off me! Fat chance of that, was there? You bloody cow.'

He threw the foil packet onto the floor at her feet. He looked so mad that Christie thought, *This is it. He's going to throttle the life out of me.* She'd deceived him. She even felt bad about it. But she didn't know what else she could have done.

'Why?' he rapped out. 'Why would you do that? You know how much I want kids. I thought you did too.'

Actually, Christie had never said so. They had never even discussed children before the wedding. Or after, come to that. Maybe if she'd talked to him, been honest, pointed out her total lack of maternal urge, then he would have understood?

No. No chance. She had seen Kenny with other people's kids, tossing them into the air, grinning, enjoying their company. Kenny adored kids. He would, of course, want some of his own. And if she had fessed up, told him the unsavoury truth about all that had happened to her in her early years, everything that had made it *impossible* for her to go there, he probably would have bailed, not gone ahead with the wedding in the first place. And then her escape route out of the Butler household would have been gone. She couldn't have risked that.

After Kenny's discovery, things cooled between them and not long after that she became aware that Kenny was taking mistresses. Her favourite perfume was Femme de Rochas, and he would come home reeking of Shalimar or Chanel No. 5. He bathed more, took even more care than usual over his appearance, dropped a stone from his big meaty body, was out more. He never mentioned the Pill episode again, but it stood between them, unspoken.

'They all do it.' Patsy shrugged it off when Christie told her about Kenny's 'outside interests'. Patsy was married herself now, to Mungo Boulaye. 'Mungo's exactly the same. And really, why worry? You've got to be straight with yourself, accept it. I have. That sort of high-powered bloke's always going to be looking for a little bit on the side. We both know it, don't we?'

Christie not only knew it, she was relieved by it. She didn't like the lies, the play-acting. Kenny might be a thug, but he had always treated her decently enough and she had sufficient common decency herself to feel badly about the way she'd used him. But what choice had she really had?

Their marriage wasn't bad. Kenny wanted sex with her less and less often while he busied himself with other women. In a way, she was pleased for him. He was getting satisfaction with those others, and she knew that he was sensitive enough – just about – to realise that it was something Christie herself found hard to provide.

26

In the summer of seventy-eight, when things were getting a little heated in London for Kenny, the Spanish – God bless them – decided to end the hundred-year-old extradition treaty that had been drawn up long ago, with Benjamin Disraeli. They said it was unworkable – despite the scheme having worked perfectly for a century – and thus they paved the way for Kenny and a great many of his mates to leave England with various police forces nipping close at their heels, and decamp to the sunny Costa Del Crime, where they were instantly untouchable.

Kenny loved the Costas, but Christie hated the heat. So, when things had settled a little, Mr and Mrs Doyle returned home to England, where Kenny purchased a plot in the Sussex hills, knocked down the crappy old bungalow that stood on it, and built a mansion.

Christie piled all her creative energy into fashioning it into an exquisite home, consulting architects, collecting paint charts, hiring interior designers. She loved pastels, mint greens, sugar pinks and sky blues, and she filled the place – *her home* – with soft colour, luxury, comfort. Kenny loved the flash of it, the sheer impressiveness of what she was creating. The baby talk between her and Kenny had faded. They lived day to day – settled, bored with each other really, dissatisfied but keeping it hidden, like so many other married couples.

There were lots of women for Kenny; and for Christie an obsession with soft furnishings and expensive curtains, collecting this and that, attending auctions, adding to the stuff she had squirrelled away as a child – Teddy, and her dad's theodolite, a collection of Wemyss pottery pigs and many other little glittery bits and pieces.

This was married life.

And it was OK.

She tried never, *ever* to think of Dex or to wonder where he could be, what he was doing.

Sometimes, she even succeeded.

27

Actually, it wasn't all bad. Kenny would chuck money at things to impress everyone, and Christie utilised that to make a fantastic home for him, for her, maybe even for their children, supposing they ever had ány, which up until her thirtieth year she had managed scrupulously to avoid.

Then Kenny came home one day and said, straight out: 'I want kids. We've got this big place, *perfect* for a family, and I want kids to fill it. All right?'

Christie could see that he meant it. He'd had enough. This could be a breaking point for their marriage and she knew she couldn't risk losing Kenny, her shield, her protector.

'All right. OK. I'll come off the Pill,' she said.

But Christie, despite agreeing to Kenny's demands, still didn't conceive. And Kenny still comforted himself in the arms of other women.

There had been one searingly embarrassing interview with a gynaecologist, after Kenny had bestowed upon her a dose of the clap, which he had caught off one of his many dalliances. The gynae, his face twisted in barely concealed disgust and disapproval, had warned her, *her*, of the dangers of sleeping around and had written her a prescription to clear up the infection.

'You're certain you've never been pregnant before?' he'd asked.

'Never,' said Christie.

He frowned. 'There seems to be scarring . . .'

'Never,' she repeated.

Then came tests, lots of them. The fault had to be with her, Kenny said. It couldn't possibly be on his side, not him, not good old Golden Bollocks. Probably he had kids running around all over the place, so why couldn't he have them with his own wife? Christie knew he must feel cheated. Kenny had married her for exactly this purpose, she realised: to get the settled home life with the woman he craved. Christie knew there was a pattern here and that Kenny was following it. His dad had apparently been a philanderer and ironically Kenny – who was exactly like his dear old dad – had despised him for it. Kenny had idolised his mum, placed her on a high pedestal, and instinctively he wanted that type of woman for himself. The demure, ever-presentable housewife. The 'her indoors' who would soak up all the misery heaped upon her by an errant husband.

He thought he'd got that, in Christie.

So, there were tests. Which Christie initially refused to have, because one, she hated people poking and prying at her body and two, she felt no desire to mother anything or anyone.

'If I've got to be tested, so have you,' she insisted.

He was outraged. What was she inferring – that he couldn't measure up?

'We both have it or neither of us,' said Christie, sticking to her guns. She might be the quiet one, but – as Kenny had long since discovered – she did have an iron streak in her.

'All bloody right,' said Kenny, and sulked, and stomped about the place, but he went with her to the doctor's and then to the private clinic and was proved, much to his unhidden delight, to be right – Christie was at fault, not his little swimmers.

'Told you,' he said, triumphant. She wanted to hit him.

There were, of course, lots of things that could be done. How about IVF? Or adoption?

Rather than put herself through the anguish of medical intervention – she detested doctors, hated the thought of them pawing at her – Christie said all right, maybe they'd adopt. But she could see a flaw to that, straight away. Kenny was the sort of bullish bloke who might never see an adopted child as truly his, because the child wouldn't have sprung from his own loins.

And as for her? Well, she might discover that she wanted to be a mother after all. She thought of a brood of boisterous boys, romping around the place, fighting like puppies, shouting and throwing stones and food and – incidentally – ruining the orderliness of her beautiful home. And a daughter, a girl? A little pink and white princess to spoil and love? Her mind stopped dead at that, as a racehorse baulks at a fence it instinctively knows is too high and may cause it to break its neck.

But she owed this to Kenny, didn't she? *This* was all part of what she'd – yes, cold-bloodedly – signed up for, and it was her problem, not his, if she now couldn't bring herself to go ahead with it. So they went through all the rigmarole and were finally offered a brother and sister who were to be taken off a drunken set of parents for their own protection. At the last minute, Christie said no. She didn't want to go ahead with it. Kenny was angry and she understood that. It had been a long hard tussle to get an offer of two children and now she was throwing it all away – but she was adamant. They weren't going ahead with the adoption.

By then, the sex between Kenny and Christie had lost any sense of pleasure or purpose. Well, on Kenny's part, anyway. Christie had always simply gritted her teeth and got on with it, sex-wise. Kenny expected it, and she expected to have to provide it. It was as simple as that. So she did. If she was too tired, too dry when he entered, she – to her shame – thought of Dex, her long-lost love and it was OK, easier. Knowing she couldn't get pregnant by Kenny, that he couldn't prove himself the big man among all his mates, she could see that Kenny lost interest more or less completely – and Christie accepted that, was relieved by it.

They rubbed along, lived life day to day, like brother and sister rather than husband and wife. Like so many couples, they grew indifferent to each other. Yoked to the same plough – their marriage – but detached from it too.

There was a poem, wasn't there, a saying? Something about being a child and then growing to adulthood and having to put childish things away. Well, she'd done that. If you didn't think too much about the past, if you remembered always to keep your mind on the present, the house, your social life – such as it was – well, how could you say that any of it was bad?

It wasn't.

But then came the day of her fortieth birthday party.

Until then, she had pretended to the outside world that everything was just fine and dandy. Everything had chugged along on the track.

But then came the derailment.

Kenny's bombshell.

28

Kenny had his fingers in a lot of pies. Businesses, car washes, dry-cleaners, nightclubs. His old mate Mungo Boulaye, Patsy's husband, had persuaded him to take a share in Mungo's, the club he'd started up in Frith Street, and it proved to be a sound investment.

Bored at home, dissatisfied on some deep level and feeling his marriage was a drag, Kenny liked to look in on the business on occasion, see the clientele there having fun. He could barely remember what fun was *like*, actually. He still took the odd mistress or two, had a few one-nighters, but he felt . . . *restless*, wondering what the hell it was all about, what it was all for. So why not pop into the place, see Mungo and share a bottle or two, have a peek at the dancers?

So one night he was there, sitting at the pole-dancing bar. Mungo was busy out back somewhere, so he was alone, drinking his whisky, while the girls twirled, topless and brazenly beautiful, over his head.

It didn't hurt to look, now, did it?

Sex with Christie was no longer of any interest to him. The last time with her, she'd acted like he was trying to *rape* her, for God's sake. She'd been cold, unwilling, dry as a nun, just bloody awful. So *this* was how he got his sad jollies these days, peering up at three sets of perfect tits, all of them bouncing pneumatically over his head and thinking, well, why not? Why the hell not?

One of them in particular – the luscious one with the cascade of blonde hair who worked the centre pole – was giving him the eye, licking her lips at him, smiling. Christ, when had Christie ever smiled at him like that, a smile ripe with promise? *Never.* Not even on their honeymoon, if he was honest.

Oh, to hell with her.

The girl on the centre pole had the most fabulous set of boobs; they weren't like the other two dancers' breasts, which although appealing were obviously plastic. The centre pole dancer's tits were *magnificent*, and while her hips were narrow her breasts were enticingly big, her nipples pink. They jutted out like organ stops, big as beer mats. Those were *real* tits – luscious. *Not* plastic.

I would like to fuck her, he thought.

'You'll go blind if you stare at her any longer,' said Mungo, coming over and slapping him on the shoulder.

Kenny leaned in to make himself heard over the roar of the music.

'Also,' said Mungo, grinning, 'if she twirls them things at you any harder, she's likely to knock herself out.'

'I'd like to meet her,' said Kenny.

'You would? Well, I'll send her over when her set's finished, OK?'

'Thanks. What's her name?'

'Lara,' said Mungo. 'Lara Millman.'

★

It was all quite sudden, really. And unnerving, too. Lara came out from the girls' dressing room at the back of the club after her set was over and sat down on the bar stool next to his. Kenny was a bit shocked to see that she hadn't covered up at all. Then he had to shout to make himself heard over the Bee Gees, chatting to her as best he could, being as *cool* as he could, with those delicious nude tits of hers not two feet from his face. When she laughed they jiggled alluringly and he wanted to touch them, touch *her*.

After half an hour of this sweet torment, he leaned in and said: 'Let's go outside.'

Her eyes teased him. She had fabulous eyes, yellow as a tiger's, bold as any top-line predator's. 'What for?' she asked.

'Because I've got a hard-on that's about to blow and I don't want to waste it,' he said, his eyes serious.

'Oh,' she said. Then – oh she was a shocker, this girl! – she slowly, seductively, dipped one red-painted fingernail into his glass of Chivas Regal on the bar top, then touched her finger to her breast.

'Lick it off me,' she said.

It was a dare. They were in a roomful of people, the jungle thrum of the music was keeping pace with his own hectically racing pulse. It was hot in here, like another world. Dazzled, he took up the challenge. He leaned in close and took one of those beguiling teats into his mouth; sucked once, hard. Felt it bloom and harden under his tongue.

When he straightened up, she was still smiling. People looked, nudged each other. Kenny saw Mungo watching across the room, not looking pleased.

He's old enough to be her father, Kenny imagined them all whispering. *Lucky dog, eh?*

'You're a friend of Mungo's, ain't cha?' she asked.

'Yeah.'

'His wife don't like me.'

'Who, Patsy?' Kenny laughed excitedly. This girl was wild, sexy, crazy – and he wanted her *right now*. 'You're young and you're beautiful. Of course she don't. Outside?'

She shook her head.

'You worked here long? Only I've never seen you in here before,' said Kenny.

'I haven't seen you, either. I've been here about a year I suppose. You don't come in here very often, do you?'

I will now, he thought. 'Come on. Outside?' he asked again.

'Maybe next time,' she said.

Next time, she *did* go outside with him.

After that, he was gone; totally and completely hooked. Sex with Lara Millman was *amazing*. After a long, dry, disappointing marriage, she was such a treat – a complete treasure. He just couldn't get enough of her and she was so willing, so bloody *welcoming*.

Before very long he was – much to his own surprise – in love with her, with Lara Millman.

Fuck Christie.

29

It was the day of Christie's fortieth birthday and this was her beautiful house, the home she'd fashioned over many years, set in a golden sun-drenched English valley. Above it on this day there hung the blue breezeless bowl of a miraculously cloudless sky. Christie's house was huge in scale and with more kerb appeal than seemed entirely feasible or fair. It stood perched majestically on one side of a valley, its grounds and manicured lawns sloping down to an old disused railway track, now a public walkway; people cycled and rode their horses down there.

There were farmers' fields on the other side of the valley. Every August, for years, Christie Doyle, wife of Kenny, had watched the crops on that side of the valley bloom and mature. She'd seen the vivid eye-splitting acid yellow of the rape, the milder custard-cream tones of the ripening wheat crops. She'd seen the farmer and his family harvesting every August, the combine working late into the night to get the crops safely in, the headlights on the big machines cutting through the deep blackness of the country night.

Her lovely turquoise-watered pool. She'd had it installed, years ago, fussed over every little detail of it, the tile colour, the precise balance of aqua to green, the chicest type of pool house, the obligatory high-powered water heater and the best automated pool covering needed to get and keep the water nice and toasty. *Her* pool was perched on the slope where the view was at its absolute best. There were people in there now: their party guests. They were swimming and shouting, splashing about. Sometimes in high summer Christie saw a little female fox swimming in the pool, cooling off. She liked that fox although the gardener Patrick always cursed her, because the vixen dug holes in the border beside the elevated stretch of the decking.

'Thinks she'll make a home under there,' said Patrick. 'Bloody thing.'

But Christie couldn't help admiring the sheer balls of that female fox. Sometimes she watched her come up from the orchard at the bottom of the plot near the railway line, a dead rabbit clamped hard in her jaws – a feast for her pups, no doubt. She'd watch the fox jump up over the gate, then out to the front of the house and away, back to her den. Tough little bitch – she always brought a smile to Christie's face, as Christie was something of a tough little bitch herself; she'd had to be.

But right now there was no fox in the pool, just people. Everyone was having terrific fun. This had been Kenny's idea, this party, not hers. He'd said they should 'make a splash'. It was her fortieth and it had to be celebrated. And he'd invited along some people that Christie herself wouldn't have invited, not in a million years.

Further up from the pool there was a vast pink, elaborately frilled marquee. Pink and white flower-decked arches lined the red-carpeted path from the folding doors at the back of the house right down to the marquee's entrance.

People were strolling about the garden, laughing and chatting. There was the merry clink of champagne glasses; there were black-clad staff going hither and thither, replenishing drinks, offering trays of indescribably exquisite foods. UB40's '(I Can't Help) Falling In Love With You' was blaring out from the DJ's mighty sound system.

It was all bloody lovely.

Christie's house, her home.

It was her bolthole. Her place of safety. All right, Kenny didn't know the seedier aspects of her history with the Butlers, but still, she was mad at him. What the fuck was he doing, inviting them here, today of all days? It made her skin creep to see the Butlers in her house. *Fuck* Kenny and his stupid 'big party' ideas. For the greater part of the day she was able to avoid them, but then to her dismay she came face to face with Aunt Julia on the lawn and the crush of people was so dense that she was unable to move away from her.

Christie had long since decided that her Aunt Julia was nothing more than a sea of acid floating under a thin film of sugar and that she *still* blamed Christie, not Ivo, for all that had happened in her household.

'Christie! What a fabulous place you have here,' she said, her eyes sharp but her mouth smiling, the fact that Christie had never once invited her to come here standing stark and unspoken between them.

'That wonderful Venetian mirror over the fireplace in the sitting room, where on earth did you get that?' Aunt Julia asked.

'I picked it up somewhere. Can't really remember.' Collecting, embellishing this wonderful home, was Christie's passion. Always had been, still was. She had nothing else. Sad, but true.

'Well, the whole place is just lovely,' said Julia. 'Isn't it, Jerome?'

'Thanks,' said Christie, aware that her home made Julia's look like a shed.

'Jerome?' Julia nudged her big, bearded husband, who was standing silent at her side.

'Yeah,' he said, and Christie was reminded that Uncle Jerome was always uneasy in these social situations.

She could remember – just – that her dad Graham was the one who had mixed happily in a crowd; even having lost him at so young an age, she knew he'd been a get-along-with-anyone type of person, the one who dad-danced crazily at parties, who roared with laughter at silly jokes, who was loved and respected by the people who worked for his and Uncle Jerome's firm.

'Well – enjoy yourselves,' said Christie, and she quickly moved away.

She thought that was the worst of the day over, but no: not half an hour later her cousin Jeanette passed her en route to the downstairs cloakroom. Jeanette hadn't seemed to improve in any way since she'd grown up. Some girls did: they started out plain, and then blossomed. But not her. Her face was still all sharp angles, her unremarkable eyes downturned, her lips thin, and the yellow-toned floral dress she wore sat horribly alongside her sallow skin.

You could almost feel sorry for Jeanette, Christie sometimes thought. She'd had, so far as Christie knew, few boyfriends, no marriages, no kids; all she ever seemed to do was loiter in the office of J & G Butler Ltd – Jerome had never changed the company name, out of respect for his dead brother – shuffling invoices from suppliers for ballast or cement or scalpings, ordering Tarmac or diesel over the phone, being taken out to lunch by middle-aged sales reps who wouldn't object to a flattery fuck with her but were more concerned with securing the big orders that a large concern like Butlers could afford to place.

If Jeanette wasn't doing all that, then she was hanging around with her brother, always keen to win his approval and never, so far as Christie could tell, succeeding in doing so.

'I guess I ought to say congratulations,' said Jeanette, catching hold of Christie's arm because it was obvious Christie was going to just walk on by.

'What for?' asked Christie.

'For your birthday of course. And for all this. Smart move, hitching up with Kenny Doyle, wasn't it. He's loaded, so you can queen it out here doing fuck all, money no object.'

Christie understood why Jeanette had never married. She was bitter as a lemon, catty, cutting, just as she'd been in childhood. And what sort of man would want a wife like that?

'Thank you,' said Christie curtly, and wrenched her arm free and walked on.

Then, not ten paces on near the buffet table, where he was hoovering up food like the greedy bastard he always had been, she stumbled over Ivo.

He was running to fat now, Christie saw. He looked shambolic, scruffy, his shirt half in and half out of his trousers, his shoes scuffed and dirty, his ungroomed hair a tangled mess.

'Hiya Christie,' he said, and she felt herself literally *flinch* in alarm. Here was the last person on God's earth she *ever* wanted to see.

'Ivo,' she said shortly, and went to pass on by, feeling her innards curdling with disgust.

'Nah, don't run off,' he said, grinning, food stuck in his teeth.

She shuddered when he touched her arm with one sweaty, thick-fingered hand. But there were people crowding all around them – she couldn't make a fuss.

'I just saw Jeanette,' she said, because she had no clue of what else to say to him. 'She looks well.'

'What, her?' He guffawed. 'You're joking. Poor cow. Never married. Don't even wear make-up, does she, but you can see why. No point polishing a turd.'

'I saw Aunt Julia and Uncle Jerome too,' she said, just wanting to bolt.

'Yeah. And they been *hurt*, Christie. You know that? Hurt 'cos you've never asked them out here. And Christie?' He loomed over her and she cringed back. 'I been hurt too. Rejected. I've called at your London gaff and I've even come here a few times, but guess what? Never no answer.'

'I must have been out,' said Christie, feeling sweat running down her back, feeling her heart thudding with sick horror in her chest.

'Yeah? Maybe. Well maybe I'll call again, what about that, eh, Christie? We're family after all, ain't we?'

Christie pulled her arm free and hurried away. She heard his mocking laughter behind her and was moving in a panic, in a hurry to just *get away*, when she reached the drinks table – and there was Kenny, thank God. He was deep in conversation with Mungo.

'Nah, stuff that,' Mungo was saying. 'I'm happy with the one club. I'm not like you, Ken; I'm not ambitious. Fair play to you though, mixing it with Cole Mason and his crew. Personally? I'd rather sleep nights. He's in tight with Primo over in the US – d'you know that? One word from Cole and there's a hitman over here, quick as you like, and then *bam*, you're dead.'

'Come and join the lodge at least,' said Kenny. 'I'll sponsor you.'

'I'll think about it.' Mungo looked up, saw her, grinned. 'Christie! Happy birthday, my darling. Another year younger, eh?'

Mungo hugged her.

'Thanks,' said Christie.

'Happy birthday,' said Kenny, and kissed her cheek.

30

There was one positive thing you could say for Kenny Doyle, Christie thought; he had a very big presence and the instant he appeared anywhere, you knew it. Kenny was big, full stop. Tall and set broad across the shoulders and now, in his middle years, rather full-bellied too. Well padded. Impressive, of course. A smooth crook to his fingernails. The sort of bloke it's hard to put down on the floor, and impossible to keep there. Okay, they might never have been love's young dream, but having just had a brush with Ivo, Christie was *very* happy to see him.

'All right then?' he said, giving her a cursory hug.

Actually, they'd both long since got sick of making too much fuss of birthdays. What to get him? What to get her? In the end they'd decided not to bother. But a party was different, a party for a big milestone birthday like a fortieth was something else. Kenny had insisted they push the boat out. He had even organised it in his usual ham-fisted way, inviting not only their wide circle of friends – *his* friends, mostly – but also the Butlers.

'What the hell did you have to go and do that for?' Christie had demanded, scanning the guest list before the event and stumbling, with horror, upon their names.

'It's your fortieth. Only right we put on a bit of a show,' Kenny said.

So she'd had to see her loathed relatives mooching about her place, examining everything, costing up the fixtures and fittings, making nice to everyone. And Ivo. *Scaring* her. The bastard.

'I want a word,' said Kenny.

'Yeah? Well so do I, as it goes,' shot back Christie. 'I wish you hadn't asked the Butlers to come here today.'

He shrugged, his eyes on her face. 'You know, I've never understood why you don't get on with them. They're *family*, for God's sake.'

'They're not my family,' said Christie icily. 'My only family are dead.'

She had a sneaking, horrible feeling that Kenny had invited the Butlers today simply because he knew it would upset her. Lately, he seemed to enjoy sticking the knife in at every opportunity. Goading her. *Annoying* her.

'So,' she asked. 'This word . . . ?'

'Inside,' he said, pasting a smile on his big suntanned face.

He was a sun worshipper, Kenny. He'd *loved* the Costas. Christie had kept telling him while they were out there to put a hat on, but hats, Kenny said, were for ponces; he wasn't wearing a bloody hat. His brown eyes were glittering and there was a shimmer of moisture across the saddle of his nose. He patted her sharply on the behind.

''Scuse us, Mungo,' he said, and turned away and started walking toward the house.

As Christie followed, she saw Ivo, still picking over the food, and he glanced up at her, grinned. She averted her eyes with a shudder.

They went into the kitchen, bypassing the chaos of the servers and cooks. There was her birthday cake, white icing, *Happy Birthday Christie* on it and – thank God – one solitary candle. People were going to and from the downstairs cloak-room, smiling, nodding, nothing to see here, everything OK.

Kenny led the way into his downstairs office. He had another one upstairs, with better views. In this one there was nothing much except a couple of good paintings of race-horses. Kenny loved the nags. He kept a couple in training over at a stables in Corhampton. Enjoyed the kudos of a win or two. He was rubbing a hand over his head, something he had a tendency to do in stressful moments. Christie followed, closing the door behind them.

'So what's up?' she asked.

Kenny turned when he reached the desk. Looked at her.

'Well?' Christie asked. She glanced at her watch. 'They'll be taking the cake out in a minute. I'm supposed to be there to blow out the candles. Well, candle. Forty would have set off every smoke alarm in the building.'

She smiled. No smile in return.

'Come on then,' said Christie. 'Spit it out. What's up?'

'I'm sorry about this, Christie.'

'About what? Sounds serious.'

'That's because it is. Sorry.'

'Sorry for *what* exactly?' Christie demanded. 'Come on, don't . . .'

'I want a divorce,' he said.

31

Someone was knocking on the office door. Christie was staring at her husband and thinking that she must have misheard. Kenny stood there, hands stuffed in trouser pockets, eyes on the floor, looking as furtive as a five-year-old caught thieving apples.

The office door opened a crack and the caterer Mrs Rawnsley poked her head around it. 'Mrs Doyle? Time to come and do the cake.'

Christie wrenched her eyes away from Kenny. 'What?' she asked the woman vaguely.

'You said two exactly,' said the caterer.

'Yes.'

'But I can put it back five minutes if you're busy.'

'Yes.'

'Yes, put it back? Or do you want to go ahead now . . . ?'

'Um.' Christie held out a hand, palm up. 'Just . . . give us a minute, will you?'

The caterer looked at her face. Then she looked at Kenny's. She nodded and closed the door.

Silence descended in the office. They could hear Abba launching into 'Dancing Queen' outside, greeted by a roar of approval from the revellers. In here, everything was still.

Then Christie said: '*What* did you just say?'

'You heard.'

'Say it again. Say it again so I'll know I haven't gone completely bloody mad, all right?'

Christie could feel her gullet contracting, could taste bile rising in her throat. A moment ago, everything had been OK. Now, she felt like the floor had just fallen away from her and she was left standing on thin air.

'I want a divorce,' Kenny said again.

'That's what I thought you said.' Christie's voice sounded thin, shocked.

'Sorry,' he said, not looking up from the floor.

Christie took a breath. She knew Kenny had never been faithful; he just wasn't the type. The sex between them had dwindled to nothing and, while certain Kenny was getting his kicks elsewhere, she hadn't much cared about that anyway. A certain type of man – *Kenny*'s type – would always look elsewhere. It didn't bother her. She hadn't wanted his physical attention anyway – cold, harsh as that might sound – and she was downright relieved to have it focused somewhere else.

'Is there someone else then?' she asked, her mouth dry.

Of course there was someone else. With Kenny's type of flash bastard, there would *always* be someone else. But did she truly care? What he'd said had surprised her, shaken her, but was she cut up about it, genuinely? On a personal level, she knew she was not. On another level entirely, she was. Kenny was – had always been – her safety net against the threat that was Ivo, and the thought of losing that was terrifying. Deeply, deeply scary.

'No. There's no one. Absolutely not,' he said, his eyes meeting hers at last.

'Right.'

'Come on, you can't pretend it's been great,' said Kenny.

'Yes. No. Right,' said Christie. This felt surreal. All those sodding years, and now *this*? She had built this home, this dream of a home, around her. Yes, they had the four-storey Georgian in Primrose Hill and the Malaga villa but *this* was home to Christie. She'd always felt safe here. Untouchable. And now, what?

'It's hard to keep pretending everything's OK when it's not,' he said.

Pretence? He was talking to *her* about pretence? She'd been pretending for twenty years, ever since she'd walked into Chelsea Register Office and thought, *Is this a mistake?*

Even the wedding photographer had spotted a problem on that day.

'You looked so nervous when you were getting out of the car,' he'd remarked, smiling, at the reception. 'Thought you were going to bolt.'

But bolt to where? To who? Back to the ones who'd raised her after her parents died?

No way. No bloody way. Back to Ivo, stalking her? Raping her? To Jeanette, making her life a misery? To Aunt Julia, looking down her nose at Christie, forever disapproving, forever blaming her, and to Uncle Jerome, a whipped dog in his own house, dominated by his bulky, despicable son?

With no choice, she'd gone ahead with the wedding. And had the marriage really been that bad? They had a fantastic home. They lived a lush lifestyle. Everything they needed was supplied by Kenny's dubious and very tangled 'businesses'. He was the ultimate invisible man, Kenny. All right, part of the deal for Christie was accepting that she had a philandering shit-heel for a husband, and that he was a crook into the bargain, but so what? She'd had what she really wanted – a safe haven.

Or at least it *had* been . . .

'Got to go and do the cake,' said Christie suddenly, feeling stifled in the confines of his office, feeling that she had to just get out of there, breathe fresh air again.

She ran for the door and was gone.

32

Memories stabbed at Christie sometimes. Sudden and unbidden they'd rise up out of the swamp of her brain and *ping* – she was shot straight through her stupid, hopeless heart. Ironic that, as she was walking back outside, Christie found herself thinking about *him* again. Her long, stagnant marriage had just been given the heave-ho and what was on her mind? Dex damned Cooper.

She was remembering one of Jeanette's planned days out at the local stables that was owned by a friend of a friend of Ivo's, way back when she'd still been a hopeful girl, and *he* had tagged along because he was a mate of Ivo's too, and he'd tapped her on the top of the head when she'd had her riding hat on, just mucking about, just one of the usual gang, making fun of her like he seemed to like to do. Then when she'd been coming back with the rest of them from their ride out he was still there, standing in the way of her horse, arms spread, grinning up at her, and she'd sent Juno – that was the horse's name, lovely soft old thing it was – barrelling, *galloping*, straight at him. Dex had leapt aside, laughing, helped her down from the saddle. And then she'd been laughing too – and then not laughing at all as she looked up at him and their eyes met, locked.

Oh *God*, she'd loved him.

It still hurt to think of it. How ridiculous was that? But he'd left her. Snubbed her. So what the hell was the point of remembering him?

'The cake, Mrs Doyle?' Mrs Rawnsley was sweating her make-up off, her smile fixed, grimly doing her job even though she could see there was something wrong, that her client was somehow uninterested, disconnected from events.

But Christie was used to making an effort, to hiding the truth. She'd done it always, hadn't she? Always and forever, like the song.

'Yes, have them put it in the centre of the table like we said,' Christie said, smiling.

'Should we wait for Mr Doyle?'

'No. Let's go ahead, all right?'

Christie blew out the candle on the cake; she didn't bother making a wish. Wishes never came true, so why bother? She cut her birthday cake – sponge, because so many people didn't like fruit – and smiled around at her guests. Kenny wanted a divorce. Maybe that was a good thing? Maybe, at last, after that, she might feel free?

But she didn't think so.

Kenny came out when they were handing the cake round on pink paper plates. He toasted her in champagne. She looked across the loaded tables and saw Patsy, her best friend, one of the 'gals', the wives of the high-class mobsters Kenny always liked to hang out with. Patsy was the same little beauty she had always been – a tiny vivacious redhead, merry-eyed and daring in plunging necklines and short skirts. Right now, though, her usual smile was missing.

'*What's up?*' Patsy mouthed.

Kenny was raising a glass to Christie and saying pretty words. *My wonderful wife, yada, yada.* Everyone was applauding. Christie smiled. Kenny smiled right back at her. The two-faced bastard. And then he came over and hugged her and whispered in her ear: 'Of course, this place'll have to go.'

Christie looked at him. 'What?'

'This place. Got to liquidate a few assets. Can't say you need a big gaff like this because you've got kids to care for, can you?'

His eyes were cruel as they stared into hers. And . . . *what* was he saying? But this was her house. This place, more than any other, was her home. *She* had made it. Lavished care and attention on it. Run it. Kept it. Polished every glass in it, looked after it, *loved* it. *She* had done all that. Not *him*. But her name wasn't on the deeds of course. She'd been a young girl when she'd married him and he had always run all their financial affairs, including the purchase of this plot and the building of this house. Legally, it was his. It wasn't hers at all. *Nothing* was.

Later, when everyone had gone home or turned in to sleep in one of the many guest bedrooms, she sat out on the deck, alone. Kenny had gone, saying he was going out, no explanation, but of course he'd be with one of his tarts or doing some iffy deal. Christie looked out over the valley as the sun set in a blaze of peach and orange above the farmland. The air was soft and warm; there was no sound but the sighing of the breeze. She turned her head, looked back at the house.

Her house. Not his. Never his.

He was going to sell it. Liquidate an asset. Her home.

Over my dead body, sprang into her mind.

But then – knowing Kenny – that could be a distinct possibility.

33

When she awoke next morning, there was a moment of utter, blissful blankness before the memory of what had happened yesterday came flooding back, consuming her. Making her stomach clench and threaten to make her throw up. God, she'd drunk too much champagne. Her head was aching. She reached out but of course Kenny wasn't there.

It was years since they'd last made love, and it hadn't been successful. She'd tried, she really had, but she'd been unresponsive, dry; he'd lost his erection. With a shiver of revulsion she couldn't quite conceal, she'd turned away from him.

'Well fuck *you*,' he'd snapped, and left the bed, left the room.

Left the *marriage*, really.

Now – much to Christie's relief – they had a bedroom each. Kenny snored like a hog and when he wasn't snoring he was out and about in the middle of the night, doing deals she had no knowledge of. With Kenny's business, ignorance truly was bliss.

She crawled from the bed, crossed to the window, yanked back the blinds. And there was the view, her view, of the soft green, brown, yellow and purple patchwork of fields. A tractor was chugging its way along the skyline, and there were three riders up there too today in the sunshine, trotting along in single file. Puffs of white cloud were drifting across the perfect blue of the sky. Down in the dip of the valley, two deer were grazing.

She remembered something from her childhood – a test card on the telly, a caption saying *Under An English Heaven* while music played. She'd always longed for that scene, longed to own it, to vanish inside it. Now, she *had* vanished, hadn't she. She'd stood on the edge of life, watching, not living but looking on, hiding herself away.

She'd exchanged one cage for another. She was numb to life. Unable to ever know it or live it. She'd been hurt too much, too young. And now she was going to lose this place and the very idea terrified her.

No. She couldn't.

She went over to the door into the adjoining suite, tapped, opened it. 'Kenny?'

He wasn't there. The bed didn't look like it had been slept in.

Christie went and showered, then dressed in jeans and T-shirt and went downstairs. The cleaners were in, tidying up the debris from the party. Out in the garden Christie could see the marquee people disassembling the huge pink tent, cheerfully calling each other cunts while the radio played Sister Sledge. Her gardener Patrick was out there on the ride-on, making a start on the lawns.

Christie made herself a mug of coffee and went out onto the deck and sat down, gazing out at that beloved view – *her* view.

'Christie? What about the chairs? Should we stack them back in the stables? Is that all right?' It was the cleaner.

Christie shook herself. 'Oh – yeah. Thanks. The one on this end. Patrick's got the onions drying on racks in the middle one. Don't touch those for God's sake – there'll be uproar. And there's the nest in the other end, don't go in there.'

The cleaner smiled and departed.

The stable block had stood empty the whole time the Doyles had lived here. Originally, Kenny had said, why not knock them down? They'd already demolished the old bungalow that had stood here for over seventy years, why not the stable block too?

But then he'd thought they might have kids, and the kids would have loved ponies, and there was room. You needed an acre per pony and they had that, all that and more . . . but there had been no kids. The stables – like this vast house – had stood mostly empty, and right now they were full of nothing but stackable white plastic chairs, onions drying out on chicken wire, and a large wasps' nest in the far end stall; they were going to have to get the pest man in to sort that out. Well, she was. Kenny didn't concern himself with the day-to-day running of this place. It was hers, body and soul. Her creation, her child, her one true treasure; she *loved* it.

Only now, apparently, it was going to be taken off her.

Fear gripped at her innards. Where would she go then? What would she do?

She thought of her estranged Butler relatives and winced. Never to them. She would have to buy a place somewhere, a small place she could manage on her own. She was frightened by the thought of that, of having to cope alone, without Kenny's backing. The spectre that was Ivo haunted her. But if Kenny was kicking her to the kerb, the least he could do was be fair over a settlement. This place was worth a fortune. Oh Christ, she would have to talk to a solicitor about all this.

And Kenny. For God's sake, where was he? They needed to at least discuss this in the clear light of day. He wanted a divorce? Fair enough. So be it. But things would have to be sorted out. It was no good ignoring the situation. It wasn't going away.

34

'Hey, doll! Wassup?'

Christie snapped back to the present, to the here and now. Patsy was coming across the decking, bustling up to the table, coffee and newspaper in hand. She slapped the paper down onto the table. Christie glanced at it, saw that John Major's Conservative government was haemorrhaging support even though the economy was recovering, and that the Women's Royal Air Force had fully merged into the Royal Air Force.

Slow news day, she thought.

Patsy and Mungo had spent the night here. Mungo had been *way* too sauced to drive home. Patsy was wearing tight denim shorts and a buttercup-yellow T-shirt that clung everywhere. She was also wearing wedge heels to give her a little height – she had always been self-conscious about being so petite – and huge designer shades. 'What was it with you yesterday? You and Kenny had a falling-out, did you? Or is it the big four-oh thing? Bit of a blow that. Thirties back there in the dust, fifty looming . . .' Patsy grinned. She was forty-one and looked ten years younger than that. Then she stared at Christie's face. Her cheeky grin vanished. 'What is it? What's wrong?'

'He wants a divorce,' said Christie, wondering if saying it again would make it seem more real. It didn't.

Patsy's jaw dropped. 'He *what?*'

'A divorce. He told me yesterday, just before I cut the cake.'

Patsy was quiet for a moment. In the background, the marquee men laughed and folded acres of pink silk away. Whitney was singing on their radio, her world-class voice soaring out over the hills. The ride-on droned past, just below the deck. The sun shone. Catering staff were walking stacked white plastic chairs down to the stable block on trolleys.

'*What?* The bastard,' said Patsy. 'What did you say?'

Christie gave a dry laugh. 'It knocked the breath out of me,' she said. 'I don't think I said anything much.'

'There's someone else?' asked Patsy.

'He says not.'

Patsy sipped at her coffee, her face averted.

'What?' asked Christie.

'I didn't say anything.' But Patsy was the picture of guilt.

'What do you know?' asked Christie.

Patsy shrugged. 'Only what everyone else does. That Kenny's a bastard for the birds. They all are, the guys. Mine's the same. Mungo has these hot-and-heavy things going on for a couple of months, then it's over and he's back to me and bringing me flowers and diamond bracelets. Then on to the next one. I always thought Kenny was the same. I always thought you knew that.'

Christie's gaze was level. 'So,' she repeated, 'what do you know?'

Patsy squirmed. 'All right! I think it's one of the girls who works at Mungo's club. Me and Mungo saw them going into a restaurant together. Not one of our usual haunts – we just fancied a change. That's how we caught them out I guess. Of course Mungo covered for Kenny straight away, steered me away but not before I summed up the situation. Mungo didn't say a thing about it, and neither did I. But I know what I saw. Very touchy-feely, they were. And afterwards in the car when I tackled him about it, Mungo admitted that Kenny had a thing going on with her. He said her name was Lara Millman and she lived in the next village from here, but that it was nothing, nothing at all. Just a fling.'

Christie nodded, feeling curiously detached. She ought to be anguished. Her husband, dining in secret with another woman. She checked herself out, the way a doctor would. No tears, no nothing. She was just *numb*. 'Well it's hardly a bloody fling is it, if he's talking divorce. What's she look like?'

Patsy squirmed. She shrugged and sipped her coffee: 'He's got a type, hasn't he? Very young. Nineteen or something? Long straight white-blonde hair, thin, tall.'

Like me when I was nineteen, thought Christie.

'Look,' said Patsy, reaching across the table and giving Christie's hand a squeeze. 'He'll come to his senses. He's done it before. They all have. They get obsessed with a new girl, then suddenly it's over. It's . . .'

Christie shook her head. 'No. He wants a divorce.'

'He'll change his mind. He won't want to lose all this.' Patsy gestured around at the land, the house.

'Or me?' Christie's smile was wry. 'But he never had me, Patsy. Not really. And you know what? The poor bastard knew it.' She tilted her head as she heard the heavy familiar crunch of Kenny's car out at the front of the house, coming into the gravelled driveway. 'And speak of the devil, here he is. D'you suppose that's where he spent the night? With her? This "Lara"?'

Patsy stood up, picked up her coffee. 'He'll change his mind,' she said firmly. 'Chin up, girl. He'll realise the mistake he's making.' She glanced back at the French doors. 'Hold on to your hats,' she muttered to Christie. 'He's coming out.'

35

'So where have you been?' Christie asked him as Patsy scarpered. Kenny sat down, taking her place at the table.

'What?' he said blankly.

'Just wondering where you went so early. To see the girl-friend?'

'I told you. There's nobody else.'

Christie thought of Patsy's words. 'Right,' she said.

So that was the way he was going to play it. He was going to lie his way out of the situation, just like he always did with *every* situation. Kenny and the truth were strangers. But then, she'd always known that. And she'd never really minded, or cared. Not until now.

Kenny scowled over his shoulder at Patrick on the ride-on. 'Does he have to do that right now? Got a head on me like you wouldn't believe.'

Good. I hope it hurts like a bastard.

'Yes he does. It's his day and he has other things to do the rest of the week.' Christie's reply was calm. She *felt* calm. Her world was busy crumbling around her, but once again she felt that curious detachment.

Kenny looked at her. 'You OK?'

'Peachy.' Christie gave a dry smile. 'Thanks for the birth-day present. A divorce! How lovely.'

'Shit, can we not do this?'

'Fine with me. Only I happen to know that, as usual, you're lying through your teeth.'

'About what?' That blank, innocent look again. Oh, he was good at this. Too bloody good.

'About Lara Millman. The girl who works in Mungo's place.'

He looked like he'd been gut-punched then. His mouth fell open and for a full minute he sat there, not knowing what to say.

'Look, I . . .' he started.

'You lied. Doesn't matter. I'm used to it.'

'Look,' he said again forcefully, rapping a fist on the teak table. 'I know this is hard for you. But it's happened and I want out of this sham marriage and . . .'

'Sham?'

'Well isn't it? Come on! You married me to get away from a rotten home – that's the truth of it. I don't even blame you for that; I never did. I know it must have been bad. *How* bad, I was never sure. You never said, did you? But you didn't like them, didn't like *any* of them. Which I never understood, really. They're your family. Anyway, I knew there was something there you were keen to get away from. Now you say I'm a liar? Well, so are you. Those vows you made at our wedding? You *lied*, Christie. You spouted on about love and honour, none of which you ever did. You bloody tolerated me to get the hell out of Dodge. That's the truth, right there.'

Christie sat there, almost swaying back, away from him, away from this onslaught. It was true, what he was saying. True and terrible, and she'd felt bad about it over the years – of course she had. But he was right: she'd had to get out of there. And Kenny had been her escape route.

'Finished?' she snapped back.

'No I bloody haven't. I haven't finished by a long chalk. All right, the truth's out but not *all* of it.'

'Christ! You mean there's more? What's happened? You sold this place out from underneath me, have you? I wouldn't put it past you,' she said.

'I haven't done that. But it's going to have to go. I told you that and I meant it. No, the other thing is . . .' He paused.

'Is what?' demanded Christie.

He paused. 'She's pregnant,' he said.

And there it was.

Lara Millman – who might have been a fling, a nothing – had suddenly acquired monumental importance in Kenny's life. Because what he had wanted, had *always* wanted, *yearned* for, was to be a dad, the great soft bastard. And Christie hadn't been able to give him that. She was forty years old now, but even in her prime she'd been unable to fall into line with Kenny's dream of a big family. Lara Millman, however, was nineteen years old and she could do it.

No contest.

Christie had to swallow hard to be able to get the words out. 'I see,' she said.

Kenny was clasping his hands together, his eyes anxious as they rested on her shocked face.

'Look, I never meant for that to happen. But it did, and . . . Christ, Christie, you know it's what I've always wanted. And it's been stale with us for a long time – you know that too. Dead in the water. We've been going through the motions, that's all. Pretending everything is fine when we both know it isn't. When I met her . . . well, then I could see what a pretence it all was and now she's pregnant and I know it's time to make a move.'

Christie nodded. 'To dump me.'

'Come on. You can't say you're heartbroken, can you. We both know that's not true.'

'So what now?' Christie asked, dry-mouthed.

He stood up. 'I'm going out,' he said.

36

Kenny vanished back indoors. Christie sat there for a moment, his words echoing around her head. There was a pain behind her left eye. One of her stress-induced migraines was coming on, just to add to the fun. Her heart was thudding hard in her chest. Suddenly she made a decision. She stood up and hurried indoors. The cloakroom toilet had been flushed and the door was standing open. Now Kenny was heading out the front door. Christie paused in the kitchen. Mrs Rawnsley the caterer was clearing up, snapping the lid closed on a Tupperware container.

'Can I borrow your car?' asked Christie.

'What?'

Christie's own car, a racy red Mitsubishi 3000GT would be far, far too noticeable. The caterer's was a discreet little black Fiat 500. 'Can I borrow your bloody car?' she said, louder.

'Oh. Well . . . sure.' She picked up her bag from a chair and handed Christie the keys. She looked at Christie's face. 'Everything all right?'

'Fine,' said Christie, and heard Kenny's Rolls-Royce crunch out over the gravel. She went to the front door and saw the big car turn left out of the drive, and she ran to the Fiat and got in and started the engine. Not even bothering with a seatbelt she shot out of the driveway after him.

He was cruising along the high street of the village, down past the war memorial, down the hill, past the church and the village hall and then into the lane where the primary school was. She followed him past fields of sheep and cows and then they were in the next village with its post office cum general store and he was pulling in outside of a detached thatched cottage. Quickly, Christie turned into a side lane and parked up the Fiat. She got out, not bothering to lock the door.

She walked out onto the main high street of the village and there, about two hundred yards along it outside the thatched cottage, was Kenny's garish silver Rolls. He was going through the gate, along a tiny overgrown pathway to the front door. Christie stepped a little closer, watching as he rang a bell over the porch and then stepped back, rubbing the back of his neck, impatient when the bell wasn't answered straight away. He was always impatient, Kenny. If he was made to wait for anything, he twitched about and then quickly lost interest.

Well he's not going to lose interest now, thought Christie. She knew exactly who was going to come to the door. And a moment later, she did. Here was the woman who threatened her security, her stability, who was going to whip her home off her and – with Kenny – any protection she had once had against Cousin Ivo. Lara Millman came out onto the front step.

And oh, she was lovely. Christie couldn't help but think that. Nineteen and fresh as a daisy. Not a mark on her. Newly minted. Her skin so tanned and clear, her hair a long sheet of white-blonde silk hanging loose to her waist. She was wearing a corduroy raspberry-pink dress, very demure, and as she stepped forward and into Kenny's arms, Christie could clearly see the bulge of her pregnancy.

A net curtain twitched in the cottage Christie was standing outside of. An elderly man peered out at her, eyes accusing. Ignoring him, Christie – driven by some urge she didn't even understand – walked on until she stood within ten feet of Kenny and his mistress.

'Well, this is damned cosy,' she said loudly.

They broke apart as if something had scalded them. Some of that healthy young colour drained out of the young woman's face as she saw Christie standing there. Kenny was obviously more practised at all this. He stared at Christie and said: 'What the fuck?'

'That's exactly what I was going to say,' said Christie. 'What, you not going to introduce us then?'

Kenny said nothing.

Christie turned her gaze on the girlfriend.

'I'm Christie,' she said. 'I'm Kenny's wife. Or maybe you didn't realise he's married?'

'Of course she bloody realises it. I told her,' said Kenny.

Christie put a hand to her chest. 'Oh, sorry. I'm not imply- ing that you're lying to her or anything. No, I think that's only something you do with *me*, isn't it.'

'I'm sorry about this,' said Lara to Christie. 'I really am.'

'Well, I appreciate that. I really do,' said Christie with sar- casm.

'Why don't you fuck off, Christie?' said Kenny irritably.

'Oh, what, ruining your little get-together am I? Spoiling the dream? Sorry about that.'

'*Fuck off!*' Kenny bellowed at the top of his voice.

The curtain twitched in the cottage next door again and Lara's face spasmed in shock. Christie guessed that she had never before heard that particular tone of Kenny's, the one that could make grown men tremble.

Kenny threw Christie a look of total loathing, put a supporting arm around Lara and ferried her indoors. The cottage door slammed and Christie was left there, standing in the road, alone. She trudged back to the Fiat. On her way there, the elderly gentleman next door opened the front door of his cottage.

'Can I help you?' he asked, his face hostile.

'Doubt it,' said Christie, and got back in the Fiat and went back to what was still – for now – her home.

37

Christie got back home and handed the Fiat's keys to the catering manager. One by one, the staff started to disperse. First the caterer and her helpers, then Patrick the gardener, Patsy and Mungo and the other remaining guests said their farewells, then finally the marquee erectors folded up the last bits of their tent and departed.

About two o'clock in the afternoon, Christie sat out on the deck, alone, and beheld the view. The view, of course, had sold them on this plot and it was always different, always fascinating. It was *her* view. The farmer was in his tractor up on the ridge, spraying a crop that had turned, over the spring, from beige to pale mint-green to a green so dark it was verging on black.

At six o'clock Christie was still sitting there, watching horse riders down in the dip of the valley. At eight, she was still there, wondering what the fuck she was going to do now. Some people had nice divorces, civilised separations, fair pay-outs, divisions of the spoils. She didn't think for a minute that Kenny was that sort of person. Kenny was a swipe-it-all-for-yourself type, grabbing greedily at life, at food, at money. If he'd decided enough was enough, then Christie was going to have to fight tooth and nail to get so much as a bean from him. And she knew that fighting Kenny was never, ever a good idea. He didn't fight fair.

At eight the sun started to go down, staining the clouds above the horizon lemon yellow, purple, vivid scarlet. That was one of the best things about this house: the sunsets.

At nine o'clock the stars winked on in the darkening sky. This was a dark place. No street lights anywhere. Ideal for astronomers who wished to gaze at the stars. Christie gazed at them now and wondered what the hell it was all about.

At ten it was full dark and she stood up and went indoors. Locked the place up. Went to bed.

She didn't expect Kenny home and she certainly didn't expect to sleep.

But somehow she did.

And in her sleep, she walked.

38

Ted Dawkins was coming back from the village pub, happily drunk on real ale, when he spotted the smoke. It was pouring out of the upper floor windows of the detached cottage next door to his own. Black, thick, evil-looking smoke, he told everyone later. And then as he stared, horrified, there came the explosion, the windows blowing out, pushed out by the force of the heat. Then came the flames, leaping up twenty feet into the pitch-darkness of the night-time sky.

He ran to his front door, unlocked it with shaking fingers, fell inside and phoned the fire brigade. They arrived fifteen minutes later and then everything was chaos while they unrolled hoses and pumped water at the fire. The cottage that was ablaze was old – sixteenth century in parts – and thatched; this was the country where normally everything was peaceful and good. Tonight, it wasn't. Tonight, there was smoke and a deadly, crushing, skin-shrinking heat and horror. Later, Ted would tell his pub cohorts that he always knew that one of these days there'd be trouble. That he could tell there was death in the air.

'Thatches are a bastard,' the fireman in the white helmet told Ted as they stood watching the building being drenched. 'Devil to put out. The thing smoulders on for days, sometimes. You know your neighbours well then do you?'

Ted had already told the fire chief that he thought the woman who normally occupied the house was away.

'You got a number for her?'

Ted hadn't.

'What's her name then?' asked the chief.

'Lana? No. Lara. Lara Millman.'

'And she told you that, did she?' asked the fire chief. 'That she was away? You're sure?'

Ted shrugged. 'No she didn't tell me. Never really spoken to her. Not a friendly sort. Not a community sort of person, her. Never joined in with village life. Bit of a tart by all accounts. But her windows were all shut up and the lights were off and the car was gone. Most weekends, she buggers off.'

Then one of the firemen wearing a breathing mask came stumbling away from the burning building and straight across to the man in the white helmet.

He pushed down the mask. Took a breath.

'There's a body. In the hallway downstairs,' he said.

39

The pager woke the detective inspector from sleep at precisely four in the morning. He sprang awake, mouth dry, heartbeat accelerating to a gallop, dread crunching his stomach into a knot. He slapped the light on the bedside clock and saw the early hour and groaned. So it would be a bad one. Because anything else could wait until eight o'clock, couldn't it? Four was when people died, when they slipped all too easily from this world into the next. All passion spent, all energy exhausted. He always thought of four as the death hour.

He crawled out of bed, snatched up the phone, tapped in the number. 'What's going on?' he asked the duty sergeant on shift at the station desk.

'Bad fire.'

'I'm off this week.' The DI looked around the bedroom. Boxes and bags of clothing were stacked against the wall; he'd barely been in this new apartment a week and had been hoping for some time to get at least a little organised. 'Turnbull's shout, isn't it?'

'Both Turnbull's kids are sick and his missus is away on a course. He can do it if he must, juggle things around, but I thought . . .'

'Yeah. All right. So what is it?'

'The fire chief thinks it's arson, started deliberately, accelerants involved. So he got straight through to us. They found a body. And there's more to it. This one's nasty.'

'The chief still at the scene?' asked the DI.

'He is. Waiting for you.' The duty sergeant gave the DI the address. He scrabbled for the jotter on the bedside table, scribbled it down. 'SOCO there?'

'Yeah, all done.'

'Thanks,' he said, and hung up; then he rang out again.

'Smith?' he said, dragging a hand through his hair.

'Sir?' His DS's voice was muffled with sleep.

'Get your arse out of that pit.' He gave Smith the details. 'Collect me in twenty minutes, OK?'

'Yessir,' moaned Smith, yawning, and hung up.

The DI went to get a shower.

*

A thatch, once it caught alight, was murder to put out. Layer upon layer of thick durable Norfolk reed made it a long job and often a recurring one. Thatch smouldered, reignited. You put it out. It heated up again, and off it went one more time. You put it out again. And so on, and so forth. You had to keep pulling it off, layer after layer, until sooner or later – probably later – the bugger stopped burning. The fire chief explained this to the DI and his DS as they stood outside in the road. Uniform had put up a cordon to keep back the villagers who had gathered in a shivering half circle in dressing gowns and overcoats, watching what was going on. Hoses were still being played over the ruined remnants of the thatch, damping it down. The air was thick with smoke.

Paulette Vardy the pathologist had arrived shortly after the DI with the police photographer and was now attending to the loading of the body into the back of the mortuary van. Mercifully, it was enclosed in a body bag. Nothing too shocking. But a murmur of horror went up from the watching crowd as the thing was brought out and loaded.

It wasn't the best of starts to the new day.

Over in the east, the sky was lightening to grey and rooks were cawing in the trees clustered around the edge of the village, disturbed by all this human fuss and bother.

One of the uniformed officers came up to the DI. 'Someone here wants a word with you, sir. A neighbour.'

An elderly gentleman had detached himself from the rest of the interested watchers and come forward.

'You want to speak to me sir?' the DI asked him.

'I knew something like this was going to happen,' he said, his voice tremulous. He blinked. His eyes were bloodshot from the smoke that choked the air.

'Did you? How is that?'

'It was a right carry-on. Young girl lived there – had a sugar daddy; I suppose he paid the rent – and she had a fat belly. Expecting. Then he shows up yesterday and then the *wife* shows up. I think it *must* have been the wife, and there's shouting and screaming in the street. You wouldn't believe it, no way to behave.'

'Do you know the occupant's name, sir?'

'Yes. Lara Millman. Tarty piece. Kept herself to herself. I knew *his* name too. Everyone around here knows that blighter.'

'And he is . . . ?'

'Kenny Doyle. Bit of a villain by all accounts. Bet your lot have heard of him.'

They had. The DI had, certainly.

'And you are . . . ?'

'Dawkins. Ted. I know where he lives. Poncy loud-mouthed beggar, got a house in the next village – big place there. Huge white house it is, everything on show, the flash git. Married, he is. And his bit of stuff tucked away here, very convenient. It's disgusting. Then the wife turns up shouting the odds. I spoke to her. Oh – and there was another one, showed up not long after the wife cleared off. Pulled up on a motorbike, this chap did, and just loitered around outside.'

'You get the number of the bike?' asked the DI.

'No. Sorry.'

'Can you describe him?'

'Yes. He took his helmet off so I could see his face clear enough. Pale. Spotty. Young. Black hair and sticking-out ears.'

The mortuary van was pulling away. The firemen still clustered around the ruined cottage, pulling out bits of thatch, damping down. The thatch smouldered. Wouldn't seem to *stop* smouldering.

'Smith?' The DI summoned his squat, dark-haired DS over. 'Take statements from all these people. See if anyone saw anything else or knew anything else about the woman who lived here.'

A car was pulling into the lane, stopping outside the cordon. A big car, a silver Rolls-Royce. A bulky and pugnacious man got out. Leaving his car door open, he hurried over to the scene and shouted: 'What the *fuck*?'

Nope, thought the detective inspector. This was not a good start to the day *at all*.

40

Christie had been distantly, dimly aware of police cars or fire engines or *something* roaring past during the night. She woke briefly when vehicles passed out in the road, considered everything that had just happened to her and quickly huddled back into sleep as a child would, pretending that if she couldn't see or hear a threat, then it couldn't be there.

At nine o'clock in the morning she came back to full consciousness and found she was not in bed. Her arm was stiff, her back aching.

What?

She looked around. She was at the bottom of the stairs, hunched over. Painfully, she straightened.

Oh Christ, it's happened again . . .

She hadn't walked in her sleep for years. The upset of Kenny's news had clearly dug deep into her brain. Slowly she straightened up, feeling pins and needles crawling up her arms as the blood flowed back in. She stood up and stretched, then went slowly, doddery as an old woman, up the stairs.

The nightmare events of her birthday were still swimming in endless circles around her brain as she showered, washed and styled her hair, put on make-up – although she hadn't a clue what she was doing that for. Then she put on jeans and a sky-blue pullover and went downstairs to make coffee. Aware of the background hum of a motor, she stepped out of the front door and onto the drive. The engine of her little red sports number was running. Frowning, she stepped up to the open driver's door. The keys were in the ignition.

Oh shit.

Christie stepped forward, turned the key. The engine juddered to a halt. She took the key out, closed the door, locked it.

I walked last night. Did I start the car? Did I?

She went to the kitchen and took her mug of coffee and a couple of paracetamols out onto the deck and sat there to reluctantly review the situation. She took the pills, sipped her drink, watched the view. Two hang-gliders soared overhead on lime and orange oblong parachutes and landed with balletic grace in the field opposite. A line of riding-school horses followed each other nose-to-tail up on the far ridge. Nothing had changed, nothing was altered. Only everything. That was all.

She heard the front door open and braced herself. Kenny was home.

She heard him coming heavy-footed – as always – through the house, heard the French doors swing open. Felt the deck vibrate under his footsteps. She closed her eyes briefly, feeling wrung out despite the night's sleep, exhausted right to her bones. Not ready for a fight, which was exactly what she was going to get. Nobody fought Kenny and won. *Nobody.*

He came around the bench and sat down on the other side of it, obscuring her valley view. Christie felt every muscle in her body tense. *Here we go . . .*

Kenny sat down and Christie looked across the table at him – and then she stiffened in surprise.

The normally well-groomed Kenny she knew so well looked dishevelled – his shirt collar was dirty, his jacket rumpled. There were smuts of soot on his chubby face and a strong smell of smoke hung around him. His eyes were bloodshot and – for fuck's sake! – they were full of tears. He looked *shattered*.

Christie experienced a split second of concern before she got a grip on herself. She guessed that when you lived with someone for years, no matter how big an arsehole you knew they were, *their* pain somehow managed to become *yours*. It was clear that something cataclysmic had happened to him, and she couldn't help but feel that jolt of sympathy.

'What's happened to you?' she asked.

Tears were slipping down his face, dripping onto his jacket. Yes, he smelled smoky; sweaty too. His mouth was working but no sound was coming out.

'Kenny?' Christie was staring hard at him. 'What the hell's happened? Did you crash the car? Are you all right? What . . . ?'

For a big man, Kenny moved deceptively fast. Most of the time, he had to. Keep ahead of the competition, he always said. Keep out of reach of the Bill. Whenever he heard a police siren, he always joked: *Damn, looks like they caught up with me at last.*

He wasn't joking now. He lunged across the table, grabbed her arm and shook her so hard that her teeth rattled.

'*Kenny!*' burst out of Christie's mouth. Her arm where he had hold of it was agony. She knew he was strong but she had never felt that strength turned on her, not once. Now, she did. His face was filled with incoherent rage and she was terrified.

'Don't give me that, you bitch. Did you do it? *Did* you?' he shouted full in her face.

Christie was trying not to scream. Her arm hurt like hell. If he carried on with that pressure, he could easily break a bone. 'Kenny! What the fuck are you talking about? Do what? What's going on?'

'Bitch! Fucking *cow*!' he said, and drew back his free hand and slapped her, hard. 'Barren useless fucking bitch, I'll kill you!'

In panic Christie groped for the mug of hot coffee and tossed the contents straight in his face. It seemed to snap Kenny out of his rage. He froze, boiling-hot coffee dripping down over his face along with tears and snot and smuts; he was a mess but his eyes had lost that wild killer expression and he seemed to come back to himself. With a jerk of disgust – Christie didn't know whether it was for her or for himself – he let her arm go.

Her face stung. Her arm throbbed. She was panting with the aftermath of fear as Kenny sank back into his seat, burying his head in his hands.

'What the *fuck*?' she demanded shakily. 'What the hell are you talking about?'

His hands dropped from his face.

'Was it you? Did you do it?' he asked her again, and there was raw pain in his voice. But this time, Christie was beyond being touched by it.

'Do what for Christ's sake?' she snapped out, rubbing her arm, shivering with shock at what had just occurred. All these years, he'd never raised a hand to her. Never. Now, *this*.

'Did you do it because she could give me a kid and you couldn't?'

Christie looked at him in bewilderment. '*What?*'

'You did, didn't you. You did it.'

'Did what? What are you talking about?'

'You know exactly what I'm talking about. You did it. You crazed, jealous bitch. You killed Lara.'

41

'*What?*' Christie stared at him like he'd gone mad.

'Lara. You know? The woman who was pregnant with my baby? My child?' Kenny was sobbing now, the words tumbling out between gasps and heaves for breath.

'Kenny – I don't know what you're talking about.'

He sprang to his feet. Christie shrank back, fearing further attack. She didn't know this man. This was a dangerous, blubbering stranger. Not tough grinning fuck-you Kenny Doyle.

'You lying *whore!*' he yelled, spittle flying. 'You were there. You were watching us together. I saw you.'

'What, yesterday?' Christie's head was swimming. 'Yes. I followed you.'

'Yeah. You did. You cow. And not in your own car. I watched you go. That was *not* your car. I'd know your car anywhere.'

Yes, she'd followed him. She wasn't even sure, in her own head, why she'd done that. Jealousy had certainly not been the motivation. Resentment of his deception? His lies? That he'd destabilised her safe and secure life, the life she had clung to so desperately despite being unhappy with her marriage to him, in one fell swoop? Maybe that. She'd borrowed the caterer's car because she'd known he would spot her own very distinctive motor easily. But then getting there, arriving at their love nest, she'd shown herself so what had been the use of subterfuge?

She knew she hadn't been thinking straight. Her marriage was miserable, plodding, and the truth was that she was slowly dying a little every day, tied to it, stifled by it, but she'd had *her home*. She didn't care for the place in Primrose Hill or the Spanish bolthole. This place was *her* house, where she hid from the world, safe and sound, an Aladdin's cave of treasures. That, at least, she had. But what Kenny had said to her yesterday about divorce had roughly stripped all that away.

So yes – the neighbour had seen her. Kenny had seen her. And Lara too.

Lara.

'You said . . . you mean she's . . . dead?' asked Christie.

He said nothing. Just stared at her.

'Kenny, tell me what's happened.'

'You bitch . . .' He was coming around the table. *Christ he's going to kill me* sprang into her brain. Christie shot to her feet and backed away, then she turned and ran to the end of the deck, down the steps, down the bank to the pool with him coming behind her, swearing, cursing her, saying he was going to drown her, stop her fucking breath, that she was a cow, a bitch, a *demon*.

Christie reached the pool, which still lay uncovered after the birthday celebrations, and snatched up the pole the pool man used to fish out debris. It was a pathetic weapon but Christie used it to shove hard at Kenny's chest and he was so upset, so blindsided by fury, that it actually unbalanced him for a second or two before he shoved it aside and ran at her. Out of the corner of her eye Christie saw someone else coming down the bank at a run. Kenny was right in front of her now and she'd dropped the pole.

'*Bitch!*' he roared out, demented, his hands reaching for her.

Christie flinched back.

'Police!' shouted the man who'd come charging down the bank. He was holding out a warrant card. 'Stop right there,' he snapped out, and grabbed Kenny's arm, which was swinging up to land a blow on Christie's head. '*Enough*,' said the man. 'I'm DI Cooper and I am warning you that you will be charged with assault unless you *stop this right now.*'

The policeman's voice seemed to penetrate the fog in Kenny's brain. He stopped moving. His hand dropped to his side. Then he rubbed one weary hand over his face and slowly sank to the ground, his shoulders shaking with the intensity of his grief.

Christie, breathless, staggering with the aftermath of panic, was left standing there facing the DI. Now another copper was coming down the bank after him.

'Smith, stay with him,' said the DI to the younger man who had followed him down. He looked at Christie. 'You – come with me.'

And it was in that moment, when she'd believed a few seconds before that she was about to die at the hands of her cheating husband, that she suddenly thought: *Hang on. I know you!*

And then she realised that she did.

Oh fuck – she did. It was *him* – wasn't it?

This was mad. This was *crazy*. But it was *him*.

It was Dex Cooper.

42

They went back indoors, into the sitting room. Christie sat down on the couch, and DI Cooper sat down on a chair opposite. Christie was rubbing her arm, where Kenny had clamped it in his vice-like grip. She was shaking, her whole body throbbing like a rotten tooth. She knew everything that Kenny was, she knew what everybody said about him and she had never, up to this point, given a single solitary damn about any of it. But now she'd seen Kenny in the raw, she knew what a predatory animal he could turn into at the drop of a hat.

'You all right?' said DI Cooper.

Christ! It was him.

Dex hadn't changed in any way that mattered. Christie stared at him and yes it was *him*, her long-lost love, older certainly, no faint remnant of madcap boyishness lingering in him. He looked far steadier than she remembered, more authoritative. He leaned his elbows on his knees and looked at her, apparently without recognition.

Christie stared at his face. The laughing blue eyes didn't laugh anymore. He was staring at her blankly, as if . . . as if he didn't even know her!

She thought of all the times she'd sat and wept over the loss of him, listening to sad songs like Harry Nilsson's 'Without You'. She'd felt like that. Wished to die, to not feel such pain anymore.

'It *is* you, isn't it?' spilled out of her mouth, because if it wasn't, what was happening to her brain? Had she cracked, finally? Lost what little remained of her sanity after all these dry, long, dusty years with Kenny?

DI Cooper tilted his head. Glanced away from her, then back. 'What?' he said.

'You . . . don't you remember me?' Her voice sounded hopeful, lost, pitiful to her own ears.

'I'm sorry?'

He sounded so cold, so formal. She remembered laughter, the warm caress of his voice in those long-ago days. His arm around her on that trip to the concert. Oh God, would she never forget that? When they laid her in her grave, would she *still* have that in her cold dead skull, that one priceless golden memory?

He didn't know her. That much was obvious. Well, he'd changed. Maybe she'd changed too. Too much. She could see she was in danger of making a total fool of herself. Maybe she had even mistaken his attentions, all those years back. Maybe he had been like that with other girls too. Maybe she'd aged terribly and he just couldn't see that it was *her*, the Christie he'd known, and not some traumatised stranger.

'Is there someone I can call for you? A friend? Anyone?' he asked.

He didn't know her. It wasn't him.

Another shock, after days of them.

In the kitchen, they could hear DS Smith talking to Kenny, telling him to calm down. Kenny was still sobbing. There was the sound of the kettle being filled. The cure-all: a cup of tea.

Lara's dead.

'Mrs Doyle, can you tell me what's been happening here?' he asked.

Christie gulped and took a stab at it. 'It was my fortieth birthday party. My husband – Kenny – showed up and told me he wanted a divorce. He said there was no one else involved. Then he told me that there was. A Lara Millman. He said he was in love with her. He said she was pregnant with his child.'

'And how did you take that?'

He said that he was going to sell my house out from under me. My home.

'Kenny and I haven't been close for a long time.'

If ever.

Christie thought of all the things she didn't like about Kenny. It was a pretty long list, because she'd had plenty of time to compile it. *Bags* of time. His binge drinking, for one. His controlling ways. The way he had of shuffling her aside when he talked to other men, like she was some sort of bloody trinket they might try to steal. God knew why that should bother him, because he didn't love her anyway. But she was *his*, wasn't she. Bought and paid for. And then, the way he laughed at things she held dear. Nice things. Things that made her feel happier and more secure. The TV programmes she enjoyed, of chic hotels and fabulous holiday destinations, which he mocked loudly all the way through, spoiling it for her.

'Only I imagine some women would be very upset by that,' the DI went on. 'Their husband fathering a child with another woman? Violently upset, perhaps.'

'I wasn't.'

'But you were seen outside Miss Millman's cottage, having followed your husband there. That hardly seems the action of a disinterested woman.'

Christie squinted at him. If she had a type, if she had *ever* had a type, this man was it. Blue, blue eyes. Treacle-blond hair with now a hint of grey at the temples. Taller than her, a solid six foot. It was him. It *had* to be. Didn't it? But he was all business. He was looking at her like she had something to hide, and maybe she did. She thought of her car, running on the drive. The door open. The keys in the ignition. And Lara Millman, dead in the next village.

'I don't know why I followed him,' said Christie.

'And in a borrowed car? As if you didn't want to be seen?'

Christie was shaking. Kenny treating her like that . . . it had brought back memories. Bad ones. Ivo, pushing her around. Hurting her. Assaulting her. 'Well *that* didn't work out, did it?' she said angrily. 'I got there and bawled Kenny out. He was standing on the doorstep with his young bit of fluff . . .'

'Who is now dead.'

Christie swallowed hard. 'Yes. She is.'

'Mrs Doyle?'

Christie stared into DI Cooper's eyes. Maybe it wasn't him. It couldn't be. Could it? No. It couldn't. She was just in shock and imagining things. That was it. 'Yes?' she asked.

'We'd better continue this down the station.'

43

It was her.

Christie Butler, now Doyle. There was no doubt, absolutely none, in DI Dex Cooper's mind that this woman who'd been trying to beat off an attack by Kenny Doyle down by the pool in the huge valley house was in fact the same Christie he had once known. Oh – and loved.

Actually he'd been *obsessed* with her, that young innocent Christie who'd flittered through the years of his youth, tempting, elusive, maddeningly reserved. But so sweet. So *cute*. She was changed now. A woman full grown. Self-possessed. Curvier. More beautiful, not less. Somehow the same but different, so different. An adult.

He caught himself then and added a mental note: *and a suspect.*

It was like someone throwing cold water in his face. Snapping him back to reality. He had a woman dead in a fire, he had an enraged lover, he had a (maybe) vengeful snubbed wife. A crime of passion, perhaps, as the French called it. Had the wife – Christie, he reminded himself; the same Christie he'd known once, long ago – found out about the mistress and simply flipped? Set light to the cottage, killing her rival in the process? He thought of the witness: the old man who'd said the wife had been screaming and shouting out in the street, threatening all sorts.

Dex didn't know Christie now. He'd barely known her then. Who knew what she'd been through, what trials life had thrown at her, how she had been hardened, fashioned by fate? He hadn't seen her in over twenty years. She must have changed a lot in that time. God's sake, she was married to Kenny Doyle, a big-time criminal who now chose to live the high and seemingly respectable life perched in this mansion in the hills. As if that arsehole could ever be anything but what he truly was – a crook.

Surely some of Kenny's badness would have rubbed off on her. It had to, didn't it? He remembered her with the Butler family. She'd always been with them but somehow apart, remote, untouchable. Maybe her coolness had been part of the attraction for him. He'd always – even as a very young man – been used to women falling at his feet. He had an easy, charming, outgoing manner. He knew it – even now – and used it. Mostly, women responded to it.

But Christie hadn't.

Way back then, he'd fallen for her big-style. He'd been so young and so had she. Eighteen maybe? Or even younger? That night in the front of one of the Butler company trucks, finally, she was in his arms and it wasn't an opportunity he was about to let go to waste. He'd kissed her all the way to the concert venue, and she had responded. God knows what show they saw that night. He couldn't remember. He remembered her ugly big bastard of a cousin Ivo driving them there, with his scrawny little mouse of a sister. They'd sat through something for around an hour. All his mind had been on was Christie, and then there would be the trip home, Christie on his lap again, being able to kiss her all over again.

Then she'd got into the truck facing her cousins. He couldn't kiss her in front of them. Accidental or deliberate?

Maybe she hadn't been as willing as he'd thought she was. But they'd been growing closer and closer, until something like the wild, passionate kissing in the front of the truck had seemed inevitable.

Well, he must have got it wrong, misread the signals. He remembered saying one anguished *no* when she did that. She'd been stiff all the way home. And then Ivo had called, saying Christie wasn't interested. Then Dex was certain that he'd misunderstood everything.

Dex had been in despair after that. Real despair. He'd had it so bad for Christie. Too bad. Previously, he'd toyed with the idea of going abroad, seeing the world. After her rejection he started to consider it as a serious option and before he knew it he'd done it – left England. Maybe to force Christie's hand, make her plead with him not to go. Who knew? He'd gone to the Butler house the night before he left the country, feeling torn, desperate. Out there in the world was adventure, the adventure he'd always craved, and yet . . . there was Christie. The thought of leaving her damned near broke him in two.

Before he went, before there was a whole ocean between them, he had to see her again. But he knew it was stupid. She'd made her feelings clear. She didn't want him. Nevertheless he'd stood there in the Butlers' fancy sitting room beneath the chandelier – and she had blanked him. Absolutely refused to interact with him in any way.

So what the fuck.

Devastated, dejected, he'd had a goodbye party with his folks, got very drunk, and then he'd left the country with a massive hangover and a broken heart. And he'd started a new life – a life without the girl he'd fallen in love with. He'd have married her in a heartbeat. Him, Dex Cooper, who flirted relentlessly, who was everybody's friend and never a slave to

love – he would have put a ring on her finger and taken
with him anywhere, everywhere, and he would have been
happy. He would have made it his life's work to make her
happy too.

Ah, what the hell. Now with the clarity of years spent out
in the world, he thought that it had probably been nothing
but a teenage obsession, what he'd felt for her then. And her?
Well, clearly she hadn't felt the same.

Far from it.

44

DS Colin Smith was interviewing Mrs Christie Doyle down at the cop shop. 'We are pressing charges for assault against your husband Kenneth Doyle,' he told her, sitting across the interview table from her, a female constable at his side busy taking notes. 'Would you like to give a witness statement?'

'No,' said Christie.

'What's been happening, Mrs Doyle?' asked Smith.

'My husband accused me of killing his mistress,' said Christie.

'Did you know of the existence of this mistress?'

'I did.'

'Where she lived?'

'Yes. I did. I followed him there, yesterday.'

'So you knew where she lived and you knew what she looked like? You could identify her, by sight?'

'Yes. I saw them both standing together outside the front door.' Christie squinted at him. Kenny had accused her of killing this girl, this Lara. 'What's happened to her?' she asked, feeling sick with nerves. It must be something bad. Something awful.

'You're telling me you don't know, Mrs Doyle?' Smith asked.

'No. Of course I don't.'

Smith looked at her squarely. 'Did you in fact kill her, Mrs Doyle?'

Christie shook her head. *What?* 'Do I need a lawyer here?'

Smith indicated the recording machine at his side. 'For the record, Mrs Doyle . . . ?'

'No. I didn't kill her. Kenny had lots of mistresses. Why would I kill this one and not the others?'

Because this one was pregnant with his child . . .

They would know about that soon enough, when they talked to Kenny.

'*Do* I need a lawyer?' she asked.

★

In the interview room next door, DI Cooper was questioning Kenny. He too had a female constable with him, and Kenny looked just about as broken as any man could be.

'Why were you going to attack your wife, Mr Doyle?' Cooper asked him.

'Christie killed her,' said Kenny. He was still mopping at his eyes. Still gulping, stifling sobs.

'Can we get you a coffee or tea, Mr Doyle?' asked Cooper.

'Water,' said Kenny, and the female constable went haring off to get it. She returned presently with a Styrofoam cup and a box of tissues. Kenny grabbed a handful, blew his nose with a loud honk and stuffed the used tissues in his pocket. He gulped down some water.

'Thanks,' he said.

'Who did your wife kill, Mr Doyle?' continued Cooper. But Kenny was staring intently at this copper's face. 'I know you, don't I? You look familiar.'

'Answer the question please, Mr Doyle.'

'Lara. Lara Millman.'

'Who is . . . ?'

'She's . . . we've been having an affair.'

'I see.'

'She was expecting my child.' And Kenny was off again, Kenny the hard man, in floods of tears. Then rage flared in his bloodshot eyes again. 'That bitch, she killed her.'

The door opened. A golden-haired youth in uniform put his head around it and looked at Cooper.

'Sorry to interrupt, sir. Call for you. Urgent.'

Cooper stopped the tape running and left the interview room. Next door, they were questioning Christie. He walked past the room where she was being interrogated, into the office the young man showed him to. He went in, closed the door, picked up the phone.

'Hello?'

'Dex?' It was the pathologist, Paulette. She was a dark-haired, endlessly meticulous matron of fifty; they had worked together a lot and there was a huge amount of professional respect between them.

'Paulette? What's up?'

'The Millman woman. You'd better get over here and take a look at this.'

'Do I have to?'

'You absolutely do.'

Dex looked at his watch. 'Give me half an hour. Then I'll be there.'

He went back into the interview room, restarted the tape. Sat down.

'Mr Doyle, how long have you been having an affair with Lara Millman?' he asked.

'A year. About that,' said Kenny.

'And your wife was unaware?'

'She was.' Kenny shook his head. 'Well I *thought* she was.'

'You say Miss Millman was pregnant.'

'She was.' He started to cry again, tears streaming down his florid face.

'Was that the reason you believe your wife killed her?'

Kenny was nodding, gulping. 'After I told Christie I wanted a divorce, I left. Yesterday I went to see Lara, tell her I'd done the deed. Christie followed me out there. Borrowed someone else's car, and why would you do that if you were kosher? Nah. The bitch did it to conceal the fact she'd followed me.'

'Wait, Mr Doyle. That doesn't add up. The next door neighbour – Mr Dawkins – says your wife was out at the front of his house, shouting at the pair of you. Hardly being discreet, was she?'

'She lost control. It's obvious. She meant to sneak around, but seeing us together, it shook her I guess.'

'If your wife loves you,' said Dex, 'you could see that it would be a shock, seeing you like that with another woman. A much younger woman than her. And pregnant with your child.'

Kenny thumped the table with his fist. The female PC jumped.

'Loves me?' he roared. 'Don't be fucking stupid. That bitch don't love me. She's made use of me, that's for damned sure. She wanted out from under the Butler lot and that's why she married me. It was only after she had a ring through my nose that I realised she was a barren, cold frigging bitch. We even thought of adoption, once upon a time. But she cancelled that. When I knew Lara was pregnant, it was a whole different ball game. I was going to be a dad. Start again with a woman who really did love me.

Christie only ever loved the lifestyle I gave her – that was all. Nothing else. Certainly not me. When I told her I was going to sell the house, move on without her, that's when the shit hit the fan.' Kenny dragged a tired hand across his eyes. 'That's when she decided to kill Lara.'

'And you were happy about the pregnancy?'

Kenny's eyes sharpened on Dex's face. 'What are you saying?'

'I'm asking if you were happy about it? Some men wouldn't be.' Dex's eyes didn't flinch away from Kenny's gaze. 'You had a settled life. A wife. Then, your mistress is pregnant? Maybe that's all a bit too hot for you to handle. Maybe she'll want something more from you. Maybe marriage, a commitment like that. Maybe that you take responsibility for your child when she delivers it. Perhaps you don't like the idea of any of that.'

Kenny's fist smacked down onto the tabletop. The female PC sitting beside Dex jumped several inches off her chair.

'What are you saying?' Kenny demanded. 'You think I killed her? Me? I loved the bones of that girl. Worshipped the ground she walked on. I was in love with her, if you have the slightest idea of what that might mean.'

'Where did you meet her, this girl?' asked Dex.

'She worked in my mate's club,' said Kenny.

'The name and address of the club . . . ?'

Kenny gave it. Dex wrote it down.

'But she hasn't worked there for some time?'

'No. When we got together, she packed all that in. I had the cottage standing empty; nobody was renting it. It seemed like a solution.'

'I'm sure it was, to have your mistress set up so conveniently and so close by Her family. What's their address?'

'Her mother . . . Christ, what's her mother going to make of this?' Tears were squeezing out from Kenny's eyes again. He gave a sigh that shook his entire frame and suddenly looked ten years older. Dully he told Dex Lara's mother's address. 'That poor bitch, she's got a world of hurt coming to her. She loved Lara.'

'Miss Millman had brothers? Sisters?'

'No. She was an only child.'

'Thank you, Mr Doyle. Now – let's get a lift organised for you. And Mr Doyle?'

Kenny levered himself tiredly to his feet and stood up. 'What?'

'We'll handle this.'

But Kenny was shaking his head. 'She's still here, ain't she? In this police station? Well make sure you *do* handle it. Lock that conniving vicious cunt up and throw the fucking key away.'

'Whatever we decide is to be done about your wife, Mr Doyle, you stay out of it. It's down to us. Don't go home. Go to a friend's house, or a relative's. You keep away from the house, and from her.'

Kenny paused. Pointed a finger at Dex. 'I *do* know you. Don't I.'

45

All the way over to the mortuary, Dex was turning the case over in his mind. If he *didn't* know anything about the woman involved – Christie – well, what would he think then?

He knew what he would think. Never mind about rattling Kenny Doyle's cage by pointing the finger at him, that was just testing a sore spot and wondering if the patient would react. What he would really think was this: *the wife did it.*

In a rage over the prospect of losing the cosy lifestyle she'd built over the years with her high-powered crook of a husband, she'd followed him out to his mistress's home, seen them together, and lost her mind. She'd gone back there under cover of darkness, set light to the place – and Lara Millman with it.

Dex considered all this. He'd known Christie Butler as a sweet young thing. In the years between, she'd grown and so had he. Surely there was nothing – well, very little – left of the people they had once been. Now he was a hard-nosed copper. It could have been prison for him, or the army, or the navy like his dad, but instead it was the police force that had stabilised him, made him grow up at last. And she . . . well, what the hell was she?

Quite possibly, she was a murderess.

She was still at the station. Smith was still questioning her. Dex knew what it was like, facing Colin Smith across an interview table. It was brutal, and protracted, and exhausting. And if he felt one iota of compassion for Christie, the Christie he'd once known, for being in this position, he quickly quashed it. That girl was gone. And the woman who was in there with his sergeant now? He didn't know her. Not at all.

Paulette was there at the ready in the mortuary, wearing scrubs, waiting, a white-sheeted remnant of humanity resting on the metal slab in front of her.

'Hello, Dex,' she said.

'Bad one, yes?'

'Bad yes. And . . . it's, well, odd, I would say. She's definitely ID'd as Lara Millman. Dental records confirmed it. And the tox report says no drugs in her system.'

'Odd in what way?'

'Come and see.'

Dex could never get used to corpses; he envied Paulette her composure around the dead. He'd told her so once and she'd said: 'Oh, don't feel bad. I never get used to it either. But I'm helping them, you see. Finding out who did this to them. That's a comfort.'

Paulette was drawing the sheet back from the head. It was scorched: inhuman. A faint odour like roasting pork wafted up and Dex swallowed hard, concentrated on Paulette's words and on keeping his churning stomach steady.

'What is it then?' he asked, when Paulette indicated the right eye of the cadaver. The blackened socket was still there but the eye was gone, the soft tissue burned away. He thought that Lara Millman once might have been beautiful; her skull was small, delicately formed. Now, she was the image of a nightmare. Something that looked like a golden-yellow teardrop was protruding from the inner corner of her right eye socket.

'Look at this,' said Paulette, and with a pair of tweezers she clasped the teardrop and pulled it up and away from the skull, bringing with it six inches of scorched metal.

'It's long and thin, see. Like a knitting needle, something like that? But it's not a knitting needle.'

Dex swallowed. 'Do you think our corpse was dead before the place caught fire?'

'No. She wasn't. Lungs full of smoke damage. The angle of the entry of this thing suggests it breached the upper palate of the mouth, didn't enter the brain. Yes, someone put this sharp object through the eye socket. This would have caused extreme pain, maybe blinding, but it wasn't the cause of death. That was the fire itself.'

'What d'you reckon it is?' asked Dex, staring at the thing, thinking – all too vividly – of Lara Millman's last moments when she'd opened the front door to her cottage and then someone had lunged at her, plunging that thing into her eye. He could imagine the agony. The horror. The sheer *fury* needed to do that.

'This was murder all right – deliberate and vicious. And I think I know what it is. Those big hats women used to wear way back in olden times?' said Paulette. 'Well, that's a topaz, don't you think? A decorative way of securing a large hat. This looks like a Victorian hatpin to me.'

46

When he got back to the station, DI Cooper went into interview room A. Smith was sitting there, a female uniform at his
side. Opposite the pair of them sat Christie. Smith glanced
up as Dex entered, told the tape all about it, then stood up
and left the room. Dex took his place. Stared across at the
woman sitting there.

Her, after all this time.

Her reticence, her wariness, had made him warm to her
all those years back – and Dex thought that Christie must
even once have made a heavy-duty thug like Kenny Doyle
come over all protective. After all, Kenny had married her.
He might hate her now, but back then, surely it had been all
wine and roses, total marital bliss.

'What do you know about Lara Millman?' he asked, when
the silence had dragged on long enough to rattle her.

Christie's shoulders slumped. 'Kenny kept a cottage in the
next village. Rented it out sometimes. Holiday lets for walk-
ers, that sort of thing. Lara Millman had been living there.'

'You knew about her living there?'

'No. Not until the day before yesterday.'

'Not before?'

'No. Not before.'

'But you knew about the cottage before?'

'I did. Kenny bought it, said it was an investment. Five, maybe six years ago? He rented it out, as I say. Short lets at first, then there was all the kerfuffle about changing the bed linen and tidying the place up and he decided long lets, proper rentals, would work better. I didn't know much about it but I was aware that he had a tenant in there. I didn't know it was Lara Millman. I didn't know she was Kenny's bit on the side.'

'But when you followed your husband there, you saw them together.'

'I did. That's correct.'

'And made a scene.'

'I confronted them, yes.'

'You were mad with jealousy?'

'No. I wasn't.'

'Really.'

'Yes. Really.'

'Then what? Why confront them, if you didn't care?'

Christie shrugged, looked away.

'For the purposes of the tape . . . ?' Dex prompted. He remembered that careless lift of the shoulders, that mulish silence. It was her. But he was going to have to ignore that fact. Bury it, and bury it deep.

Christie's sea-green eyes came back to his. 'He told me the house would have to go. My house.'

'What, so he could buy somewhere better than a small cottage to live with this mistress of his? That must have hurt.'

'It did. Yes.'

'Enough to . . .'

'No. Not enough for that.'

'And yet Lara Millman is dead. Killed deliberately in a fire. She's died and so has the child she was expecting. Did you know about the child?'

'I found out the day before yesterday.'

'And you are childless, Mrs Doyle?'

'Yes. I am.'

'Never wanted children?'

Christie stared into his eyes. 'I don't think that's any of your damned business.'

'For the purpose of this investigation, it is.'

'I couldn't have them,' said Christie.

'So when your husband found that his mistress was pregnant and told you so, how did you feel about that?'

'Gutted.' She shrugged.

'Feeling that you were losing him.'

'Feeling that I was going to lose my home.'

'So your husband and you . . .'

'We weren't close. Kenny's one of those men who has to have kids to prove himself to be the big I-am. When he found I couldn't have them, I suppose he felt cheated. He had a lot of affairs. Not just this one. Maybe he tried to have kids with all of them. How would I know? Maybe he failed. Then with this one, he succeeded.'

'That sounds pretty bleak,' said Dex.

Again, the shrug. 'We've been married for over twenty years and I was pragmatic about it. We settled for each other, as a lot of couples do. I had the lovely house – *houses*, actually – he had his women. I thought maybe we could maintain that status quo, but it seems Kenny thought different.'

'That's cold-blooded,' said Dex.

'It's how it was, that's all.'

'So you felt upset about the whole thing. Destabilised.'

'Yes. Correct.'

'Enough to kill Lara Millman?'

Christie looked directly into his eyes again. She paused, and he thought he saw a half-smile play around her mouth. Dex felt his stomach tighten. It was the same smile, unnervingly, that had touched her mouth years ago, when they'd both been so young. Sometimes they'd played chess together. He'd taught her a few moves, but she had never taken the game seriously. He'd always been a better player than her, far more cunning, infinitely more long-sighted. Full of deadly deductions. A hint there maybe of the detective he would one day become. When he'd just made a particularly smart move, she'd always acknowledge it with that very same smile. Before, usually, flicking his pieces – and hers – off the board with a laugh.

'No,' she said finally. 'Not enough for that.'

Dex was silent, watching her face. Could she have done it – a vicious, spiteful, cruel thing like this?

Finally he reached for the switch on the tape machine.

'Interview terminated at . . .' He glanced at his watch, stated the time. 'Mrs Doyle? You're free to go,' he said, and stood up and left the room.

*

When Christie stepped outside the station and inhaled fresh air again, she felt a moment of relief – and then Ivo was there in front of her.

'You'll be wanting a lift,' he said.

'No,' said Christie. 'I won't. Have you been waiting out here, waiting for me?'

'I have. You need your family around you at a time like this.'

'No I don't. That's one thing I definitely don't need.'

She started to walk off, along the road toward the parade of shops. Maybe there was a cab office there, and she'd get a taxi. Ivo grabbed her arm, pulled her to a halt.

'Oh come on,' he said, grinning.

'I said *no*,' said Christie, yanking her arm away from him and approaching a burly sergeant who was just getting into a police car. 'Officer? Is there a cab office over there?'

She glanced back. Ivo was already gone. One sniff of police, and he was away. Thank God. She was shaking. The sergeant showed her exactly where the cab office was, and she went home.

47

'It's cut and dried, wouldn't you say?' said DS Smith, who was waiting in Dex's office.

'What?' Dex came in, went behind his desk and sat down. The image of her face – Christie's face – was, disconcertingly, swimming in front of his mind's eye. She'd barely changed at all. And wasn't Smith now repeating exactly what he'd already thought, himself?

'Oh come on. Jealous wife kills mistress. Textbook,' said Smith.

'Pretty much circumstantial at the moment,' said Dex.

'Shouldn't this have been Turnbull's shout?'

Dex explained about the sick kids, the absent wife.

Smith shrugged unsympathetically. He was single and fancy-free, and every time he heard about what marriage involved, he was damned glad of that.

'Still,' he said. 'Rubbing her nose in it like that. Got to hurt. And then her turning up, ranting in the street?'

'Maybe.'

'You haven't charged her then? Detained her?' asked Smith.

'No. Not yet.' Because Dex didn't believe she'd do that. Which was stupid. *He didn't know her.* Twenty years had gone by. How could he possibly know her now?

But he couldn't tell Smith that. He couldn't tell anyone that. His credibility as an investigative officer would be instantly compromised if he revealed that far-distant connection to her. And anyway, was it really a connection at all? Once, they'd flirted. Definitely, there'd been a strong attraction there. Christie Butler had sat on his lap and he had kissed her. Then she had rejected him.

For quite a while before that night when they'd kissed, he'd been thinking of going abroad, seeing the world – just kicking the thing down the road and seeing if he liked it, but then, feeling bleak, raw, *destroyed*, he'd brought travel to the front of his mind and thought: *Why not? Why the fuck not?*

Now a lot of time had passed by. He had to smother those memories and be dispassionate. Keep his mind on the now, not the then.

'So what next?' asked Smith. 'What about the errant husband? All the tears and stuff, but is that a real reflection of how he's feeling or just a blind? Saying oh look, I'm so upset, she's dead, boo-hoo.'

'You're all heart, Col,' said Dex.

'I've had all that bollocks knocked out of me, sir. We've seen them in here, haven't we, time after time. No I didn't do it; I would never do something like that. Then boom! They break down and confess it was them all along.'

'You've filled in Debbie and Bill on the basics?' asked Dex.

'I have. They're waiting.'

'So you suspect the husband? Kenny Doyle? Not the wife?'

Smith did an imitation twirling of an imaginary moustache. 'I suspect no one and I suspect everyone,' he said in a bad French accent.

Dex was thinking that he could withdraw from the investigation. Declare an interest, tell the super and he would understand. Of course he would. Of course he *could*. But something in him was resisting that impulse. And Smith was right. Kenny could be in the frame, and he might deserve to be there. It wouldn't be the first time a thwarted lover had lost control.

But . . . Kenny had wanted kids. Desperately, according to Christie. She hadn't been able to give him any. Kenny had been delighted when Lara Millman had got up the duff. So why then go and kill the poor tart?

'This Lara Millman,' he said. 'What do we know about her? Her family, her friends? Who are they, where are they? How did any of them feel about a young woman like Lara Millman hooking up with an older married man and a pretty disreputable one at that?'

Dex sat down behind his desk and glanced out of the window. Dusk was coming in, tinting the grim grey land-scape of the police car park to a soft gold. He thought of Kenny Doyle, rattling around loose out there, apparently – but really, who knew? – full of vengeful rage. Kenny was no fool. He was a crook and a very successful one, evading prosecution for any number of perceived or real offences. For a long time he hadn't been in Dex's immediate orbit, but Dex had heard plenty about Kenny through the grape-vine, and he didn't like the sound of any of it. This greasy hair-trigger thug was married to Christie. And now all Dex could think of was Christie, over there in her palatial valley home. Alone.

He flipped open his notebook. Lara Millman's mother's address was there. He heaved a sigh.

'Come on,' he said, standing up, snatching up his jacket.

Dex led the way out into the main open-plan office where DC Debbie Phelps, a middle-aged blonde, and DC Bill Jensen, a comfortably padded young man with a black beard and a bald head, were seated at their desks. They looked up expectantly.

'We're designating the Lara Millman case as Operation Rainbow,' said Dex, halting in front of the wall where a map of the crime location had been set up, alongside pictures courtesy of the SOCO team – shots of the burned-out thatch, the scorched hallway, the corpse, bright yellow numbered markers dotted here and there.

'I want both you three and uniform on door to door in that village,' Dex went on. 'Find out if anyone – apart from that one neighbour – saw or heard anything unusual, anything suspicious over the past forty-eight hours. Does anyone have CCTV, security cameras? That could help. All clear?'

'I had a nice evening planned,' said Bill with a sigh. 'Popcorn on the sofa.'

'Tough luck, Bill,' said Dex. 'We've got work to do.'

And not very pleasant work, either.

48

It was the bit of the job he hated most, but like everything in life, you do it often enough, you grow a hard shell over your heart and in the end it's easy. You detach, take yourself off somewhere while you do the talking, sit the person down, tell them it must have been over very quickly – even if it wasn't – and you're sorry for their loss. Very sorry indeed.

Lara Millman's mother looked like Lara herself might have looked, had she lived, in thirty years' time. Mrs Millman's long thin blonde hair was peppered with white strands, the olive-toned skin was wrinkled from too much sun. The eyes, surely once beautiful gold-yellow eyes – like the daughter's that were smiling out of framed photos on the mantelpiece – were red and puffy from all the tears she'd been crying ever since Dex had arrived at her door like the angel of doom and broken the news of her daughter's death.

'I saw it on the lunchtime news. The thatched cottage, all burned out. In the same village as Lara and I thought, no, it couldn't possibly be her place, it couldn't. Oh God. Oh God. I told her not to mix with him,' she said, after the uniformed female PC who'd accompanied Dex to her door had made them all tea in the chaotic little kitchen.

'Is there someone we should call for you? A friend? A relative?' asked Dex.

Mrs Millman shook her head, hugged herself. It was hot in the room, but she looked cold, strained.

'You shouldn't be alone,' said the female PC.

Lara Millman's mother gave the woman a scornful glance. Then someone was coming in the back door into the kitchen, rushing into the living room – a pale-faced youth with a mop of black hair. 'Is this . . . ?' he asked, looked at Dex, looking at the female PC. 'I saw a thing on the news. The village Lara lives in. What's going on?'

'And you are . . . ?' Dex asked, standing up.

'This is Andy Paskins,' said Mrs Millman. 'He lives next door. He was Lara's boyfriend, back in the day. They went to school together.' She paused, looking up at the younger of the two men. 'You better sit down, son. It ain't good news.' Her face crumpled again. 'She was my only child,' she said to Dex. 'My beautiful little girl. I want to see her.'

Dex felt an instant of recoil at this. He pictured again the pitiful burnt remains he'd seen in the mortuary. 'No, Mrs Millman. Trust me, you wouldn't want to do that.'

She was crying again, huge gulping sobs. The boy sank down onto the sofa beside her, put an arm around her thin shoulders. His face was peppered with acne, his nose over-long, his ears sticking out like radar scanners. He had soft eyes, dark as a doe's.

Gently, Dex gave him an outline of what had happened while thinking of what he'd seen outside when they were waiting on the front step to be admitted to the house – a motorbike, parked in the alleyway between the two houses.

'She was all I had,' said Mrs Millman while Andy Paskins sat there, numb, disbelieving.

Dex was silent, letting her cry. She'd be doing a lot of that over the weeks to come, and slowly, finally, the tears would dry up. The pain wouldn't go away, but bit by bit, it would fade.

'Mrs Millman?' he said at last. 'Can I take one of those photos? That's Lara, yes?'

She tucked the soiled tissue up her sleeve and looked at him. Nodded.

Dex pocketed one of the small framed photos. 'Have you any idea why anyone would want to harm your daughter?'

Andy Paskins answered for her. 'No one would want to hurt Lara. She was a great girl. Fantastic.'

Mrs Millman was shaking her head. 'I warned her against him. That Kenny Doyle bastard. I told her, don't mess with people like that. Everyone knows what he is. But she was dazzled by the flash git. She was so young, and he was an older man. You know. Experienced. Liked to show her a good time. And her head was turned by that.'

'Mrs Millman, were you aware that your daughter was pregnant?'

Her eyes widened. Dex watch a dull flush creep up Andy Paskins's spot-mottled cheeks. Shock? Anger? Slowly, Mrs Millman shook her head. Then Dex saw the meaning of it sink in, bit by bit. A grandchild. Her grandchild. One she would never see, never hold, never walk to school.

'You didn't know? Really?'

'How would I? Lara and me, we fell out. I told her about mixing with people like Kenny Doyle but she wouldn't have it. He was a married man for one thing. It wasn't right. I didn't raise her that way, acting the tart with someone like that. But she wouldn't hear a word against him. Thought he was like the second ruddy coming. He could do no wrong in her eyes.'

She cried again, wrenching, bitter tears, while Andy sat there feebly patting her back.

'You argued about it,' said Dex.

'We did. God, it all seems so stupid now. She said she was going and she wasn't coming back. And she didn't, did she? She never came back.' This brought on a fresh bout of weeping.

'We were told that Mr Doyle met Lara in a club run by one of his friends. Is that right, do you know?' asked Dex.

'Yes, that's right. Mungo's, that place in Soho.'

'I know it.' Dex knew who owned it, too. Another dodgy bastard by the name of Mungo Boulaye, a close business associate of Kenny Doyle's.

'I didn't like her working there. I told her so. We argued. We were always arguing. It all seems so damned silly now. All the time we wasted going at each other's throats, when time was ticking away, when *this* was waiting round the corner.'

49

Shortly after Andy Paskins left Mrs Millman's place, Dex left too. But instead of getting back into the car, he and the PC went and knocked on Andy's door. The motorbike was still parked in the alleyway between the two houses.

Andy was startled to see them there.

'This must be very upsetting for you,' said Dex.

Andy Paskins folded his arms over his skinny body as if he was cold. 'It's horrible.'

'Mr Paskins,' said Dex. 'A man matching your description was seen outside Lara Millman's cottage yesterday.'

He shrugged. 'Well it wasn't me.'

'Wasn't it?'

'No.' He stared truculently at Dex.

'I think we'd better discuss this at the station,' said Dex.

All the colour left Andy's face. 'I didn't do nothing.'

Dex stepped forward. 'No? OK. Let's go inside and talk about it,' he said.

*

Gut feeling? After an hour and a half of 'chatting' to Andy Paskins, Dex was undecided. Andy was a past boyfriend of Lara's and jealousy was a powerful emotion, particularly when it struck at such a young age. Andy looked guilty as hell about something, for sure. Stalking, maybe. Hanging around wherever he thought he'd catch a glimpse of her? That was a possibility.

At around five o'clock in the afternoon, Dex went and knocked at the door of the big house in the valley. There was a sporty red car parked in the drive, nothing else. The house was silent. It was massive. Bloody impressive, actually. Dex thought of his own apartment, which could fit into this beast ten times over.

The door opened.

Christie stood there. She stared up at him and said: 'So – are you still pretending you don't recognise me then?'

Dex didn't respond to that one. He hadn't been pretending. He'd been blindsided by seeing her again after all this time. Truth was, he didn't know how to react to the actual fact of Christie Doyle, née Butler, standing right there in front of him.

'Come in,' she said, and stood aside.

'This is some place,' said Dex as she closed the door behind him. Ahead, through a set of wide-open double glass doors he could see a vast sitting room and a bank of floor-to-ceiling windows. Beyond that, a decked terrace, a massive teak table and chairs set out upon it beneath a gargantuan cream-coloured parasol, and then beyond that, the luminous green and yellow and corn gold of the valley turning to amber in the soft light of late afternoon.

'Wow,' he said.

Christie followed him into the sitting room and they stood by the windows, staring out at the view.

'Did you want to ask me more questions?' she said, her voice tired. 'Or have you come to arrest me? Is that it?'

'Did you know Lara Millman?' Dex asked, not looking at her face. He found looking at her downright disconcerting. It was Christie, yes, but at the same time, not. Back then, they'd been so young. Now they had both changed and those days, he reminded himself, were long gone. 'I mean, before the day of her death?' His eyes went to the pool. Something in there. Red-brown. Swimming. 'What . . . ?'

'There's a fox. She lives out the front somewhere, up in the woods. When it's hot she likes it in the water.'

'You should put the cover on at night.'

Kenny had often said the same thing, complaining: 'You're losing all the bloody heat. That heat's costing, you know. And there it is, wafting away into the open air because you leave the cover off all night for a bloody *fox*. I'll get the gardener to put some stuff down, see the bastard thing off.'

Christie had told Patrick not to put stuff down for the fox. Patrick, who was a nice man, a friend far more than an employee, had happily complied.

'Lara Millman? No, I didn't know her. Not even slightly,' said Christie.

'Have you thought about changing the locks here? I mean, Kenny . . .' His voice trailed away.

Christie gave a faint smile. 'The locksmith left about half an hour before you arrived. It's done.'

'Safest until things are sorted out.'

'Yeah? When will that be?'

'When we get to the bottom of what's happened here. When we find who killed Lara Millman.'

Christie stared at him. Dex kept his eyes firmly on the view.

'I can't get over it,' said Christie.

'Over what?' asked Dex. Eyes front.

'You. A detective.'

He turned and looked at her. 'What, is it so surprising?'

'Surprising? It's bloody shocking,' said Christie. 'Back in the day, I thought you might be many things. A crook, possibly. No, definitely. Hanging around with the Butler lot like you did. A policeman? Never.'

'Well, I . . .'

'When you left, what did you do? Where did you go? Were you a Mountie or something? I think you mentioned Argentina once. Did you have a horse? Mind you, you never could stay on one for longer than ten minutes. You kept scaring the poor things. Moving about too fast. Horses don't like that.'

Dex almost smiled at that. She'd been better than him on horseback; more patient, gentler. He'd been rubbish. Too fast-moving, far too rough. He had *literally* frightened the horses.

*

'I didn't have a horse,' said Dex. 'I wasn't a Mountie.'

Christie stared at him in surprise. And then she remembered that awful visit from him when she'd been married to Kenny for just three days. When she'd realised how thoroughly her life had fallen apart; how disastrous it had all become. How sick to her stomach she'd felt, because her fear of Ivo had forced her down the wrong path with the wrong man. She was married, Dex would be gone – *again* – and there was nothing she could do about it but go on and live a lie.

'You came back, do you remember? A flying visit to see your folks,' she said. Her mouth felt dry. 'You called in, you remember? At the Butler place. And I happened to be there.'

'Yeah. I did. I do.'

Did he remember that horrible encounter just like she did? His face gave nothing away. Nothing at all.

'I got homesick I suppose. Came back that time to see Mum and Dad and my sister and brother and realised I didn't want to travel as much as I'd thought.'

'So what *did* you do then?' she asked, curious.

'You were right about Argentina. I spent some time there, worked on a cattle ranch on the pampas. Then I went to New Zealand and spent a while shearing sheep. I came home again and didn't know what to do next. I considered the army, the navy, the air force. Then there was a recruitment drive on with the police so I joined them instead.'

Christie felt like she'd just been gut-punched. She was literally winded. So a lot of the time when he'd been gone, he'd been here in England. Probably not even too far away. His parents lived just a few miles down the road. His nice, sweet, friendly parents, who'd welcomed her into their home on brief occasions, family parties, Christmas, Easter. They'd welcomed her even after Dex had gone away on his travels or whatever – and stubbornly, she had never asked after him. He'd as good as told her to fuck off, after all, and his parents – politely, not wanting, she guessed, to tread on anyone's toes – had offered her no information about him.

'Well, good for you,' she said tightly. 'I hope you've been happy.'

'What does that mean?'

'It means I hope you've been happy. Married now I suppose?' Her eyes went to his left hand. No ring. 'Or maybe not.'

'The police force may be a good career, but it's disastrous for marriages.'

'Right,' said Christie. He hadn't answered her question. 'Well, have you anything else you want to ask me now? Or have you asked me enough? I didn't know Lara Millman.

And frankly I could only pity the poor cow, if she was getting involved with Kenny. He's a flashy son of a bitch and whatever she may have believed of his bullshit, he'd never stay faithful for long.'

'I questioned him about their relationship,' said Dex. 'He seemed heartbroken.'

'I don't think Kenny has a heart to break,' said Christie. She went over to a big cream-coloured couch and sat down. 'So go on. Ask me whatever you want. I've told you most of it. I didn't know Lara. And I didn't kill her.'

*

All Dex could think was that she looked so small, sitting there on that vast sofa. So alone.

He felt that he was walking on eggshells here, or on thin ice – maybe, yes that was it, *very* thin ice. And at any moment he was going to plunge through it and into the wakefulness of reality below.

He tried to conjure it up in his mind: this new fully adult Christie standing there on the cottage doorstep, coolly ringing the bell, and then when pregnant Lara Millman opened the door, stepping forward and briskly plunging that hatpin into the girl's eye. Then calmly, dispassionately, pouring petrol all over her body, standing back, throwing down a match. He could picture the *whoomph* as it ignited. Could see it all, in his mind's eye, the rush of the flames, the dead crushing *heat* of them. Then Christie turning, walking away into the dark unlit streets of the village, getting into her car, going home.

Job done, yes?

Mistress dead. Kenny's child, dead.

But . . . Christie? Really?

He had a feeling of things moving beyond his control, and he didn't like that. But . . . there was doubt. Cut and dried, Smith had said. No. No way was it cut and dried.

'I don't have any more questions for you,' he said, his voice sharp. She looked up at him. The eyes of a killer? He couldn't believe it. But he just didn't know.

'Why not? I thought you'd have loads,' she said.

He felt irritated at that. What was she doing, wanting him to stay longer? Throwing him a bone? She'd rejected him, long ago. Was she toying with him? Playing him? Didn't she know he was too smart to fall for moves like that?

'Turns out I don't have any more questions right now,' said Dex. 'Let's face it, the situation's far from clear at this point.'

'Meaning?' She was staring at him.

'Meaning, Christie – we both know you've got form, don't we? As a fire starter.'

50

After Dex was gone, Christie sat there in the vast echoing silence of the house, all the wind knocked out of her.

We both know you've got form.

She'd almost forgotten it, personally. Her brain had a way of editing things out that she really, really didn't want to remember, but still – some things crept through. A snatch of an old Everly Brothers song. A woman – her mother – crying. There were plenty of such things. A hospital. Something about a hospital. Occasionally, much as she didn't want them to, these things would pop to the surface.

Oh yeah – oh Christie, don't you remember that?

The confines of the petrol-stinking car, her mother in the front seat, whispering something to Christie's dying father.

Her first night in her aunt and uncle's house, Ivo in the doorway of her bedroom.

Her, wetting the bed.

There were plenty of horror shows available in the back of her brain and sometimes they just darted out, *surprise!* and presented themselves to her with clownish glee: *hey, remember this one, Christie? Funny, yes?*

No. Not funny at all.

The grounds of the Butler household had stretched to over five acres and now she was remembering the huge workshops and storage sheds there. One of them accommodated two very costly JCB diggers, two massive HGVs and three dumper trucks, which were used by the company.

She'd found the red petrol can in there, sloshing with fuel. She'd taken up the matches, uncapped the can and emptied the contents onto some rags by one of the machines. Then she'd stepped back – she knew the vapour was dangerous with petrol. It was the vapour you had to beware of as it could float in the air and fry you to a crisp if you weren't careful.

She recalled that day, now that Dex had reminded her of it. She remembered standing well back and tossing in the lit match.

Boom!

Spectacular. Tongues of flame, leaping up.

Then Ivo running in, putting out the fire with the extinguisher.

Kenny had been there that day.

Then her uncle, sitting her down, saying why did you do a thing like that, Christie? As if she could tell him. How could she tell him that her rage at Ivo had to find an outlet, somehow? She remembered the furtive look in Aunt Julia's eyes; Aunt Julia knew exactly what had been going on in the house; Christie's pregnancy, the abortion . . . and had she been ill after that, infected? Jerome knew nothing. *Glandular fever,* Julia had told everyone. For a while, Christie had fully expected to die. *Had* she been in hospital? But she was surprisingly strong and she survived.

'She's fucking crazy,' Cousin Ivo had said, slouching in the doorway.

'Shut up, Ivo,' said Aunt Julia.

'Well it's true.'

How strange that Christie had almost completely forgotten that incident, but Dex had remembered. Something to do with having a detective's brain, she thought. She sat there, wondered if she ought to go on up to bed. But sleep was frightening her just now. She was afraid she might walk. Truthfully, she was afraid of what she might do. At the back of her brain, there was a suspicion, a tiny little worm of fear, nibbling at the edge of reason.

Had she sleepwalked – no, had she *driven* while asleep, over to the cottage where Lara Millman her husband's mistress lived, and had she burned down the place with Lara Millman in it?

'Oh Christ,' she murmured, dropping her head into her hands. It was possible. She had form. Dex knew it, and so did she.

There came a rattling from the front door and Christie's heart leapt into her mouth. Someone was trying to get in. But the locks had been changed. She bolted to her feet, went out into the hall. Dry-mouthed with panic, she stared at the door. She hadn't heard Kenny's Roller out on the drive, crunching heavily over the gravel, a sound as familiar to her as her own breathing.

She crept close to the door. Someone on the other side of it slapped the paintwork. She stopped breathing. Oh Christ, it was Kenny, come to get her. Or – oh please, sweet Jesus please – not Ivo.

'Hey! Christie? You in there?' said a female voice.

Christie sagged.

It was Patsy.

51

Christie flung open the door. Patsy was standing there, key in hand, gawping up at her. Not waiting for an invitation, she surged inside. Dazedly, her heart still throbbing like a drum, Christie shut the door. Locked it.

'The bloody key didn't work,' said Patsy, heading into the sitting room.

Christie followed her. Years ago, she'd given Patsy a key. Patsy would call in, keep an eye on the place whenever she and Kenny were away. Stock up the fridge for their return. Kenny didn't really like people in the house when he wasn't there. A crook himself, he was deeply suspicious of everyone, convinced that they would be rifling through his belongings, maybe pinching things, who knew? But Christie had insisted that she trusted Patsy. She'd known her since school. She was a mate.

'I had the locks changed,' she told her.

Patsy turned, wide-eyed. 'What for?' She dragged an agitated hand through her hair. 'Look, what is going on? Kenny's over at ours ranting about killing you; Mungo's trying to calm him down. What the hell's been happening?'

Christie sat down. She felt so tired. Wrung out.

'You mean you don't know? They haven't told you?'

Patsy flopped down onto the couch, shaking her head. 'No.' She put the useless key back into her Gucci handbag, clicked the clasp closed.

'Not much point you keeping that,' said Christie. 'It's no good now. And I'm not handing out any new ones.'

Patsy looked offended.

'No, Pats, don't get me wrong. It's not because I don't trust you. It's because I can't trust *him*. Kenny threatened me, and what's to stop him getting hold of a key if I give you one, and coming back in here and doing something drastic? No. I'm not chancing it.'

'But,' Patsy pointed out, 'he could phone any locksmith and get them to let him in, couldn't he? Gawd, there must be one on the payroll, for sure.'

He could. Christie hadn't thought of that. Failing that, Kenny could break the damned door down if he wanted too. Ram it with the Roller. Or walk straight through it. He was strong enough, mad enough.

'That girl Kenny's been knocking off?' said Christie.

'What, the Millman girl?'

'Yeah. That one.' Christie heaved a sigh.

'What about her?'

'She's dead.'

Patsy stared at Christie's face. 'You . . . what?'

'Dead. There was a fire. She died.'

'You're fucking kidding me.'

Christie gave a tired smile. 'I wish I was.'

'Kenny's over there in our kitchen, crying his eyes out,' said Patsy. 'I never seen him cry. Not once, not ever. It's bloody frightening. Like the world's collapsing.'

'He thinks I did it.'

'You . . .' Patsy seemed momentarily at a loss for words. 'You?'

Christie nodded.

'I followed him out there after my party. Made a bit of a scene in the road. People saw. A neighbour. I've been down the police station, answering questions.'

'But you wouldn't do a thing like that. I know you wouldn't.'

'They don't know it,' said Christie. 'The police.'

Christie couldn't tell Patsy about the shock she'd had, finding Dex to be the investigating officer. She could barely process the matter herself, how the hell was she going to explain it to Patsy? She thought of sitting on his lap all those years ago. Kissing him. Oh, the feel of him, her fingers on the nape of his neck, his skin so warm and smooth. Feeling that the world was not all horror and regret after all. That the nightmare images that had scalded themselves into her flinching brain might not always be there. That some good could happen. She'd almost believed that, then.

She didn't now.

'It's fucking horrific, seeing Kenny like that,' said Patsy, shaking her head. 'He's always the boss, isn't he? Always the one in control.'

Christie nodded. It was what had drawn her to Kenny in the first place, the feeling that he was totally in charge. That her aunt and uncle – and, more importantly, Ivo – shook in their boots every time he appeared. That had comforted her. Drawn her to him. Yes, they were afraid of him – and she'd always liked that.

'What the hell are you going to do?' Patsy asked.

'Clear off out of it I suppose. Go down to Cornwall or somewhere, but I can't leave the country. The police warned me of that.'

Let Patsy go back and tell Kenny that Christie was going to Cornwall. She would – Christie didn't doubt that. Yes, she was Christie's friend, but her husband's business, her whole existence, pivoted on keeping Mungo – and therefore Kenny, his mate – sweet.

'God, what a mess,' said Patsy.

'Isn't it,' said Christie.

52

'Oh for fuck's sake!' said Patsy when she got up the following day. She was flushed with temper.

Mungo Boulaye looked up as his wife came in the French doors and crossed their shiny super-deluxe kitchen. She was in her dressing gown and so was he; he was reading the morning paper at the table, sipping freshly ground coffee from the cafetiere – Mungo would never touch instant.

'What's he doing now?' he asked her, exasperated, and she shook her head.

'Mungo, if I told you, you wouldn't believe me.' Patsy went to the sink, found a cup, went to the table, slapped the cup down and poured herself a coffee.

'Try me.' By this point, Mungo felt that nothing would surprise him.

'He's in the hot tub, crying. I think he's been there all night. Oh – and you know that bottle of Macallan Lalique fifty-five-year-old Single Malt you had put by for a special occasion?'

Mungo stiffened. That bottle had cost him over a hundred quid. Granted, he had plenty these days, but for God's sake! 'He didn't.'

'He bloody did. Bottle's empty by the side of the tub.' Then she tossed the landline phone onto the counter. 'That was beside it.'

Mungo frowned. 'He's been making calls on my fucking phone? Has he been phoning abroad? Who's he been calling?'

'How the hell should I know?' demanded Patsy.

'Fucker!' Mungo sprang to his feet, spilling coffee over his *Daily Mail* and swamping the nightmare tale of Fred and Rose West.

He crossed the kitchen and went out through the French doors. There at the end of the terrace – a pretty palatial terrace, and he was rather proud of it – was the hot tub, burbling away, steaming like a good 'un. And there, head slumped forward on his naked chest, arms dangling outside the tub, was Kenny.

'Oh, mate,' sighed Mungo, exasperated.

Mungo stopped the bubbles. The thing fell silent. Kenny didn't respond. Teardrops slid down his face, into the water.

'Mate,' said Mungo. 'You got to get out of there. You got to pull yourself together. You dig me?'

Kenny didn't answer. So it was down to Mungo to haul a pretty damned drunk Kenny up onto his feet, down the shallow steps beside the tub and back onto solid ground. Kenny was stark naked, not even a pair of bathers on. Mungo reflected that the tub was going to need a very thorough clean after all this. He grabbed a towel with difficulty because he was holding Kenny upright, wrapped it around Kenny's waist as best he could, and ushered him indoors. Halfway across the kitchen, the towel came off and Patsy grabbed it, secured it more tightly around Kenny to at least preserve his modesty.

'Thanks, babe,' said Mungo, and puffing and panting he half-carried and half-dragged Kenny up the stairs and into the spare room where he was supposed to have spent the night and hadn't.

Half an hour later, Mungo was back downstairs, dressed, shaved, ready for business.

'And what the hell am I supposed to do about him?' asked Patsy.

'Let him sleep. Check on him every half an hour. I've put him on his side. Watch he don't roll onto his back and choke his stupid self.'

'I've never seen him so upset about anything.'

'The Millman girl was carrying his sprog. That was the thing, really. You know how Kenny was about kids.'

'Poor sod.'

'You'd best keep away from her now.'

'Her?' Patsy echoed. But she knew exactly who he meant. Her was Christie.

'Babe, we got to know where our loyalties lie. We got to show it, too. What, you been over there?' He frowned. He didn't like that idea.

'Sure I have. She's my best friend.'

'You got to get a better class of friend. She's bloody demented – I think Ken's right. If she did this, with a kid involved, an unborn kid, well, it's fucking evil. That's all you can say about it.'

'So you're just going to leave me here lumbered with him? You're – what – going to the club?' Patsy was furious. She didn't even like Kenny, and here she was facing the prospect of a day playing nursemaid to the sod.

'Of course I'm going into the club. Business don't run itself, does it?' Mungo grabbed his wife's arse and planted a kiss on her cheek. He smelled clean, damp from the shower, perfumed with Acqua di Parma.

'Look after him,' said Mungo firmly.

'Yeah, whatever.' She sighed.

Mungo left the building, got into his Porsche, started the engine. Bob Marley blared out of the sound system but this morning he didn't feel much in the mood for humming along. He switched it off. That fucking Millman girl had caused far, far too much trouble. One day surely even Kenny would see that it was just as well she was dead.

53

While Kenny Doyle was sleeping off the excesses of his night in Mungo and Patsy's hot tub, Gustavo Cota had responded to a call from Primo Ecco in New York and was now flying in first class from New York to Gatwick, London. He had completed one very satisfactory assignment in Aspen, Colorado, then taken an exemplary and very comfortable five-hour flight back to his Manhattan hotel, where a message awaited him. A new contract.

He called the number he'd been given, spoke to what sounded very much to his ears like a man who was drunk and nearly incoherent. No matter. He'd done lots of work for Primo in the past and any connection Primo passed him was welcome. Primo was the don. He usually gave clear instructions as to his requirements and was a prompt payer. But this Doyle person was clearly very upset.

That didn't matter. Once Gustavo had landed in England, he'd check in with Mr Doyle and be sure he'd got things right. It was always possible that, in the cold light of day, Doyle would be his usual sober self and might reconsider. Not a problem. Of course he would foot the bill for Gustavo's flights, taxis and hotels – that was only to be expected if the trip should prove to be a wasted one. Doyle would understand that. He certainly wouldn't dispute it. Nobody ever disputed one of Gustavo's bills, not even Primo, who was a scary man and always to be treated with absolute respect. When you met Primo, you weren't only expected to kiss his hand – you kissed his *arse*, if he so desired.

Gustavo refreshed himself. Took a shower, got reception busy booking him a flight out of JFK to London the following morning. He enjoyed a leisurely meal, had a massage, swam in the hotel pool, rested; and then he packed up, went down to reception when they called, checked out and got into his yellow taxi, which took him along the busy New York freeways to the airport. Everything was running smoothly, and he liked that.

When he landed at Gatwick, he took a black cab through the rain-soaked streets to the Langham in Portland Place, where he checked in and settled down in supreme comfort. There was no rush. Gustavo never did anything in a rush. That was the key to his success as a hitman.

54

'Oh! You're up,' said Patsy in surprise.

She'd come into the kitchen mid-afternoon after Kenny's unwelcome stopover at their house, to fix herself a coffee. And there was Kenny Doyle himself, sitting at the table, dressed in the shirt and trousers he'd arrived in yesterday. His suit jacket was slung over one of the chairs, part of a purple suit with a gossamer thread of electric blue running through it. Hideous. But very much Kenny's style. Iridescent, like a poisonous bug – that was Kenny. The suit colours clashed nastily with the greenish tinge on Kenny's face.

'Want some?' she offered, filling the kettle and the awkward silence. The last thing she wanted was Kenny bloody Doyle occupying her space.

'Nah.' He stood up, seemed to weave a little on his feet, then steadied himself. 'Got to shoot.'

He left the kitchen. Shortly, Patsy heard the Roller purr into life on the driveway. Was he even *fit* to drive?

Not her business, she decided, and carried on making her coffee.

★

Kenny took a slow drive up to his place in Primrose Hill, planning to stay there overnight. Then he took a cab across town and walked by the river, passing strolling couples, mothers with pushchairs, a couple of out-of-work tossers pretending to be statues, the better to encourage idiot passers-by to chuck their loose change into hats on the pavement. He sat down on one of the benches and looked out over the grey sluggish waters of the Thames toward the Houses of Parliament.

Presently, a tall thin man, a *grey* man, sat down at the other end of the bench.

'Mr Doyle?' said the man in a strange accent. Spanish maybe. Mexican? Something. Didn't matter, anyway.

'Mr Cota?'

The man nodded. Yeah, he was grey, Kenny thought. You'd pass him on the street, he was that innocuous. Which, of course, made him all the more deadly.

'I've heard a lot about your work,' said Kenny.

The man said nothing.

'You come highly recommended,' said Kenny.

'You're certain about this?' asked Gustavo.

'Yes. I am. Why do you ask?'

'Because when we spoke on the phone you sounded drunk. Perhaps today you have thought again? Reconsidered? In which case, I shall expect my travelling expenses to be paid and then we will part company and that will be the end of the matter.'

The bloke was a cold fish. He spoke like a cash register. Kenny felt his back go up, just a little, at Cota's thin nasal tones. But then, what had he expected? You couldn't look down the barrel of a gun or wield a knife at a human target and feel nothing, not unless you were a fucking psychopath. Which Gustavo probably was. And Gustavo Cota was right of course – Kenny *had* been drunk when he'd called; sorry, pathetic, tearful drunk and peeing in his mate's hot tub. He thought maybe he'd thrown up in there too, at one stage. But the drink altered nothing. That cowing cold bitch – his wife – had deceived him, cheated him of a full life, a *family*, killed the woman he truly loved. And he wasn't about to let her get away with it.

When it had first happened he had charged in foolishly, all emotion. Now, at last, he was thinking. And thinking *straight*.

'I haven't changed my mind. I *won't* change my mind,' he said. 'She's got this coming. Years she's been running rings around me, *using* me.'

'Good.' Gustavo sounded like he didn't care much, either way. 'Now tell me all about the target. Her habits. What she does every day, where she goes, anything like that.'

Kenny told him about Christie going into town then coming home, picking flowers in the garden to decorate the house; going for a morning swim, every day. 'Forgetting' to put the cover on the pool overnight, because a fucking fox swam in there sometimes, of all bloody stupid things.

'And the target's location?' asked Cota.

Kenny passed over a piece of paper with the address of the valley house, the house *he* had paid for, *his* bloody house, scrawled on it. 'It has to look like an accident or suicide.'

'I understand.'

'I don't want to know the fine details. Just make sure it's done.'

Gustavo turned his head. Grey, expressionless eyes stared into Kenny's for a long moment.

'And we are clear on the price? As we agreed?'

Kenny nodded. 'Thirty thousand sterling goes into your account today. And another thirty when the job's done, and I want proof it's done, you get me? Maybe a photograph?'

Gustavo stood up. 'Very well, Mr Doyle. Goodbye,' he said. 'You know, I've never been inside Westminster Abbey. Very fine architecture, I believe. And all those kings and queens buried there. I've an interest in death, as you might realise. I think I'll go take a look,' he said, and walked off.

55

That evening, Ivo phoned up.

'What do you want?' Christie snapped at him.

Her nerves were shot. Kenny was out there somewhere, no longer her friend but her enemy. And Ivo, ever the opportunist, was pushing, looking for an entry, for a way back into her life now she no longer had Kenny's protection.

'Now that's not nice,' said Ivo. 'I'm just calling to see you're OK.'

'Like you care.'

'Of course I do. We're cousins.'

Christie stared at the phone. 'You're nothing to me, Ivo,' she said, and slapped the phone back in its cradle.

It rang again, a lot of times.

She didn't answer.

Next morning, Christie woke up to someone banging on the front door. She lay there and the whole thing came crashing back in on her. Kenny trying to attack her. Ivo trying to creep back into her life now Kenny was gone. Dex! Dex, for God's sake, after all this time. And him a policeman, a detective. And Lara Millman, dead. In the space of a few days Christie's whole world had been turned inside out. She sat up in the bed, feeling shaky. The knocking went on. She tried to summon the will to get up. Couldn't. She slumped back across the pillows, pulled the covers over her head.

Finally, the knocking stopped.

Good.

Silence.

She was just tipping back into sleep when she heard a car out on the gravel drive. Then there was a scrabbling at the front door. And then . . .

'Christie?'

It was *his* voice. It was Dex. Inside the building. In her hallway.

Ah *God.*

There was no way she could cope with this. Not now. And how the fuck had he got past the new lock on the front door?

She pulled herself back up to the edge of the bed, reached for her robe, caught a horrifying glimpse of her sleep-dazed face and tangled hair in the dressing table mirror. She staggered out onto the landing, went to the banister and peered over.

Dex was standing there in the middle of the hall.

'What the fuck?' she demanded, thinking of some old poem, something about love laughing at locksmiths. Love? Hardly. The sod had abandoned her years ago.

He looked up. 'I was concerned. You weren't answering the door.'

'Yes. Because I didn't *want* to. How . . . ?'

'You didn't answer, so I got the locksmith out.'

'Isn't that breaking and entering or some damned thing?' asked Christie.

'I didn't break a thing. And I entered because I was worried you might have topped yourself.'

'Why would I do that?'

His eyes were very serious. 'I dunno, Christie. Guilt? Remorse?'

'For what? I haven't done anything.' *I think.*

'Look, can we talk?'

Oh God.

'Hang on,' she said, and went back into the bedroom, pulled on jeans and a pullover, yanked a brush through her hair. Then she went back out onto the landing. No sign of him. She went downstairs, into the sitting room. He was there at the French doors, staring out.

'It's spectacular,' he said, as she joined him there.

'Yes. Marvellous. Not really what's concerning me, right now.' She looked at him there, framed in sunlight. For God's sake – she felt her heart actually *lurch* in her chest. But she wasn't a teenager anymore, in love for the very first time. She got a grip on herself. 'I didn't do it,' she said, very low but with her voice filled with urgency. Trying to convince *herself* as much as him.

He turned his head and looked full at her with those blue eyes. Time tilted; years fell away. Christie turned her gaze from his and looked at the view instead because she really, really didn't feel strong enough to be looking at him, not right now.

'I didn't,' she repeated in a whisper, thinking of her car on the drive, the engine running, the keys in the ignition. No. She couldn't have done a thing like that. She *couldn't*. Could she? 'I didn't. You've got to believe me.'

'Maybe I do,' he said.

Christie's head whipped round. She stared at him. '*What?*'

He sighed. 'Look. I knew you. And doing a thing like this? You? Unless you've gone through a complete personality change, I can't believe it. So maybe you *didn't* kill Lara Millman.'

Christie swallowed. Her eyes felt moist all of a sudden. She couldn't speak,

'The only problem is, of course, proving it,' said Dex.

'What? I . . .'

'Because you've got form, as we said. That youthful misdemeanour of yours didn't go on record, but I know damned well that you have got form for lighting fires. And you're married to a villain. That could have changed you. Kenny could have influenced you over the years, made you different from how you used to be.'

'I didn't do it.' Oh God, she hoped so much that was true.

'I've talked to the super. He thinks it's an open-and-shut case. Even my DS thinks that. But neither of them realise that we knew each other in the past.'

'You're going to have to tell me everything that's been happening,' said Dex.

'Since when?' Again it was there in her mind – her car with its engine running, the keys inside, the door open.

'Since we last met. For instance – and this is pertinent, Christie – what are you doing, married to Kenny Doyle? I mean – what the fuck?'

Christie stared at him. God, how she'd loved him. And he'd rejected her and then, *worse*, a thousand times worse, he'd come back three days into her marriage, when it was all done and dusted, when it was all *too bloody late.*

Christie shrugged, feeling the hurt of it all over again. 'You wouldn't understand,' she said.

'Christie.' He reached out and, to her surprise, gave her a slight shake. 'You have to *make* me understand. Do you see that? I'm the senior investigating officer on this case, which means you've struck lucky because if it had been anyone else, *anyone*, you would be *fucked*. Even now I'm thinking I should admit an involvement and withdraw from the investigation.

I have to be very sure of what's been happening here. If you didn't do it . . .'

'I didn't! I *told* you.'

'Then whoever *did* is still walking about out there, free as a bird. And they might do this again.'

'Stop shaking me, will you?'

Dex dropped her arm. He swiped one large, square-fingered hand through his hair. The gesture was familiar, heartbreakingly so. Christie felt her innards flinch.

'Sorry,' he said.

But he was right. Lara Millman was dead, murdered in cold blood, consumed by the flames, and that was bad. Even worse would be that same fate befalling anybody else.

'All right,' she said. 'I'll tell you what's been happening in my life. OK?'

'Good. OK.'

*

Christie talked, while Dex listened. He made no comment while she told of her long and pretty uneventful marriage to Kenny Doyle, and when she said: 'That's about all of it, really,' he left, handing her a card.

'That's my direct number,' he said.

Of course, it hadn't been *all* of it. She hadn't told Dex about deceiving Kenny over the issue of children. Hiding the Pill from him – yes, *lying* to him. She hadn't told him the *real* reason she'd married Kenny – to escape Ivo Butler. In fact, she'd told him just about fuck-all.

The doorbell rang again not five minutes after Dex left. He'd forgotten something. Wanted to ask her more questions. She sprang to her feet and nearly sprinted out into the hallway, uncomfortably aware of her own racing heartbeat, her own surge of relief and – yes – a stupid, senseless feeling of something like *happiness*, because she was about to see him, speak to him, again.

She flung the door open, about to say, *what did you forget?*

But it wasn't Dex standing there.

It was Ivo.

56

Dex drove over to the next village. There were police cars out on the road, and he could see Debbie and Bill standing on doorsteps, talking to residents. Smith was at the far end of what passed for the high street and it was to him that Dex went.

'Anything?' he asked.

'Nothing at all, yet. Except the fact that nobody liked her and she, in her turn, didn't give a flying fuck about any of them.'

'And CCTV? Security cameras?'

'You must be bloody joking, sir. Safe as houses out here. Nothing's ever happened for a hundred years. People trust each other, watch out for each other.'

'They didn't watch out for Lara Millman.'

'An exception to the general rule, I grant you. But you see that one over there?' Smith pointed to a large cream-painted house with a showy flashing security box up under the eaves.

'I do.'

'A dummy. The vast majority of them are dummies, just a nod towards a deterrent. A couple are operational down the end there, but they're not even switched on at night. Bill and Debbie are going to carry on for a bit, and uniform, but I'm wrapping it up now.'

'Right. Then go on up to Mungo's.'

'Mungo's?'

'Frith Street. Where Lara worked. Talk to the girls she worked with.'

'Right.'

Dex went back to his car, and sat in it, and looked at the wreckage of Lara Millman's cottage and thought about murder. And Christie.

Slowly, he drove away.

57

'Ivo . . . ?' Christie managed to get out, and then he was pushing past her, coming in, his sheer size shoving her to one side like she was nothing. Like he always had, really. And – this chilled her to the bones – she didn't have Kenny standing in front of her for protection, not anymore. All that was over. Lara Millman was dead, and so were all her hopes of hanging on to even the faintest thread of the precious security she had always counted on.

Slowly she closed the front door, feeling that she would rather bolt out of it and up onto the road, shouting for help. She didn't. She closed the door and followed him into the sitting room. His bulk was blocking out the light by the French doors. He was standing exactly where Dex had stood not long since.

Ivo spun around and looked at her. 'Was that Dex fucking Cooper I just saw leaving?' he demanded. 'I'm dreaming, ain't I? Was that him or did that fucker just *look* like him?'

'What?' Suddenly her mouth was dry.

'Was it?'

Christie nodded. 'Yeah. It was. It was him.'

'What the fuck? It's been all over the news. That Millman tart dead in a fire and they're saying it was started deliberately. That she's linked to Kenny somehow.'

'She is.' Christie swallowed. 'Was, I mean. They were having an affair.'

'You knew?'

Christie shook her head. 'There were other women. Lots of them. But I didn't know about her in particular. Not until all this blew up.'

'Was the place hers? The thatched place that went up in smoke?'

'No. It was ours. His, I mean. Kenny's.' Kenny was always very careful to keep only his name on any legal documents – never hers.

'Very bloody cosy.' Ivo's eyes were speculative as they gazed into hers. 'You do it?'

'I didn't.'

'Why was Dex Cooper here?'

'He's investigating the case. He's a detective.'

'Jesus! Really? You're fucking kidding me! Always thought he'd wind up on the *other* side of the fence. But damned lucky for you, wouldn't you say?'

'Would I?'

'Yeah. He'll go easy on you. Never could keep his eyes or his hands off you, I recall.' He smirked at her nastily. 'Mind you, it was reciprocated, wasn't it. You were sweet on him.'

Christie said nothing. She wasn't discussing any of that with Ivo. He tainted everything he touched – he always had – but he wasn't touching her thoughts, her innermost feelings. Those were her own and he wasn't allowed to intrude on them, not now, not ever. She was aware of her own breathing, panicky and shallow. When he turned, he turned quickly, lunged toward her as if he was about to attack. Then he stopped in his tracks. Christie yelped, put a hand to her chest. She could feel her own racketing heartbeat, feel the fear. Ivo grinned, pleased. He liked to scare her. He always had. She shouldn't have let him in. But somehow she knew she couldn't have done anything else.

'So what are you doing here, Ivo?' she forced herself to ask him.

He shrugged. 'Just showing concern for a member of the family,' he said.

'I'm not a member of your family, Ivo,' said Christie flatly. 'I never was.'

'Oh, so she's got something to say for herself after all,' said Ivo, smiling, as if she'd pleased him.

When he moved this time he didn't stop; he kept coming. Christie found herself grabbed by the hair and suddenly he was shaking her like a dog with a rat. His eyes were murderous and his pouty little mouth was clenched with fury.

'You want to watch that attitude of yours, Christie,' he warned her. 'You don't want to get yourself in trouble, do you?'

Christie tried to shake her head but she couldn't. His grip on her hair was tight, agonising.

'Sorry you did it? Sorry you said that?' he demanded.

She tried to nod. She could barely move, but she tried.

Enough. He was satisfied.

He let her go.

Christie stumbled back, fell across the couch.

'I'll call again, OK? Just to make sure you're all right.' He smirked down at her. Her eyes were streaming with tears of pain. 'Bye then, little Christie.'

And then – thank God – he was gone.

58

When she was absolutely sure that he was really gone and not just lingering outside, Christie grabbed her car keys and her bag, ran out of the house and got into the Mitsubishi and started the engine, floored the accelerator and took to the road with no single idea of where she was going or what she was doing. All that mattered was *getting away*.

Christie drove and drove, haring down country lanes, veering wildly around the bends, scarcely caring anymore. She could remember as a girl how she had prayed at nights not to wake in the morning, and that it would be wonderful. She would see Mum and Dad again; she'd be reunited with them.

Once, she had been walking through Harrods and a girl on the make-up counter had sprayed her. She had stopped dead, smelling peaches in that perfume, and roses and jasmine. She had grabbed the girl's wrist and had seen alarm leap into her eyes.

'What the hell is that?' she'd snapped, because she *knew* it. It was the scent that had wafted around her in her childhood, embraced her when her mother, dressed up for an evening out, had cuddled her; it was that smell. The smell of her mother.

'It's Femme de Rochas,' said the girl.

Christie released the girl's arm. 'Sorry. Sorry. Can I take a bottle of that please?'

Now, she wore that same perfume every day. Somehow it comforted her.

Slowly, oh so slowly, the panic was subsiding. It was all right, she told herself. Ivo was gone. Her life might have descended into chaos, but she would survive it, just as she had survived so much already.

But I'm so tired of doing that, she thought.

Finally getting her bearings, recognising the road she was now travelling on and seeing the junction coming up ahead, she touched the brake, changed down a gear.

Nothing happened.

59

The junction was coming closer by the second, and cars were shooting past on the main road.

She *stamped* on the brake.

There was nothing there; no grip at all, no traction.

The panic she'd felt with Ivo returned in a hideous flood. She was going to die, she was going to career straight out onto the main road and hit another car. She was going to die just like her parents had. Maybe she had been *meant* to die on that same day, but somehow she'd survived. Her mouth dried. Her eyes were staring, fixed; there was nothing she could do. This was *it*. And wouldn't that be a relief, really? To have an end to it . . .

It was all such a mess. She was in the frame for murder. Married to a man she detested and who blamed her for his mistress's death. Terrified of Ivo . . .

No.

She thought of Dex, how they had once been, together. That golden, magical time, all too brief. So long ago. He was back now, but he was her enemy wasn't he, no matter what he said about believing her. He was an arresting officer – no longer her friend.

She stamped on the brake again. No result. One moment immobile, unable to act, now she was thrown into desperate action. She changed down through the gears, the gearbox screaming in protest. Was the car slowing? No. Not much. Maybe a little? Shaking, she lunged for the key in the ignition, switched it off. The engine died. But the car, going downhill toward the junction, was not dropping speed fast enough. She was going to shoot out onto that busy road and hit something. Kill herself, and maybe kill someone else too.

What else, what else?

Handbrake!

Flooded with panic, she grabbed it and yanked it up.

Now the car was spinning, wheels whining in protest, and Christie could hear herself screaming as the car whirled around, presenting her with a dizzying view of the green hills all around her. The Mitsubishi spun like a top and she was gripping the steering wheel with one hand, clutching the handbrake with the other, powerless, unable to control it. Giving herself up to the fates.

The car flew off the road, up over a broad grass verge, and tipped violently sideways as it hit a ditch, smacking the roof into a tall hedge, yanking Christie hard against her seatbelt. Suddenly, the car was still.

Christie sat there, gasping, unable to believe that she was still alive.

She ought to be *dead.*

She was staring out, panting with shock, through the tilted windshield. She could see cars, lorries, all hurtling past down on the main road. If she hadn't stopped the car, she'd have been a goner. She could hear the clicking of the engine as it cooled down and now someone was knocking at her window.

She looked up. There was an elderly man peering in at her, his face ashen with shock and concern. '*Are you all right?*' he mouthed, and yanked the door open.

Christie unsnapped her seatbelt and grabbed her bag. The man held out a hand and hauled her up, out of the driver's door.

'My wife and I were following behind you,' he was saying. 'We saw the car spinning. My God, are you all right?'

Christie took a breath. She could feel her legs shaking with aftershock. Suddenly she sat down on the verge, inhaling great gulps of air, aware that she hadn't properly drawn a breath from the first moment the brakes had failed.

'I'm fine,' she told him, and was astonished to find that she really was. She drew in more air. She was alive. 'Can . . . can you call the police please?'

60

The elderly couple gave her tea from a flask. She sat there. They all waited. Finally, the police came: two uniformed coppers who'd seen and done it all.

'Have you taken alcohol in the last twelve hours?' asked one.

'No,' said Christie, still sitting on the verge. The kind old man and his wife departed after giving witness statements.

The police breathalysed her anyway. All clear.

'The brakes didn't work. I was getting toward the junction and they just *didn't work*,' she said. She thought about that. About her car sitting, untended, out on the driveway at home. 'I think someone might have tampered with them.'

That brought other thoughts, even more unwelcome. If they'd been tampered with, who had done it? Ivo? He'd been at the house and the car had been right there, not in the garage or down in the double car port beside the workshop. But why would Ivo do that, and lose a victim to torment? Her heart chilled in her chest as she thought of the other possibility. *Kenny.* Kenny had a host of lowlifes just hanging around, eager to do his bidding, to worm their way into his good books. Any one of them, for money, for drugs, or just for kicks, would do this. No questions asked.

And the police? Christie knew damned well that Kenny had people inside the law, on his team. Maybe these two?

And my God, here she was on a roadside, no witnesses now, the evening drawing in, just the two of them and her. But it seemed they were OK. They arranged for a tow truck, took down all her details. They wanted to drive her home. She felt so weak, so worn out, that she didn't feel able to manage to refuse a lift. If they killed her on the way, then so what? Then it would all be over, wouldn't it – her nightmare life.

'Take me to my friend's house, will you?' she asked, because she couldn't, right now, stand the thought of being alone in her own home, the house she had always so treasured and adored.

They drove her where she'd asked to go, didn't talk to her but didn't make any hostile moves toward her either. They left her on Patsy's doorstep. She rang the bell. Maybe Patsy was out? Her mate was a shopaholic; Bond Street was her Mecca. Christie was turning away, wondering what the hell to do next, when the door opened.

'Thank God, you're in,' said Christie, and surged forward. She stopped dead when she saw the expression on Patsy's face. 'What?' she asked faintly. 'What's wrong?'

'Christie? You . . . you can't be here,' said Patsy.

'What do you mean?' Christie was half-smiling, wondering if this could be a joke. Patsy loved jokes.

'Are you kidding?' Patsy's face was grave. This wasn't her bubbly, jokey little pal. This woman looked like a stern-faced stranger. 'Look – if you'd shown your face here yesterday, Kenny would have been here and he'd have ripped your head right off your neck.'

'He stayed here?' asked Christie faintly.

'Damned right. He was here overnight, sitting in our tub. Drunk as a lord. Threatening to do all sorts to you. Thank Christ you've missed him.'

Christie stood there, speechless.

Finally she was able to say: 'I was driving and I think . . . I think someone tampered with my car.'

'You *what*?'

'You heard. And what about Mungo? What's his take on all this?'

'Mungo's out. He's none too pleased at the situation, I can tell you. Mungo and Kenny have been tight together for years – you know that. Whatever Kenny does, Mungo will always back him up. Look, I don't know when – or if – either of them'll be back and what if someone sees you and reports this back to them, you coming here? Christie – with the best will in the world – I can't let you in. I just *can't*.'

Christie drew in a breath. 'Patsy, the brakes failed on my car. I damn near crashed. I damn near *died*. The police just dropped me off here because I said I wanted to be with you, my friend, and not alone at home.'

'What do you mean, the brakes failed?'

'I was heading for a junction and I couldn't stop. I switched off the engine, put on the handbrake and spun off into a ditch. I'm lucky to be alive.'

'Look, Christie, I can't get involved, you understand? I can't get into any of this. I'm sorry. I can't even be seen talking to you. I'm bloody sorry, but I can't. Hold on.'

Patsy went back into the hall and returned with an orange card, gold-lettered, deckle-edged.

'That's the cab company I always use. They're sound. Phone them. They'll come and get you. But don't stand about out here in front of the house. Piss off and wait further down the road, will you?'

Patsy closed the door in Christie's face.

✦

Once Christie got home, she tried to calm down, to regain her shattered senses. She took a shower, made tea, tried not to dread the night to come. At every sound, every creak of the eaves, every brush of a branch against a window, stirred by the rising wind, she jumped. She'd always been known for her calm, her composure, but it seemed to have deserted her now. Deserted her, just like Patsy had. Her best friend of so many years had turned on her, cast her aside.

But who could really blame Patsy for that? She had to side with her husband. And her husband sided – always – with Kenny.

Had someone really tried to kill her?

Maybe not. Christ, she hoped not, because having failed they would no doubt try again – perhaps with more success this time. No. It could have been a total accident. She was just jumping at shadows. Unable to concentrate on the TV, she went to bed at eight, read a book, failed to take in a single word.

Had someone tried to finish her?

Kenny?

She lay down in the darkness and tried to sleep.

She couldn't.

I could be dead, right now.

She was asleep, drifting, reliving old bad memories. Her parents. The car. Her mother, crying in the front passenger seat, crying less and less, finally falling silent. Her father behind the wheel, dead. The stink of the petrol, the *drip, drip, drip* of the liquid.

Oh God.

Finally she slept, all that night and much of the next day. In sleep, she escaped.

61

Bright sunshine was scorching its way through the thin fabric of the curtains at the bedroom window when Christie came back to herself. The doorbell was ringing. Someone was leaning on it and her mind, her heart, every pulse in her body, jumped first to Kenny – and then to Ivo.

No. Go away. I can't take another thing, not after yesterday. I just can't.

'Christie!' A voice, outside. She knew the voice.

Not Ivo this time. Not Kenny either, nor Patsy. She wondered if Patsy would ever call again. Or anyone else, come to that. She'd had few friends when she'd married Kenny Doyle, and all his pals and their wives had absorbed her into their circle, tolerating but never really welcoming her. Now, she'd be cast into the outer darkness. Like Patsy, none of them was going to want to be seen within a mile of her. She was bad news. She was *tainted*. It might be Kenny who'd had the affair, but Christie was the one all his mates – *and* their wives – would blame for it.

'Cold bitch,' they'd say. 'Arctic blonde Christie? She always did seem like a chilly little cow. No wonder Ken wanted some outside entertainment.'

Now she was in the frame for his mistress's murder.

'*Christie?*' That voice again, insistent.

She didn't feel equal to any of this; not today. But she crawled from the bed, snatched up her dressing gown, hauled it on, and went out onto the landing, down the stairs, and across the hall to the front door. She opened it. Dex was standing there, hands on hips.

'Why didn't you just let yourself in? You did last time,' said Christie.

'Why . . . ?' He seemed to draw breath. Paused for a beat. Then he said: 'I didn't want to scare the crap out of you, that's why. You all right? I heard you had an accident in your car yesterday.'

'How did you hear that?'

'Two coppers picked you up, right?'

'Yes.'

'You said the brakes had failed.'

'Yes.'

'They took your car to a garage.'

'That's right.' Christie dragged a hand through her hair. She looked a mess. And why was she bothered about *that*, right now?

Because this was Dex Cooper. Because it was *him*.

Oh, Christie, for the love of God, grow up!

'The mechanic who checked it over phoned us this morning in a panic. They patched him through to me, as I'm SIO on the Lara Millman case and being as you're Mrs Kenny Doyle you're closely connected to that. He said the brake cables were cut.'

'I think I need to sit down,' said Christie, going over to the sofa that was tucked under the stairs. She sat. Dex came in, closing the front door behind him.

'You all right?'

'Someone tried to kill me,' said Christie. 'Of course I'm not all right.'

'Just breathe,' he advised.

'*You* just breathe. It was bloody terrifying. I thought I was about to *die*.'

Dex sat down too. 'What did you do?'

'Only the obvious. I switched off the engine. Put on the handbrake. Slipped up there a bit. Put it on too hard, forgot to pump it. Just slammed it on and I spun off into a ditch.'

'You were lucky.'

'Somehow I can't feel very lucky right now.'

'Was this Kenny, do you think? Your brakes being sabotaged was his revenge?'

'Maybe. Who the hell knows. But if that's the case, you know what? I'm a sitting duck. If Kenny wants a result, he generally gets it.'

*

Dex went to the windows and looked out on the valley, trying to make sense of it all in his own mind but – to his utter consternation – failing. Because this was *her*. This was Christie. The sight of her, the *nearness* of her, was peppering his normally logical thought processes with a meteor shower of emotion. He hadn't expected that would happen. Meeting her again by this crazy chance, he had not anticipated that he would react with anything other than his usual composure. That he wouldn't still be – crazily, unbelievably – so *hot* for her, as hot as he ever was, after all the time that had gone by.

He ought to step aside on this case. But he couldn't. He realised that he simply *could not* place her fate in the hands of anyone else. So he was stuck with it. And he wasn't sorry. The man in him wanted it that way. He wanted to feel fully in control and he wanted – and this was lunacy, this was trouble with a capital T – to stay close. He was, in fact, scared of letting her out of his sight. If he relinquished the case, placed it in Turnbull's perfectly capable hands as he knew he should, then he was afraid of what could happen to her.

She could be charged with the murder of her husband's mistress and she could go down for it.

Means, motive, opportunity.

She had it all.

She even had form for starting fires. No one else in the force would be aware of that. He had inside knowledge from back in the day when he'd still been picking a side. Ivo Butler's lot had gabbled about it in high excitement and he had heard their chatter. He'd very nearly chosen the criminal path himself, the one that paid better. But unlike Christie, whose life had been knocked off course early on, he'd had good, decent parents and had he wanted, really, to make them suffer the distress of their son getting in deep with the gangs? He couldn't do it to them. So he'd chosen the force instead. And it was the right choice, for him.

He could smell Christie's perfume, something with peaches in it. She was so close. She had always smelled sweet. The sun was flooding through the Velux windows above the stairs, lighting up her silver-blonde hair, and her eyes were clear as gemstones. He felt, then, a stab of remembered desire so acute, so visceral, that it snatched his breath away.

Then he said: 'Fuck it, Christie, what happened? Where did it all go bloody wrong?'

62

'Why'd you bail on me? Why'd you do that?' Dex asked her.

Christie sat up and stared at him, frowning. 'What?' She had no idea what he was talking about. *He* had left *her*. Rejected her. That was all she knew.

'Ah, nothing. It doesn't matter, does it. Not now.'

What good would the answers do him, after all this time? No good at all. He let out a sigh. He felt confused, overwhelmed. He always questioned everything. Not only her feelings – and hadn't she, long ago, made them pretty plain? – but his own too. His job now was to disentangle the events that had led up to the murder of Lara Millman. Getting himself involved with Christie Butler – no, Christie *Doyle*, he reminded himself, wife of that slippery bastard Kenny – was the surest way to cloud his vision, make his job impossible to do.

So hand it over to someone else, said an annoying voice in his brain.

He wanted to. But he couldn't trust Christie's welfare to another cop, however skilled. Couldn't let the puzzle go, either. Whatever happened now, he knew he was going to have to go with it, right to the end, no matter whether it turned out to be bitter or good.

What if she's guilty? popped into his mind.

He couldn't believe she had changed that much. She *couldn't*.

He was going to have to put any residual feelings for that old Christie aside and concentrate cold-bloodedly on the case, thrash out the facts, find the killer of that poor girl – *whoever* the killer happened to be. And if it should turn out to be Christie herself? This new, tough, closed-off gangster's wife? She was married to Kenny Doyle and she seemed hard-faced, tough as nails, and why wouldn't she be? Married to *that*, how could she be anything else?

So if it was her, then so be it. She'd get the book chucked at her; nothing less would do.

'What's the view like from upstairs?' he asked.

'What? Oh . . . well, it's great. Go up and take a look if you like.'

Dex went up there, glad of the chance to get away from her. He found the master bedroom and admired the view. It was truly spectacular. Beyond the bedroom was a small dressing room and he went there, looked inside. All Christie's stuff was in here, spread out in a jumble: a hatstand laden with velveteen scarves, straw summer hats, silver neck-laces. There was a half-glassed door looking out onto the valley and beyond that there was a balcony with two chairs and a table overlooking that fabulous view, ready for cof-fee in the morning, stargazing with a glass of wine at night before bed.

Jesus, she sure does live in style.

And he had to remind himself what had paid for this life-style – Kenny Doyle and his scams. Shockingly, she had mar-ried into all that. Beside the dressing table on a metal tripod was a thing he recognised as a surveyor's theodolite. On the dressing table itself there was a hairdryer, brushes tangled with long strands of her hair, combs. A smiling porcelain pig painted with cabbage roses. A scraggy old teddy bear with no eyes. A couple of Wade brewery flasks for gin and whisky. And . . .

Oh fuck.

He stood there and stared. What he was looking at was like those things you used to see Seventies parties – there'd be half a grapefruit wrapped in foil, with cheese and pineapple on sticks pressed in all over it, so it resembled a hedgehog.

No, he thought. *Shit, no.*

But there it was. Right in front of him. It wasn't grapefruit but foam, covered in tin foil. The thing was festooned with six-inch-long pins, many of them topped with precious jewels in rainbow colours, some with intricate and exquisite enamelling, others with tiny silver animals, or cobwebs, or snowflakes. And there at the centre of the thing was an indentation.

They were hatpins, weren't they.

Victorian hatpins.

And one of the damned things was missing.

63

Smith was knocking at the front door of Mrs Millman's house, just like DI Cooper had told him to when they'd parted earlier in the day. Just following orders, doing his job. They'd both been shocked by the news that had roared through the department, about Christie Doyle's car being tampered with. Smith was ninety-nine per cent sure that Christie Doyle had in fact killed Lara Millman, and now someone was making sure she got comeuppance for her crime. But DI Cooper – although he hadn't actually said so – clearly wasn't convinced, and so here Smith was, still digging around as instructed.

Last night he'd been at the club, Mungo's, where Lara had worked, talking to the girls who'd worked with her. He had already passed the information to Dex that without exception the girls who had worked with Lara Millman had despised her because she was a great deal prettier than they were; and she, in her turn, had despised them. No love lost on either side. And Mungo himself, the owner, hadn't been there to talk to.

The same tired-looking weepy-eyed woman opened the door and stared at him. 'Yes?'

He flashed his warrant card.

'Oh. Sorry. Yes. Didn't recognise you.'

The woman was swamped with grief, vacant, bewildered – decimated by the loss of her daughter. Or covering some sort of guilt with this huge show of dazed remorse? Who knew?

'Um – can I come in?' asked Smith. 'I just need a moment.'

She led him in to the dreary little sitting room. He sat down. So did she.

'I want to talk to you about Andy Paskins,' said Smith.

Her face was blank.

'The boy next door. Who dated your daughter, I believe, at one point?'

'Oh. Yes.'

'They were close, you said. When they were teenagers.'

'Yes. They were.' Mrs Millman's mouth grew thin. 'I always thought she should have stuck with Andy, you know. That was always my girl's trouble. Wanting to better herself. Wanting to rise above her place in life. And now look!' Mrs Millman's voice broke. 'She's dead. Killed! Mixing with all sorts at that bloody club . . .' Her voice tailed away. She fumbled for a tissue up her sleeve, drew it out, blew her nose loudly. 'Sorry,' she said, gathering herself.

'That's all right,' said Smith. He'd sat through a thousand such interviews; a few tears didn't bother him.

'Mixing with Kenny Doyle in particular,' he said, wondering if she'd bite.

'Yes! Him.' Hatred twisted her tear-blotched face. 'He's twice her age. I warned her about him. I said he was bad. She *knew* it really. She wasn't a fool.'

'Andy Paskins . . . ?' Smith reminded her.

'Oh!' She let out a shaky sigh. 'Poor Andy. He's heartbroken, you know. Ripped to bits by this. Because he hoped that . . .'

'Hoped what?' asked Smith when she hesitated.

She shrugged. 'I don't want to cause the poor lad any trouble. But he hoped she'd see sense. Put all these crazy dreams behind her. Kenny Doyle was a married man and a bad one. I told her that, over and over. Warned her. But she wouldn't listen.'

'Did Andy talk to Lara about it?'

'Oh yes. They argued. Just a few days before she died, I heard them.' Mrs Millman's eyes lifted to Smith's and suddenly they were furtive. She'd said too much and she knew it. 'Not that that means anything,' she said quickly. 'Andy's a good boy. He loved Lara.'

Smith got out his notebook and pen. 'Can I just check this – where does he work? What does he do for a living?'

When she answered, it came as no surprise to the world-weary Smith. He put his notebook back in his pocket and bid her goodbye.

★

Andy Paskins was at work in a Bermondsey garage underneath the railway arches, wearing an oily blue boiler suit. 'Cool Sisters Don't Walk Away' was playing on the radio. His mates, who were mostly bent over open car bonnets staring at an assortment of motor parts, paused when they saw DS Smith pull up, get out of his car and stroll in. The boss paused too. Huge and oil-stained, he stepped in front of Smith. He could see that Smith was filth, of course. Could smell it on him. Andy was down in the pit under a Mercedes and when he saw Smith coming he turned visibly pale and looked like he might try to bolt.

'I wouldn't, Andy.' Smith showed Andy's boss his warrant card, then when the boss man drew aside, Smith crouched down and showed it again to Andy, just to jog his memory, just in case he had forgotten their last meeting at Mrs Millman's place two days ago. 'It's not just motorbikes you like playing with is it Andy? You like tinkering with cars too, don't you?' He smiled coldly. 'You been tinkering with Christie Doyle's?'

'I dunno what you're talking about,' said Andy.

'Oh I think you do.'

All the other mechanics and the boss were frozen, watching.

'Andy Paskins, I am arresting you on suspicion . . .'

That bit was easy. A result! But Smith knew the rest of it was going to be far, far more difficult.

64

Mungo Boulaye worked hard, played hard, and Patsy knew damned well that he didn't like taking personal calls when he was at his 'office' at the club, so when she phoned him there, he was abrupt.

'Pats? What is it?'

'I've had Christie round here.'

'I told you I don't want that cow in my house. I told you that before I left home, so what the fuck?'

'I didn't invite her,' said Patsy. Her voice was shaking. 'She just showed up. She said she'd been out in her car and the brakes failed.' There was a pause, then: 'Christ's sake, Mungo, you don't know anything about this do you? 'Did he do it? Kenny? Was it him? I know you two are super tight together. Would he do that? Would you cover for him? I've been thinking about it, Mungo, and I think you probably would. All right, you don't want me talking to her, being friends with her, anymore. Yes, OK. I understand that. I can see it makes life difficult for you being as it's Kenny who's involved. But Christ! Come on! *This?*'

'Don't talk such fucking rubbish,' said Mungo and put the phone down.

He dialled straight out again. The phone rang and rang and Mungo thought, *He's drunk still, he's out of it, he's not going to pick up.* Mungo was about to hang up when Kenny's voice said sharply: 'Yeah?'

'It's me,' said Mungo. 'Pats just told me . . .'

*

Once he'd got rid of Mungo, Kenny straight away put a call through to Gustavo.

'I told you not to get in touch with me until the job is done,' said Gustavo, cool as a cucumber. 'When it is, I will contact you.'

'Just wait a minute, you arsehole. I'm paying the bloody bill. What is this, amateur hour? Cutting brake lines?'

'I have no idea what you are talking about,' said Gustavo.

Kenny filled him in.

'Whoever did that, it wasn't me. And I am offended you imagine I would employ so crass a method.'

Kenny squinted at the phone. 'It wasn't you?'

'Certainly not.'

'Then who . . . ?'

'I have no idea. Don't contact me again, Mr Doyle. Good-bye.'

'Wait . . .'

Gustavo was gone.

65

'What the fuck's going on?' asked Dex when he came back downstairs.

'I don't know what you mean,' said Christie.

Dex took Christie's arm and led her up the stairs. He marched her into the dressing room.

'What the . . . ?' she started.

'Don't, OK? Just tell me what's going on here.' He was pointing at the display of Victorian hatpins.

'What? Those?' Christie was frowning up at him. 'Well . . . they're hatpins, that's all. I thought they were pretty. I started collecting them, years ago.' Christie wasn't about to explain that she had started, ever since her parents' death, hoarding lovely things because having them around her made her feel safer; made her feel that there was some stability in the world. 'What's this about?' she asked.

Dex stared at her. 'Look. You can see one's missing,' he said. 'Where is it?'

Christie looked at the hatpin display. He was right. One *was* missing. One of her favourites, actually, the one with the pale golden-yellow topaz set in its tip.

'Christie, come on – where is it?' asked Dex again.

'I don't know.' Christie was hugging herself, feeling under threat. He looked furious.

'You don't *know*?'

'I don't. Last time I looked, it was there.'

'When did you last look?'

'I don't know. I don't do a daily bloody inventory,' she snapped.

'*Think.*'

'Does it matter?' Now she was getting exasperated. She didn't understand what he was driving at. Was he making some sort of accusation?

'Yes it matters. *Think.*'

'Well. Maybe the day of my party. That morning. I got dressed in here. I looked at it then I suppose. And I think they were all there.'

'You think.'

'I can't say for sure. I wouldn't swear to it.'

'That the best you can do?'

'What more *can* I do?'

'What the hell is this?'

Of course, if she was innocent then she didn't know about the hatpin's part in Lara Millman's death. If she was guilty, she was hiding it well. But – dammit – she'd almost *invited* him to go upstairs, to look at the view. So what was that? The arrogance of a stone-cold killer? Or simple, uncompli-cated innocence? Dex dragged a hand through his hair and stared at her in agitation. Did he know her at all? No. He did not.

'I've got to go,' said Dex. He couldn't think straight up close to her. It was no good. She had only to look at him with those heartbreaking eyes, the way she was looking at him now, and he was lost. A woman had died. Died hor-ribly. He thought of that twisted, blackened corpse. And he could be standing here, right now, with her murderer. Really, he should be hauling her down to the station.

He should be saying the words: 'Christie Doyle, I am arresting you on suspicion . . .'

But he couldn't do it.

★

Christie was staring at Dex. Was he about to charge her with something that involved the hatpin? Was it . . . oh God, was that somehow connected to the death of Lara Millman? His face was so grim: so set.

He was going to do it! He was going to take her in.

For a moment they stood there and Christie waited for the axe to fall, sure he was going to lock her up.

But then Dex just moved past her without a word. The front door slammed behind him. He was gone.

66

Christie spent the day alone and barely slept that night. Her mind was whirling. When the next morning came, bright and clear, she put on her swimsuit, grabbed her sarong and towel, and went down to the pool. She hadn't put the cover on – the weather was still pleasingly warm and there was the little female fox to consider – and there were a few dead leaves floating in the otherwise clear turquoise waters, shed from the sycamores in the heat.

Patrick the gardener was just driving in the front gate and down the long driveway at the side of the house. She waved to him as she left the deck and went down the grassy slope to the pool. He parked his van in the car port by the workshop, walked over to the ride-on mower, which was also parked up there, then unlocked the workshop door to fetch petrol. He waved back to her. Then he paused, looked across to where she was standing. Christie thought that the water looked so inviting, so cooling and it would calm her down, a swim; it was just what she needed. But there was something floating around by the bubbles beside the pump outlet and now Patrick was running across the grass, shouting something.

Christie paused, her eyes on the thing in the pool.

It was the fox.

Christie hurried forward but she could see straight away, with a stab of real sorrow, that it was dead. Patrick was running forward, shouting louder now. Christie bent down, stretched out a hand. The poor thing. Had that *bastard* Kenny done this somehow, got one of his rotten mates to shoot the vixen – or had he put down some poison himself, as he had often threatened, if Patrick had refused to do it? Kenny would do anything to hurt her, the mood he was in. *Anything*. To kill the fox would delight him.

'Mrs Doyle! Don't!'

She knelt at the side of the pool, reaching . . .

Patrick came tearing up, white in the face, and grabbed her arm so hard it hurt.

'No!' he panted out. 'Don't do that. Don't touch the water. It looks like a light's blown, you could get a bad shock.'

Christie straightened and came staggering to her feet. Her eyes were fixed to the dead fox. It was bobbing, eyes glazed, teeth bared in one last snarl, in the bubbles from the pump outlet.

'Poor bloody thing,' said Patrick, eyeing the animal. His eyes turned to Christie. 'You all right, Mrs Doyle? You want to sit down for a bit?'

'I'm . . . fine,' said Christie. *If she'd touched that water . . .*

'You want me to phone the pool people? The electrician? Get them out to fix it?'

If Patrick hadn't arrived on the scene when he did, she would have pulled the fox out. Or tried to. And . . . there was no doubt about it.

She would have been electrocuted.

She would be dead.

67

'Did you hear about the Doyle woman?' asked Smith next day.

Dex was sitting behind his desk, and behind him on the wall of his office was an array of photos you would never want to show to anyone of a nervous disposition. Various shots displayed the effect of the devastating fire on what had once been a picturesque chocolate-box cottage. Various other shots displayed very clearly what could happen to a human body when it got caught up in an inferno. None of it was pretty.

Dex looked up at Smith but his mind was elsewhere – on Christie Doyle, his old teenage crush. His *adult* crush too, he realised. One look at her and he was gone. Well, no more. Enough of that shit. Christ, hadn't he worked hard enough, long enough, to get to where he was right now? He was a DI, highly respected. He had a flawless track record and that hadn't been easy to achieve, not for a boy from his humble background. Once, way back then, he'd mixed with the wrong sort of people. Skated along the edge of the criminal underworld. And through them, he'd met Christie. Hung around with them simply because he couldn't see enough of her. But that was then and this was now. Now, he had to shape up. Knock it on the head. *Forget* her.

Smith was still staring at him, waiting for a reply.

'What about her?' asked Dex, while his stomach clenched and roiled into mush and all he could think was *has something happened to Christie?*

He shouldn't care. Caring fogged his vision. He'd left what could be vital evidence in her dressing room yesterday. He hadn't been thinking straight. He hadn't been thinking *at all*.

'She phoned in asking for you but you weren't here,' said Smith.

'And?' snapped Dex.

'She said one of the lights on her swimming pool had blown. Glass cracked or some such shit, and the whole thing was live.'

'You *what?*'

'She went down for a swim and there was a dead fox in there, got a big blast from the electrics. The gardener yanked the Doyle woman back before she got a blast too. She's going to get the electrician out, make it all safe. The pool people too.'

'And she was phoning me why?' No way did Dex want Smith sussing out what was *really* going on here with him and Christie. And what was that, exactly? Truth was, he didn't even bloody know.

'Dunno. Hardly a police matter is it.'

'Hardly,' said Dex, and bent over his papers again. 'Anything else?'

'Nope,' said Smith, staring at the photos of the burned, twisted remains of Lara Millman. 'How much would you have to hate someone, to do a thing like that?' he wondered aloud. Then he said: 'You going to call her?'

'Leave it with me,' said Dex, thinking that no, he wasn't.

With Smith gone, he turned and looked again at the wall of photos. Looked at the wreckage of the fire, the shrivelled remnant of humanity that was Lara Millman. Looked at her *closely*. What he was going to do was get a grip. He was going to go back there and see Christie again but this time there would be no mishaps, no misunderstandings.

The past was the past, dead and gone.

Just like Lara.

68

The electrician told Christie that it had taken a considerable impact, a *hard* one, to break the specially toughened and reinforced glass on the underwater pool light.

'We had a birthday party a few days ago,' said Christie. In fact, it felt like a hundred years had passed. 'There were a lot of very drunk people in the pool.'

'What, with hobnail bloody boots on?'

'They were drunk. Fully dressed. They had shoes on, certainly. Stiletto heels on the women. A few Cuban heels on the men. It could happen I suppose.'

'Wild party then.' The electrician smiled, probably thinking *rich tossers*. And that someone must have a kick like a mule to do that much damage.

He looked around at the massive house, the grounds, the view. The pool people had arrived in their big blue van and had opened the sluice. Water was now gushing out down onto the lower level of the gardens. The gardener was on the ride-on, cutting the grass in the orchard down at the bottom of the plot, weaving among the Bramley's and Cox's apples and Victoria plum trees, out of the way of all this poolside excitement.

'Trouble is, people have these things fitted and then they leave them there for years,' he said. 'No checking if they're safe or not. Careless. And in the end something like this happens. How long would you say these have been in?'

'Nearly twenty years I suppose.'

'Serviced? Checked?'

'Not that I know of.'

She hadn't even thought about it. He was right. That was careless. That was *stupid*. And now the poor bloody fox was dead and she could have been too, if not for Patrick's quick thinking. Patrick had asked if Christie wanted him to stay up here and talk to the electrician and the pool people, but she had refused. She was used to do everything on her own; it was nothing new. But now she wished she'd let Patrick handle this bloke; he radiated sexist disapproval; thought her a 'silly little woman'.

'Well, it's all earthed now and safe. I'll be back tomorrow, when it's all completely drained and dry, then I'll crack on and replace all eight, OK?'

'OK. Thanks.'

The electrician walked away across the grass to the turning circle by the workshop, where his van was parked. He got in, started the engine, drove away up the long slope of the driveway. Then Dex's Merc came in.

Oh Christ, she thought.

He got out of the car and now he was crossing the lawn, coming toward her. The dead fox was gone. Patrick had taken it with him on the ride-on; he'd buried it down in the orchard. Christie wondered if the vixen had cubs somewhere up in the woods out the front of the house, waiting for her return. Only, she never would. And if they weren't old enough to fend for themselves, they would starve. God, everything was going wrong. Everything was a bloody disaster. Suddenly she felt deathly tired.

Dex came and stood beside her, looking at the water draining out of the pool.

'What happened?' he asked.

She told him.

Dex was silent for a long while. Then he said, thinking of the brake lines on her car: 'So it was an accident? Someone broke one of the lights somehow?'

'The electrician said it probably was. Probably happened at my party. There must have been thirty people in the water at one point. You could see how it might happen.'

Dex could see that. He could also see that she was shaken, and beautiful, and thoughts of *that* took him right back to two days ago when he had suddenly felt feverish, *desperate* with lust, and it was an effort to get his mind away from that, but he did it. He had to.

'Come on.' He glanced at the pool man, who was standing close by, all ears. 'Let's talk indoors.'

69

Dex went straight through the lounge and up the stairs. Christie followed more slowly, wondering what the hell he was up to.

'Dex?' she called, when she lost sight of him.

'Up here.'

She found him standing in the dressing area, staring down at the Victorian hatpins on the dressing table, at that one tell-tale missing space where the topaz-topped one should have been.

'For fuck's sake,' he said. There was a scene playing over and over in his mind now: the killer coming up the path to the cottage, the door opening, Lara standing there and then that shadowy, mystery person – her? Him? – lunging forward. The hatpin in which hand, left or right? The pin had been lodged in Lara's right eye. Impossible to say for sure, wasn't it?

What he'd been *hoping* – and this troubled him – was that Christie would have disposed of the damned things before he could get back here and bag them up. But no. They were still here. Either she was completely innocent or she was a bloody fool or – worse – she was guilty and just playing it cool, denying all knowledge.

'What is it?' Christie asked.

Dex heaved a sigh. The hatpins being still there, the decision was made for him. He fished out a pair of gloves and an evidence bag from his jacket pocket. Angrily he snapped on the gloves. Christ's sake! He was a DI. He was supposed to be cool, controlled; solve the crime at all costs. The way he had *always* been.

'Look,' he said flatly. 'I need to take these hatpins.'

Christie shrugged. She looked startled and hurt by his tone. 'OK.'

Why didn't you get rid of them? he wondered. He wanted to say it out loud. Couldn't. He stared at her, at those wide sea-green eyes. Innocent? Or just extremely bloody convincing? He'd looked at a thousand faces in the course of his work. People lied. They blagged. They wept. They pleaded. *Not me, I didn't do it.* Then it would turn out they did. But Christie just stared at him; innocence personified. But – oh shit, what if he got this judgement wrong?

Other people could die.

And that would be on him.

Silence fell. A long, waiting silence in which their eyes locked, held.

Then Dex said: 'I need another list of everyone at your party. I need to see if anyone's been missed. *Everyone.* Staff included.'

'Right.'

'CCTV in this place?'

Christie shook her head. 'No. There isn't any. Sorry.' He was slipping the hatpins into the evidence bag. 'That missing hatpin. Is that something to do with Lara's murder?'

'I can't answer that.'

'Why not?'

'Why *not*?' He closed the bag. 'God Almighty, Christie. Don't push me. Can you get that list of guests now?'

'Sure. In the downstairs office.'

'Let's get it then.'

He followed Christie downstairs and through a door at the far end of the lounge. Inside was a big walnut desk, filing cabinets, pictures of glossy bay racehorses. She went to the computer, turned that and the printer on, and the printer spewed out two sheets of A4. Christie passed them to Dex, and he pocketed the list of the party guests.

He could see that she was upset. Well, good. This chill between them was a good thing. It would make it easier for him to focus, do his job, see the whole thing more objectively.

The fingerprint people had already checked everyone's dabs and dusted the whole area upstairs for prints – although what use that would be was debatable. There must have been people upstairs on the day of the party. And Christie's and Kenny's dabs would be everywhere.

'Andy Paskins. Lara Millman's old boyfriend,' he said.

'What about him? I don't know the man.'

'Well he knows you and he thinks you did for his old flame. Your accident in the car? He's admitted cutting the brake lines.'

Christie took that in. She'd been *sure* it was Kenny. 'And . . . ?'

'You don't seem too surprised.'

'With all that's happened to me this past week? I think I'm beyond that.'

'Well, we're pressing charges.'

*

Christie found herself thinking of the dead fox, the dead girl. The wreckage of her own life, the ruination of this boy

Andy's. He'd felt something for this Millman girl. Enough to kill for her. 'We're releasing Lara Millman's body for burial tomorrow,' said Dex.

Christie felt herself go pale. 'So soon?'

'We have all the facts we need. It seems fair and decent to let Lara Millman's mother get on with the business of burying her. I'll see myself out.'

70

That evening, Christie got a telephone call from Patsy.

'You still talking to me then?' asked Christie.

'Don't be like that. You know the situation I'm in. You know that Mungo's got to stand with Kenny.'

'So what do you want?'

'I'm just checking you're OK. There's been talk. Our pool man was gabbing on to the cleaner about a big house out in the hills and the lights in the pool had all fused and someone could have got hurt. *Killed*, in fact. And then I realised that he was talking about your place. He gave me the details. And I thought, well, we're mates, ain't we? Have been since primary school. I just wanted to know you're all right.'

'I'm fine,' said Christie.

'Good. Good!'

'The police have told me they're releasing Lara Millman's body for burial.'

'Oh, you know about that?'

'What do *you* know?' asked Christie.

'They've got the funeral planned for tomorrow. I don't think there's going to be a big fuss made. The family don't want many people there. Actually Mungo thought I'd better tell you . . .' Her voice trailed away.

'Tell me what?'

'To stay away from the crem.'

Christie looked at the handset. 'So *this* is the real purpose of the call?'

'No, but . . . it would just be a really bad idea to show up there, that's all.' A pause. 'You wouldn't though, would you? I mean, that would be totally bloody inappropriate. Half the population think you did for the poor cow. You . . . wouldn't, would you?'

Christie said nothing.

'Did you see that detective on the news, asking the public for information about that girl Millman getting herself killed in that fire?' asked Patsy.

'No. I didn't. What about him?' Patsy *must* be talking about Dex, and right now Christie couldn't bear to go there.

'He looked like that boy you used to have a crush on years back, you remember? The Kevin Costner lookalike. What was his name . . . ?'

'Dex Cooper,' said Christie.

'*That's* the one. Thought I was going mad. Thought it couldn't be, but . . .'

'Well it is,' said Christie sharply. 'It is Dex Cooper.'

Christie put the phone down.

She paused there for a moment, then she picked it up again and dialled out. It didn't take her five minutes to get the information she wanted. Then she put the phone down again and it rang.

She snatched it up. 'Hello?'

Breathing.

'Hello?' she said again, feeling her pulse starting to jump with nerves.

Nothing but breathing.

She slapped the phone back into its cradle and, when it rang again, she didn't answer.

71

Next day Christie dressed in a black Chanel skirt suit and went to the crematorium. She loitered in the car park, eyeing the arched and rather impersonal front of the crem building as the mourners started to arrive for the ceremony.

She couldn't have said, if asked, why she felt she had to be here. It was a cold day, a brisk wind gusting across the crem's too-open grounds. There was a gaggle of press people, camera, sound man, presenter, all hanging around not far from where she stood, all smoking and talking. *Big sensation!* she thought. Some poor bitch gets herself done to death and here they are. Let's see who we can catch on camera, weeping copious tears. The mother maybe. Or maybe . . .

Christie saw the silver Roller pull into the crem's entrance and park up. Kenny! She shrank back among the cars, feeling her heartbeat quicken. He got out, strode over to the crem's entrance, talked briefly to other people there, went inside. Lara's mother arrived, propped up by a dark-haired young man. The woman looked like she was about to have a total meltdown. Then the hearse pulled in, bearing its sad load – the coffin, draped with pink flowers spelling out LARA.

What the hell am I doing here? wondered Christie.

The six undertakers were unloading the coffin, lifting it shoulder high. Christie tried not to think about what was inside it. The thought of young, lovely Lara who was now nothing but burned shrivelled flesh and blood was painful. A sickening stab of doubt hit Christie's midriff.

Oh God – did I do it? Could *I have done that?*

Dex was right, wasn't he. She had form as a fire starter. She walked in her sleep. So had she done it? Had she *driven* in her sleep, over to Lara Millman's place, and killed her? She thought of Dex's odd interest in the missing hatpin. What was that all about? Somehow it *had* to be connected to Lara's murder.

She watched the men move indoors with the coffin; watched the film crew move closer to the entrance. They wouldn't go in, would they? Surely not? But the doors closed behind the coffin and the film crew remained outside, huddled there in the gusting breeze, chatting, shivering, waiting for the pay-dirt shot no doubt – waiting for Lara's mother to come out.

'What the fuck?' asked a voice by her ear.

Christie jumped a full yard off the ground. It was Dex. She'd been so absorbed with watching the hearse and the film crew that she'd missed his arrival. She hadn't expected him to come here today, but then he would, wouldn't he? He'd be watching the mourners, seeing who looked genuinely grief-stricken, and who – horrible thought – looked secretly pleased.

'What are you doing here?' he asked her. He looked mad enough to spit.

'I don't know. I just wanted to be. That's all,' she replied lamely.

'You got your car here? You drove here?' He was talking coldly, as if to a stranger.

Christie looked at him. Bastard! 'No I fucking parachuted in,' she snapped. 'Of course I bloody drove here.'

'Then get in your car and go home,' he said flatly.

Something in Christie's brain seemed to go off with a bang. 'You don't get to tell me what to do,' she informed him. 'That missing hatpin. Can you tell me one thing? What does it have to do with all this?'

'What?' He seemed taken aback.

'The hatpins you bagged. And the *missing* one. I don't get it. I thought Lara Millman died in a fire?'

'That's information I can't share with you,' he pointed out.

'What, after all that bullshit about wanting to believe I'm innocent? I think that *you* think I did it. Deep down, you do, don't you? What, did someone stab her with it, and *then* set her alight? Is *that* what happened?'

His expression told her nothing. 'Christie. For fuck's sake, piss off home, will you?'

But Christie walked away from him, over to the crem entrance. She went inside. A recording of sombre organ music was drifting out from speakers placed at each corner of the crematorium's interior. There was a lot of red-stained wood on the ceiling and the walls, and around fifty chairs were spread out in neat rows, most of them empty. A small huddle of mourners – Kenny was there, among them – were gathered up at the front around Lara's mother, a hunched and pitiful figure. At the far end of the room was a big stained-glass window in the shape of a cross and in front of that stood a balding middle-aged man wearing a khaki-green tweed suit and heavy horn-rimmed glasses; he was standing behind a lectern, fiddling with bits of paper. Ten feet away from him was the coffin, neatly perched on a travelator, red curtains edged with gold to either side of it.

Christie took a seat at the back, well out of the way. She watched Dex slide into a seat over to the right. He didn't even glance at her.

The service began. It was horrible, punctuated by gasps and moans and wails of despair from Lara's mother. When the coffin slid away and the curtains closed, Christie thought that Mrs Millman was going to faint off, fall to the floor. Instead the woman lurched up, staggered a few steps, tried to snatch at the coffin as it slid out of reach. The dark-haired young man with her was trying to get the mother's hands off the thing, and Mrs Millman was resisting. Shouting *No! No!*

I shouldn't be here, thought Christie. *This is too bloody cruel.*

She had attended very few funerals. The image of the two coffins at her parents' burial was forever there, branded into her brain. Sometimes she dreamed of it, saw that day all over again. Since seeing her parents buried at such a tender age, she had avoided death, funerals, cremations, whenever she could. So today was a new and unusual and pretty damned ghastly experience. It shocked her, seeing this much raw grief up close.

But *something* had brought her here. Maybe the almost, *almost* cast-iron certainty that she, Christie Doyle, was no killer. No matter how powerful the motivation, not even if she had *loved* Kenny Doyle – and she never had – not even then did she truly, in her heart, believe herself capable of such an act.

But there remained a sliver of doubt.

What if she was *wrong*?

She had form. Dex was right.

There was no Mungo here today, Mungo who had been Lara's employer. No Patsy either. And none of the girls that Lara had worked with at Mungo's club. Just the small, tragic family group, and the boy who had loved Lara enough to want revenge, to fix Christie's brakes, and Kenny the deceased girl's lover. Aware of Dex's attention on her now, Christie stood up, went to the door. The reporters were there, and she walked straight through the midst of them, anxious to get away from this place, from this unbearable spectacle of grief, and she barely heard the cry go up from inside the front of the crem.

'It's *her*!'

72

Suddenly they were all crowding around her. The black hole of a massive TV camera was being thrust in her face, the sound man was looming over her, the keen-eyed reporter, her face avid with delight at this unexpected bonus, was shouting questions: 'You're Mrs Doyle, aren't you? Are you Mrs Christie Doyle? Mrs Doyle, are you guilty? What are you doing here today, Mrs Doyle? Miss Millman was your husband's mistress. What do you have to say about that . . . ?'

Christie didn't answer. She could hear all hell breaking out inside the crem and then she was being jostled, pushed, overwhelmed. Suddenly, shockingly, the dark-haired young man – was this Andy Paskins? – was up close, his body and others shoving her, almost knocking her flat to the stone-cold pavement, and there was stark hatred in his eyes, this boy who had already tried – and failed – to kill her.

'You bitch! What you doing, coming here to gloat? Ain't you done enough?' he roared in her face, spittle flying.

Christie could see Lara Millman's mother clinging on to his arm, trying to restrain him and failing. He seemed demented by his grief. And Christie was not one hundred per cent sure she didn't deserve this attack. She knew herself – didn't she? But she also knew that it was, horrifically, possible that she was guilty. That she had sleepwalked, just as she had when she was a young and troubled girl. That she had got in her car, driven over to the next village and killed Lara Millman. Not meaning to. Of *course* not meaning to. But maybe the wish, in her subconscious brain, had been there, and the wish had been enough.

Yes, maybe she had done it.

No. Over and over again, her brain rebelled, kicked the thought, the horror, out. *She couldn't have.*

Could she?

'Get back. Mr Paskins, get back, stand clear.' It was Dex's voice, snapping and harsh, and then through the crush she saw DS Smith rush across the car park and up to the teeming, thrashing group outside the crem door – the group she was in the middle of.

The reporter was still flinging questions at her. Winded, she couldn't even think about an answer. Dex grabbed her arm and pulled her out of the scrum and away while DS Smith held out his arms and shouted to everyone to just *'calm down, okay?'*

Dex was hustling her across the car park. 'Your car?' he asked.

Christie pointed. She was too breathless to speak.

He walked her over there.

'Key?'

Christie groped in her bag, opened the car door. Dex nearly threw her into the driver's seat and glared down at her.

'Go home,' he said. 'And for fuck's sake, stay there.'

Then he was gone. Christie sat there for a moment, her eyes on the melee at the front of the crem. Her breath was coming in gasps. Jesus, that look in Andy Paskins's eyes. The *hatred.*

Did she deserve that?

Whether the answer to that question was yes or no, she had to find out.

She *had* to.

She started the engine.

But she didn't go home.

73

As soon as she could she stopped the car and phoned Patsy. Patsy – of course – asked why she wanted to know that particular address. But Christie wouldn't tell her that.

'Look, on second thoughts, whatever you're up to, just *don't* tell me, OK? And I told you not to call here anymore, didn't I? Mungo won't have it.'

But Patsy did give her the address she asked for, and Christie went there. She parked the car a couple of streets away and then she followed small groups of black-clad people inside the narrow council house, took a glass of sherry from a tray on a small occasional table in a tiny hall. She whopped it back. Her hands were shaking from the shock she'd had at the funeral. At least she hadn't come face to face with *Kenny*. That would have been the absolute end. She hoped to God he wasn't going to show up here as he had at the crematorium. She didn't think he would – funerals were a pet hate of his, just as they were hers – but maybe for Lara Millman he might break the habits of a lifetime and attend a wake?

She took another sherry, drank that too. Dutch courage. Then she moved on, into the lounge, but it was shoulder to shoulder in there and people were starting to look, starting to realise that she was here, amongst them. No Kenny. She couldn't see Mrs Millman and she wanted to talk to her, to say that she was sorry, that this was awful, that she hadn't done it, she *couldn't* have.

It was so hot in the overcrowded little house. The weather had turned cold today but the heating was going full blast. Christie felt herself starting to sweat, not only with nerves now but with strong alcohol and the insane heat of the place. Jostling among the bodies, she moved through, toward another door. A kitchen. Not a show home, not at all what Christie herself was used to. Just a basic little blue and white square with a sink, a fridge, a cooker and a washing machine. At the centre of the room there was a table covered in sandwiches, sausage rolls, little quiches, small cakes, all of it covered with clingfilm, ready for the funeral feast.

It was cooler in the kitchen. Christie leaned against the table, wishing she'd bypassed the sherries. God, what was she doing? Dex was right: she should just go home. This was crazy. She turned back toward the door and was suddenly face to face with the dark-haired young man who'd been supporting Lara's mother at the funeral. They stood there, staring into each other's eyes. Christie took a gulping breath. It was him. Andy Paskins.

The boy who'd cut her brake lines.

'I'll go,' she said, moving to pass him, to go back out the door into the super-heated lounge, but he pushed the door closed and stood in front of it. Blocking her way. God, this was a mistake. This was *stupid*.

She looked down.

There was a knife in his hand.

She stood there, staring, unable to move an inch. Was this how it was going to end then? Maybe it should have ended when her parents died in that car crash, so long ago. Maybe she should have died too, but somehow, by some odd quirk of fate, she had lived. There had been times since then when she had *wished* she had died too. Lots of times. And perhaps now was the moment for it to finally happen, for her to join them, to be free.

She was looking death in the face. She could see it in his eyes. He wanted her gone. He took a step forward, towards her. His skin was so pale it was almost blue. His eyes were enormous, dark, blank with intent. The knife glinted beneath the glare of the harsh fluorescent light overhead. In the next room she could hear the merry clink of glasses, the chatter of voices, the odd burst of very un-funereal laughter, quickly suppressed so as not to show a lack of respect.

Christie swallowed hard. She was sweating. She could feel moisture worming its way under her breasts and trickling down her spine. But her mouth was dry. Her tongue felt swollen to twice its normal size but somehow she got the words out.

'Andy, I'm sorry,' she said. Her voice sounded thin, strained.

He held the knife out, blade toward her. 'You did it then. I was right, we were *all* right – you did it.'

Christie shook her head.

'You did,' he said.

'No,' she said.

He moved the knife, the slightest lunge. Took another step forward. He was going to kill her. Strange how calm she felt about that. Somehow, now, her voice was steady.

'I've died a hundred times already, Andy. You think once more's going to scare me? You're wrong,' she said.

'She was worth ten of you,' he said, and his voice broke. Tears filled his eyes.

'I didn't know her,' said Christie.

'Well she was. *Ten*. And you know what? They used her. She couldn't see it. *Wouldn't* see it. But it was the truth. She was dazzled by them. All that money. All that stuff they could give her, things she could never get from me. I was strictly second best but, fuck it, I *loved* her. And them? They just passed her around like she was a piece of meat.'

'Who did?' Christie asked. This was something new. Of course she knew about Kenny, but what was this – there were *others*?

'You know.'

'I only know about Kenny. That's all.'

'It was Mungo Boulaye too. Look.' He took a photo out of his jacket pocket. Shoved it at her. Flinching slightly, Christie took it, and looked. It was the cottage in the next village to the one where she lived. Intact, not burned out. The love nest bought by Kenny at first to house holidaymakers and tenants – and then Lara Millman. And there was Mungo Boulaye at the door, grinning, leaning into Lara, who was just saying goodbye to him, or greeting him as he arrived? Hard to tell. But one thing obvious was that Mungo was about to kiss her. And the other thing? She didn't look pregnant.

Christie blinked in surprise. Good God. *Mungo*. Then she said: 'I didn't do it, Andy. And I really, really want to know who did. Maybe it was Mungo? Or maybe it was you? What are you doing, covering your tracks?'

His face froze. 'You bitch, you take that back!'

'Andy?' It was Mrs Millman, pushing open the door behind him. Christie could see into the room beyond. There were curious faces, people staring. Mrs Millman stepped into the kitchen, closed the door, leaned against it. She could see at a glance what was going on. Her eyes opened wide, fearful.

She put out a hand, laid it urgently on Andy's hand that held the knife. 'What are you doing?'

'Aunt Dottie . . .' he started.

'No!' Mrs Millman's voice cracked like a whip. 'You put that away *this instant*,' she said. 'What, you think I want more bloodshed? More disaster? Haven't we had *enough*?'

Christie watched, mesmerised, while Andy turned into a small boy. His expression guilty, chastened, he put the knife away in his jacket pocket. She guessed he'd been living next door to the Millmans for a long, long time. Mrs Millman was Aunt Dottie to him. As good as family. Tiny, mouselike Mrs Millman had very probably just saved her life.

'Now,' Mrs Millman rapped out, turning her gaze on Christie. 'You. Out. Go the back way. I don't want any more upsets. Out you go.'

Christie went. She still had the photo in her hand.

74

Half an hour later Christie was hammering at Patsy's door. When Patsy opened it, she looked like she'd found a fresh turd on her doorstep instead of her lifelong friend.

'Oh Christ not again! I *told* you to stay away. Mungo don't want . . .'

'I don't care what Mungo wants,' said Christie, and surged past her, into the hallway.

Patsy closed the front door.

Patsy's expression was all the answer she needed; she couldn't fake the blank look of total shock.

'*What?*' demanded Patsy.

Christie shrugged. 'Can you really say you're all that surprised? You've said it before: that's what our men like to do. They like the nice home life, the pretty wife, all lovely and tidy – but they also like the young hotties. The ones like Lara.'

'I don't know anything about that.'

'I've seen proof.'

'I don't believe you.'

'Yes. You do.'

Patsy clamped her arms around herself, hugging her midriff. She gave a shrug.

'Look. All right. But that's up to Mungo. I know he plays away. So does Kenny. Come on, Christie – we both know the score.'

'Oh, the score was fine,' agreed Christie. 'Right up to the moment when someone decided they were going to kill Lara Millman over it. Then a bit of fun on the side took on a whole new meaning. And now *I'm* in the frame.'

'Look, Christie . . .'

'No, *you* look. This isn't funny anymore. Not even a little bit. The police are taking things out of my house. They're thinking maybe I did it. I don't like that.'

'Oh come on. You can't think *Mungo* . . . ?'

'Kenny thought the baby was his. He was ranting and raving at me about it. He's always wanted kids. You know that. It was a big deal between us. You know what? When he knew Lara Millman was carrying his kid, he was over-joyed. I mean, the poor sap was *ecstatic*. But the big joke is this, isn't it? *It might not have been his at all.* Now I'm thinking the father might have been the boy she grew up with, Andy Paskins. Very passionate young man, that Andy. Almost killed me over it – twice – but he's yet to succeed. Or it could even, looking at the photo he showed me, have been Mungo's.'

'Mungo's?' Patsy had gone pale. 'Oh come on! No, I don't . . .'

'You don't know, do you. Neither do I. I want to talk to Mungo about this. Where is he? At the club?'

'Well . . . ah . . .'

'Of course he is. Look, Patsy. Lara's dead and gone and nobody knows the truth, do they? Except whoever killed her. And whoever did for her, they're hoping that particular secret is gone with her.

75

Christie drove into Soho and parked up near Frith Street. She fed the meter and didn't let herself think too hard about what she was planning to do. It was full dark when she walked over to the main door of Mungo's and saw Terry, one of the bouncers she knew, standing guard there. Terry had been at her party, admitting those who were there by invitation only, letting no one else past the gate. He knew her on sight. And he looked awkward, as if she was the last person he wanted or needed to see here, tonight.

'Hi, Terry,' she said breezily. 'Mungo in?'

'Yeah. Sure,' he said after a beat, and waved her inside.

Christie went through the foyer and was immediately enveloped in the hot underworld-dark feel of the inner club. As she went deeper, she was nearly deafened by Grace Jones pounding out of the sound system, saying she was a slave to the rhythm. Up above the crimson-lit bar, three of the dancers were already at work on their poles, wearing silver thongs and nothing else.

Mungo was sitting at the far end of the bar, thumbing through a newspaper, sipping on what looked like Scotch. He nearly choked on it when he saw Christie stroll in.

'Can we talk?' she yelled up close, to make herself heard.

Mungo looked at her. 'What's to say?' he wheezed.

'Plenty. Can we go in the office?'

Shrugging, Mungo slid off the bar stool and led the way. Once inside his office, with the door shut, the level of noise became bearable. Mungo leaned back against the door and stared at his best mate's wife.

'What d'you think you're doing?' he asked flatly.

'I could ask you the same question,' said Christie, feeling anger bubbling up inside her. She was being fitted up. She was almost sure of it, almost *convinced* of it, and if this bastard had done it, and now thought he was going to get away scot-free, well, he wasn't. No way.

'Meaning?' said Mungo, pushing himself away from the door and going around the desk to sit down in his big high-backed red leather chair.

He indicated the chair on the other side of the desk, but Christie remained standing. She'd startled him, walking in here; but now he was back under control, leaning back easily on his throne, king of all he surveyed.

'Meaning this.' Christie threw the photo of Mungo in a warm embrace with Lara Millman at the cottage door down onto the desk.

A guarded expression came over Mungo's face. He reached out, picked the photo up.

'It's a copy,' guessed Christie. 'Not the original. That's in safe hands.' As she said it, she wondered again how 'safe' Andy Paskins's hands could be. Half the time he seemed demented, any logical thought fragmented by his grief over Lara.

'So? What does this prove?' asked Mungo, who had obviously decided to front it out.

'You're just about to kiss her. And it doesn't look like it's going to be a peck on the cheek.'

Mungo tossed the photo back onto the desk. 'This doesn't prove anything.'

'No? Well then I'll show it to . . . oh, let's see . . . to *Kenny*, shall I? See what he makes of it?'

Mungo's expression altered. Lost its smugness. Then, abruptly, it was back.

'You won't be talking to Kenny anytime soon,' he said. 'Word is, he's just about ready to kill you. Wouldn't surprise me if he did. You're no fool, are you? So you won't be talking to Kenny. It's more than your life's worth, doing that.'

'Hey.' Christie stared down at him. 'Look at the photo, Mungo. That ain't no casual hello. Your hand is on her *arse*. You're about to stick your tongue down her throat. And now you're trying to call my bluff? To bet I won't show that to Kenny?'

'Yeah,' said Mungo. He smiled. A cat's smile, just before it pounces on the mouse. 'That's what I'm doing.'

'OK. How about the police, then? You think *they'll* buy your innocent act?'

The smile vanished. 'Look . . .' he started.

Someone rapped hard on the door. Then Terry poked his head around it, looked at Mungo, looked at Christie.

'*What?*' snapped Mungo.

Someone pushed Terry to one side. A big man, a bruiser in a flashy shot-silk suit.

It was *Kenny*.

76

Instantly Christie swept the photo up, stuffing it in her jacket pocket. Mungo surged to his feet. He looked guilty as hell to Christie's eyes, furtive, but Kenny's attention was fixed on her.

'What you doing here?' he asked, and Christie wondered at his expression. Anxiety? Anger?

Christie glanced back at Mungo. She had him by the balls and he knew it. *Your move, Mungo. You want me to tell Kenny . . . ?*

'She just called in, thought Patsy might be here,' said Mungo quickly. He came around the desk, his hands up in a gesture of appeasement. 'Now come on, mate. I know things have been said, things have happened, but let's keep it civil shall we?'

'Civil?' Kenny snarled. 'This whore did for Lara. I know she did.'

'I'm hardly a whore,' said Christie calmly. 'I am Mrs Kenny Doyle. Your wife, I think you'll find.'

'You . . .' Kenny stepped forward, hand raised.

Christie looked again at Mungo.

'Now come on,' he said, and stepped between husband and wife. His eyes, full of desperation, met Christie's. 'Bugger off, will you? Just go.'

'OK,' said Christie, outwardly cool but inwardly wondering if even Mungo could restrain Kenny when his blood was up. She swept out of the room, back down the side of the bar by the dancers and out. When she got outside, she realised she was drenched in sweat and shuddering with nerves. Kenny close up in a rage was not something anyone would want to confront. And now she realised something else: the expression on Kenny's face when he saw her in Mungo's office, the one she had struggled to identify, had not been anxiety or even the anger she might have expected.

It was *shock*.

77

'Do you remember a girl called Christie Butler?' Dex asked.

He'd called in late in the evening and now he was in his mother's conservatory, which led off her sitting room and out into the garden. He had grown up in this house. It was a semi in the suburbs of Ealing, a vast rabbit warren with big rooms and high ceilings and a warm family feel about it. Here he'd been born, and his younger brother and his sister too. Dad was gone – too many cigarettes and a shade too much rum during his time in the navy had done for him several years ago – but Joyce, Dex's mum, had stayed on here, and the house still retained its cosy, chaotic feel.

At his question, Dex's mother looked up with some surprise. Joyce was a handsome woman in her sixties, neatly dressed, hair butter-yellow blonde and barely a wrinkle on her face. Her eyes were blue – like Dex's – and now she looked at her eldest son with sharp inquiry. She put down the tea she'd been drinking on the glass-topped bamboo-framed circular table that matched the rest of her loud tropical-style conservatory furniture.

'Remember her?' Joyce laughed. 'Course I remember her. Broke your heart, didn't she? Back when you were very young. Sent you a bit mental for a time, I recall.'

'Oh have a day off,' said Dex. 'I have never been anywhere near mental.'

'No? Well, I think that was the closest you ever came to it. She was all you could think about and it seemed to me you weren't quite sure how to approach her, were you? I can still remember the way you used to look at her whenever she came over here. I was a bit afraid for you, truth be told.'

Dex was startled. 'Afraid? Why?'

'Because.' She shrugged. 'I could see you'd fallen hard. And Gawd, that family. The Butler crowd. Not good people. They were bad 'uns and I was worried you were getting in deep with them and dragging your little brother in with you. You worried me to death back then. I was sure you were going to get cautioned or convicted of something. It was nothing short of a miracle that you never were. And she was part of that whole set-up, wasn't she.'

'I don't think Christie was ever part of the Butler crew. Not really.' But through them, she'd met Kenny Doyle. And married him. Now what the fuck had she done *that* for? Yeah, because he was rich. That was it.

'Her parents were Butlers,' Joyce reminded him.

'Graham Butler, her father – I heard that he was all right. Didn't Dad always say that? He said Graham was a decent sort, but he didn't get on with his brother Jerome.'

'He did say that, but well, who really knows? Graham and Anna Butler are long dead, poor souls. And Christie? Somehow she survived. Car crash, wasn't it. She was just a baby, wasn't that the case? Three or four years old? Tragic. Losing both her parents like that.'

'But she did survive.'

'And grew up pretty, I recall.' Joyce smiled. 'And she was your obsession, wasn't she. All through your teenage years.'

'Maybe I was obsessed. A bit,' he said, thinking of silent, beautiful Christie as he'd known her then. How he'd hung around the Butler crew to be near her. He'd tried to reach her but somehow he hadn't ever been able to. He hadn't been used, even at so young an age, to failure with women. And Christie? Joyce was right. She *had* broken his heart.

'A bit? Come off it. You were in torment over her. You hung around that Butler lot and you didn't even really like them, did you. You were one of the gang, part of their crowd, but that wasn't the real attraction. It was *her* you were after.'

'She was so young.'

'Ah, young love.'

'It isn't funny,' said Dex, but he was smiling too.

'That DS of yours, that Smith – he still trying to fix you up on a date?'

'Nah, I think he's given up on that.' Since Dex's marriage to Tammy – five, or was it six years ago? – Smith had tried to coax his boss out on double dates, but Dex hadn't been keen. He was restless, uninterested, concentrating on the job, moving from apartments to houses and now into a more upmarket Thameside place – as a DI he earned pretty well – but really? There was nowhere – except this place, his mum's house – that he had ever truly thought of as *home*.

'When I last saw him he told me half the female officers at the station were drooling over you.'

'Smith's full of bullshit. Mum?'

'What?'

'The case I'm working on. It involves Christie Butler.'

'Christie? Seriously?'

'Only she's not Christie Butler now. She's Christie Doyle. She's married to Kenny. You remember Kenny Doyle?'

Joyce puffed out her cheeks. 'Remember? Sure I do. He was in charge of that Butler boy and his gang of thieves, wasn't he. Liked to lord it around their place. I suppose that's how he met Christie?'

Dex nodded.

'And married her? Good God. He didn't seem her type. Not at all.'

'That's not the end of it,' said Dex. 'In fact, that's just the beginning.'

Dex explained to his mother about all that had been happening. Kenny's mistress getting herself killed. And Christie being in the frame for the murder.

'She was such a quiet girl,' said Joyce thoughtfully, when he'd finished. 'She seemed perfect for you. I hope you don't mind me saying that but she did. You were all mad and fiery, but she calmed you down. I liked her.'

'She liked you too.'

'Missed opportunities,' said Joyce, her merry, gentle eyes on her son's face. 'Shame.'

'She's involved in this case. Right up to her neck.'

'And . . . ?' asked Joyce.

'The case. It's bad. She's prime suspect.'

Joyce's eyes opened wide. 'Oh come on. What, Christie? Little Christie who would never say boo to a goose?'

'That's the one.'

Joyce was silent for a while. She was gazing at her son's face. 'Then maybe you should step aside. Pass it on.'

'I thought of that.'

'And?'

'I don't think I can. Put her in the hands of someone else, who might not take the care I would? I can't.'

Dex's mother stared at him. 'First cut is the deepest,' she said thoughtfully.

Dex's mouth twisted in a wry smile. 'What's that, the gos-
pel according to Rod Stewart?'

'It's true though, isn't it.' She paused, thinking. 'I saw how
it tore at you all those years ago. *Crushed* you. I felt for you,
son. I really did. You know, when you're young you sort of get
over the loss of a love, on the surface anyway. You think to
yourself, I'll find another one. It'll be OK. I saw you thinking
that, lots of times. It made my heart break to see it. You were
trying to convince yourself. To get your mind, get your *heart*,
off Christie. Even your marriage to Tammy. One year that
lasted, didn't it?'

Dex flinched a bit at that. Tammy had deserved better; but
their divorce had at least been amicable.

'You told yourself it was just puppy love with Christie,
didn't you. That there would be others,' Joyce went on. 'You
made yourself believe that. But the sad part is, son, sometimes there just never is. Sometimes that first one is *the* one.
There never is another to take its place. Another love never
happens. And then? All that's left is regrets.'

78

'I told you not to get in touch with me. Correct me if I am wrong, Mr Doyle, but didn't I say that?' asked Gustavo. It was late. He sounded irritated.

Cold bastard, thought Kenny. He stared at the phone. His head was swimming with drink. How much he'd drunk he really couldn't recall. But yes – a lot. And yes, the hitman had said, *don't contact me.* But for fuck's sake! There was Christie, still walking about, large as life. She'd been in Mungo's and she was still – hatefully and inconveniently – *not dead.*

'Listen, arsehole,' said Kenny. 'I walked into my mate's club tonight and there she was chatting to him as if everything was just fine. She was *there.* You were supposed to sort this.'

'And I will,' said Gustavo.

*

It was annoying, thought Gustavo, that the pool lighting system hadn't done the trick. It would have looked like the perfect accident. People swimming around the pool at her birthday party, someone kicking the light, loosening the cover – and then *her,* diving in one morning and getting fried to a crisp. End of problem. Cue pay cheque. But no. It hadn't worked. Time to think again, time to find the solution to the ongoing problem that was Mrs Christie Doyle.

Gustavo wasn't about to tell Kenny that his first attempt on Christie's life had failed. No client ever heard about a failure from Gustavo. He counted himself as a highly valued asset of Primo Ecco, New York's most elite mob boss. Only success was broadcast; and success, he knew, would come.

'So what are you doing? What's being done?' asked Kenny hotly.

'Planning,' said Gustavo. 'And when I have successfully completed my plan, you, Mr Doyle, will be informed. Until then – as I believe I have already said – you don't make contact. I will contact *you*.'

Gustavo put the phone down. Then he wiped the handset clean, then every surface he had touched in his suite. He packed up, checked out and moved to another hotel, irritated but finding it necessary, because what if that oaf Kenny Doyle had phoned from the valley house, and what if the police had a tap on that wire and could trace it straight to this hotel, this suite, and therefore to Gustavo?

Amateurs.

You had to watch out for them, *think* for them.

But – damn it – they paid the bills.

79

Sometimes the dreams still haunted Christie, sent her chasing down dark corridors in the dead of night, her skin wet with sweat, her nostrils full of that particular smell, that *dreaded* smell. Tonight – after she'd seen Mungo and Kenny at the club – was such a night. Before she turned in, she saw a note from Patrick the gardener on the worktop in the kitchen, but she didn't pause to properly read it, or the newspaper he'd left there for her. Glimpsing the front page, she saw that the Channel Tunnel had been officially opened and someone called Denis MacShane had held the seat for Labour in the Rotherham by-election. She didn't care. She wanted her bed. More than that, she wanted *oblivion*.

Patrick was a comforting fixture around the house. Maybe the *only* one. He came in every weekday morning to heat his soup in the microwave and they chatted about the garden, about the acquisition of new tools to cut the hedges because Patrick was getting on in years and needed aluminium rather than steel to work with these days.

'Lighter, see?' he'd told her.

Maybe that was the note. Prices for new tools. The least she could do, really, for the man who'd saved her life. But all the recent happenings had changed the way she viewed this house, her home. Her *precious* home. Was it really a home at all? Mostly it was empty, when it should have been a family place, children playing in the gardens and filling the house with noise and laughter. Or was it – she didn't want to think this way, but she couldn't help it – was it really just a fancy mausoleum for a marriage that had always been more dead than alive?

Sleep was so much better than waking, right now. She fell into sleep for escape, but instead of sweet release tonight there was once again the torment of that old, familiar dream. The petrol odour choking her, the stench of burning. And a new horror. The door to Lara Millman's cottage opening and she, Christie, was surging forward, plunging *something* into Lara's flesh, and then the flames, the flames . . .

Something was different this time. Not only this new scene, not only heat, not only smell, but also *noise*.

Christ, such a noise.

She snapped awake and was sitting up instantly, alert, heart thundering in her chest, staring into the dark wide-eyed, blind.

The *noise*.

She sat there, panting, sweating, and then reached out a fumbling, shaking hand. Snapped on the bedside light. What the hell . . . ?

It was the smoke alarm out on the landing.

And – oh God – now she could smell it. She could smell *smoke*.

This wasn't a dream. This was real.

She almost fell from the bed, ran to the closed bedroom door, threw it open. The noise escalated, deafening, shrieking at her. Out here the smoke smell was thicker. The air felt dense, warm. She looked down, over the banisters and into the hallway below. Nothing. She threw open one door on the landing, then another, then another and . . .

Shit!

This was the small room that Kenny used as a second office. It would have been hers, had she actually *done* anything. Crafts or something. But she didn't, so it was Kenny's. There were books lining the walls although Kenny never read books. Appearances were all to Kenny. There was a desk, a blue leather captain's chair behind it. A computer, which mostly went unused. The air was thick with smoke in here. She stumbled forward, gasping, switching on the overhead light to see that the air was grey and chokingly dense. There was a tangle of white wires snaking under the desk and the smoke seemed to be curling up from there. She ducked down and looked. A four-point extension lead was under there, stacked with plug after plug after plug, one on top of the other, extension upon extension. Madness. As she stared, there was a snap of sound and flames started to erupt.

Christie turned on her heel, coughing, and dashed out onto the landing, down the stairs and into the kitchen. She snatched down the small extinguisher in the utility room, ran back upstairs in the dark and nearly fell onto the landing.

She went back into Kenny's study and had to stop, had to look again at the instructions on the side of the extinguisher because she'd never used it before. The flames were now creeping up over Kenny's display books, blackening them. The shriek of the smoke alarm went on and on, drilling into her shattered senses.

Finally she got the extinguisher to work, shot a jet of white foam onto the flaming tangle of wires, hosed down the books.

Within seconds, the fire was out.

She slumped down in the captain's chair, dropped the extinguisher onto the floor. She coughed, her throat feeling raw. Looked at the plug in the wall socket, reached down and snatched it out.

Stupid bloody Kenny, putting all those plugs into one lead, was he mad? Didn't everyone know that you never did that? That this was *exactly* how house fires started. And what if she hadn't woken up? What if that damned alarm hadn't jolted her out of sleep and into wakefulness?

Christie swayed back to her feet, went back onto to the landing, into the master bedroom's en-suite bathroom and grabbed a towel. She went back out onto the landing and whirled the thing about her head to try and stop the alarm. Not succeeding, she went into the smoke-stinking study, holding her breath against the stench, and threw open the windows. Then she went back out onto the landing again, swiped at the smoke alarm some more. Suddenly, the alarm stopped.

Silence.

Christie snatched up the extinguisher and gave the plugs and the books another dose. Then she went into the master, grabbed the quilt off the bed, and went downstairs. It was gone three in the morning. She put all the lights on in the sitting room and then lay down on the couch, draped the quilt around her. She lay there wide-eyed, shuddering and sweating, that smoke-scent still thick in her nostrils.

What if I hadn't woken up?

That thought turned over and over in her brain.

And the answer was obvious.

The answer was there, stark as a neon sign blinking on and off in her aching head.

I'd be dead.

When dawn came, she realised that she'd been putting off an important decision.

She'd lavished such love on this place, so much attention, but now? She felt under threat here. She couldn't deny it any longer.

She was going to have to leave the house.

80

She *did* sleep, somewhere around dawn. And awoke to noises coming from the kitchen. She tensed. *Kenny?*

She shot off the sofa like a cat and left the sitting room, walked through the hall. The kitchen door was open, the lights on. Faintly, she could hear movement.

The microwave?

She stepped into the open doorway and Patrick turned and gave her a hesitant smile.

'Oh! Sorry. Didn't know you were already up Mrs Doyle.'

'That's OK.' She couldn't bring herself to even start explaining about what had happened in the night.

The microwave 'pinged' and Patrick took his soup out, placed it on the worktop, got out a spoon. 'Can I make you a coffee? Tea? Toast?' he asked her.

'No. Nothing thanks.' Her stomach heaved at the thought of food.

'Thought I smelled smoke in here.'

'Oh? Oh yeah. I burned a saucepan last night.'

'Ah, right. You got my note?'

'Note?'

Christie dragged a hand through her hair. Patrick turned and held up the slip of paper that had been sitting on the worktop. 'This one. You look like you had a rough night. You OK?'

'I'm fine,' she lied.

'Look, I know you're going through a tough time. If there's anything I can do . . . ?'

'You already do plenty,' said Christie. She held out a hand. 'The note . . . ?'

'About the BT engineer. Here.'

Patrick handed her the note, took a spoonful of tomato soup. He was a regular sort of person, Patrick. It was tomato soup or nothing. Always.

'What engineer?' Christie unfolded the note. Saw Patrick's looped handwriting. *BT engineer called to address the fault on the phone upstairs in the office. Says all sorted. M.*

Christie felt her blood turn to ice.

'There was an engineer here? Yesterday?'

'There was. He said you'd reported a fault.'

'How long was he here?'

'About twenty minutes, while you were out. He said it was all fixed, all fine. Then he left.'

Christie swallowed hard, trying to work some spit into her mouth; suddenly it was very dry. She hadn't reported a problem with the phone upstairs. She hadn't reported *anything*. So probably this 'engineer' had been one of Kenny's boys, and he'd been in there pretending to be a BT engineer, poking about in the study upstairs, piling all those plugs into that extension lead, knowing it wouldn't take the load. Waiting, in fact, for a fire to start; and for that fire to kill her in her sleep.

'What was he like?' she managed to ask at last. 'This engineer?'

Patrick looked puzzled. 'Um . . . medium height. Balding. Fortyish. Had a hooked nose. Clean-shaven. He had ID. Sort of bloke you'd pass in the street I suppose. Not very remarkable.'

'Patrick.'

'Yeah?'

'Don't let anyone else in the house. Always check with me first.'

'Why? What's happened?'

'I just don't like strangers in the house right now.'

'OK. Sure.'

Leaving Patrick in the kitchen with his soup, Christie went upstairs and opened the study door. The scent of burning was there, still strong in the stagnant air. She left the windows wide open, looked around her at the detritus of spent fire extinguisher, melted plugs, blackened books. She went back out of the room, closing the door after her, and went to take a shower, wash the smoky smell of the fire from her skin. She couldn't seem to get rid of it. And then she thought: *maybe that was what Lara smelled as* she *died*.

81

Smith was feeling pissed off. Yesterday the boss had come in first thing, tossed what looked like a mini Sputnik in an evidence bag onto the desk, told him to get that off to forensics. And today his DI had presented him with a fresh list of all the people and staff who had been in attendance at Christie Doyle's birthday party.

'Anything turned up on that first list?' Dex asked when he had assembled Smith, Debbie Phelps and Bill Jensen in the big main office.

'Nothing,' said Smith. 'We got statements off the catering staff – one of them's gone off on holiday, the caterer's daughter Gemma Rawnsley.'

'I'm seeing the catering company owner – Mrs Rawnsley – tomorrow at her place in Clapham,' said Debbie.

'When is the daughter due back?' asked Dex.

'Day after tomorrow. I'll catch her then.'

'Nothing else? All those dubious bastards there, and *nothing*?'

They all shook their heads.

Dex turned to the wall of photos and stared bleakly at the heading 'Operation Rainbow'. Thought of someone, full of hate, plunging in that hatpin and then dousing the injured woman with petrol – and coolly setting her alight.

It was fucking *horrible*. Truly, the stuff of nightmares.

What about the trajectory of the blow? he thought. *What about that?*

'I want to know everything about those people who were there on the day of Christie Doyle's birthday. *Everything.* If any of them have got form for anything, even for a parking ticket, put them on the top of the pile. Make sure you talk to them all. Once, twice, a third time. Rattle their cages. Leave no one out, not the waiting staff, not the cleaner, nobody. I want everyone accounted for. Where were they on the day, what did they see, who did they speak to, and was anyone seen going into the upstairs master bedroom? Was anyone behaving suspiciously? Did anyone see any of these—' Dex indicated the photo on the wall, of long hatpins stuck into the tinfoil of the Sputnik thing '—being carried about the place? It's unlikely but who knows? Maybe someone did. Also, talk again to everyone in the club that Mungo Boulaye, Kenny Doyle's mate, owns. Talk again to the bouncers, the other dancers, everyone. No fresh news on door to door around Lara Millman's place?'

'Nope,' said Smith. 'The consensus was that she was a tart. Beyond that? Nothing.'

'Right. I'm going to talk to Christie Doyle,' said Dex, because Christie had just phoned through and said she had news about Lara. News that involved Mungo Boulaye.

First Christie's brakes had been tampered with.

Then her pool had gone live, turning it into a death trap.

That was two 'incidents' too many.

He was a professional. He could handle this. He could talk to her and forget the rest of it, forget the fact that he was still – alarmingly, amazingly – hungry as hell for her, as if the years in between their first parting and this time right now were nothing at all. All he had to do was focus on the job. Forget the rest.

82

'I'm sorry,' said the girl behind the counter at the petrol station. 'Card's declined. Try another one?'

Christie had driven out to the local market town, stopping on the way for petrol. Anything to keep busy, to stop panic from setting in. And now her card had been turned down. Yesterday, it had been fine.

'Sorry,' she said to the impatient man who was twitching in the queue behind her. She handed over another card.

'Um – that one too,' said the girl.

Christie tried two more.

'Is this going to take much longer?' the man behind her demanded.

Christie paid cash and walked out of the petrol station shop and got back in her car. She still had half a tank of fuel left. Kenny – the bastard – had clearly stopped all her cards. Everything was in Kenny's name, of course. *The Lord giveth and the Lord taketh away,* she thought grimly. Because everything she had was Kenny's, wasn't it. And now he'd decided she was to have nothing.

She drove back to the house. Patrick was down in the orchard now, weaving the ride-on mower between the apple and plum trees.

She went upstairs to her dressing room and opened the dressing table drawer. Inside a little blue book she kept in there, she had a thick stack of twenty-pound notes. She pulled them out, stuffed them in her purse. This was the cash Kenny gave her week by week to pay the window man and the house cleaner, to pay Patrick. It was also sometimes, she grandly imagined, her 'fuck you' money – the little stash of loot she had accumulated over the years in case she ever got up the nerve to try and leave Kenny Doyle.

But she hadn't left him.

He had left *her*.

She thought of that strange but very definite expression of shock she had caught on Kenny's face when he'd walked in and found her talking to Mungo at the club. Apparently he was not only dooming her to poverty but also trying to wipe her out. All these 'accidents'. Had he paid Andy Paskins to cut the brake lines on her car? And what about the pool? She thought of the fox, floating dead in there, electrocuted. Had that *really* been accidental? And then the BT engineer who was not an engineer at all. No way had there been so many plugs in that extension lead before. Just four, if she recalled correctly. But *did* she?

Increasingly, her brain felt as if it was being fried over a low light. She didn't know if anyone could be trusted anymore, not even, if she was entirely truthful, *herself*. And for God's sake! Patrick, letting fake tradesmen into the house. She could have *died*.

And what if one day, not knowing the full story, he let her cousin Ivo in. One of her family, after all. Patrick wouldn't see any harm in that. Why would he? He didn't *know*. She thought of the heavy breather on the phone. He'd called several times. It *had* to be Ivo – didn't it?

Christie went into the bedroom, threw open the wardrobe and snatched out her suitcase.

The phone started ringing.

She stopped, stared at it like you'd stare at a poisonous snake.

Ivo . . . ?

She knew he was out there, circling, moving ever closer. He thought her protection was all gone and he was right. Kenny would be *glad* of anything happening to her. She knew that. Ivo knew it too, now. And she thought he was going to make his move soon. Reclaim her. Take her back. Make her *his* again.

Finally, the phone stopped ringing.

She unfroze her limbs and carried on packing, stuffed underwear, clothes, whatever she could, into the case. Then she went downstairs, scrawled a note for Patrick and stuck it to the side door where he couldn't miss seeing it. She made a call from the phone in the sitting room. Then she left her refuge, her precious home. But not hers, really. Never hers. Always Kenny's. His name on the deeds, his payments on the mortgage. She closed the front door behind her and wondered if she would ever go back inside the place again.

What she had to try and make herself believe was this: someone at her party had come upstairs and into her dressing room, taken one of her Victorian hatpins and used it somehow in the killing of Lara Millman – her brain offered up all sorts of grisly images, but she still didn't really know precisely how, and Dex wasn't saying.

But is that what happened? Or did I sleepwalk over there and do the job myself?

No. She could never have done that.

Never.

The sweet little vixen floating dead in the pool.

The tangle of wires, smouldering in the office upstairs.

No, right now she didn't think she could ever set foot in her home again. She had to go somewhere else. Somewhere she could feel *safe*.

But where the hell was that?

83

She went to a dingy hotel on the edge of the nearby market town – not the sort of hotel she'd got used to as Mrs Kenny Doyle. This place was two-star, shabby, the staff uncaring and the standards of cleanliness questionable. Ants marched in line back and forth to a never-emptied trash bin under a tiny desk in her room. There were tacky nylon sheets on the bed and dustballs under it. But it was OK. Nobody knew her here. Nobody expected her to be here. She booked in, went along the hall to her ground-floor room, crawled into bed fully clothed, prayed that there weren't any bed bugs in there with her, and slept the sleep of total exhaustion.

*

She woke at six in the evening, coming back to herself by slow degrees. She could hear a TV playing loudly in the next room. She sat up, yawning, groggy from too deep a sleep. She looked around. A tip of a place, but she felt happier here, more secure, than she had at home.

She knew she'd been fooling herself. Ever since Lara Millman had breathed her last, Christie's time out there in the valley house had been done and her marriage – such as it was – over. She had just refused to see it. She'd been clinging on to whatever sense of security she could, as usual. She'd done it all her life. Been scared shitless, she could admit that now to herself, all her life. But now? Maybe she'd been fooling herself. Maybe there was really no security, anywhere. Maybe that was just a fact of life that she had – belatedly – to learn.

She got up, showered in a meagre bottle of lather-free shampoo, put on a grey robe that had the texture of card-board and scratched her skin wherever it touched. The phone started ringing as she sat on the bed and dragged a comb through her hair. She looked at it like you'd look at a venomous snake. Then, finally, she picked up the receiver.

'Yes?' she asked.

'Someone in reception to speak to you,' said the same surly receptionist who'd booked her in.

But nobody knew she was here. Nobody except Patrick, and she'd left strict instructions that he was not to tell a soul about it.

'Who?' she asked.

'It's the police,' said the receptionist, sounding offended, as if this was a *respectable* establishment, and Christie was somehow lowering the tone.

Christie thought about that. She hadn't heard from Dex for days. Maybe he'd done what they had talked about – passed the Lara Millman case on to one of his colleagues. And perhaps now this colleague had come to do what Dex hadn't: to charge her – at last – with Lara's murder.

Whatever, she had to face it.

'I'll come down,' she said.

*

It *was* Dex. He was sitting in an alcove by the window oppo-site the empty bar. The metal shutters were down on the serving station. No staff were in evidence. When he saw her in the doorway, he stood up.

'Your watchdog didn't want to tell me where you were,' he said as she joined him, and they both sat down.

'Patrick? No, Patrick wouldn't. I told him not to.' Christie spoke coolly, but her stomach was in knots. Stupid to feel this way – glad to see him. Relieved, really. But scared too. And hurt. It was stupid, but seemingly beyond her control. 'How'd you get it out of him?'

'Leaned on him a bit. Said he was impeding a police investigation, and perhaps we'd better go to the station and discuss it further. He did his best, but in the end, he caved. What do you have to do to get a coffee in this place?'

'Probably die of thirst? And even then, if you collapsed right here on this horrible swirly carpet, I doubt they'd rush to give you sustenance.'

Dex's mouth twitched in a half-smile.

That smile! It shook Christie, sent her spiralling back through the years. It was disconcerting; one moment he was a threatening stranger who might jail her, the next some slight movement, some expression – like this one – could remind her of the jokey, cocky, overconfident and frankly *loud* youngster he had been, the one who had flirted with a shy, vulnerable girl about a zillion years ago. And of course that girl had found his bouncy self-confidence attractive; he had been the opposite of her in every way, and she was bound to admire him for it.

'Why here?' he asked her.

'It felt safe. Anonymous.' Christie looked at his face. 'Did you know about Mungo Boulaye and Lara Millman?'

'What?'

Christie took the crumpled photo of the pair of them out of her pocket and laid it on the table between them. Dex looked.

'That puts a different complexion on matters, I'd say.'

'So would I. Andy Paskins gave me that. I wonder if my beloved husband knew about it.'

Dex's eyes narrowed. 'What – you think *Kenny* might have done the deed?'

'He was besotted with her. You can see he might be annoyed, Mungo being all over her like this. And she doesn't look like she's raising the slightest objection, does she?'

'I do see that, yes. And this picture? Further proof of stalking behaviour by the Paskins boy.'

'Dex – I didn't do it. At least I don't *think* I did.'

His eyes sharpened on her face. 'What the fuck does that mean?'

'Doesn't matter.'

'Did Kenny have other women, besides Lara?'

'Hundreds, I should think.'

'You call him your "beloved husband",' said Dex.

'I was being sarcastic. Or flippant. Actually, both.'

'Christie, I have to ask these things.'

'Ask away.' She shrugged.

'So – were you happy in the marriage?'

There were two things that Christie never wanted to talk about. Her upbringing with the Butlers, and her marriage. But Dex had leaned on Patrick, and she could see from the set of his face that he was now more than ready to lean on her, too, if he had to.

'I've already told you all about my marriage to Kenny So can we talk about something else?' she asked.

'No,' said Dex, 'We can't.'

84

There was a silence and then Christie said: 'Well, were you happy in yours? I bet you *have* been married at some point.'

'I asked first.'

'All right.' Christie paused, gathering her thoughts. 'I was happy with all that he gave me.'

Dex leaned back in his chair, his eyes intent on her face. 'That sounds cold. Calculating. It's just . . .'

'Just what?' asked Christie.

'When I knew you, you were different. You wouldn't have married *anyone* for that reason.'

'Just a minute. You think I married Kenny for his *money*?'

'Sounds like it.'

'Well – I didn't.'

'For what then?'

'Hardly matters now, does it.'

'Humour me. You're the suspect and I'm the detective. OK?'

'Or we'll continue this chat down the station?' Christie smiled ruefully.

'Or that, yeah. Christie – why'd you marry a bent bastard like Kenny Doyle?'

'A bent *rich* bastard,' Christie chipped in. 'Don't forget that.'

'Yeah, rich – from the proceeds of crime,' said Dex.

'Very likely. I never looked into any of that. Never even thought about it.'

'As I said,' said Dex. 'Cold.'

'How dare you say that to me?' said Christie flatly, feeling anger stir. What the hell did he know? He was a *man*. He'd lived his life free from fear. He didn't know what it was like to look over his shoulder, to know he was weak and could be under threat from someone stronger. *She* knew that, though. Only too well.

'That's better,' Dex congratulated her.

'Shut up,' she snapped. She'd risen to the bait and she hated herself for it. And there was nothing cold in this conversation. There was heat and there was passion – a volcanic flare of it was rippling red-hot along every word they uttered to one another, every glance they exchanged. She felt it, and she knew damned well that he felt it too. Maybe he was fighting it, but it was there.

Dex folded his arms over his chest. 'Whenever you're ready . . . ?' he prompted.

'What, you want me to say I hated him? That I hated Kenny?' Christie let out a bark of laughter. 'I didn't. I still don't. I think he really loved this Lara girl, and I pity him because he's lost her, hasn't he. She's gone for good.'

'What, then? You're telling me you loved him?'

'I was *grateful* to him.'

'For what?'

'For the life he gave me.'

'What are you talking about? If you don't mean the money, what the hell *do* you mean? What was wrong with the life you *had*?'

Christie stood up. 'Look – we've already established the fact that I'm a cold bitch, not the girl you once knew. So you had a lucky escape when you snubbed me and took off on your travels, didn't you. Maybe I *did* marry Kenny for the lifestyle he could give me. Why not? People do. Let's just leave it at that, shall we?'

Dex stood up too. 'I didn't . . . look. Hold on. You're hiding something,' he said. 'What are you hiding?'

'Well, you're the detective. You should be able to wheedle it out of me,' said Christie.

'I will,' he said, and his eyes were flinty with purpose. 'Count on it.'

'Whatever,' said Christie, and shoved back her chair, out of the way.

'In the meantime, I'll be pulling in Mungo Boulaye for questioning,' he said as she turned and walked away.

'As I said – whatever,' Christie flung back over her shoulder. Then she paused. Turned.

'The missing hatpin,' she said.

'What about it?'

'It *was* used in the murder of Lara Millman somehow, wasn't it?'

Dex didn't answer.

'Yeah. Thought so,' she said, and left the bar.

85

But Dex wasn't about to let this go that easily. He followed her out to the reception area.

'Hold on,' he said, while the receptionist stopped thumbing through her magazine and watched them with interest. She was humming the Wet Wet Wet song from *Four Weddings and a Funeral*. Dex glanced at the girl, then said to Christie: 'Where's your room?'

'Down that corridor, right on the road. Traffic passing all night long. It's *fabulous*,' she said, not without sarcasm.

'Come on.'

*

'Was there something else you wanted to ask me?' said Christie when they were alone, in her room. 'Only, Dex, I have something I want to ask you.'

'Oh?' Dex was wandering around the shabby little box of a room, looking unimpressed. 'Go on then.'

'Why the police? When I knew you, you were hell-bent on a life of crime, weren't you? You were mates with my cousin Ivo and that Millican crowd of wasters.'

'Yeah, that's right.'

'So . . . why?'

Dex paused. Finally he said: 'Why? Because I loved my parents, I guess.'

'What does that mean?'

'I was going bad. It upset my parents, hurt them. I was their eldest child and they expected better. They were decent people and they were scared for me. It got close. *Bloody* close.'

'How close is that?' she asked, curious.

'You really want to know?'

'I'm asking.'

'You remember the Millicans then? Lonny and his little brother Ian, who used to hang around with Ivo at the Butler house?'

Christie wrinkled her nose. Yes, she remembered them. A pair of complete tossers, always headed for trouble. Just like she'd thought *Dex* was.

'They did a job. High-end motors. They were in the act of shipping them out to Saudi when customs caught them.'

'Right.'

'I was with them.'

'Oh Christ.'

'I was *right there.* I hid behind a container and I thought, *That's it, I'm done for.* Then one of the customs men came strolling past. He saw me. I must have looked as scared as I felt, because you know what? He just turned and walked away, as if he hadn't seen me at all. The Millican boys were charged, convicted and sent down and lucky for me they kept schtum, left me right out of it. After *that*, I thought I'd pressed my luck far enough. The irony was, of course, that I never hung around with any of those lads to keep in with them. It was always just to see you.'

Now Christie was pacing back and forth in front of Dex, arms folded over her middle.

'I loved your parents. And your brother and sister.'

'Dad passed two years ago,' said Dex.

Christie stopped pacing and stared at his face, startled. 'I'm so sorry,' she said. 'He was lovely.'

Dex shrugged. 'He was a great guy and he had a good life. What's to regret? He had a successful career and he found the woman he loved and married her. What could be better than that?'

'Still, you must miss him.'

'I had him for a lot of years,' said Dex. 'I was lucky and I'm grateful for that.'

He was grateful! There were echoes here of that long-ago boy she'd fallen in love with; that can-do positive attitude hadn't faded away. He still saw the good in life, not the negative.

'And your mum? How is Joyce?' she asked.

'She's fine.' He smiled. 'Scatty as ever. Still inclined to fall on her arse while dancing and laugh her head off about it.'

'I loved Joyce,' said Christie wistfully. 'After you . . . you know, had gone . . . she used to invite me over and feed me Florentines. She never talked about what you were up to, though. And I never asked.'

'I didn't know that. She didn't say. Florentines? Those things with nuts and chocolate? She still loves those. Tooth-busting little bastards.' He looked at the floor for long moments and then his gaze was fixed on Christie once again. 'Earlier, you said you didn't *think* you'd done it. What did that mean?'

'Nothing,' said Christie. She was pacing again.

'For God's sake. Come on.'

'No. I've really nothing more to say on the subject.'

'How can I help you if you refuse to open up?'

'I don't want to talk about it.'

'You have to.'

Christie stopped pacing and fastened her eyes on his face. 'All right. I get *episodes*, I suppose you'd call them. I don't sleep well. I dream. Rotten horrible dreams.'

'About what?'

About the crash. And other things. The drip, drip, drip of petrol or rain or some damned thing, and something else, some other sort of drip, something to do with hospitals.

She shrugged. Ivo crawled leering into her dreams sometimes. She couldn't tell Dex that. She was embarrassed to even *think* about that bastard and the disastrous effect he'd had on her life. Because of Ivo, she'd married Kenny. 'About the crash. The deaths of my parents. About that.'

'And so you don't sleep well.'

'And I . . . well, sometimes I get agitated in the night. Restless. And . . .' Her voice trailed away.

'And what?'

'Look – I sleepwalk. Sometimes.' She had never told anyone outside of the Butler family this before. It felt like revealing something shameful, awful. And dangerous, too. Dex was, after all, police.

Freak, she could hear Ivo whispering.

Moron, Jeanette would chip in.

You're a head case, Ivo would sneer before slipping halfnaked, horrible, into her bedroom.

She supposed she was. She walked in her sleep and didn't know what the hell she got up to while she was doing that. She'd wet the bed into her teens. And there was no way, literally no way at all, that she was going to tell Dex Cooper about that. She watched his face, waiting for the shock of her revelation to sink in, for him to start looking at her like she was a lunatic.

He didn't.

'So what I mean is, yes – I could have done it. Couldn't I?' she shot out. She walked up to him and glared up into his face. 'That hatpin was *mine*. I could have done it. Taken that and the petrol can out of the workshop. Driven over there. Set fire to her, to the cottage.'

'Is the petrol in that can at the same level as it was before Lara Millman's death? Would you know?'

Christie shook her head in frustration. 'There's no way of checking that. Patrick's been mowing the lawns with the ride-on, there's no way of knowing where the levels should be. Unless *he* checks the levels, which he must do to a certain extent I suppose, but we're talking big differences here if it was used to set fire to . . .' Christie's voice tailed away. She couldn't even say it.

Dex was frowning. 'OK. I'll check that with the gardener. What else?'

'Oh Christ,' moaned Christie.

'What? Go on. Say it.'

'The morning after Lara died I found my car out at the front of the house, the driver's door open, the key in the ignition, the engine running. Dex, for God's sake! This is what I mean! I could have done it.'

'Or someone could be setting you up,' he said.

Christie threw her hands up in the air. 'You want to believe that? Go ahead! But I'm beginning to think . . . I'm really afraid that I . . .' If she'd done that awful thing, how could she live with herself? 'And there's something else I have to tell you. There was a man at the house yesterday, pretending to be a BT engineer. He overloaded a socket in the upstairs office, and it caught fire when I was asleep. It was just luck I woke up. That's why I've moved out. I didn't feel safe in the house anymore.'

'Why didn't you call me?'

'I wanted to get away. I didn't think of doing that.'

'You think this was a deliberate attempt to kill you?'

'I do. Yes.'

'By who?'

'Maybe Kenny. He was in love with her. He really was.'

'Did you tell *anyone* where you were going, when you left the house?'

Christie shook her head. 'Only Patrick. The gardener.' She started to shake, remembering the fear, the feeling of being utterly alone and at risk.

'Christie.' Dex stepped forward, grabbed her arms, held her steady.

For a long moment they stood like that. Then Dex said: 'Fuck it, Christie, what happened? How did it all go so bloody wrong for us?'

'How can you ask me that? *You* dumped *me*, don't forget.'

'Why the hell do you keep saying that? That,' he said firmly, 'is *not* true.'

'Yes it is. Ivo came back and told me *you* said I was to piss off. That you weren't interested.'

'*What?*'

'He did. And then you went abroad . . .'

'Hold on! Ivo came to me and said much the same thing to me. That you weren't interested. So I backed away. You think he was being overprotective or something. Is that it?' asked Dex.

Or something . . .

'Probably,' she said, thinking that Ivo's interference in her relationship with Dex had been far from protective. Ivo had been keeping her for himself. It was as simple, as *disgusting*, as that.

86

Ever since they'd met again Dex had been keeping his guard up, frightened – yes, shit-scared – of that huge depth of feeling he'd once had for her. As scared as a high diver would be, at the prospect of leaping into a massive unknown pool of water.

He knew this was crazy. This was madness. But there was no way he could stop this whole thing unravelling. From the minute he'd seen her with Kenny trying to brain her, he'd wanted this. He'd wanted this for *years*. Yearned for her, lost her, somehow put the memory of her aside. Gone to the bad and then veered back to the good. Now he knew that every other woman – Tammy included – had been nothing but a sad and ineffective sticking plaster over the gaping wound that the loss of Christie had torn in his heart. And now? He was going to have this, no matter what.

He pulled her into his arms and suddenly he was kissing her. He was holding her so tight that he knew he must be hurting her, and he didn't even care.

'Bed . . . ?' he asked against her lips.

Whatever else might happen to her, to him, then they at least would have this, the thing they'd been cheated of.

★

Christie nodded. 'Yes. Bed,' she murmured, feeling almost frantic, *consumed* by lust, after that kiss. It was shocking – and wonderful – that he could still make her shake with desire after all the long, dry, awful years that had separated them, to realise that *nothing* had changed between them. That the long dark shadow cast by Ivo hadn't altered this, not in the least.

'Slowly,' said Dex, as Christie lifted her T-shirt, dragged it over her head, tossed it aside.

She smiled into his eyes, understanding. Having been denied this for so long, he wanted to savour it, draw the experience out until they were both fully satisfied.

'The jeans,' he suggested.

Christie kicked off her trainers, unbuttoned her Levi's and slid them down, slowly; then she kicked them aside.

'Nice,' said Dex, admiring the lemon-coloured pants and bra she wore.

He went to the bed, sat down, took off his boots and socks, his jacket, and put them aside, while watching her.

'The bra,' he suggested.

Christie felt breathless, racked with desire. This was wonderful – nothing like those early days with Kenny, nothing like the horrors Ivo had subjected her to. This was *Dex*.

With unsteady fingers she reached back, unhooked the bra, slipped it aside while shielding her breasts with one arm. Smiling, she dropped the bra to the floor.

'Teasing,' said Dex. 'I like that.'

'I can see you do,' said Christie, feeling herself moistening, becoming ready, as she saw the hard bulge of his arousal rise beneath his trousers.

'I am going to give you *such* a seeing-to in a minute,' Dex warned.

'I do hope so,' said Christie, and let her arm fall to her side, baring her breasts for him.

She saw the hard flash of sexual hunger in his eyes.

'You're beautiful,' he said, peeling off his shirt.

'So are you.' Christie stared at the well-defined muscles on his chest and arms as his hands went to his belt, unfastening, unzipping.

'Come here,' he ordered.

Christie drifted over to the bed and Dex grasped her hips, pulling her in between his thighs. Then his big hands were sliding over her skin, cupping her breasts, caressing her rock-hard nipples. Christie closed her eyes in ecstasy.

'I think these can go now,' he said, and she felt his hands smooth down over her belly, felt them ease down her panties, push them to the floor.

'Oh God,' she moaned and first his hands and then his tongue probed between her legs.

She grasped his head in her hands, holding him there, marvelling at the sensations he was causing to ripple through her body.

But all too soon he eased her back, away from him. Christie groaned in protest but then he was yanking off his trousers and boxer shorts and she saw his cock rearing eagerly up. She reached for it in wonder, smoothed her hands over it and then Dex, all control gone, grabbed her around the waist and tumbled her onto the bed, pushing her legs apart, needing to be inside her right now.

'Oh God,' she cried out as he pushed into her, filling her. 'Yes. Dex. Yes.'

She had never felt anything like this: a total surrender, an uncaring need. She'd had a long marriage to a man she didn't love and now miraculously Dex was back. She was here with the man she had always loved; he was touching her, loving her. The sheer shock of her orgasm was so extreme that she screamed and, in that same instant, Dex came too, pushing himself into her frantically, sweat welding their bodies together.

'I love you,' Christie heard herself murmur.

Oh shit, was that wise? Didn't you have to play coy with men, the way all women did? Wasn't that part of The Rules, that you held back, admitted nothing even if you were crazy for him?

Yes, that was how she should have played this.

But she couldn't. She did love him. She always had. And she'd said it, out loud.

He didn't say it back though. He moved back, away from her. She knew what he'd be thinking. She knew he'd be regretting this already. This would fog his judgement. Make him doubt himself. But she didn't regret it in the slightest. She had never felt anything so right. She curled in against him, running her hands over his broad chest, feeling safe, happy.

God alive! When had she last felt like that? When had she *ever*?

But he'd be off, away, any minute now. And – whatever his personal feelings – he would put her in jail if he had to. His honesty and doggedness wouldn't allow for anything but the truth. And then she would lose him all over again.

As quickly as joy had seized her, now misery set in and all at once she was crying. She had *never* really cried, not even as a tiny child after losing her parents. Four years old! It was monstrous, cruel.

'Hey! What is it?' Dex asked, smoothing her cheek, alarmed by this sudden unexpected storm of weeping.

Christie gulped but couldn't speak. She cried, the tears pouring out of her like rain.

She tried to regain control. 'It's . . . oh God, it's just that . . . oh, you know what? I thought that was *it* for me. That there would never be anything, ever again, after you left and I married Kenny.' She heaved in a sobbing breath, swiped at her eyes. 'I thought it would always be the same, just feeling *numb*, I suppose. Locked away. Does that make any sense?'

'Yeah. It does. Christie?' He kissed her brow, stroked her tears away. 'I think maybe I know something that could help.'

'Help what?' she asked.

'You,' he said.

87

'What do you mean?' she asked.

'When we split, all those years ago,' he said, cuddling her close.

'Hm?' She was only half-listening, still sunk deep in bliss.

Dex lifted her chin, looked into her eyes. 'I was in bits,' he said. 'I was frantic to forget you, to find some sort of direction in life. I started drinking too much. My parents were very worried. My brother and sister too. I'd come reeling home, drunk out of my mind.'

Christie was watching his face, listening intently now. She hadn't known any of this. If she had been shattered by their parting, now she was discovering that he had been too. And until now, until he had burst in on the disaster that had become her life, she hadn't had a clue.

'I'm sorry,' she said feebly.

'Then I got married to Tam but it didn't last. How could it? It was a school reunion that finally saved me. Of all things. David was an old mate and he had always been a bit "experimental", a bit off the wall, and when we were out drinking together, tearing up the town, he could see I was in trouble and he said if I cared to be a guinea pig and try something, he'd like to help. He liked the idea that hypnotherapy could dig out old bad things, clear them away, and he was working through his qualifications, reading great bloody tomes on the stuff, and looking for mugs to experiment on. Well, I was one of the mugs. He says this about psychotherapy now, about CBT – he's not a fan. He says you unearth all this stuff, but then what? It's left lying there, on the surface. Whereas with hypnotherapy, it's tidied away. Expunged, he says. Dumped, just like it should be, so you can carry on with a clean slate. And all that old stuff doesn't have the power to hurt you or even touch you anymore.'

'D'you suppose I'd ever get to that stage?' said Christie, doubtful. So much had happened to her. *Too* much.

'You will. I did. Although I was very sceptical. I thought it was just Dave and his wild ideas, but at that point when I was trying to drink myself to death to escape the reality that I'd lost you and that you'd gone off and married Kenny Doyle of all fucking people, I quit the drinking. Just stopped dead, after two sessions. I don't know who was more amazed: me or my family. Whereas before my brain had been a mess, suddenly it was calm and I could carry on with my life; I could forgive you for what you'd done to me and move on.'

'I hadn't done anything,' said Christie, appalled to hear all this, to know how the loss of her had wounded him.

'Yeah. I know that now.' Dex reached over, turned out the bedside light. 'Try and get some rest. You must be worn out.'

She was frightened of sleep now. Scared of the nightmares.

But somehow that night she did sleep, wrapped securely in Dex's arms – and she didn't dream. And in the morning, she told Dex she would try it; she would see David.

88

There was something odd going on. DS Smith was convinced of it. The boss was acting strangely. Smith had been a detective for quite a while and he had a nose for trouble. First he'd done five years at Hendon and then straight into uniform on the Met; then exams, lots of them, and he was – much to his gratification – drafted into CID, then *more* exams and he was a detective sergeant, first assigned to work with an old chap who was bitter and who – to his relief – quickly retired; then Smith was assigned to DI Cooper's team to work alongside DC Bill Jensen and DC Debbie Phelps. Smith was happy on the team, the cases were absorbing and mostly this boss was easy to work with.

But now? Suddenly Dex Cooper was like a bear with a sore arse, snapping and snarling at Smith and the others. Something was wrong – Smith knew it. He was, after all, a detective. Such things were instinctive. Still, he carried on with the job and with the assistance of Jensen and Phelps he was still industriously trawling his way through the intricate details of each and every attendee at Christie Doyle's birthday bash.

It got tedious, this sort of assignment. First you had to get all the personal details of whichever person you were focused on, then question them intensively. Did they see anything out of the ordinary, anything suspicious? Did they go upstairs in the house that day?

'Why would I do that?' said one after the other.

'Go to the loo?' Smith suggested.

'There's a loo downstairs.'

'If that was busy. Someone else in there?'

'It wasn't. I went in the cloakroom downstairs, then back out to the party.'

'Proper rogues' gallery,' said Debbie Phelps when they were back in the office, sifting through the backgrounds of what seemed to be half the criminal fraternity. 'He mixes with dubious people, this Kenny Doyle.'

'There was a loud rumour that he could have been one of those involved in Brink's-Mat,' said Bill Jensen.

'It was rumoured,' agreed Smith. 'Never proved. Slippery as an eel.'

'The catering woman's come up with something interesting though,' said Phelps. 'She didn't mention it the first time she was interviewed, didn't think it was important. She said it was her car the birthday girl borrowed.' She stood up, gathered up her shoulder bag. 'I'm off to have another word now.'

'Have fun,' said Smith, and then he was called out to the front of the station; someone had asked to see the officer in charge of the Millman investigation.

'He's out,' said Smith.

'You'll do,' said the duty sergeant, and Smith went down the corridor and out into reception – and there, waiting for him, was Kenny Doyle.

89

It was very disappointing when a plan didn't work out. *Very* annoying. Gustavo drove past the big valley house in his hire car, expecting the place to be incinerated, and what did he find? The place was intact. Not a mark on the building, nothing at all. The target's red car wasn't in the drive, in its usual spot. She was out, then. So she'd survived – again.

Really annoying.

All he could see, parked in the drive that led down the side of the house, was the gardener's van. He'd already noted the big turning circle at the bottom of the drive, right in front of the workshop beside the big oak-framed double car port.

He drove on past the house and parked the hire car a long way down the road, tucked out of sight by a huge hornbeam hedge. Then he walked back up to the house and down the drive.

*

Some people only cut their hedges once a year, but that, as far as Patrick could see, was folly. To keep the shape nice and retain the proper level of density, he favoured twice a year and it was this that he was preparing for now. One cut in spring, another in the autumn, and everything stayed beautifully neat, just the way he liked it.

He was sitting in the neatly fitted out workshop, the grinder
running loudly as he held the cutting blade against it, honing
it to perfect sharpness prior to starting work. The workshop
door was wide open, giving him a view out over the top lawn
and across to the pool, so when someone stepped into the
doorway, the light dipped and Patrick turned off the grinder,
anticipating Christie but instead, to his surprise, seeing this
man he was sure he'd seen before. Tallish, plain, bald. The
sort you'd pass on the street and not even notice. He realised
it was the BT engineer who'd called here before. And this
was worrying, because Christie had said, quite specifically,
that he wasn't to let anyone enter the house again, to clear it
with her first. And Christie wasn't here.

'Hello,' he said. 'Can I help? What's up? Phones again?'

'Yes, the phone,' said the man.

'Well, Mrs Doyle isn't here today, I'm afraid,' said Patrick.

'No matter. You have a key, yes? Just let me in and I'll sort
it out in no time.'

Patrick stood up. 'Sorry, mate, can't do that.'

The man smiled, his expression bemused. 'But why? You
let me in before, didn't you?'

'Mrs Doyle doesn't want me letting anyone else into the
house when she's not here.'

*

For Gustavo, this was not good news.

So the woman had survived the night and was now tightening up on security.

Irritating.

'No problem,' said Gustavo. 'Give me her number. I'll
contact her and then I can get on with my work.'

'I can't do that, either. Sorry, mate.'

Gustavo's smile lost its warm edge. 'Why is that? Where is she then? Attending some secret assignation? Only I have a job to do, and she did ask me to come out, to fix the fault.'

'Look, she's not here, all right?' He could see that the gardener was getting annoyed. 'I'm not going to go giving out her phone or her whereabouts either. She'll just have to rearrange an appointment, and the best thing you can do right now is tell your office that and the whole thing will have to be rescheduled. OK?'

Gustavo shrugged, help his hands up. 'Look. Come on. Just tell me where she is and I'll sort it out with her directly.'

'I told you. I can't do that.'

'But you can,' said Gustavo.

'No,' said Patrick.

'I really think you should.'

'Pal, you're starting to get on my bloody nerves. I told you, no.'

Gustavo stepped inside the workshop and pointedly closed the door.

'That's unfortunate,' he said, taking one of the pristine spanners down off the workshop wall. 'Because I am telling you *yes*.'

90

The wedding caterer *Ma Petit Choux* was, despite its fancy Gallic name, being run out of a strictly non-glamorous and rubbish-strewn trading estate in Clapham. When DC Debbie Phelps entered, she was confronted with a line of large steel tables and twenty women wearing hairnets and plastic gloves and white overalls, all of them diligently assembling mini sandwiches, tiny quiches, sausage rolls. A radio was playing and Manchester United Football Club were singing 'Come On, You Reds'. Several of the ladies were trilling along to the track, bumping and grinding at their work stations, smiles on their faces.

'This looks like a happy work environment,' Phelps commented to the middle-aged woman who left the table and joined her.

'I hope so,' she said, smiling.

'I'm DC Phelps,' said Debbie, showing her police ID. 'Mrs Rawnsley?'

'I'm she. Come on through to the office. We can talk there.'

Mrs Rawnsley led the way past the tables to the far end of the room. There a half-glassed office was tucked into a corner. The boss could see the workers from there, and the workers could see the boss. It might be a happy work environment, Debbie reflected, but Mrs Rawnsley's sharp eyes flicked often to the big room beyond, to make sure nobody was slacking.

'Must keep you busy. Weddings. Parties,' she said, sitting down.

'Certainly does. Can I get you a tea? Coffee?'

'No thanks, I'm fine.' Debbie dipped into her handbag, extracted pen and notebook. 'If we can run over what happened on the day of Mrs Doyle's fortieth? What time did you get there?'

'Nine o'clock, to get everything set up.'

'You and . . . ?'

'Me and my daughter Gemma; we generally do all the kitchen preparation on these occasions. And three waiting staff I usually hire in from an agency, they're very good. You need smart people, neat, discreet; they're not that easy to come by.'

Mrs Rawnsley gave her the name of the agency.

'Thank you.' Debbie paused. 'You said on the phone that Mrs Doyle asked to borrow your car next day.'

'That's right. Me and Gemma were packing up, clearing away.'

'But Mrs Doyle has her own car, am I right?'

'You are. That's why I phoned in. I thought it was odd.'

'And how was she, when she asked to borrow your car?'

'Strange. Sort of wound up. She snapped at me.' Mrs Rawnsley smiled. 'I'm used to being snapped at. Around weddings and other special occasions, everyone's on hyperdrive. Tempers can fray.'

'So you gave her the keys to your car.'

'I didn't see any harm in it.'

'No, of course not. You've heard about the fire in the next village. The death of Miss Lara Millman in the blaze.'

'Everyone has. It's been on the news. It's awful.'

'Have you anything else you think you should tell me, Mrs Rawnsley?' asked Debbie.

'No. I think that's all.' Mrs Rawnsley's eagle eye had spotted two of the workers not working at all. She stood up, rapped at the glass. They jumped like spooked deer and got back to work.

'Never employ anybody,' Mrs Rawnsley advised Debbie with a weary glint in her eye. 'You've got to watch them like a hawk, all the time, or they skive off and take the piss.'

'I'll bear that in mind,' said Debbie, thinking of something her own boss had said to her just this morning. 'Did you see anyone go upstairs on the day of Mrs Doyle's party?' she asked. 'From the kitchen in the house, there's a glass door, isn't there? From inside the kitchen, I believe you could see the hallway, the staircase?'

'Yes that's right. I could.'

'So . . . ?' prompted Debbie.

'I don't think . . .' Mrs Rawnsley pondered. 'No, I don't think . . . well, there was something. I saw a couple go upstairs together.'

'Did you know them?'

Mrs Rawnsley gave Debbie an old-fashioned look. 'I didn't know anyone there, apart from Mrs Doyle herself, and Mr Doyle because he booked us to cover the event.'

'So what did this couple look like?'

'Um. Well he was tall. I mean, *really* tall. Dark-haired. And she was tiny. Red hair. Pretty.'

'And their ages?'

'Oh, around thirty-five, forty, I should say.'

'Were they up there long?'

'Long enough to do the deed, I imagine. I saw them come back down. Half an hour.'

'You think they'd had sex?'

'They looked flushed. Yes, I think they had. And good luck to them. They were certainly having more fun than I was.'

'Meaning?'

The woman shrugged. 'It was just a bit awkward on the day. Something going on with the birthday girl and the hubby. Bad atmosphere.'

'Is your daughter here today, Mrs Rawnsley? Did she see this couple too?'

'No, she's not here today; she's at home with a bad cold. But yes, she saw them go up and come back down too. We had a bit of a giggle about it.'

'She lives with you?'

Mrs Rawnsley nodded.

'And your home address is?'

Mrs Rawnsley gave it.

'Did the two of you see anyone else go up there?'

'No.'

Debbie put her pen and notebook away. 'I'll be calling on your daughter today, if you can let her know to expect me . . . ?'

'Yes. Sure. Although she's not very well. If this could . . . ?'

'It can't wait, Mrs Rawnsley. This is a murder inquiry.'

'Yes. Of course.'

Debbie drove back to the station and bumped into DI Cooper at the front desk. She told him about her interview with Mrs Rawnsley, about her intention to get back out there and see the lady's daughter, Gemma, who was at home nursing a cold now she had returned from her holiday.

'Good,' said Dex, who was intent on his next job: checking out Lara Millman's personal effects, paperwork, bank statements. He was – very carefully – *not* thinking about having made love to Christie, *not* thinking about the way she'd cried and said she loved him.

'Oh, and the caterer and her daughter saw someone go upstairs on the day.' She repeated the description of the couple Mrs Rawnsley had provided to her. Very tall man, dark hair. Little redhead. 'They were up there for about half an hour. Having sex, she supposed. Came downstairs giggling.'

'Very tall? How tall?'

'Six-seven.'

'Ages?'

'Thirty-five to forty, both of them.'

'That's interesting.'

'In what way, sir?'

'I think I know who matches those descriptions.'

'Really?'

'That's Mungo Boulaye and his missus.'

91

Dex was on his way along the corridor to his office when Smith met him.

'Kenny Doyle's been in,' he said.

'Oh?'

'Making a complaint.'

'About what?'

'About you knowing his wife from years back. About, apparently, you always having a soft spot for her. Being *sweet* on her, was how he quaintly described it. And he said that meant you had a clear conflict of interest and ought to be yanked off the case.'

'Right.'

'I've told the super.'

'OK.'

'He wants to see you.'

★

The super was a tall, thin, suntanned man of fifty with eyes as sharp as a shit-house rat's. He watched Dex come into his office and sit down. The super was clicking his ballpoint pen – open, shut, open, shut.

'The Millman murder,' said the super. 'Kenny Doyle's filed a complaint about you handling it. Do you know his wife, Christie Doyle?'

Lie or truth?

But Dex's hesitation was all the super needed. 'I'm pulling you off this then. Handing it over to Turnbull's team. They should have been on it by rights from the start anyway. And we're nine days into Rainbow and the press are sniffing around. That's too bloody slow.'

'Not yet,' said Dex quickly.

'When, then, do you suggest?' asked the super blandly. 'When it's all blown up in our faces and we can't get a damned thing past the CPS, can't make a fucking thing stand up in court? Get real for God's sake.'

Dex thought of Lara Millman's stuff, which was still being sifted through, thought of the Sputnik with the missing hat-pin, guests still being worked on.

'Give me another week,' he said.

The ballpoint clicked faster: in, out, in, out.

'You're fucking kidding me.'

'Just one.'

The super was silent. He threw the pen down on the desk.

'One week. That's all.'

'Nope,' said the super.

'The team's getting there,' said Dex. 'Turnbull's lot would have to start from scratch. 'Seven more days. That's all.'

The Super let out a gust of air. Threw down the pen.

'All right then. And don't for fuck's sake give me cause to regret it.'

92

Christie left her car at the hotel and Dex drove her over to the valley house to pick up some clean clothes, winding his way through the quiet country lanes, bypassing cyclists and horse riders with practised ease and consideration, while Christie sat there in the passenger seat and had to mentally pinch herself every couple of minutes because she could still hardly believe he was there.

All the time, she was transported back to those miserable days after she'd lost him, to Harry Nilsson on the radio singing 'Without You' while she sat miserable, bereft. But now he was here! And he wanted to help her. She could see that. But also – she could see that he would do his duty if he absolutely had to. If she truly was guilty of Lara Millman's death, he would put his own feelings aside and would not flinch from doing whatever he had to do. She knew that.

'What the hell?' Dex said as they drew nearer to the house.

Blocking the road ahead were two fire engines, firemen unravelling hoses, barking out orders, running. Christie sat up straighter. Above the high roofline of the house she could see smoke rising. Dex parked the car, switched off the engine and was gone, hurrying toward the firemen. Christie followed more slowly, full of dread. Reaching the entrance to the driveway, she stared down the long stretch of Tarmac that led to the workshop and double car port, which was where the smoke was coming from. Firemen were haring down there, past Patrick's van. Meanwhile up on the road there stood a fiftyish woman with a weather-beaten face and a cap of steel-grey hair, holding tight to the leads of two fat golden retrievers.

'I saw the smoke coming up from down there while I was walking past,' she was telling the fire chief. 'And then there was this noise, this awful *boom*. And I could see flames coming up.'

Christie stood rooted to the spot. 'Patrick must be down there,' she said to Dex, and the panic that filled her then was overwhelming. She started forward, heading down the driveway.

Dex kept a firm grip on her arm. 'No. It's not safe. Stay here.' He showed the fire chief his ID. 'When did you get the shout?'

'About half an hour ago, from this lady here.'

The hoses were filling, roaring into life.

'I can't,' Christie said to Dex. 'What if he's hurt?'

'They'll handle it. Just wait.'

The smoke was getting denser, steam rising as the hoses were deployed. They could just see the edge of the worktop from the top of the drive, could see the firemen playing the gushing water over and over the burning building.

If he was inside when that caught fire, then he's dead, thought Christie in anguish.

Dex was talking to the woman with the dogs now, but Christie hardly heard a word. It felt like hours but it was only minutes before the chief said to Dex: 'All out.'

The firemen were coming back up the long slope of the drive, winding up the hoses. The chief went down and met them halfway. They spoke, then the chief looked back over his shoulder and beckoned to Dex, who turned to Christie.

'This lady's upset,' he said. 'Take her inside, will you? I'm going to talk to the chief.'

Christie didn't point out that the woman looked far from upset – in fact, she looked as if this was the most excitement she'd had in years. But the dogs lumbered to their feet and Christie ushered the woman and her pets indoors. Made small talk, somehow. Made tea. But really she just waited, sick with anxiety, until Dex came to the side door. She let the woman and her dogs out as he came in.

'Well?' she asked. 'Did you see Patrick?'

'Sit down, Christie,' said Dex.

And then she knew it was bad.

She almost collapsed onto the sofa. 'He was in there?' she said, dry-mouthed, horrified.

'I'm sorry.'

Blue lights were flashing outside. Through the hall window she could see police cars pulling up. A large dark-blue van too. Dex raised his head when he saw that. It would be the pathologist, she guessed. Here to take the body away.

'Oh Jesus,' Christie moaned. Patrick had been a friend, a helper. He'd been here for years. And he'd saved her life, stopped her putting a hand in the pool water and suffering the same fate as the fox. 'Oh no. God no.

'Well, no one can say you started *this* fire,' said Dex on a sigh. 'You were with me. And there goes any chance of checking the fuel levels in the can. That explosion? That was the petrol going up, I guess.'

Someone was knocking on the front door.

'I'll get it,' said Dex.

Christie put her head in her hands.

Patrick, dead?

She couldn't believe it.

93

It had been happening lately, and it was entirely regrettable. Gustavo knew that it was a fault, a funny little glitch. In his youth, he had *never* lost his temper. He had been cool – all right, cold. He could acknowledge that. Always in control. But nowadays, well, things happened. *Unfortunate* things. He was a very focused person, *completely* focused, and when someone – anyone – put an obstacle in the path of him achieving a goal, he could sometimes, these days, well, not to put too fine a point on it, he could *lose* it.

He wasn't comfortable with that, of course. He disliked lack of detail in anyone else and always strived for personal perfection in every task. Maybe his age? Maybe his patience had finally worn thin, and then bad things could happen. Not his fault, really. Just a glitch.

So he went back to his hotel, wearing the thick overcoat he had carried in the boot of the hire car, to cover the blood-stains from any prying eyes when he passed through reception. The rest of it, the tool he'd used, the damage, well, all that would be covered by the fire to a certain extent. Not covered enough to fool the police though, and he regretted that.

'Having a good day, Mr Taylor?' asked the receptionist, smiling her practised smile.

'Wonderful. Thank you,' replied Gustavo Cota, and smiled back, and then he went up to his room, stripped off the coat and removed every stitch of clothing underneath it. He stepped into the shower and washed the blood away and tried to forget about the glitch that had made him lose his temper, but it was hard. His mind always went back to his uncaring parents when he thought of the glitch, and sometimes he thought, *Am I normal?*

Well, there was only one possible answer to that: no.

He was, he supposed, a psychopath.

He'd killed both his parents, after all, when he was twelve years old. Covered his tracks too, very neatly. And decided then and there that this could be his profession. But now? Ah, the glitch. The fault that was not in his stars but in his bloody *head*.

He got out of the shower, packed all the clothes he'd been wearing into a hotel laundry bag and stuffed that into his suitcase. He took out fresh clothes, fresh underwear, and began to feel a little better about everything.

He'd order a nice room service meal and chill out. Forget the glitch. Forget the screams too? Oh, he could live with those. Actually, he rather liked them. And the day hadn't been entirely bad. After all, he'd got the target's whereabouts from the man in the workshop.

94

Having driven Christie back to her hotel, Dex went on over to Mungo's club, flashing his ID at the doorman and swiftly being admitted. It was getting late. Club House was roaring out of the sound system as he followed the doorman's vast bulk through to the back office.

Mungo was there. He rose from behind his desk and seemed to keep going up and up; he was a real tall guy, easily six feet seven inches but not with that crane-like skinniness such very tall men often displayed. Mungo was bulky, strong. A cap of densely packed black curls clung to his enormous head and his eyes were a deep, dense brown. All his features were exaggeratedly large – big wide-apart eyes, big hook nose, cushiony lips. He was elegantly dressed in a white silk shirt, black cord jacket and neatly pressed grey trousers.

Dex showed the ID again and Mungo indicated a chair and sat back down while the doorman exited, closing the door behind him and dropping the sound level down by twenty decibels.

'How can I help, officer?' asked Mungo cordially. His voice was booming and seemed to come from somewhere deep in his boots.

'The day of Mrs Christie Doyle's birthday party,' said Dex. 'You were seen going upstairs with a woman.'

Mungo sat back, his eyes fixed to Dex's face. 'So?'

'Who was the woman?'

'My wife. If it's any of the police's business.'

'Does she know about your relationship with Lara Millman? The woman who was the victim of a fire – you remember her? She used to work as a dancer here?'

Mungo stiffened. 'I don't know what you mean.'

Dex tossed the photo Christie had given him onto the desk. There they were at the cottage door – Mungo and Lara Millman, looking very cosy. Mungo looked at it, then up at Dex.

'It was nothing,' said Mungo.

'It doesn't look like nothing,' said Dex. 'But then, you still seem on good terms with your wife too, don't you. Does *she* know about this?'

Mungo tensed. 'All right. She doesn't. And now Lara's gone? There's no reason why she should. And I don't want this going any further. I don't want *this*—' he poked the print with a fingernail '—getting into the wrong hands.'

Dex read it then: the flicker of unease in Mungo's face. Like everyone else, he was wary of crossing Kenny Doyle. Mate or no, he feared him.

'What, like into the hands of Kenny Doyle? Is that what you mean? Yeah, I can see you'd want it kept dark. After all, Kenny was having a serious affair with this girl, who was incidentally expecting his baby. He was serious enough about her to tell his wife on the day of her fortieth that he was divorcing her. Or – I wonder – *was* it his baby at all? It could have been the boy next door's, poor dopey little Andy Paskins. He was pretty cut up about her death. Or – how about this? – it could have been yours.'

'Now just hold on . . .'

'What were you and your wife doing upstairs in the Doyle household?'

'Patsy was showing me the view from upstairs. She often went over there to see Christie. They're old mates from way back. It's a helluva house. Sensational view.'

'Is that all?'

'What else?'

'You didn't *take* anything from upstairs?'

'What? Kenny's my mate. That's his house. I don't pinch off my friends.'

'How about Patsy?'

'No.'

'You don't think she knew about you and Lara Millman?'

'No. I was careful. It was a *fling*, all right? Just a few weeks of humping. She was handing it to me on a plate; I wasn't about to refuse. I hate to speak ill of the dead, but she was a tart, you know. A real little one-nighter.'

'You weren't careful enough, because Andy Paskins took this photo of you together. Would you object to me seeing the club's accounts, Mr Boulaye?'

'What? No. Of course not. Why would I? Patsy takes care of all that, not me.' He fidgeted anxiously. 'Listen. Me and Lara, it's *well* over now.'

'It certainly is. She's dead. No prospect of her causing you any trouble, is there?'

'Hey! I don't like your bloody tone. What are you suggesting?'

Dex put the print back in his pocket. 'And your wife is where, tonight?'

'At home.' Mungo told him the address. Then he looked shifty. 'She doesn't have to know about Lara, does she?'

'Maybe she already does,' said Dex, and after Mungo had given him the past year's accounts he left the club with Mungo's shocked face still imprinted on his brain.

Dex was getting into the car when his phone rang. 'Yes?' he snapped. He wanted to get the Patsy interview over and check back in with Christie.

It was Paulette, the pathologist. 'Dex?'

'Yep?'

'Come over, can you?'

95

The Lysol-scented city morgue was quiet late in the evening; Paulette was there, gowned, masked, bending over the big channelled steel table that was essentially her work desk. She looked up as Dex entered.

'Something?' he asked, coming closer. Not too close though. She had yet another horror laid out in front of her: another burned cadaver. Ridiculous that he could still feel nausea and pity after all these years, all that he'd seen. But the burned ones were the worst: twisted, agonised. He hated seeing the burned ones. They turned his stomach.

'Something, certainly. Look here.'

He went to the table and looked down. There was little to suggest that the scorched thing lying there was in any way human, but he very definitely was. This was Patrick, Christie's gardener. The poor bastard that Dex himself had 'leaned on' just yesterday, to get Christie's whereabouts out of him.

'Look here.' Paulette's gloved hands held a scalpel, and she used this to indicate the point of interest. 'Left arm, see this? There's a break in the humerus. And here. Right arm. Radius broken. Very clean break.'

'Right,' said Dex.

'And here too.' Paulette moved down the table. Using the scalpel as a pointer, she leaned over the corpse's legs. 'Here we go. Left leg, tibia's broken. Fibula still intact. Right leg, same again. Broken tibia, fibula sound.'

'Meaning . . . ?'

'These breaks are commensurate with heavy blows, probably from a metal instrument. A hefty one. Something like a wrench? Or a large hammer? The instrument that was used to inflict these breaks is probably one of the tools that were to hand there. I say probably. Maybe this poor man's attacker could have brought the tool along with the intention of using it to torture him. There's no doubt that he *was* tortured, prior to death. And why would his attacker do that?'

'To get information,' said Dex.

'Yes.'

Information about what?

But he knew. It had to be Christie's whereabouts.

Apart from himself, who else had known where Christie was? Only Patrick the gardener. The one she trusted, left notes for, confided in.

'It was a violent assault,' said Paulette, shaking her head, her dark eyes serious over the blue top of her mask. 'Deliberate and prolonged. And then I would guess the perpetrator set the fire to destroy any evidence. Nasty, Dex. Really nasty.'

96

It was gone eleven and Christie had just got out of the shower and was about to turn in for the night in her shabby little hotel room when she heard her phone ringing on the little desk by the window. She dragged one of the big scratchy bath sheets around herself and hurried out there and snatched it up.

'Christie?'

It was Dex's voice. He sounded *tense*.

'Yeah? What is it?'

'You at the hotel?' he asked quickly.

'Yeah. Just going to see if I can get some sleep. But after today, I don't know. I don't think I will.'

'Don't go to bed,' said Dex.

'What?'

'Don't do that. Just get out.'

'*What?* I'm standing here nearly naked.'

'Never mind. Do it.'

Hearing the urgency in his voice, Christie dropped the towel and snatched up her jeans and T-shirt, struggling into them one-handed, her damp skin resisting, the phone an encumbrance. That accomplished, she scuffed her feet into her trainers. 'I was in the shower . . .'

'Just get dressed and get out of there.'

'What, just get in my car and . . .'

'Don't get in the car. People know that's your car and it might already be booby-trapped in some way.'

Christie stared at the phone, horrified.

'Get dressed and get out, go to the nearest busy place and stay there and I'll come, OK?' said Dex.

'Dex! Nowhere's busy right now – it's nearly midnight.'

'Is there a nightclub near there?'

'I don't think so. I don't know this area too well. There's a store on the corner, that stays open all night I think.'

'I remember that. Go there. Stay there.'

'OK. If you say so. Why . . . ?' Her mouth was dry with fear, her heart thwacking hard against her chest wall.

'Don't ask questions. Do it. I think your gardener told whoever attacked him exactly where you are. Just get out, quick.'

Christie felt her stomach twist into knots. 'Patrick wouldn't do that,' she protested.

'Patrick didn't have a choice. It was beaten out of him. Now for fuck's sake, stop with the questions. Get out of there.'

What? 'OK, I . . .'

The lights went out.

97

'Christie?' said Dex when she stopped speaking. 'You OK?'

'The lights,' said Christie with a gulp, 'they've gone out.'

'Get out of there,' said Dex. 'Just *go*.'

He hung up.

Christie listened to the dial tone. She was blinking, trying to get her eyes accustomed to the semi-dark in the room. Not too sure of her surroundings, she blundered over to the window, barking her shins on a small table, but she barely felt the pain. She yanked back the curtains she had closed earlier in the evening before eating or at least *trying* to eat her meagre and badly cooked room service meal: a scorched steak and a jacket potato. The steak had done for her. She'd left most of it and retched her heart up in the bathroom afterwards, thinking of Patrick dying, which still didn't seem possible.

She'd always hated change. Loathed it. But now, in the space of a week, everything she had known as normal and good and *settled* had been thrown into complete disarray. And Patrick's awful death was the final straw. And now – what was Dex saying? Someone had *killed* Patrick, and before that they'd beaten her whereabouts out of him?

Shaking, nearly gagging with terror, she stared out of the window.

There were street lights out there. Some traffic passing. Not much.

In here, in the hotel, there didn't seem to be any movement at all. The place was awful; it was no surprise really. Many of the rooms seemed to be unoccupied. She stood there, undecided. And then she heard movement, across the room.

She couldn't place it, at first.

And then she knew.

Someone was trying to open the door.

98

If someone was at the door, then her way out was barred. And who was it? Maybe a hotel staff member, announcing that the sudden power outage was going to be fixed shortly? But if that was the case, why hadn't they called out, tapped on the door? The movements sounded *stealthy*.

What was it Dex had told her?

Someone beat her whereabouts out of Patrick.

Her heart in her mouth, Christie was suddenly galvanised into action. If the doorway was blocked, it was the street-level window, or nothing. With trembling fingers she fumbled around the window frame. She hadn't noticed, when she'd drawn the curtains earlier, exactly where the catch was.

Oh God, what if it doesn't open? What if it's locked?

The noises behind her went on. Furtive. Stealthy. Did he – whoever *he* was – have a master key, snatched from reception along with the number of her room?

Her stumbling fingers found the window catch. She tried to turn it.

It wouldn't turn.

Behind her, the noises were growing louder.

The damned catch was painted shut. Or locked. There in the semi-darkness, her heartbeat thrumming through her head, almost deafening her, she couldn't tell which. It just *wouldn't open*.

Then the noises stopped.

Christie froze, her eyes locked onto the door now. Was that handle turning? She thought it was. Or maybe she was imagining it. She couldn't really see. Her eyes were playing tricks on her. She stumbled a couple of steps back, came up against the solid little oak table that she'd bumped into once before.

The door was starting to open. She wasn't imagining it. She knew she wasn't. She could see a tiny pencil-thin strip of light coming in from the hallway outside.

She snatched up the table and flung it at the window. The noise it made when it hit was huge, shocking. The glass held. Not daring to look behind her, she scrabbled for the table again and this time smashed it harder still into the window, as hard as she could, nearly sobbing with effort.

The window shattered.

The strip of light at the door was wide now and growing wider. And she could hear footsteps. Uncaring, desperate, she felt a hand touch her back and launched herself out of the window and hit the pavement outside hard, dragging shards of glass with her, the jagged frame catching on her jeans, tugging at her T-shirt.

As she hit the pavement she staggered to her feet and started to run, gasping, shuddering.

Did she hear footsteps behind her? She thought she did. But she couldn't really hear a thing past the frantic beating of her own heart. She ran like she had never run before. She had wings; she was flying along past the small – closed and in darkness – parade of shops. Cars were passing. Should she stop, try to flag one down? But she didn't think she'd dare stop long enough to do that.

When she reached the vividly lit all-night shop on the corner, she crashed through the door, sending the bell above it jingling. A middle-aged man was behind an elevated counter, staring at her. The freezer cabinets hummed. Shelves were stacked high with brightly coloured crisps, biscuits, packets of pasta, soft drinks. Everything looked *normal*.

But nothing about this situation was that.

'Help!' she gasped out. 'Someone's following me.'

Christie looked out of the big windows at the front of the shop. She couldn't see anyone. Not yet. But he'd be out there. Probably it was the fake BT engineer. The one who'd killed Patrick. The one who was now intent, according to Dex, on killing *her*.

The man behind the till didn't look too interested. 'Who?' he asked. 'Husband? Father?'

If she said yes to either of those, he might even approve of her pursuer. She couldn't be sure.

'Do you have a room where I can hide? A stockroom?' she asked.

'No,' he said.

Christie's eyes stole back to the front of the shop, to the dark pavement outside. In here, all was brilliant light and normality. Out there, a killer was stalking her. And if he came past those windows and saw her standing here talking to this unhelpful man behind the till, he might just come straight in and God knew what would happen then.

'I need to hide. You've not seen me, OK?' Christie panted out.

The man was going to say no again, that he wouldn't collude with her, wouldn't lie. She could see it in his face. Desperately, with shaking fingers, she reached into her jeans pocket and pulled out a wad of fivers.

'I'll pay,' she said.

He hesitated – then reached down and snatched the money. Then he nodded to the far end of the shop and started walking that way. Quickly, Christie followed. He came down a small set of steps, led her to a door, leaned in, switched on a faint yellow-tinged light. Christie stepped through into a tiny room stacked high with cardboard boxes. There was a chair, and a kettle on the floor with some teabags and two tin mugs. Through another half-open door she could see a sink and a foul-smelling toilet.

'More,' said the man, and held out a hand.

Christie handed over the last of the fivers. The man, seemingly satisfied, went back out into the shop and closed the door behind him.

He's got the money and now he'll say I'm back here, she thought.

There was nothing she could do about that. Aware that she was trembling all over, Christie ran her hands over her face, tried to calm herself. She had the feeling, overwhelmingly powerful, that she had cheated death back there in the hotel room, and that the Grim Reaper was still out to get her; that she wasn't out of trouble.

Instead of settling on the seat among the boxes, she went into the filthy toilet, closed the lid on the brown-stained bowl and sat down there, pushing the door closed behind her.

There was a lock on it. A tiny bolt. Ineffective, probably, against a determined assault, but she flicked it closed anyway.

She sat there and waited.

She was either going to die, or Dex was going to arrive.

She wasn't sure which.

She sat there and debated her fate. She'd had the living shit kicked out of her, one way or another. Losing her mum and dad. Ivo, giving her nothing but abuse, raping her, lying to her about Dex, scaring her into a dead, hopeless marriage to a man who now hated her. But she clenched her teeth and *willed* herself to stay strong, to survive, to get through this.

She *had* to.

99

Ten minutes later, there was a knock on the door and Dex's voice said: 'Christie?'

Christie stood up on unsteady legs, shot back the bolt, opened the door. She had never, in her entire life, been so glad to see anyone as she was right then to see him.

'You all right?' he asked, his face concerned.

Christie took a gulping breath. 'The lights went out in the hotel and then someone was coming into my room. I smashed the window and got out. The shopkeeper let me hide in here.'

Dex nodded. 'Good.'

Christie thought that it wasn't so good, not really. She knew damned well that if she hadn't paid a large amount of money over, the shopkeeper would have happily hung her out to dry.

'Can we get out of here?' she asked, shuddering.

'Sure. Come on.'

★

Dex took her back to his apartment and left her there.

'Help yourself to anything you need,' he said, and then he was gone.

Christie sat down on his big dark brown couch and looked around the apartment. Minimalistic didn't quite cover it. There were bare boards, white walls, no photos, no pictures. Boxes stacked everywhere. She wandered through to the bedroom. Same there. An overwhelming feeling of a man always on the move, unsettled. A king-sized bed covered with a cigar-brown throw and not much else.

God, they really were opposites. She thought of her own magpie habits, her random collections of this and that, and how it would contrast with this. *Not very well* was her conclusion.

She felt she badly needed a shower after her stint in the corner shop toilet, but looking at the massive cubicle in Dex's bathroom, she wasn't entirely sure she could even turn the thing on. And besides, she felt shaky. She really didn't feel like she wanted to be alone, in a shower, in a strange place, in the early hours of the morning. So she stayed there on the couch and was almost dozing when she heard Dex's key in the door. Then she shot to her feet, panicking, wondering if it was going to be Dex at all.

But it was.

He came in, closed the door, locked it. He looked at her standing there and then Christie ran across the room and flung herself at him. He held on to her tightly, smoothed her hair, kissed her neck.

'It's OK, it's all right,' he murmured, over and over against her trembling flesh. 'I've been back to the hotel. The night porter said a fuse had flipped in the cellar. I asked if anyone had been in reception looking at the list of guests.'

'And?' asked Christie, cuddling into him, absorbing his heat, his strength.

'He said someone had come in asking for a room just before midnight, shortly before the lights went out. A bald man. Very plain. He said he couldn't really describe him. No luggage. The night porter said this man was peering at the guest list and somehow he didn't like the look of him. By the way, the night porter is pretty pissed off that you broke a window.'

Christie let out a ragged laugh. 'I had to. Someone was coming in the door.'

'Christ,' said Dex.

'I'm all right,' said Christie, as if *he* was the one needing reassurance, not her. She reached up and kissed him on the lips.

Dex's arms tightened around her and the kiss deepened.

'Come on, let's . . .' said Christie, and led the way. She was sweaty and, now that shock was setting in, she was really shivering.

'What do you think of this place?' asked Dex.

'It's hideous.'

'I only moved in a fortnight ago,' said Dex, turning on the shower then flinging his clothes off.

'That explains the lack of décor I suppose,' said Christie. She was still shaking with reaction, a core-deep shuddering that she couldn't seem to overcome. But then – she *had* overcome, tonight, she reminded herself. Once again, she'd survived. And she was here, with Dex.

He flashed her that quick, cavalier grin. 'Come on then. Hurry up and get naked.'

*

Later, in bed, Dex said: 'I talked to Dave.'

'Oh?'

'Usually it's six sessions and that would take six weeks. But because of the circumstances, he's going to do the whole thing faster. If you're agreeable.'

'Oh.' Christie felt apprehensive about that. And she still suspected that the whole thing would be a waste of time.

'It can be difficult,' he said. 'Stressful.'

She didn't even believe it would work, so that didn't trouble her.

'You start tomorrow,' he said. 'It's all arranged.'

'All right,' she said wearily. It was all hokum, all nonsense.

Much later, wrapped in Dex's arms, she slept.

100

Kenny had to admit to himself that yes, OK, he'd been just a little hasty. He was sitting in Mungo's night club, topless pole dancers twirling in bored indifference above him – remembering *her*, Lara, how beautiful, how daring, how scandalous she had been. He was drinking a Scotch. The TV over the bar was on, showing repeats of this and that, and he was taking absolutely no notice of any of it until the news came on and there were pictures of a house. Jesus! *His* house, smoke rising from the workshop at the bottom of *his* driveway.

What he'd been thinking, before that reporter started talking about someone having died in a fire in *his* workshop, on *his* premises, was that yes, he had indeed been hasty. Actually, what he thought was that he had been half out of his mind with grief. He thought again of Lara and tears filled his eyes. They would have been so happy together, them and the baby.

Now, all that was gone.

But – yes – he had overreacted.

He'd attacked Christie. He wasn't too sorry about that, not really; actually he thought she'd deserved a good clump in the jaw, for all the miserable years he'd wasted with her, all the lies she'd prattled off in the register office all that time ago, swearing to love and honour, all that shit. She'd done *none* of that.

Oh, she'd devoted a lot of time and effort into making a grand home – *three* grand homes – for them both. But he could see now that she'd been interested in just that one place in the valley: that home, *her* home, not in him, never in him. It should have been a *family* home. Fat chance of *that* with her, the cold cow.

He now knew, with the clarity of a few days' grace, that he should never have pleaded with Cole Mason for the details of a hired assassin. That he should never have let Cole go ahead and contact Primo Ecco across the pond, should never have taken on Gustavo Cota, should have *cooled down*. He'd phoned the Langham, hoping Gustavo might still be there, and he'd talk to him. He'd be reasonable. He'd just call the whole thing off because the truth, the absolute bitter truth, was that he'd gone completely over the top. There was no calling Lara – or his child – back from the dead. And what had hiring a hitman achieved, except to call attention to Kenny himself?

Make it look like an accident, he'd said. *An accident, or even suicide.* What he had *not* said was, fuck up royally and in doing so, call unwanted attention to the aggrieved husband: to Kenny Doyle.

No, it was all getting too bloody complex. He knew he had to call off Gustavo before the twat did some irreparable damage to Kenny's nearly flawless reputation as a wide boy who was far too clever to ever be caught again and banged up at HM's pleasure.

Kenny didn't fancy doing a long stretch for setting Gustavo on Christie. Kenny liked high living too much, and in the nick you couldn't do that. But he couldn't get hold of Gustavo and in truth – and this surprised even Kenny himself – in *truth*, he was finding Gustavo creepy. Damned sinister. Downright bloody scary, in fact. When you looked into those blank grey eyes of his you just knew that the bastard would kill you with as much compunction as he would squash an ant.

The thing was, Kenny did have contacts on the other side of the pond. *Mafia* contacts. He was in tight with them ever since he had signed on with Mason's crew. He had the plum jobs from them. He looked after their security when they came over for a visit, which they frequently did. He wasn't scared of them. Well, not much. Not really. So having failed to call off Gustavo in person, he now decided that he would go straight to the top. You cut off the head and the job was done, right? So he would contact Primo in New York and let *him* call off that mad bastard. He went into Mungo's office and placed the call to New York; sent out a plea for assistance. Gustavo was in the don's pocket. This was *obviously* the right thing to do.

'Bastard's running amok,' Kenny told Primo when the don finally came on the line.

'Mr Doyle,' said Primo. 'What can I do? And how is your charming wife? Christie, yes? I enjoyed meeting her the last time we came over to your beautiful country, Dora and I. *Such* a lovely woman.'

'Yeah. Yeah.' Was Primo not listening? 'But this Cota geezer, he's off the wall, do you see? I wanted a nice neat job doing, and what do I find? He's overdoing it. Putting me in the frame. Acting like he's holding all the cards. "Don't contact me, I'll contact you," he says, and I'm supposed to be content with that when the fuckwit's causing chaos? I just saw my home on fire, on the bloody news. You believe that? Well I say fuck *him*. I'm not happy, Primo. I mean Mr Ecco. Sir. Not at all.'

Primo listened to all this and then said: 'Mr Doyle. I have thought of you in the past as a reasonable man, but perhaps I have been mistaken? Listen: you don't grab a tiger by the tail and you don't interfere with Gustavo when he's at work.'

Kenny stared at the phone in wonderment. Was this arsehole *rebuking* him?

The don went on: 'Personally, I wouldn't have hired the shmuck in the first place but Cole said the matter was urgent and I did this, made the connection, for him as a favour. But I did warn him. I told him, I didn't use Gustavo too much anymore because the truth of the matter is, he ain't what he was. Got PTSD or some damned thing. My advice is you let him proceed as he would and then you pay him. End of story. You start fucking with him, phoning him, altering your initial instructions, you will find yourself in trouble because he ain't the most stable of personalities. You get me?'

'No, wait. Maybe you don't understand what I'm getting at here,' said Kenny, trying to hang on to his patience.

Talk about Chinese whispers! Cole Mason hadn't said a single fucking thing about Gustavo Cota being loopy.

'Look! This bozo's going so far off-piste that he's stirring up things that should be left alone. He is starting to implicate *me*, and I can't stand by and let that happen.'

'You never did tell me your target's name,' said Primo.

'What? Well it's *her*, isn't it. That bitch. Christie.'

Primo was silent.

'This bastard's getting me further into this thing than I want to be and I thought you would understand my predicament,' Kenny charged on.

'What, you're making war on your own wife?' Primo sounded scandalised.

In frustration Kenny barked out: 'Let me make myself crystal clear: I say fuck *him*, and I also say fuck *you*, Mr Ecco.'

Kenny slammed the phone back onto the cradle. He was breathing hard with temper.

There was a tap on the door. It opened.

'Hey, Ken?' Bruce, one of the club bouncers, appeared. 'Visitor for you,' he said.

Bruce ushered in a young dark-haired cop holding out his ID.

'I'm DS Smith. You remember me, Mr Doyle? I need to discuss the fire at your house with you. Can we do that now please?'

That *shitter* Gustavo, thought Kenny.

'Sure, sure,' he said smoothly.

But now at least he was reassured that the New York don would see sense and give Gustavo's scrawny arse a *very* thorough kicking.

101

Don Primo Ecco put the phone down in his swish old colonial Fifth Avenue apartment and sat there looking out at his spectacular Central Park view. For a while he couldn't quite believe what he'd just heard. That Christie Doyle, that sweet girl, was the target for that maniac Cota. And had that fucking rat bastard Englishman actually said *fuck you* to him, *him*, Primo Ecco, godfather, don, top man?

Had he *really* just said *fuck you*?

Yes. He really had.

Primo picked up the phone again.

He made a call.

★

Christie was at Dex's place, alone, and her phone was ringing but she ignored it. She ignored it because it wasn't just the heavy breathing anymore. Mostly, she simply didn't answer the damned thing these days because she knew who it would be. Ivo. Not just the breathing now but whispering stuff, *disgusting* stuff, in her ear.

You're mine, he'd say.

Are you wearing jeans? That's bad, Christie. You know I like to see your legs. I like to feel them wrapped around me. I'm getting all hot just thinking of that, of back when we were young

and together that way . . . don't you? Remember that, Christie.
Remember how I could make you moan . . .

She wouldn't listen to it.

She *would not*.

And how did he know she was wearing jeans? Was he out there, was he watching her?

Yes. She thought he was.

She sat indoors, alone. As always.

Safer that way.

She dozed on Dex's sofa, awoke, wished he'd come home, roamed around the big empty place, lay down, dozed some more. And dreamed. The dripping water, the stink of petrol, the sound of her mother crying in the front of the car.

She snapped awake, heart thumping, full of dread. Got up, fixed herself a coffee in his bleak modernistic kitchen, then tipped it down the sink. She thought of what Dex had planned for her today and his – probably deluded – belief that it would help drive out the demons that seemed always to plague her.

Yes, it was true that she was afraid to look at the past. But maybe she *had* to.

102

The place Dex took her to wasn't at all what Christie had expected. What she had expected was a clinic, somewhere expensive-looking, professional, all glass and clean lines. This was an ordinary nineteen-thirties house in a normal street. Now Christie felt that she was wanting – needing – to turn away from this, to say, *No, I've changed my mind. Let's go back to your place. I don't like this idea.*

But it was too late. Dex was knocking at a side door. There was a small brass plaque on the wall beside it, saying: David Cottrell MIAEBP DHyp. A man opened the door straight away. It jammed a little, and the man gave a curse, then a smile. He was tall, dark-haired, vaguely scruffy, around forty, with warm crinkling hazel eyes. His shirt was cream-coloured and neatly pressed, his trousers dark brown cord.

'Hiya, Dex,' he said, and reached out a hand.

They shook.

'This is Christie Doyle,' said Dex, giving her a subtle but decisive push in the small of the back.

'Christie! Hello there.'

He shook her hand and then led the way into a tiny unfurnished hallway. To the right there was an open door leading into a no-nonsense cloakroom. David led the way and at the end of the short passage they stepped into a tiny room. There was a window with Venetian blinds closed against the warm spring light. There was a moss-green velvet-covered recliner, a wheelback chair, a small desk holding papers and a brass lamp that was switched on and was at the moment the only source of light in the room. Underfoot, there was a carpet in the same muted tone as the recliner. Nothing else – except a box of tissues on an occasional table beside it.

'Time I wasn't here,' said Dex, and left.

'Take a seat, get comfortable,' said David, and he settled her into the recliner, tipping it back so that she was half-lying.

David ran through a few exercises with her. 'What's your favourite colour?' he asked.

'Turquoise,' said Christie.

'What pets do you have?'

'None.'

'Why?'

'I wouldn't want to lose them.'

'You're married?'

'Sort of.'

'Children?'

'No.'

'Why?'

'That's personal.'

'Why, though?'

'I don't know.'

He smiled at that, reached out, switched off the table lamp. Darkness.

Then David's voice, saying very gently: 'What we are going to do, Christie, is this: I am going to count down from ten and you are going to descend into a lovely peaceful garden at dusk . . .'

He went on, but Christie was tense, thinking: *I am sitting here in the dark with a man I don't know.* But Dex wouldn't have left her with anyone dodgy, would he?

No.

He wouldn't.

David was counting back. 'Eight.'

A weird feeling of peace stole over Christie. His voice was nice. Counting down . . .

'Five . . .'

'Two . . .' he said.

'And . . . one. Now, can you tell me your earliest memory?'

Was this bullshit?

Was it?

She could picture in her mind's eye . . . lights, strobing lights.

Her mind skittered away from that.

Ivo, loitering by her bedroom door.

Wake up, little Susie . . .

Christie writhed in the deep comfort of the chair.

No, away with that. What the hell was he doing? All she wanted to know – she'd discussed this with Dex – was about the night Lara Millman died. She wanted to know if she'd driven over there in her sleep and killed her. Left the car engine running on her return, gone back indoors, woke up on the stairs, unaware that she had committed murder. That was what she wanted answers to. Not all this additional shit, not all this about her earliest memories. All that was done and forgotten. Wasn't it?

'What do you see, Christie?' asked David's voice.

Christie moistened her dry lips. 'My cousin Jeanette and me. Singing in the garden.'

'Singing what?'

'A song from a film. Tony Curtis. *The Great Race.* A love song.'

'A happy memory then?'

'No. Jeanette had an accordion, a Christmas present.'

'And you didn't?'

'No. I didn't.' She'd got nothing that Christmas. Aunt Julia had said she'd been bad.

'Who else was there, when you were in the garden, singing?'

'My cousin Ivo. And Aunt Julia and Uncle Jerome. Aunt Julia was praising Jeanette, saying how well she played, how nice her voice was.'

'And what about yours? You were singing too.'

'She never praised me. Never.'

'This was in your uncle and aunt's garden?'

'Yes it was.'

'Not your parents'?'

'No, they . . .'

Wake up, little Susie . . .

'What were they doing? Were they there?'

Christie couldn't speak. She shook her head.

'Let's find another memory. Can you do that, Christie? Forget the garden now. Let's go and find something else.'

Brilliant lights, flashing, hurting her eyes.

A mind-numbing impact and then drip, drip, drip.

Rain?

No. Not rain. Something else: something worse.

'I can't . . .' she murmured, twisting in the chair.

'Your cousins. What about them?'

She was four years old and terrified. Her parents were gone and she was moving in with her aunt and uncle. She was going to be one of their family now.

'I moved in with my cousins,' she said – and to her horror and embarrassment felt tears slip from her eyes.

'You didn't like your cousins.'

'I hated them.'

'Another memory then, Christie. Come forward. Let's find a happy day. A birthday?'

The day of her fortieth. Christie breathed a little easier. This was the meat, the bit she really wanted to chew on, the bit she had to know about. Had she sleepwalked and, all unknowing, killed Lara Millman?

'My husband organised a big party for my fortieth,' she said.

'A happy day?'

'He wanted a divorce. One last big blowout, then he was off.'

'That was tough.'

'I didn't love him,' she said.

'Still. A shock?'

'Yes. A shock.'

'And we're coming out of this now, Christie. It's all fine and you're going to wake up very soon and feel better. Rested. At peace. Ten . . . nine . . . eight . . . seven . . .'

Christie moved, yawning.

'Six . . . five . . . four . . .'

She opened her eyes and saw the dim outline of David sitting there on the wheelback chair in front of her. She felt sleepy but somehow untroubled. Had she been out of it? Unconscious?

No. Surely not.

'Three . . . two . . . one.'

She was wide awake now.

'And we're back in the room and everything is fine,' said David, switching on the light.

Christie stretched. David stood, came forward, straightened the recliner.

'All right?' he asked her, smiling.

She *had* been out of it. Back in the far-distant past. No. She didn't want that. She wanted just that one night, the night Lara died. Nothing else.

But that song, in her head . . .

Wake up, little Susie . . .

'You've done well,' he said.

103

DC Debbie Phelps was at the home of the catering manager Mrs Rawnsley, trying to coax a conversation out of Gemma, the daughter, who was nasal with cold and coughing fit to bust, having picked up a virus on her way home from her holiday. Debbie was concerned that she might catch a bad dose and be off work for a fortnight if she sat less than six feet away from her.

Having reluctantly admitted Debbie to the family home, Gemma was now sitting on the sofa, wrapped in a thick pink-spotted white dressing gown. She wasn't a pretty girl, and the bad cold she was suffering from didn't add to her looks in any way. Her square face was feverish, flushed. Her eyes were red. Her squashed little nose was scarlet. Her mid-blonde hair was thin and stuck up in tufts, like a fretful baby's. At intervals she sniffed, sneezed, blew into a tissue.

'So,' said Debbie, taking out her notebook and pen. 'You were at Christie Doyle's fortieth birthday party. Helping out your mum in the kitchen.'

'That's right,' said Gemma, coughing. 'Sorry.'

'It's OK. Can I get you anything? Tea? Lemsip?'

'No. Thanks. When we're done here, I think I'll go back to bed.'

'Good idea. Gemma, did you notice anything odd on the day of the party?'

'Odd?' Gemma frowned.

'Yeah, anything that seemed sort of out of step. Strange. For instance . . . did you see anyone going upstairs that day?'

'No, why would I?'

'Well, from the kitchen in the house there's a good view of the staircase. So I wondered, did you notice anyone going up there? Anyone maybe who shouldn't have been doing that?'

'Mum saw a couple going up there. Tall man, little redhead. I didn't really notice; I was over by the oven. She laughed about it. A bit of afternoon delight, she called it.' Gemma grimaced. 'All right for some.'

'But you personally didn't see them?'

'No.'

'Or anyone else going up there?'

'What's the big deal about people going upstairs?' Gemma said, then sneezed heartily into a tissue. 'Sorry.'

'So you didn't? See anyone else go up?'

'No. I don't think so.'

Debbie made a note. Smith was right; Christie Doyle had done it, and they were all running themselves ragged over this damned thing, trying to find the perp when in fact the perp was right there in front of them. The jealous wife. The one that apparently their boss *didn't* want to find guilty of the crime.

'Fancies her like crazy,' was Smith's take on this when they'd chatted about it. 'He's pushing us all on this because he wants to prove she didn't do it. And what do we all think?'

There had been a gaping silence.

'Exactly,' said Smith.

'You don't *think* so?' said Debbie to Gemma Rawnsley. 'What does that mean?'

'What it says,' snapped Gemma. She closed her eyes. 'Sorry. I really don't feel well.'

'You don't sound certain. Did you see anyone go up there, or not, at any time during the day of April the twenty-third?'

Gemma shrugged. 'How should I know? I was busy.'

Debbie stifled a sigh and consulted her notes. 'And there were how many catering staff there on the day? Including you and your mum?'

Oh . . . four.'

Debbie looked at her notes. Mrs Rawnsley had said five, including herself and Gemma.

'Your mum said five,' she pointed out. 'So there's you, your mum, and who else? People from an agency, I think she said . . . ?'

'That's right.'

'Five people. Not four, Gemma.'

'Sorry. Got it wrong.' Gemma paused. Coloured up a little. 'There were two from the agency, and one other.'

'Who was the other?'

'To tell the truth, Mum was pissed off with me over it. We had words on the day. She don't like him much but *I* do. He's done waiting before, he knew the job and he needed extra cash and – well – I was keen on him once. We went to school together. I still like him.'

'His name?'

'Andy Paskins.'

Debbie stiffened. Was this the same Andy Paskins who lived next door to Lara Millman's mum? *That* Andy Paskins? She told Gemma the address and she nodded.

'That's him. Andy.'

'And he was upstairs on the day of the party?'

'He's an old school mate. Always on the lookout for extra work.'

'But why would he go upstairs?'

'Dunno. Maybe the toilet downstairs was busy.'

'Was he up there long?'

'No.'

'How long?'

'Maybe ten minutes.'

Lara Millman's old boyfriend, her boy-next-door, the one who had tampered with Christie Doyle's brakes and against whom Christie had refused to press charges. He'd been up there quite long enough to pick up one of those hatpins.

'Gemma,' said Debbie when Gemma finished another hacking coughing fit. 'Did you definitely see Andy Paskins go upstairs that day?'

Bleary-eyed, Gemma nodded.

Great, thought Debbie. Turns out the whole world and his fucking wife had been wandering around upstairs that day.

104

Dex took the call from Debbie when he was on his way to Frith Street again to see Mungo.

'Does the caterer's daughter know why he was up there?' he asked.

'She says not. Could be he was just looking around, being nosy. Or maybe the loo downstairs was busy, as she suggested, so he went upstairs to find another.'

'Or could be he was up there picking up that topaz hatpin, thinking that it would be another nail in the coffin, would put Christie Doyle right in the frame for the murder,' he commented.

'Who knows? Should I pull him in?'

'No, not yet. Thanks, Debbie.' Dex parked up, left the car on the rain-drenched street and hurried into the club. He showed his ID to one of the hardmen on the door and was led back into Mungo's office.

'You again? What can I do for you, officer?' asked Mungo. 'Only I'm pretty busy just now.'

Mungo didn't look busy. He was lounging back in his king-sized red chair and looking very relaxed indeed.

Dex took a few sheets of paper out of his jacket pocket and laid them out on the desk. Mungo looked. 'What, the club accounts? I told you, I don't touch them. Don't go anywhere near them. Patsy sees to all that.'

'Yes,' said Dex, pointing. 'But look at this. This is Lara Millman's bank statement, and it shows a regular payment going into her account from your business account.'

'Her wages. Yeah.'

Dex shook his head. 'Not her wages. The wages are here, see? This is a *bigger* payment, paid in every month to her from the Mungo's account. Five hundred pounds. Every single month.'

'*How* much?' demanded Mungo, swivelling the papers round so that he could take a closer look. He looked at the proof, right in front of his eyes, and then up at Dex. 'What the hell's that for?' he asked.

'That,' said Dex, 'is what I want to know.'

105

Christie was silent when Dex picked her up and took her back to his apartment. He spoke to her, asked how it had gone, but she didn't answer. She had nothing to say; she couldn't trust herself to speak until they were in the flat and then she burst out: 'What the fuck, would you mind telling me, was *that*?'

Dex threw the car keys into the dish on the table by the door and looked at her in frank surprise.

'What?' he asked.

'All that shit! Delving back into the mists of time about my family, all that *rubbish*. Didn't you tell him that we wanted to know about the night of my fortieth? That that was *it*?'

'I didn't tell him anything. That wasn't my place. I left it between you and him.'

'I don't believe you!' Christie flew at him. 'Of all the fucking wastes of time!'

Dex squared up to her. 'Look. Just because he hasn't addressed the problem *this* time, that doesn't mean that he won't in another session . . .'

'*Another?*' Christie let out a dry laugh. 'Are you kidding? I'm not going back there, *ever*.'

'Six sessions is the norm, Dave tells me,' said Dex.

'He can fuck off and so can you. I'm . . .'

'Only it sounds like he touched a nerve,' said Dex.

'How *dare* you put me through all that stupid mumbo-jumbo?' Christie yelled, and hit him, punching his chest again and again, which was useless, like hitting a wall.

'Don't do that,' said Dex, catching her wrists, stopping her. 'All I wanted to do was help you find some answers. That's all.'

Christie hung there, caught by his more powerful grip, feeling tearful, thwarted, nearly incandescent with rage. After a moment she came back to herself and she stared into his eyes and said, her voice thin with strain: 'And what if he finds out I did it? What if your pal discovers in the dim dark recesses of my mind that I took one of those hatpins, took the petrol can out of the workshop, took some matches, got in the car that night, drove over to the next village, rapped on Lara's door and killed her? What then?'

Dex was staring into her eyes, his expression very serious. 'I don't believe you did that. I don't believe you could.'

'Dex – you don't even know me.' *You don't know what I've been through.* Memories were crowding into her brain now. Things she didn't want to know about. Things she thought she had forgotten, and good riddance. *Horrible* memories. *Wake up, little Susie . . .* 'You knew me as a teenager, as a young woman, and then you were gone and I was married to Kenny, and Dex, *you just don't know me at all.* Not the me I am now.'

'I didn't even know you then,' he said, a sad edge to his voice. 'Not properly. I would have changed that, given the chance. Safe to let go now?'

Christie sagged tiredly and nodded. Dex released her wrists. They stood there, weary combatants, a foot apart.

'Are you going to go on with the sessions with David?' asked Dex.

Everything in Christie wanted to cry out *no*.

But the mystery surrounding Lara's death. She might not want to go on with this, but didn't she owe Lara the effort? The pain?

'I'll go on with the sessions. So long as he's clear what we're looking for and he doesn't start rooting around in stuff I don't want to talk about. Understood?'

'OK,' said Dex. 'I love you,' he murmured against her hair and she clung to him.

Slowly, they made love and afterwards Christie lay listening to his breathing, thinking that things were moving very fast now, hurtling toward some sort of a conclusion. She was going to have to be brave.

She was going to have to press on.

106

'Dex said you were pissed off with me,' David told her next day when she dragged herself into the torture chamber he called his consulting room.

'It's just that all I want to know about is the night of my fortieth birthday. It's pointless going back further,' she said.

'You think so? Really?' He looked dubious as he settled her in the chair, tipped the recliner back. 'Comfortable?'

'Yes. And I do think so.'

'OK. Look, Christie – I know it's hard. And we're having to rush through this, so it's very intense. But let's see how we go, shall we? You're in a safe environment here. Everything's fine. And if you feel at any point that you really can't continue, then say and we'll stop.' He sat down, switched off the small lamp on the table.

This was far from fine, she thought. Those memories, stirred at the last session, now kept bubbling to the surface of her brain with an almost relentless power. Snatches of old songs. Strobing lights. A hospital ward. Things she hadn't ever thought about, didn't *want* to think about.

'Now,' said David in a soothing voice. 'We're counting back, and you are stepping down into a beautiful garden at dusk. Everything is peaceful, Christie; everything is good. Ten . . .'

Christie tensed.

'Nine.'

She started counting down too, in her head. Tried to pic-ture that lovely dew-soaked garden in the muted light of sun-down, to hear the birds settling in to roost, to see the moon rising high above her . . .

'Give me a memory, Christie. Any one you like,' said David.

Christie felt tired, peaceful. Relaxed, all of sudden.

Wake up, little Susie . . .

She frowned. *No.*

'The night of my fortieth birthday.'

'All right, that one. Big party, yes? Happy?'

Christie thought of the crowds of people there – mostly Kenny's deadbeat mates and their wives. And the Butlers, who it had been *Kenny*'s idea to invite, not hers. Never hers.

'I suppose,' she said.

'You don't sound very sure of that.'

'Kenny told me he wanted a divorce.' She sighed.

'And that upset you.'

'Yes. It upset me.'

'You love him.'

'I don't love him. I never did.'

'Then why . . . ?'

Christie said nothing.

'Another memory?'

'My car door was open. The engine was running.' Chris-tie's hands clenched on her lap.

'And you thought . . . what?'

'I sleepwalk sometimes. When I'm upset. I thought I might have driven . . .'

'Does that happen?'

'Strange things do. People cut up sandwiches, eat them. Take the dog out for a walk. All sorts of weird stuff.'

'So you think you drove over . . .'

'I think maybe I drove over to the next village and . . . oh fuck, oh *fuck*, I could have killed her. I could have killed Lara Millman.'

'Do you really think you did?'

'I don't know. I woke up on the stairs. The car engine was running. *I don't know.*'

'You think you got into the car . . .'

'Petrol. I'd have needed petrol, wouldn't I.'

'For . . . ?'

'To set fire to Lara. To the cottage. And matches,' said Christie, her voice almost dreamy.

'Where would you get the petrol?'

'In the workshop. Patrick kept some there for the ride-on mower.'

'Then where's the petrol can? Was it still in the car? In the boot?'

Christie shook her head.

'Maybe I put it back in the workshop.'

'In the middle of the night? And the matches, where were they?'

'They weren't in the car. Or in the house. I looked.'

'The workshop?'

'I didn't check in there, not for the matches. But I could have thrown the packet into the fire at the cottage. Destroyed the evidence. Couldn't I?'

'Do you think you did?'

'One of my hatpins . . . I collect them, keep them in my dressing room. One was used . . .' Her voice tailed away.

'For what?'

Christie felt her heartbeat accelerating. *Wake up, little Susie . . .*

'I . . . I think someone stabbed Lara with it. Dex won't say but I think that's what happened. Someone stabbed Lara. With the hatpin.'

'Someone?' asked David. 'Not you?'

Christie was shaking her head. *No, no, no.*

'No. I didn't do it. I *couldn't* do it.' Now she was gasping, like she'd just run a mile.

'Another memory now, Christie. Let's leave that one. Take me back a little, can you? Just a little bit.'

But hadn't she said . . . ?

'I can't think of another one,' she said.

'A nice memory. A *good* one.'

Mum and Dad at the beach. Rock pools. Tiny crabs and sea urchins, and she was gathering them up in her little bucket . . .

'The beach.' She shrugged. The sun and the shriek of gulls and Mum's little red tranny. Ice cream and laughter.

'You like the beach?' asked David.

'No. Yes. I did.' Her heart was racing again. She could feel sweat breaking out on her brow.

She didn't go anywhere near beaches these days. Beach holidays were out, she hated them. If she took a holiday it was never with Kenny – Kenny was always far too busy with work to spare time for fun trips. He couldn't ever relax when he was away. Always he was on the phone, kicking his heels, waiting for the holiday to be over so that he could get back to normality, to the business of fleecing some poor bastard. Usually – if she holidayed at all – she went with Patsy. They'd go traipsing around Milan's fashion hub or exploring Cretan ruins or visiting the Uffizi Gallery in Florence or taking in the pyramids via a cruise up the Nile. Christie didn't do beaches. They made her feel sad, uncomfortable. She couldn't think why she'd just said she liked them.

'When did you like the beach, Christie? When you were a child?'

Christie nodded. She felt too choked to speak. This was weird.

'And now you don't like the beach?'

Christie nodded again. She felt a tear slip down her cheek.

'I hate it,' she managed to get out.

'What do you hate about it?'

'Oh, memories. That's all.'

'Memories of what?'

'I don't want . . .' She was squirming in the chair.

'OK. We're walking up the steps from the garden now. It's dusk; it's beautiful. You see it, Christie?'

It calmed her. The garden filled her mind's eye and she felt peace descend again. It was OK.

'I'm going to count down now, here we go . . . ten . . . nine . . . eight . . .'

Christie felt herself relaxing, stretching, coming back to herself.

'Three . . . two . . . one. Back in the room now, Christie. Everything's fine.' He switched on the lamp. 'All right?'

'The beach,' said Christie, shaking her head, gulping, wiping a tear away.

He nodded. 'There's something else there, isn't there.'

'No,' she said.

'Christie – there is.'

'All right. Maybe an old song. *One* old song. The Everly Brothers.'

'There's something buried there. *Half* buried, anyway.'

'I don't want to go back there,' said Christie.

David gazed at her face. 'You don't have to – unless you want to. Or need to.'

'What does that mean?'

'To get rid of all the old rubbish. Everything that's held you back. To kick it out, once and for all.'

'Right,' said Christie, and David helped her up from the recliner and she said goodbye to him with a feeling of deep relief because she was never, ever coming back to this room again.

107

That night Christie snapped awake in the early hours, sitting bolt upright in bed. Dex was there beside her, and he was awoken by the sudden violence of her movements. He was reaching out for her – but for a moment she didn't realise it was Dex and she cringed back, away from him.

'What is it?' he asked, and she came back to herself then, realised she was sweating with some unnamed terror, realised where she was, realised that it was Dex in bed with her – and not Ivo.

'What the hell has he done to me?' she murmured, swiping her hands through her hair, groping for the light, only being fully convinced that she was safe when it was turned on and she could *see* Dex there beside her, could know for sure that he wasn't *anyone else*.

'Who, honey?' asked Dex, smoothing a hand down her bare arm, soothing her.

'Your damned friend. I just . . .' She shook her head, unable to explain. Something in those sessions with David had stirred up old, dusty memories, snatches of conversations, things that made her shudder and wince.

'David said it would be hard to do. To look at all the old stuff. He said that.'

'Oh yeah.' She let out a harsh laugh. 'But it's worse than that. It's crucifying.'

'You don't want to go on with it?'

'No. I don't.' Christie shook her head, thought about that. But if she *didn't* go on with it, was this then the way it would always be for her? Now she couldn't even sleep. She writhed in the bed while her mind kept throwing up nightmare images, horrible memories, things she couldn't live with.

'You don't have to. If you don't want to,' said Dex.

'The night of Lara Millman's death – I'm pretty clear on that now,' she said.

'You are?'

She looked into Dex's blue eyes. 'I didn't do it. But some-one . . . I think someone left my car's engine running, left the door open and the keys in the ignition, to make me think I did. They were screwing with my mind.'

'Someone who knew you used to sleepwalk,' said Dex.

Christie stared at his face. And who knew that? Kenny, of course. He'd had to guide her back to bed a couple of times, early on in their marriage. The Butler clan – they all knew it. Her Butler cousins had mocked her over it, all the time. And Patsy – and probably Mungo too, because Patsy, God bless her, was such a blabbermouth that she would not have been able to restrain herself; for sure, she would at some point have told her husband about Christie's night-time meanderings.

'So, in a small way, Dave's already helped,' said Dex.

'I'm not going back there,' snapped Christie.

'Back where? To Dave's place?'

No. To the past.

108

'Your wedding day. What about that? A happy day, am I right?'

She'd gone back there. She hadn't wanted to, hadn't *meant* to, but the nightmares were bad and something deep in her brain was telling her that this somehow – miraculously – might begin to fix it.

She was in the recliner, the room was darkened, and David's voice was soothing.

'No,' she said, and sighed.

'The day you married Kenny Doyle – you weren't happy?'

'I didn't want to. I had to.'

'You were pregnant?'

She shook her head: no.

'What does that mean, then? You "had" to?'

'Oh, for reasons . . .'

'What reasons?'

'Things. You know.'

'No, I don't know. Tell me.'

'Things were difficult. At home.'

'Describe them.'

She was silent, unable to say it, unable to think it.

'You're safe here, Christie. Perfectly safe.'

'They were afraid of him.'

'Who was afraid of who?'

'My relatives. The people I lived with after . . . they were frightened of Kenny.'

'And is that why . . . ?'

'That's why I married him.'

'You didn't love him.'

'No. Not at all.'

'Wasn't that cruel?'

'What else could I do?'

'What was happening, at home?'

'Oh, nothing much.'

'Something, surely?'

'Just . . . arguments. Disagreements. Things.'

'Arguments about what?'

'Oh – business.'

'What business was the family in?'

'Building.' She was sweating again. Her throat was dry.

'It was a family business, then? Run by them?'

'J & G Butler Limited,' said Christie.

'Who were they? The J and the G?'

'My Uncle Jerome and my dad Graham.'

'Your dad and his brother, they didn't get on?'

'No, I . . . my dad died years ago, way back . . .' Christie gulped. 'The arguments, they were between me and my cousins.'

'Tell me about those arguments.'

'Oh, nothing really. Just kids being kids. A bit of bullying I suppose you'd call it. They resented me being there.'

'Why were you living with your cousins? Was this something to do with your dad's death, Christie?'

'Um . . . when he died, him and my mum . . . my uncle and aunt, they were my godparents and they became my legal guardians. I moved in with them.'

'How old were you, Christie? When your dad died?'

'Young. Very young. Four.'

'That's tragic. I'm sorry.'

'I haven't thought about it in a long time,' she said, and there it was again, a snatch of that song. 'Wake Up Little Susie'. It was playing in her brain. The Everly Brothers. A flash of lights. The smell . . . *petrol*

. . . and the rain coming down . . .

'Tell me about your cousins then,' said David.

'I'm sorry, I have to go,' said Christie, and scrabbled out of the recliner and stumbled to the door, flinging it open. She stumbled into the tiny cloakroom and vomited into the toilet bowl.

109

David had said it would be hard. But it was *too* hard. There was no way she could face that little room again, no way she could dig around in her aching brain and find the answers he wanted her to find.

'It's your decision,' said Dex, and took her home.

'Happens a lot.' David had kindly brushed aside her apologies. 'When we're getting near to something.'

So, she was supposed to go back.

But she *wasn't* going back.

Only . . . now she couldn't rest at all. Now the nightmares were there all the time. Bad things. *Horrible* things. Then Dex awoke one night to find her standing in the kitchen, staring at the tiled wall. He guided her gently back to the bed, settled her back in. Next morning he told her she'd walked in her sleep.

But she wasn't going back.

Never, never.

Around dawn, she woke up screaming.

That morning, she had another session with David.

*

'Down into the garden,' said David's voice. 'It's peaceful, it's dusk, and we're stepping down into it, ten, nine, eight, seven . . .'

She was back there.

'Where are you now, Christie?' he asked.

Tears were streaming down her face.

'Christie?'

'The woman,' she managed to say.

'Which woman is that?'

'She hurt me. She said it would all get better but it didn't.'

'What would get better?'

'The woman who did the abortion.'

David was quiet. Then he said: 'That's all over now, Christie. You are safe. You are well. You were pregnant then?'

Christie nodded.

'And you had an abortion.'

'Yes.' Christie sighed, feeling something let go of her – some deep, awful, sorrowful *something* that she had been carrying inside her for so long.

'It was Kenny's child?' he asked.

She shook her head. Was silent.

'Whose child was it, Christie?'

'I don't know.'

'I think you do.'

'I . . . no. I don't know. They were frightened of him, I had to marry him, I had to get out.'

'Who was the father?'

Ivo coming into her room.

The abortion had gone wrong. She'd been sick. She'd been in hospital. Good Christ, that was right, she could *see* it. She'd been in *hospital*, and her mind had totally blanked it. But now she remembered. She'd spent two weeks in there, feverish with pain, thinking that she would die, that she would *like* to die, to be with Mum and Dad, to get out of it all.

But no such luck. Back 'home' then. Back to the Butler house.

'I didn't know who the child's father was.'

'Yes you did.'

Christie cried harder.

'Christie? It's all right. No rush. In your own time.'

She took a breath and nearly *screamed* it. '*It was my cousin Ivo's.*'

'And you were ill after the abortion.'

'Very ill. God yes. I was.'

'And you couldn't have children after that?'

'No. I couldn't. One of the doctors I went to said there was scarring. It was unlikely I could conceive. Kenny wanted kids. But I couldn't. And I didn't.'

'Bearing in mind what you'd been through, that's no surprise.' A pause. 'Well done, Christie. Maybe that's all of it,' said David. 'Do you think that's all?'

The Everly Brothers, singing.

Petrol . . .

'Yes.' She was shaking, feeling nauseous. This was *awful*. 'No. Oh Jesus . . . I think there's more. Further back. I think there's more. I keep hearing this song. "Wake Up Little Susie". And I smell petrol.'

'Why petrol, Christie?'

'We were in a car . . .' And there it was. Her mind literally *leapt* away from the truth that was there, right there, waiting for her to see.

'Maybe that's enough for today. Do you think so, Christie?'

She nodded. Shivered. *The night was wet, the strobing lights, the whoosh of the windscreen wipers . . .*

It was warm in the little room but she literally *shivered*.

'Let's go back up the steps. We're leaving the garden now, Christie, and we are full of a sense of peace, full of contentment and happiness. Everything in our world is good and the sun is shining. You feel the sun, Christie?'

She nodded. She really did. It was amazing.

'Counting down now, coming back into the room. Ten, nine, eight . . .'

A moment later she was back in the recliner, and David was straightening up her seat, patting her on the shoulder, then sitting back down. Switching on the lamp, driving back the shadows in the little room. 'All right?' he asked.

'I think so,' she said, grabbing some tissues from the box, mopping at her wet cheeks. Then she thought of what they had unearthed. That stay in hospital after the abortion, how the hell had she simply wiped that from her mind? Obliterated it? And there were other things coming back to her. Things about Ivo who had dominated, ruined, *wrecked* her young life, and was haunting her still.

'But there's more,' said David.

Now she didn't even try to deny it. She knew there was more there, that it had been buried, rotting away there, poisoning her system, for long enough.

'Yes. There's more,' she said.

'We'll find it,' said David. 'And when we've done that, Christie, then we'll get rid of it, once and for all.'

Ivo couldn't believe what Kenny had told him. But here was the proof. He sat in his car and watched Christie and the man coming out of the house. Kenny had said the man was a copper and that he had been part of their old gang during the Sixties and Seventies – Dex Cooper.

Ivo stared at the man intently as he got back into his car with Christie.

Shit yes.

It *was* Dex Cooper.

Ivo felt rage take hold, firing him up. He *liked* the feeling, usually, but right now, he was pissed off. *Seriously* pissed off. Dex bloody Cooper, tramping on *his* territory again? Oh no. Forget *that*. He thought he'd seen that bastard off years ago, and now he was back.

No. He wasn't having this. No way.

Christie had always been, *would* always be, his, Ivo's, no one else's. And now that Kenny was history, Kenny had turned on her, she would be Ivo's again.

He was going to make that plain to her.

Very plain.

III

Smith drove over to Dex's place, ready to have all this out with him. He'd spoken to Doyle, heard the complaint, noted it. He often dropped in to see his boss of an evening when they were on a case, just to chew the fat, have a pint, talk things through. But this time when he drove over to the boss's new place and pulled into the dockside road where Cooper lived, he got a shock. Saw something he could scarcely even believe.

There was Dex Cooper outside the big block of converted dockside warehouses, getting out of his car – and there was a woman with him, an Arctic blonde in a turquoise coat. Smith instantly recognised her as Christie Doyle, their prime suspect in the Lara Millman murder, Kenny Doyle's wife. And – oh shit – here was the worst thing. DI Cooper was being all touchy-feely with the woman, putting his arm around her shoulders as they walked up to the block and vanished inside.

*

Next day, Smith went into DI Cooper's office, shut the door behind him, and sat down. Dex was there at his desk, staring at the wall of photos at the back of the room, thinking about the arc of the hatpin falling. Dex looked round at Smith, then at the closed office door, and put down his pen.

'Something?' he asked.

'Boss, I saw you,' blurted out Smith. 'You and the Doyle woman. Last night. Outside your place.' He paused, groping for the right words, and suddenly said: 'What the fuck's going on?'

Dex let out a sigh. 'We know each other,' he said.

'You were all over her like a cheap suit. And she wasn't exactly beating you off with a stick was she?'

'We know each other from years back. It's complicated.'

'What the hell . . . ?' Smith shook his head. 'I ought to report this. You *know* I ought to do that.'

'It's already been done.'

'God's sake!'

'We're getting close to something. And the super's given me a little more time on it.'

'You're getting close to *her*. I could see that,' snapped Smith. He saw the sudden flare of cold anger in Dex's eyes and added: 'Sorry, boss. But you should have handed the case on to someone else. Don't you think?'

'I thought that I would. But I couldn't. Personal reasons.'

Smith was shaking his head, over and over. 'I don't know what to do with this,' he said.

'Then do nothing. The super's aware. Give me a bit more time – like he has.'

112

Christie wished she had never signed up for any of this. She knew that no one ever took all this woo-woo hypno non-sense seriously, so why was she? But that thing about the hospital stay? Her brain had *buried* it. She couldn't deny that. She had always vaguely remembered Ivo's abuse of her, but never clearly. Partially, she supposed she had buried that too. Lived day-to-day life in her luxurious home as Mrs Kenny Doyle, kept her mind on the *here*, on the *now*, refused to think about all that had gone before and how it had marked her.

It *had* marked her. She thought of Aunt Julia, who had been more than happy after the disastrous abortion she'd put Christie through to put all of the blame on Christie herself and none on Ivo, her beloved son. That raping son of a bitch *bastard*.

Now she could remember Aunt Julia saying: 'You led him on, didn't you. Admit it, Christie. It was you, wasn't it, play-ing the slut.'

But she'd never 'led Ivo on'.

So now she was in the little room again, in the recliner, and David was stepping her down into the garden, the peaceful garden where all her secrets could be found. She hated this. And she was frightened of it. If she'd told Patsy about it – her dearest friend, the one who now didn't seem to want to be her friend at all – she knew precisely what Patsy would say. 'Hypno*what*? You crazy? You don't fuck about with things like that. It's like voodoo or something, isn't it?'

But it had worked. It *was* working. Christie had never believed that it would, but now she knew that it did and that was terrifying. What else was she going to find?

'You know there's something more back there, don't you Christie?' asked David. She could see the dim outline of him there beside the table. The lamp was out. The semi-dark enclosure in the room was peaceful. Her eyes fluttered closed.

'But here, in this room, everything is fine; everything is safe and good. So give me a memory, Christie. Your earliest – how about that?'

A rock pool. Tiny exquisite creatures swimming. A crab, she found a crab and put it gingerly, careful of its flailing claws, in the little red bucket. She showed it to Mum, but Mum was quiet. Distracted, she told David.

'How old are you, Christie?' asked David.

'Four,' said Christie, her voice high, almost child-like.

'Your mum wasn't interested in what you'd found?'

'No, she . . . they were talking a lot. Her and Dad. I don't like this . . .'

'What, Christie? What don't you like?'

'They were talking about the firm.'

'Firm? What firm?'

'The family firm. My dad and Uncle Jerome, they ran it together. And . . .'

Wake Up, Little Susie . . .

'What were they saying about the firm?'

'Cooking,' said four-year-old Christie.

'I thought you said it was a building firm?'

'No, cooking. I thought it was funny. I laughed but Dad was . . . He didn't smile. Cooking, he said. He didn't smile. I wanted him to smile but he didn't.' Christie felt tears slipping down her face. It had been a lovely day, on the beach. But there was a cloud over the sun. Her parents had been worried. Unhappy.

'He said he had to say something,' she gasped out.

'To who? About what, Christie?'

'To Michael.'

'Who was Michael?'

'The accountant. Dad said he had to say something to Michael. And when we were on the beach Dad said it would all come out, about the cooking.'

'What sort of firm was it again, Christie?'

'A building firm.'

'Was your dad cooking the books, Christie?'

Christie shook her head, hard.

'Not Dad. Uncle Jerome was doing that. That's what Dad said. He was upset. He'd looked at the books and he could see Uncle Jerome had been cooking them. Cheating him. He called it emb . . . embez . . .'

'Embezzlement.'

'He kept saying it, over and over on the beach, when we were eating ice creams. "My own brother," he said. "He's robbed me blind. *My own brother.*"'

113

Christie came staggering out of that session. Her legs shook under her as she got back in Dex's car and they drove back to his place. Once indoors, she went and washed her face, refreshed her make-up and thought about what had come out this time. She thought about the lavish lifestyle that the Butlers had enjoyed, Jerome and his snooty wife Julia and their hideous kids. The luxury motors, the crystal chandeliers, the unbelievably expensive holidays abroad, the lavish parties at the great big Victorian house set in its lush acres of grounds; they'd had the very best of everything.

She contrasted it with the life her parents had lived when she was little. She remembered a modest house, nothing fancy. No chandeliers. Plain carpets. A grey Ford Anglia saloon to drive around to the sites in. Holidays to the Isle of Wight, or down to Devon for a stay in a rented caravan. The business was growing, but Dad wanted it to really thrive. He'd ploughed a lot of what he'd earned back into the business. Later, he always said, they would live it up. They would be made.

'One year for growth, the next for consolidation,' he'd said.

But Jerome and Julia hadn't wanted to wait for either of those things.

They'd wanted it all *now*.

So they'd used the business, the *joint* family business, as their own personal cash cow. Scooped handfuls of money out of it – thousands upon thousands of pounds – and tucked it away, treated the joint family business like it was theirs and theirs alone. Jerome as managing director, Julia as the secretary and treasurer, handling all the transactions, and Dad who was also a director but was far too trusting and too busy working, working *hard*, touring around their many building sites to talk to the foremen and check out the site plans, to iron out any snags, to see everything was going along just as it should, poring over paperwork late into the night, liaising with councils, slogging his guts out; too busy ever to look up long enough and see what was going on right under his nose.

Christie stared at herself in the bathroom mirror and shuddered. Who knew what had made her dad, her poor hardworking dad, ever smell a rat and take a look at the books? Strictly honest himself, he would never have suspected that his brother could be anything but the same. How wrong he'd been. And now tomorrow she had to go again, see David again.

Session six.

Dex couldn't take her there; he was busy on the Millman case. It was all coming to a head, he said. So next day he kissed her goodbye and she took a taxi over to David's place, and asked the driver to wait for her outside.

The very last session. The worst one, she knew, because she was going to have to think about *that*. The crash. The one that had killed her parents – and left her, at four years old, all alone in the world.

114

First, down into the garden, the peaceful, beautiful garden and it was so vivid, so amazingly *there*, that Christie could smell the roses, could see the dew settling on the grass, could feel its cool wetness beneath her naked feet, could hear the sweet deep trilling of a blackbird.

'Another memory, Christie,' David said.

Already, she was shaking with fear.

'You're safe here,' he said. 'What's happening, Christie?'

'The car, it crashed.'

'Tell me about that.'

She didn't want to. For a long time she was silent. Then she said: 'Mum had her little red tranny on her lap. I could see it when I leaned forward, between the two front seats. She wasn't singing along. She usually sang along.'

'Why wasn't she singing along, Christie?'

Christie shook her head. 'They were worried. Dad said he'd have to *say* something. He'd talked to Jerome about it. And Uncle Jerome had said no. He'd denied it. But Dad said Uncle Jerome was lying because he'd seen the books and this was serious.'

'Go on.'

'There were lights, flashing lights. Cars coming. And it was raining, there was water on the windows and I was listening to the tranny, the Everly Brothers, "Wake Up Little Susie" . . .'

'Then what?'

'So many lights, coming toward us. Dazzling. Then there was a van, a big grey van and I could see . . .' She drew in a gasping breath.

'What could you see?'

The big grey van crashed into us and the noise, the noise . . .'

'It's OK. Go on.'

'The car spun around, over and over and I saw a tree, we crashed into a tree and then Mum was crying and then she stopped crying and there was dripping. The rain was coming inside, and I could smell the stuff, the p-petrol, the . . .' Christie ran out of breath. She sat there, panting, horrified.

'Everything's all right. You're here; you're safe.'

'I saw, I saw . . .'

'What did you see, Christie? Can you tell me what you saw?'

Christie told him.

115

Dex was busy in town, but it was no problem. Christie had said she would take the taxi back to his place – he'd given her a key – after the final session with David.

Everything had come out into the open this time and she felt odd. Free, somehow. She had never felt free in her entire life. Always, right back until that day at the beach, she had felt scared, anxious, waiting for some unnamed blow to fall.

'You will feel compassion for all living things,' David told her, and she really felt, as she got into the taxi and gave the driver the address she wanted to go to, that it was true. The anger that had been stirred up in the early sessions, the unease, the screaming for revenge, had all gone and now there was just this deep, enfolding, amazing *peace*.

She sat back, enjoyed the ride. Almost dozed.

She wasn't even aware of the car that slid in behind her taxi, of Ivo, hunched over the wheel, watching her, following.

★

When Dex got back to the apartment he was surprised to find that Christie wasn't there. Her session was long over; she should be home by now. He phoned David.

'She left here over an hour ago,' said David.

Dex looked at his watch and felt an uneasy bubble of panic rise in his gut. Where the hell was she then?

But maybe she'd done some inconsequential thing. Gone shopping to celebrate the completion of her treatment maybe? But Christie wasn't a keen shopper. And those hypnotherapy sessions had drained the life out of her. Left her tired, wanting only to sleep on the sofa, to recover, to process all that she'd been through.

'Thanks, Dave,' said Dex and put down the phone.

He stood there, undecided.

Her course of treatment was concluded.

So . . . where would she go?

He picked up his car keys and left.

He thought he knew. He had answers now. Lots of them.

Everything was starting to make sense.

116

Jerome was coming through the kitchen at the Butler house. Jeanette was at the sink, washing her hands. He paused. 'Where's Ivo?' he asked.

Jeanette shrugged, reached for the towel, dried herself.

'How should I know? He wasn't due out to any of the sites today. He's probably following Christie around again. He does that a lot. Honest to God, he's like a dog after a bitch.'

Jerome looked stony-faced at that. 'Wash your mouth out, Jeanette. He's her *cousin*.'

'Oh, come on, Dad.' Jeanette slumped against the sink and stared at her father in amazement. 'You can't be unaware, surely?'

'Unaware of *what*?' Jerome demanded.

'You knew about the abortion she went through. You must have known about that.'

Jerome looked uncomfortable. 'We don't talk about that, Jeanette.'

'No, we don't talk about *anything*, do we?' Jeanette smiled bitterly. 'But we all know that it was Ivo's, wasn't it. That sick fuck.'

Jerome paced back and forth, shaking his head. 'Don't talk about your brother that way.'

'Why not? It's what he is. A *sick fuçk*. And why the hell would you stick up for him, eh Dad? For *either* of them.

Mum or Ivo? Who's the boss in this house? It sure ain't you. It's Mum. And Ivo runs the firm, not you. So what you got left, Dad? Hm? Anything?'

Jerome took a step forward and slapped his daughter, hard.

Julia, coming in from the hallway, saw this and launched herself at her husband's back.

'What the hell are you *doing*?' she roared.

Jerome turned, panting, enraged. 'You didn't hear what she said,' he spat out.

'I was saying about the kid Christie got aborted. I was saying it was Ivo's,' Jeanette told her mother, clasping a hand to her reddened cheek.

'We *don't talk about that*,' shouted Julia.

'No, because it's a bloody scandal,' Jeanette shouted back.

'I'm out of here,' said Jerome, and nearly ran out of the kitchen door and into the garden and round onto the drive where the Jag was parked. He loved that car, with its floating super-smooth ride, its walnut dashboard and its cocktail cabinet in the back. It was pure *status*, that car, and then he thought of what Jeanette had said. *What you got left, Dad? Hm?*

He had nothing.

He climbed into the car and sat there, hugging the tan hide of the wheel as you'd hug an old friend, for comfort.

Jerome thought of Graham, his brother, his dearest friend, lost to him, gone so many years ago, thought of the price he'd had to pay for his wife's ambition – oh, and his too; he couldn't say that he'd been totally innocent of blame either – the price that had shattered him. It had been far, far too high.

No.

He wouldn't have this.

He was still head of this household. Whatever any of them said, he was still man of the house and that dirty bastard Ivo was going to have to be made to *respect* that.

So that *sick fuck* – yeah, Jeanette was right about that – that *sick fuck* was still following Christie around, was he? Looking to do again what he'd done in the past? Well – Jerome was still guardian of his brother's daughter, and he wasn't having it. No way.

Sweating, flushed with temper, Jerome started the engine and pulled out, onto the road.

117

Christie had paid off the taxi driver and he'd driven away when there was the heavy crunch of tyres on the gravel behind her. She was just getting her key into the door of the valley house, when she turned – and there was Kenny's big silver Roller pulling to a halt not two yards away.

He got out and came at her very fast, snatching the key from her hand, jamming it into the lock, shoving open the door. *Pushing* her inside her gilded prison.

That was how she thought of it now.

It was odd, really strange, but this – the fear of Kenny coming at her, threatening her, assaulting her – no longer seemed to fill her with the same constant low-level dread. That calmness that David had talked about was still with her. She looked at Kenny, unkempt, unshaven, smelling a bit ripe. He wasn't wearing one of his flashy suits, just a days-old shirt with a stained and crumpled collar, some shabby jeans and an old pair of trainers.

Having shoved her inside, he now didn't seem to know what to do. He just stood there in their huge, glamorous hallway. Christie could smell smoke, lingering from the fire upstairs. She could smell Kenny, too. She turned away from him and walked into the sitting room where the big panorama of fields awaited. She crossed to the French doors, unlocked them, stepped out onto the deck.

Down on the right, behind the big turning circle, was the burned-out workshop, the POLICE – DO NOT CROSS tapes still strung up there. *Patrick died there,* she thought on a fresh wave of sorrow for her old friend, who'd got mixed up all unknowing in the Doyles' dirty business.

Patrick, I'm so sorry . . .

Ahead, there was the view – *her* view – beautiful, timeless. Horses were being ridden up on the ridge at the far side of the valley. Christie inhaled and thought: *OK – if Kenny does it now, then I'll die in the place I love.*

She turned – and Kenny was just stepping out onto the deck, coming after her. His face looked grim, set.

My husband is about to kill me, she thought.

It didn't seem to scare her anymore. She looked at him, the *state* of him, and felt . . . pity.

You will feel compassion for all living things . . .

Kenny was decimated by Lara Millman's death and convinced she was responsible. It was the place she *should* die, maybe. In her home. Looking at *her* view. Overlooking *her* pool.

Why not?

Why the hell *not*?

118

'Why'd you do it?' said Kenny, and there was real pain, *unbearable* pain, in his voice. 'Why'd you have to go and kill her?'

Christie shook her head. Everything seemed clear to her now. 'I didn't kill her, Kenny. How can you think I would do that?'

'No.' Kenny was shaking his head, gulping back tears. 'You did it. I know you did. There's no other explanation. It was you.'

'I didn't, Kenny. Seriously.'

He was coming closer, closer, and where was the panic this time, where was the fear? She looked at him and thought *poor bastard*. Her big impressive bull of a husband was reduced to a blubbering wreck because of love. But she had felt a similar pain long ago. That pain was an old, old friend. So yes – she pitied him.

'Bitch,' he said.

'I didn't.'

'You did.' He advanced on her.

And then, over his shoulder, she saw movement.

Someone – a bald man with cold grey eyes – was moving up the steps from the garden, coming up onto the deck.

'Kenny?' she said, 'Who . . . ?' She was looking beyond him, at the bald man.

'Nice try,' Kenny said, and almost grinned but couldn't quite manage it. His mouth trembled. 'Really nice, you cow.'

Maybe she didn't care anymore. Maybe she was ready at last to give up, let go.

No. She wasn't. Kenny had lost his chance of happiness but she, miraculously, had regained hers. Dex was back in her life. She'd been parched and starved of happiness for so long, but now she'd found it again. She *couldn't* die now. Could she?

'*Kenny,*' she said again, more urgently.

At last, he turned. And saw.

'*You,*' he said, his eyes on the bald man. 'Gustavo fucking Cota. What the fuck are *you* up to, you tosser?'

Gustavo looked at Kenny, looked at Christie.

Then there was a tiny *phut* of noise – so inconsequential, hardly a noise at all.

Gustavo's head exploded.

119

Even Kenny flinched.

There was a shower of blood and brain and Gustavo went hurtling back down the steps and lay at the bottom, on his back, arms outstretched: dead.

'What the fuck?' said Kenny, but unlike Christie he hadn't seen what was coming out from the French doors behind him.

He hadn't seen what she could see – a tall man, dressed all in black, his face covered, an aura of compact athleticism about him. In his right hand was a long gun – a handgun with a silencer, Christie thought. That's what it was. She'd seen loads of them in the movies. Strange – really, unbelievable – to be seeing one now, here, on her own deck at the back of the house. Kenny couldn't have shut the front door. He'd been so worked up, so intent on harming her, maybe even on killing her out of revenge for Lara, that he'd left the door unlocked.

Kenny turned – and now he too could see the man who was emerging from the house onto the deck.

'Kenny Doyle?' the man said. He had an American accent.

'Who the fuck wants me?' said Kenny.

The man raised the gun. 'Don Primo does,' he said.

'*What . . . ?*'

'The don says hello.'

'You f . . .'

The man pulled the trigger and Kenny flew back, hit the table, fell across it; his chest was red, wet with blood. The man in black stepped forward, stood over Kenny's gasping collapsed body and fired again, one careful businesslike shot, into his skull.

Kenny stopped breathing.

Christie stood frozen not six paces away as the gunman turned to face her.

Here it comes, she thought.

She was calm.

She was cold as ice.

She was about to die.

Then someone else was crowding out onto the deck from the French doors and was saying: 'What the *hell*?'

120

Ivo stood there in the open doorway and looked out and saw Christie, saw the dead hitman at the foot of the steps, saw Kenny laid out dead on the table – and the live hitman turning, levelling the gun in his hand at this new target.

Christie looked at her cousin and thought, *What, are you going to save me, Ivo? After all you've done? Now that would really be just splendidly ironic.*

Ivo's chubby face twisted into a mask of horror. He spun on his heel and, arms outstretched like a blind man, ran back into the sitting room.

Again there was that low, deadly *phut* of sound. So quiet – but Ivo flew forward and fell onto the cream carpet in there as if struck by a ton weight. The hitman stepped in closer and again there was the noise. Christie thought she would hear it in her sleep tonight. *If* she slept.

But no. What was she thinking? Her cousin was lying unmoving, not breathing – dead.

The grey man – dead.

Kenny – dead.

He won't want any witnesses, she thought to herself, very cool.

The gunman turned and looked at her. Pointed the gun at her head.

For a long moment their eyes locked, Christie's and the killer's.

*

Don Primo had said *not the woman with the white-blonde hair.* She was a lady, Don Primo had said, kissing his finger, *bellissima!* Mrs Christie Doyle. The assassin looked at her and thought that the don, with his plain little wife Dora, clearly had a place in his weathered old heart for this beauty – and who could blame him? Suddenly he lowered the gun and turned away from her. He went down the steps, stepped over the body lying there and was gone.

Christie stood there, staring after him.

She was still alive.

Had all that just happened?

Or was it just another nightmare, another crazy dream?

Suddenly she started to shake. She pulled out one of the heavy wooden chairs, moved it away from Kenny's dead body. Slumped down into it.

She couldn't believe it – but she was alive.

121

Afterwards she couldn't have said how long she sat there, head in hands. It was shock, she supposed. She was in shock. It was only when she heard movement indoors, heard a weird low keening noise, that she was able to stir herself, to look up.

Through the open French doors she could see Uncle Jerome kneeling, cradling Ivo's bloody form in his arms. Out here on the deck, flies were starting to buzz around Kenny's fallen body, settling in the sticky mess of blood, feasting. The sun was beating down on her back, and she was beginning to feel as if she was going to be sick.

'My boy, my boy,' Uncle Jerome was saying, over and over. 'My boy, my *son*, oh what have they done to you?'

Christie finally was able to lurch to her feet, look all around her. The body on the steps. Kenny. Ivo.

I could be dead right now, she thought.

On trembling legs she went to the French doors and stepped inside the house. Uncle Jerome looked up at her. The front of his white shirt was soaked through with Ivo's blood. His grey-bearded face was drenched in tears. His features twisted into hatred as he looked at his niece.

'*You,*' he said. 'You! This is all down to you.'

Christie stared at her uncle.

'You should have *died,*' Jerome moaned. 'You should have died with Graham and Anna. You *shouldn't be here.*'

Christie stared down at the pitiful scene – the huge lumbering form of Ivo, clasped bloody and dead in his weeping father's arms. She thought back, *way* back, to her parents' funeral. At four years old she had stood there in the church, Aunt Julia holding her hand, and Uncle Jerome had been crying then too; sobbing, sick and heartbroken. She remembered him standing up in the pulpit giving a speech about her parents, what great people they'd been, but he'd broken down, unable to go on. He'd dashed from the church and everyone inside the building had heard Uncle Jerome being sick in the bushes outside because he'd been racked with grief.

Only, it *hadn't* been grief, had it?

'You should have died with Graham and Anna and then none of this would have happened,' Jerome sobbed, kissing his son's brow, hugging his unresponsive form.

'You're right,' she said coolly, and pulled out her phone. 'But you know what, Uncle Jerome?'

He looked up at her like a man drowning.

Christie tapped in the number she needed.

'You really shouldn't have killed them,' she said.

122

The day after the shooting at Christie's place, DI Dex Cooper with DC Debbie Phelps in attendance sat down in interview room A, with Jerome Butler and his solicitor. Dex switched on the tape and stated the facts. Then he addressed Jerome.

'Mr Butler, did you kill your brother and his wife?'

Jerome sat there, slumped. For an instant Dex thought he was going to say *no comment*, but then a sigh like a gust of wind escaped Jerome and he scrubbed a weary hand over his face and grey beard and said: 'I didn't mean to. You have to believe that.'

Tears started leaking out of his eyes. He had the dazed look of a man who had peered through the gates of hell and knew full well that he was going to pass through them very soon now.

'What does that mean?' asked Dex.

'I loved my brother. I *loved* Graham. But by Christ he could be a pedantic sod. "Let me have a look at the books," he was always saying, and – well – I didn't want to do that. Me and the missus had been dipping into the company funds more than we should. I *knew* that. But it had got to be a habit, you see. We'd never had much. Julia especially. Not much at all. Suddenly there was all this cash sitting there, untouched, and it was just *crazy*, I know, but we started spending and then somehow it got out of hand. It was too much . . .'

'How much did you embezzle from the company, Mr Butler?' asked Dex.

Jerome glanced at his solicitor, who nodded.

'Around a hundred thousand pounds,' said Jerome. 'I started scaling it all back, because Graham was asking, always bloody asking, to look at the books. He must have suspected. We . . . Julia liked the high life, you see. She didn't have the sense to be subtle. The house was kitted out like Buckingham fucking Palace. And the clothes she wanted. Designer stuff. Madly expensive. But I can't say it was all her. I had Jags, a new one every year. It was stupid. Maybe I *wanted* to be caught in the act. Who knows?'

'Did you?' asked Dex. 'Did you want to be caught in the act?'

Jerome was shaking his head tiredly.

'The minute Graham demanded the books from out of the safe, *demanded* to see them, I knew the game was up. I let him look them over and he could see it was all bollocks, he could see clear as day what had been happening. He was furious. He said he'd been working himself to death and not spending, ploughing all he had back into the business to make it stable, and here was I, wrecking the bloody thing.'

'Which was true, yes?'

Jerome nodded.

'For the purpose of the tape . . . ?' said Dex.

'Yes. That was true. Julia wanted it all and I just fell in with it, started living that way, and it just . . . it just ran away with us.'

'What did your brother say about the state of the company's accounts?' asked Dex.

'He said—' Jerome sighed '—that he was going to call the police. That I'd betrayed him. That he'd see me in court.'

'And then?'

Jerome shook his head, hard. 'I couldn't let that happen, could I? I told him, I said, "Graham, believe me, I'm going to pay it all back, all of it, if it takes me forever," but he was so mad, he wouldn't have it, he wouldn't . . .' Jerome's voice tailed off. He stared at the tabletop. Tears slopped down off his beard and dripped onto the metal surface.

'I loved my brother,' he said on a sob.

'What happened on the day of the crash, Mr Butler?' asked Dex.

'Oh God, oh God . . .'

'Just tell me.'

123

'They'd driven down to Bournemouth beach. I knew they were going there,' said Jerome. 'It was the day after Graham had seen the state of the books and he yelled at me that he was taking the day off and I could just go fuck myself, and he said that: "*Go fuck yourself Jerome, you cheating bastard.*" He said he hadn't had a break for a damned year while I'd been swanning around like a lord. He was bitter. He said we were brothers; we were *partners*. He was *furious*. I'd never seen him like that before.'

'And what then?'

'We argued out on the drive and then him and Anna and Christie all got back into his old Ford Anglia and he drove off while I was still trying to talk to him, to apologise, to say I would put it right. I didn't know how, but I would do it.'

'So he left.'

Jerome slumped forward, crying hard now.

Debbie Phelps nudged a box of tissues over by his elbow.

'Do you want to pause for a while?' asked Dex. 'We could take a break.'

Jerome shook his head, grabbed a wodge of tissues and blew his nose. 'No. I'll go on. I want it out now. I just want it out. You've no idea what it's been like. All these fucking years. And the kid, the kid looking at me every day. *Being* there. Reminding me.'

'So what happened?' Dex asked, trying not to think about the fact that 'the kid' was Christie. Trying not to think of all this *fool* had put her through.

'I was desperate, didn't know what to do,' said Jerome. 'Julia – my wife – I told her what had happened, about Graham seeing the books, about him knowing what we'd been doing, driving the firm to the edge of bankruptcy. She thought . . . she suggested maybe I should follow them, try to catch them up. We talked about it for a long time. Asking was it a good idea, was it not? I was in a state, didn't know *what* the fuck to do, really. So I went down, hours after they'd left it was, down to the coast. I'd find them there. Julia said it would all be OK. I could talk Graham round, make him see . . .'

'Make him see what?'

'That I couldn't help it. Julia had wanted all this *stuff*, and I liked it. I fell in with it; it wasn't all her. I can't say that. It wasn't.'

'You set out after them?'

'I did. I did, yeah.'

'And you found them?'

Jerome shook his head.

'I was getting more and more desperate, more keyed up. I was climbing the walls. I *had* to talk to him, to change his mind about dobbing me in. I was his brother but he was so *honest*, Graham. I just knew he'd do it. So I followed on. Couldn't wait for them to get back. I was that wound up, tight as a coiled spring. I'd go there, talk to him. My whole world was falling down around me. It was a nightmare. Graham was like that, you see. If he said he was going to do something, he did it. He was straight as a die, my brother. He was.'

'And then?'

'It should never have happened,' sniffed Jerome. '*Never*. But . . . oh God . . .'

'What, Mr Butler? What happened?' asked Debbie.

'It was sort of twilight. I had the headlamps on in the van. It was raining. And I . . . God help me . . . it was a long straight stretch of road. Not much traffic on it. I saw Graham's car coming back toward me.'

'You want to take a break?' asked Jerome's solicitor.

He shook his head.

'What happened?' asked Dex, very low. Thinking of Christie – hardly more than a baby – inside that car.

'I didn't *intend* to do it. You have to believe me, I didn't. It was crazy, a moment of utter madness. I just suddenly thought that all I had to do was veer a little to the right and that would stop him. Just *nudge* him off the road, stop all this silly business about calling in you lot. The van was big; their car was small. I never intended it, I swear I didn't. But I just jerked the steering wheel and . . . oh Jesus . . . it was too hard, much too hard. It smashed into the driver's-side wing of their car and it spun off the road and I just carried on. But I looked back in the rear-view mirror and I could see that it had ploughed into a tree.'

Jerome was crying again, struggling to get the words out.

'What did you do with the van, Mr Butler?' asked Dex.

'I . . . I didn't know what to do. I drove home. The front axle was twisted. I *limped* home with the bloody thing; it was all bent out of true. The headlamp was smashed; the side panel was buckled. I drove home and . . . I didn't know what to do. So Julia said, hide it away, put it in the shed right down the bottom where all the crap was kept, cover it, padlock it, forget about it. No one will ever know.'

'Go on.'

'But the weird thing? The kid would walk in her sleep and sometimes I'd find her there, right there outside that very shed. It freaked me out. Having her there, a reminder of it, that was awful.' Jerome looked at Dex, at Debbie. 'Look. I didn't mean to do it!' he shouted suddenly. 'I just wanted to scare him, that's all – just to scare him and stop him from ruining everything.'

'Where's the key to that shed?' asked Dex.

Jerome told him.

'Interview paused at eleven fifty-eight a.m.,' said Dex, and left the room before the urge to punch Jerome and just keep on punching overcame his common sense.

124

Later that same afternoon, Julia Butler was brought into the station and questioned as an accessory to murder in interview room B. By four-thirty Dex, Smith, Phelps and a team of uniformed police were out at the Butler house. Jeanette, who had been working in the office next door, opened the safe because that was where Jerome had told Dex the key was.

'What's this all about?' she asked him.

'We're investigating a crime,' said Dex.

'*What* crime for God's sake?'

'Just stay here in the office.'

Dex took the bunch of keys Jeanette gave him and they all trudged down to the bottom of the plot. The shed door was padlocked. Dex tried all the keys in it, but it was rusted shut. One of the uniforms fetched the bolt cutters and sliced the chain securing it open. Dex applied the door key and yanked. The door creaked open with a noise like someone opening a crypt after long, dry centuries. It jammed from disuse and he had to force it before he could step inside.

The gloom in here was dense, the one window caked with years of grime, only the light from the open door to see by. Dex, wearing gloves, tried a light switch and looked hopefully up at the fluorescent tube over his head, but nothing happened. He looked around, his eyes adjusting. The place was full of old bits of machinery – ancient chainsaws, engine parts, a rusted block and tackle, an ancient Suffolk Punch lawn mower, a cobwebbed low-loader like something out of a Thirties movie, and a big tarp-covered *something* up against the back wall.

The team picked their way back there.

The headlamp was shattered, the front axle all bent out of true.

Dex went to the left-hand side, the driver's side. He lifted the tarp.

It was a Ford van, light grey, very old – and yes, severely damaged from an impact.

'Fuck,' said Smith.

'Why the hell didn't he just get rid of the thing?' Debbie Phelps wondered aloud. 'Burn it out upcountry somewhere? Say it had been stolen?'

Guilt, thought Dex. Jerome had killed his brother and he'd been sick with it; all he wanted was to hide the van away, forget it, forget all that had happened. His neck might be saved but his brother was dead, and the awful torture of that had to be lived with and endured. Dex wondered what it must have been like, when Jerome realised that Christie had survived the crash and would be there, every day for the rest of his life, a constant reminder of the hellish thing his desperation had forced him to do.

'Let's get forensics out here,' said Dex.

125

It had been a long, long day and by the time Dex got home he was shattered but Christie was there, waiting. Alive and well.

'How'd it go?' she asked, anxious, knowing where he'd been, what he'd done.

'Let me grab a shower first,' said Dex, and went and washed the stink of the day away.

When he emerged from the bathroom in his dressing gown, she handed him a glass of wine and they sat down on the sofa, snuggled up close.

'Hungry?' she asked.

'No. Not yet.'

'What happened?'

'What you said was absolutely right. Jerome *did* crash into the car. We found the van that Jerome used to drive it off the road. It was there, in the shed right at the bottom of the grounds. He'd hidden it in there. Forensics are on it. They'll find paint from your parents' car on the impact site, no doubt about it.'

Christie nodded, went to sip her wine and then put it aside.

'I can't imagine what it must have been like for him – living with the knowledge of what he'd done, day after day,' she said. 'And then – my God, it must have been awful – having to take me in, having to be seen to do the right thing, knowing all along that he'd killed my mum and dad.'

'Let's hope it hurt,' said Dex grimly.

Christie thought of her Uncle Jerome, now sitting in a police cell, all his grandiose dreams in tatters. She thought of all that she'd remembered under regression: the dark bearded man at the wheel of the big grey van, ploughing into her parents' car. That had driven it off the road, into a tree – killing them. But *she* had survived. And, finding that scene hidden away in her mind, she had remembered it too. Dug it out, brought it into the light. Justice had been a long time coming for Jerome; but finally, today, it had arrived.

'He should have got rid of it,' she said.

'I guess he couldn't bring himself to do it,' said Dex. 'He was terrified of discovery, sick with fear, ruined by remorse. He wanted it all tucked away, forgotten. But I guess he never *could* forget, could he? Because *you* were always there to remind him.'

Christie huddled in closer to him with a shudder.

'It's been horrible,' she said.

'It's over,' said Dex firmly.

'Is it though? What about Kenny? And Ivo? And that man the gunman shot?'

'There's nothing to be done for Kenny, the poor bastard. *Or* Ivo. We've got an APB on all points out of the country, but what did he look like? You don't know, do you?'

'I couldn't see his face.' Christie sipped her wine, thought of those terrifying moments on the deck. Kenny, shot dead. And then Ivo. Then the bald man with the horrible blank grey eyes. Finally the gunman turning, looking at her – and then slipping quietly away, leaving her alive.

'Exactly,' said Dex. 'So I think it's unlikely we'll catch him. From what you tell me, it sounds like a professional hit. And people who do that sort of work usually have an exit route worked out well in advance.'

'What about Lara Millman?' asked Christie.

'Yeah. About that.'

And then he told her the shocking truth about Lara's murder.

'It's all there, isn't it. It's straightforward, obvious,' said Dex.

'Obvious to who? Certainly not to me,' Christie objected.

'The accounts.'

'What accounts? J & G Butler?'

'No. Mungo's.'

'*What?*'

'Large regular payments going out from the business, straight into Lara Millman's account.'

'For what?'

'Bear with me here. It's simple, really. Who stayed at your house on the night of the party?'

'Quite a few people who didn't want to drive home tanked up.'

'Who had keys, access, to your home and your car?'

Christie shrugged. 'Patrick?' It still hurt her, horribly, to think of Patrick.

'Who was seen going upstairs on the day of your party?'

'Didn't you say Andy Paskins . . . ?'

He shook his head. 'Whose husband was fooling around with Lara Millman behind Kenny's back?'

Christie was staring at Dex. 'Oh no,' she said weakly.

'I'm afraid so.' He drained his glass of wine, stood up, hauled her to her feet. 'Come on, let's get to sleep. You've had enough for one day. And I'm completely done in.'

Patsy Boulaye was just coming out of her house the following morning, off to her spin class, when she saw the tall figure of Dex Cooper coming up the drive, a short dark-haired man at his side.

'Mrs Patsy Boulaye?' said the DI.

Patsy nodded.

'I'm DI Cooper . . .'

'I know who you are. I remember you. Dex Cooper.'

'. . . and this is DS Smith. Can we have a word, Mrs Boulaye? Down the station?'

'Well, I . . . OK. Sure,' said Patsy. 'Is this about what's been happening over at Christie Doyle's place? I saw it on the news last night.'

'It's related to that, yes,' said Dex.

'Only I'm pretty busy right now.'

'We're all busy, Mrs Boulaye. I am arresting you on suspicion of the murder of Miss Lara Millman. You do not have to say anything now but anything you do say . . .'

Dex carried on reading her rights. Patsy stood there, stunned. Her face was a blank. Then with fumbling fingers she shut the front door and followed Dex and his DS down to the car.

*

Interview room A again. Dex was sitting across the desk from chirpy little Patsy Boulaye and her sober-suited female lawyer, who had hotfooted it down here after Patsy called her in.

'This is all a mistake,' Patsy kept saying, fidgeting, tossing back her thick red hair.

Christie's old friend. Her only *friend.*

At Dex's side sat DC Debbie Phelps, who had a bad cold and so was cursing Gemma Rawnsley and who had, incidentally, heard all this bollocks about a million times before.

Dex placed a piece of paper on the desk between him and Patsy. It was a bank statement.

'For the purposes of the tape, I am showing the suspect item number five four six, a bank statement for Mungo's nightclub. Mrs Boulaye, you do the accounts for the club. Is that correct?' asked Dex.

'I do, yes.'

'Then can you explain this regular payment going out? This one here? Five hundred a month – that's a lot of cash. Being paid directly into Lara Millman's account.'

'Extra shifts, I expect. I'd have to check back. I don't carry all that around in my head, you know.'

'You do the books for your husband's club,' said Dex.

'Up to a point, yes. But we have a book-keeper too.'

'Then you must know exactly what this amount is for.'

'Sorry. I don't.'

Dex decided on a different tack. 'You went upstairs on the day of Christie Doyle's fortieth birthday party, with your husband.'

Patsy said nothing.

'We have witnesses who can corroborate that fact.'

'Well, all right. I went up there with Mungo, wanted to show him the view.'

'And is that all you did, upstairs?'

Patsy shrugged. 'We fooled around a bit. Then we came downstairs.'

'Did you take anything from upstairs?'

'No, what do you mean?'

'A Victorian hatpin with a topaz head?'

Patsy looked down. 'No.' Her blue eyes flashed upward then, met Dex's. 'It's different for Christie.'

Where's she going with this? he wondered. 'Different in what way?'

'She didn't love Kenny. It's horrible, all this stuff on the news, Kenny getting done, but you know what? She won't care because she didn't love him anyway. She married him for money. Well she's free now, ain't she? Free as a bird, 'cos poor old Ken's gone, and she's got all the loot too. Christie's quids in.'

Debbie shifted in her chair, seemed about to speak. Dex shot her a glance. *Let her talk.* Debbie subsided.

'She always said that place was a "gilded prison" – you know that? She didn't even *like* Kenny, much less love him. So – yes – it was different for her.'

'In what way?' asked Dex.

'I love Mungo,' said Patsy with sudden passion. 'I mean, I really *love* him. I couldn't stand to lose him. I *won't* lose him.'

Dex took a stab at it. He thought he knew, now. He had to say it.

'Mrs Boulaye, were you being *blackmailed* by Lara Millman?'

Patsy sat silent, her eyes glued to his.

'Oh, what the hell.' She sighed.

'Mrs Boulaye . . .' warned her solicitor.

'No!' Patsy started up, clutching at her seat, her eyes still fixed on Dex. 'It was about a year ago, just before Christmas.

I was planning all sorts. We were going to Barbados. Mungo loves it there; his dad comes from Bridgetown. We were going to stay at Sandy Lane and have a fabulous time. Then I get a knock at the front door and what do I find? Lara *fucking* Millman, standing there bold as brass and she told me, she told me . . .'

Patsy seemed to run out of breath. She stopped, panting, clutching a hand to her chest. Then she went on: 'She told me her and Mungo had been at it and I told her she was crazy; he wouldn't do that to me. You know what that cow said to me, right there on my own bloody doorstep? She said "You're pushing forty. He wants a bit of young honey now and he can have me. I'm young, see? And I'm gorgeous." That's what she said.'

'And what did you say to that?' asked Dex.

'I said she was dreaming. That Mungo wouldn't do that. But I didn't really believe it. I sort of knew she was telling the truth. He always had women and up until that point none of them were a serious threat to me. And then she said that she'd stay away from him, but I was going to have to pay her for the privilege. Five hundred a month, she said, and she'd leave him alone. So I paid up. I took it out of the company account because nobody ever looks there; nobody checks. Mungo certainly doesn't. It was a small revenge, too, wasn't it. He loved that bloody club of his so much, and I was milking it for money to pay off his girlfriend. It sort of *fitted*, you know? He trusts me. And the book-keeper knows not to ask questions or I'd fire her arse.'

'So you paid Lara,' said Debbie. 'And what happened then? Everything was OK?'

Patsy shook her head. 'No. I caught them in the back room of the club one night, doing it. I got sort of paranoid about it. I'd call in at odd hours, looking to catch them, and I did. Her with her pants round her ankles and him – *my husband* – cock deep, the bastard, bending her over the desk. Mungo was embarrassed and he swore it wouldn't happen again but that cow was *smirking* as she left the room. I knew it would go on, and I was *paying* her not to do it, and she didn't give a fuck about what I wanted or needed; it was all *her*.'

'Go on,' said Dex.

'Can we take a break? I need to speak to my client,' said the solicitor.

'Of course,' said Dex, and signed off on the tape.

128

Half an hour later, they resumed. The tape was set and running. Now Patsy seemed positively chatty.

'So what did you do?' asked Dex. '*Did* you take anything from upstairs on the day of the party?'

'It didn't matter, did it?' Patsy said brightly. 'Christie was miserable in her marriage anyway. How could it hurt her, being banged up for a bit?'

'Maybe life,' Dex pointed out.

'Life?' Patsy shrugged. 'Maybe. I suppose.'

'Did you take the hatpin, Mrs Boulaye?'

Patsy smiled faintly. 'It was the same colour as that cow's eyes. She had eyes like a tiger's. Predatory. Hungry. She was going to eat up Mungo and she didn't care if that hurt me. We were going back downstairs, me and Mungo. He was in front of me, and I saw the thing on Christie's dressing table with the hatpins in it and I saw the topaz one, yellowish, gold-streaked, the *exact* same colour of Lara's eyes and right then I thought, yes, I'll get you, you little bitch. Let's see who's young and gorgeous *then*, shall we?'

'So did you take it?'

'Yes. I took it.'

'And what about the car, the Mitsubishi, Mrs Doyle's car? What did you do with that?'

'Christie's a bit odd,' said Patsy. 'That crash with her parents when she was little, it scarred her. She used to sleepwalk. End up down the garden. Sometimes even as an adult she'd do that, if she was under stress or unhappy.'

Dex knew this to be true. He'd seen it with his own eyes. Bright, bubbly, chirpy little Patsy had used her lifelong knowledge of Christie's behaviour to beat her.

'It was practically perfect, wasn't it,' said Patsy. 'After I'd been over there and seen to Lara, I left the engine running on Christie's drive overnight, the driver's door open, the keys in the ignition.'

'To make her think that she had, in her sleep, driven over to Lara Millman's place and killed her?'

'That's right. And she did, didn't she? It worked. It would have worked *beautifully*, if you hadn't come poking your nose in.'

'Christie Doyle would have done time and you wouldn't.'
'Correct.'
'Your friend.'
'Also correct. Yes, all right.' Patsy puffed out her cheeks. 'I've been pals with Christie for years and I was a bit sorry to do it to her, but as I say, it didn't really matter that much. Because she didn't love Kenny. And I love Mungo. I really do.'

Dex straightened in his seat. There it all was, nice and neat and tidy. So why did he *still* feel he was missing something vital? Frowning, he leaned forward, spoke, stopped the tape. He stood up. *The hatpin. The trajectory of the hatpin.*

'Just taking a short break,' he said, and left the room. He went to his office. Looked at the wall of photographs. Then he went down the corridor to where Smith and Jensen sat at their desks.

Smith looked up. 'What?' he asked.

'It looks like she did it. She's *confessed* to doing it.'

'Yeah. So?'

'Everything points to her,' said Bill Jensen.

'But there's one thing that's bugging me,' said Dex.

'And that is . . . ?' asked Smith.

'The angle of the hatpin. The *trajectory* of the damned thing. Paulette told me it was angled down, missing the brain, penetrating the upper palate.'

'And . . . ?' asked Smith.

'Patsy Boulaye's a small woman, isn't she. Barely five feet tall. And Lara Millman was bigger. Even standing on the step at the cottage, I don't think Patsy could have achieved that angle. You know what I think? I think it was done by a taller person, someone who was looking *down* onto Lara Millman when she opened the door that night.'

'So . . . ?' said Bill.

'Christie could maybe have done it. Just about.'

'But she didn't. Right?' said Smith.

'That's right. She didn't.'

Smith's mouth dropped open. 'So . . .' he started, then his phone rang. He snatched it up.

'Yep?' he asked, then he listened.

Very gently, he replaced the phone on its cradle.

'There's someone waiting to see you,' he said to Dex, 'in reception.'

Dex went out and found Mungo Boulaye waiting there, pacing the floor.

'Mr Boulaye,' said Dex. 'How can I help you?'

But he knew; he knew it all now. Everything was clear, even before Mungo said the words.

'I did it,' said Mungo. 'It wasn't Patsy. It was me.'

129

'Everything Patsy knew about you, Mungo knew too. They were husband and wife. They shared most things,' Dex told Christie later that day. 'Lara *was* blackmailing Patsy, but Mungo knew about that. Maybe it was the final straw, for him.'

Mungo.

Christie could barely take it in. 'So . . . it was all about jealousy then? About which of them could have Lara Millman – Kenny, or Mungo?'

'It was. Mungo kept saying throughout the interview that Kenny was a "gutty bugger" who wanted everything, wanted the world. Mungo said his own ambitions were smaller. He had the nightclub, he had Patsy – but then he got keen on Lara Millman, and she was playing the two men off, one against the other. She started threatening Patsy that she'd take Mungo off her and demanding money, and Mungo said Lara threatened to tell Kenny that he'd come on to her – and *everyone*, even Mungo his old mate, was scared of Kenny, so it all got out of hand. I asked him, why the fire? And he said he wanted her finished, finished for good. And also . . .'

'And also it pointed the finger even more surely at me, the girl with the rep as a fire starter,' said Christie. 'So it wasn't Patsy who lifted the hatpin on the day of the party.'

'No. It wasn't. It was Mungo. Mungo's great height accounts for the angle at which the hatpin entered Lara's eye.'

Christie winced. 'Oh God. So *that* was it? That's how it was used in the murder.'

'Did I not tell you about that?'

'You know damned well you didn't.'

'Anyway – Patsy's confessed that she'd been leading the way downstairs on that day but she had *seen*, out of the corner of her eye, when Mungo took the topaz hatpin. She probably never had any idea what Mungo did with it, not then anyway, but she knew all about the car running on the driveway, the keys in the ignition, things she had access to and through her, so did Mungo. She *knew* Mungo had murdered Lara. Maybe he told her he'd seen the payments to Lara, out of the company account? Maybe he confessed everything to her, every gory little detail, later on. Anyway, she set out to protect him. She was desperate to cover for him and things were getting scary so setting you up for a fall was the obvious way to do it. She did regret it, I think. Implicating you.'

'My God,' said Christie. 'So . . . it's over, then.'

'Yeah. It's over,' said Dex, and kissed her brow, and thanked God for it.

130

Next day, with the Lara Millman case officially closed and Mungo in custody, Dex took Christie out.

'Where are we going then?' she asked him, getting into his car, expecting a country pub, lunch, then home – she hoped – and straight to bed. Starved of him for years, she couldn't get enough of him now.

'It's a surprise,' said Dex, tossing a small pink paper bag onto the back seat.

When he pulled up in front of a row of suburban semis, Christie started to smile. Dex reached back, handed her the bag. She peered inside and laughed out loud. They went up the pathway to the front door and Dex knocked. Dex's mum Joyce opened it straight away, her face wreathed in smiles. She'd been waiting for their arrival.

'Sweetheart!' she said and embraced Dex. Then she looked past him and her eyes were suddenly brimming with tears. 'Oh for goodness' sake! Christie! After all this time.'

'We bought you some Florentines,' said Christie, and held out the bag.

Joyce took it, half laughing, half crying, and then stepped forward and pulled Christie into a warm hug. 'I'm so pleased you're back with us. Come in! Alex is here. And Andrea. Put the wood in the hole behind you.'

This, then, was what it was like to have a proper family, thought Christie as she was hustled indoors, hugged, kissed, smiled at. Oh God – *this* was what happiness felt like. They had lunch then spent the afternoon in the garden, and went home at teatime. On the way back to his place, Christie asked Dex to make a detour.

'You sure about this?' he asked her.

'Yeah. Very sure.'

★

Within half an hour of leaving Dex's mother's, they were at the Butler house. Curiously, looking at it now as they drove in, Christie thought that the house looked somehow smaller, shabbier, far less impressive than it ever had before. The bottom of the drive where the sheds were lined up and the lorries turned was cordoned off with POLICE CRIME SCENE – DO NOT CROSS tapes. Down in that far shed, the van used in the killing of Christie's parents had been found, the front fender bashed in, traces of grey paint that matched her parents' Anglia deeply embedded in the metal.

Dex refused to wait in the car so they went inside the house together and found Julia at the kitchen table, hunched over. Her usually immaculate make-up was gone, her face bare. Her black-dyed hair was showing an inch of white roots and looked as if she'd been dragging her fingers through it. She had on her dressing gown, tea stains down the front of it. She looked *shattered*.

Somehow then Christie remembered what David had said to her on her final session.

You will feel compassion for all living things.

And she did. She didn't want to feel it, not for Julia and probably not for Jeanette either, but she did.

'Julia? Are you all right?' she asked.

Julia looked up, said nothing.

'Where's Jeanette?' asked Christie.

No answer.

'Can I call someone for you? Get someone to come?'

Julia started to smile. A sour, mocking little smile with her eyes fastened on her niece.

'Why didn't you just die?' she asked in a flat monotone.

'Julia . . .' Christie started.

'Oh why didn't you just *die*?' Julia's fist came suddenly down and thumped the table. 'Why did it have to be Ivo and Jerome? Why not *you*, you *cow*?'

Christie didn't have an answer for that.

None at all.

Dex touched her arm, and they left.

EPILOGUE

On a blustery day a week later, Christie bought flowers and took a taxi to a place she had never been before. Julia had never taken her there; she had never asked to go, either. Truthfully, she had no idea how she would feel when she saw it. This wasn't a trip she relished. But she needed to do this and she realised that now she was strong enough, that the past couldn't hurt her anymore.

She walked slowly among the stones, searching for the name Butler, and in the end she found them; they lay side by side in the shadow of a large yew tree that was dancing in the breeze, dappling their final resting place with slivers of sunlight. Two headstones, not one. Anna Louise Butler, beloved wife and mother, was carved into the first. Graham Butler, husband and father, adorned the second.

At peace with the angels, each headstone said.

She sat down on a bench nearby and thought of the years lost, thought of losing them at just four years of age. She thought of all that she'd suffered since they'd left her. After a long, long while she got up, laid the flowers on her mother's grave; then she took a single rose from that bouquet and laid it on her dad's.

Then, at last, she was able to cry for them.

★

She stayed for nearly an hour, until there was not a single tear left, and was walking back toward the cemetery gates when she saw Dex standing there beside them, waiting.

She hurried up to him, kissed him. Dex put his arms around her and pulled her in close. That mad, unstoppable, all-consuming undercurrent of heat and desire still crackled between them, every time they touched. This was the start of her life, this, right here, right now. Her and Dex, together at last.

'OK?' he asked.

She nodded. Soon she was going to have to talk to him, tell him the full story about Ivo and her panicked flight into marriage with Kenny. That would come, later. For now, finally, she was free and filled with a new strength and a new energy to start living her life with the man she loved. Who could possibly ask for more than that?

'OK,' said Christie, and together they went home.

END

ACKNOWLEDGEMENTS

Huge thanks to the team that supports me. You know who you are.

An invitation from the publisher

Join us at www.hodder.co.uk, or follow us
on Twitter @hodderbooks to be a part of
our community of people who love the very
best in books and reading.

Whether you want to discover more about a book
or an author, watch trailers and interviews, have the
chance to win early limited editions, or simply browse
our expert readers' selection of the very best books,
we think you'll find what you're looking for.

And if you don't, that's the place to tell us what's missing.

We love what we do, and we'd love you to be a part of it.

www.hodder.co.uk

@hodderbooks

HodderBooks

HodderBooks